The Sword of Cherubim

Scott P. Hicks

Copyright © 2025 by Scott P. Hicks

All rights reserved.

No part of this publication may be reproduced, distributed, or transmitted in any form or by any means, including photocopying, recording, or other electronic or mechanical methods, without the prior written permission of the publisher, except as permitted by U.S. copyright law.

The story, all names, characters, and incidents portrayed in this production are fictitious. No identification with actual persons (living or deceased), places, buildings, and products is intended or should be inferred.

Book Cover by Scott P. Hicks

ISBN: 9798281220613

Chapter 1

Dr. Helena Carter stood in the subterranean passage under the Temple Mount with a flashlight trembling in her hand. She pressed her palm to the damp, time-worn wall, her heart pounding like a warning drum. Darkness stretched ahead, broken only by the hazy glow of portable lanterns placed at intervals along the jagged corridor. Her archaeological team—eight dedicated souls—fanned out behind her. each as apprehensive as she felt.

She reminded herself that the Temple Mount had been explored for centuries. It was a layered site, full of secrets that might be lurking beneath the surface. Yet, the labyrinth beyond this recent cave-in was uncharted territory, discovered only by chance during a structural survey. Rumors had circulated among local experts that something extraordinary waited below. Whispers of a hidden chamber. possibly sealed before the Crusaders even set foot in Jerusalem, had spread like an irresistible call. Still, rumors were one thing. Hard evidence was what she craved.

Up above, the late afternoon sunlight burned hot across the Old City. Crowds bustled through narrow streets. Yusef Nasir, a resourceful teenager from the area, caught wind of the dig from two Temple Mount guards who joked about "treasure hunters" crawling through dusty catacombs. Those remarks sent the boy racing to the edge of the restricted zone. where he now hovered behind barricades. He peered down into the excavation site, straining to see if the archaeologists had found anything remarkable—or dangerous.

Below ground, Helena could almost sense that each breath carried the weight of centuries. The air had a staleness that pressed on her lungs. She nodded to Ibrahim Mahdi, her liaison from the Israeli Antiquities Authority, who was kneeling by a support beam. He wore a tense expression. concern etched into his brow. Their path forward was blocked by rubble from a partial collapse. Stone chunks the size of small boulders lay scattered across the corridor, forcing them to rely on metal braces and temporary beams to keep the rest of the ceiling from crashing down.

"I'm not sure how stable this section is," Ibrahim murmured, checking a section of cracked mortar. He wore a battered helmet with a bright lamp attached. "One more shift in the rock, and we may have a bigger collapse.".

Helena's gaze traveled across the battered walls, their surfaces carved with faint inscriptions that looked like time-worn Hebrew. She brushed away a layer of dust and made out shapes resembling wings or stylized cherubs. "We need to proceed," she said. "If we stop now. we might lose the chance to study these carvings. They don't appear anywhere else in this subterranean network.".

He nodded, swallowing his anxiety. "Yes, but we mustn't push our luck. How about we set up additional supports first?".

Behind them, a muscular man named Amir hammered a stabilizing bracket into the wall. The metallic clang reverberated through the passage. Helena checked her watch. They had already lost two hours clearing debris to reach this point, and sunset would come soon. The authorities had granted her team only certain-hours access so they wouldn't disrupt the flow of visitors above. She wanted to use every minute of that permission before bureaucracy slowed them again.

Just then, a tremor pulsed through the corridor. Grit sifted down from the ceiling, and Helena instinctively pressed herself against the wall. Her colleague Dr. Lorraine Marsh let out a startled gasp.

"Everybody stand still," Helena commanded, her tone clipped. They waited in silence. Dust swirled in the lantern light. The tremor subsided without bringing the ceiling down. She exhaled, wishing her heart would slow. "I think the substructure shifted a bit, but it seems to be holding.".

From outside the corridor, a crew member called through a handheld radio, "Any injuries down there? We felt that up here too.".

Ibrahim answered into his device, "We're all right. Stay ready in case we need help.".

"Roger that.".

Helena signaled for two team members to move forward with picks and small shovels. They began carefully dislodging loose stones that blocked a low archway. Every scrape of metal on rock made her shoulders tense. This was delicate work. A single misstep could bury them all. She fixated on the inscriptions. leaning closer to interpret their meaning. The winged motif was repeated in intervals, always accompanied by figures that looked like they were either kneeling or protecting something. Parts of it reminded her of the biblical descriptions of cherubim. She felt a stirring in her gut—excitement tempered by apprehension.

Dust rose in a thin cloud as Amir and Lorraine cleared a path beneath the partially collapsed arch. A narrow space beyond that opening invited them deeper into the darkness. Helena knelt to examine the threshold. The rock floor was pitted with age, but her flashlight revealed more carved symbols. The script was too worn to read fully. but she recognized the partial shapes of Hebrew letters that might translate to "glory" or "holy." A chill raced up her spine. If these inscriptions were genuine, this could be a site tied to the earliest era of the First Temple, or even older.

Ibrahim edged closer. "Helena, do you see what I see?" He traced a small chunk of text with his gloved fingertip. "That's a mention of cherubim. And it's describing—" He paused, eyes wide with excitement. "It might be referencing guardians of some sacred object.".

"That's my guess," she replied, her voice trembling with possibility. "Maybe an time-worn storeroom or shrine.".

Lorraine offered a hesitant grin. "You're suggesting we might be near an undiscovered holy site? Maybe something from biblical times?".

"It's a possibility," Helena conceded. She hated jumping to grand conclusions, but every sign pointed that way. "Let's see what we find in there. Carefully.".

They ducked under the arch, emerging into a larger chamber. Their flashlights revealed a musty room strewn with rubble. Sections of the walls held faint reliefs depicting figures carrying rods and a rectangular chest. Helena's heart sped up as she mentally compared these shapes to historical accounts of the Ark of the Covenant. In the back of her mind. she recalled the biblical stories: the gilded chest said to contain stone tablets from

Moses, rumored to hold supernatural power, protected by cherubim over its lid.

For a fleeting instant, Helena pictured the time-worn descriptions of the cherubim atop the Ark—those winged guardians said to brandish a flaming sword of judgment. Legends claimed that blade blazed so brightly it carved daylight into cavern darkness, an omen that the relic answered only to divine command.

She dismissed the notion with a wave of logic—countless explorers had chased the Ark for centuries. If it truly existed, would it be here, waiting beneath the Temple Mount? But her eyes came back to those carvings. In them, two winged shapes hovered over a rectangular object. It was unmistakable. She glanced at Ibrahim. who stared at the relief with parted lips.

Outside, Yusef shifted from foot to foot, worried about the tremors. He had approached the edge of the restricted zone, hoping to catch a glimpse of the archaeologists. Guards had been posted to keep curious bystanders away, but they seemed more concerned with each other's conversation than with a determined teenager. Yusef crouched behind a half-collapsed stone railing. straining his ears for any sign of the team's status. All he heard were muffled echoes. He pictured them far below, risking their safety to chase a hidden treasure. He didn't see how any of that could be wise. Yet the mere thought of time-worn wonders beneath the holy site stirred his imagination.

Back in the chamber, Helena directed the team to set up additional lights around the perimeter. Each new bulb revealed more details. She ran her fingertips across a carved panel showing silhouettes of robed figures carrying a box on wooden poles. She recognized the style: a classic rendering from biblical times. Fragments of Hebrew text curved around the scene. though centuries of weathering had eroded key portions.

She studied the relief for a long moment, then spoke gently, "We may have stumbled onto something more significant than we ever anticipated. Let's proceed carefully, note everything, and do nothing to disturb the integrity of this place.".

A collective hush fell over the group. Even Amir, not usually prone to wonder, looked moved by their discovery.

As they swept the chamber, someone shouted from the far corner. "Dr. Carter! There's a crack in the floor.".

Her stomach clenched. "Is it serious?".

A stocky grad student named Kyle responded from across the room. "It looks intentional. Like a seam in the stone that was covered up. Might be a door or trap panel.".

Helena strode over, kneeling to examine it. Sure enough, rectangular lines cut through the floor's center. "All right," she said, beckoning for a crowbar. "We'll try to open this carefully. Everyone stand back.".

Kyle wedged the tool into the gap and pushed. At first, nothing happened. Then, with a scraping noise, the slab lifted slightly. Two more workers joined to pry it up, revealing a narrow staircase descending into an even deeper chamber. A puff of stale air hit them. reeking of mold and earth.

Ibrahim aimed his flashlight down the steep steps. "It goes about four meters. I see a landing. Something metallic is reflecting the light.".

Helena exchanged a look with him, then nodded. "I'll go first. Everyone else, be cautious. I don't want any sudden movement.".

One by one, they descended the steps, hearts thudding. The deeper they went, the more the environment seemed to press in, as though the walls themselves had secrets they refused to surrender easily. The landing opened into a room smaller than the one above, but better preserved. Its walls had smooth stone blocks. and in the center stood a boxlike shape draped in rotted cloth. It looked like it had once been concealed or protected under heavy fabric. A hush spread as they realized the object itself seemed to be constructed of polished wood banded by tarnished gold.

Every detail matched the biblical descriptions swirling through Helena's mind, yet it was so surreal that she froze, uncertain if she should even move closer.

She forced herself to inhale. "We need to document everything," she managed, her voice husky with awe. "Photography first. No one touch it.".

They clustered around, adjusting lighting and snapping photos. Helena's chest constricted. The sense of presence in that chamber was overwhelming. Her scalp tingled. She had read accounts of explorers who claimed the Ark might still exist, and she had often dismissed those stories as legends. But faced with this chest. with its ringed corners and elaborate moldings that suggested biblical cherubim, she felt tremors of belief. She didn't want to let superstition cloud her judgment, yet she couldn't deny the tension gripping every nerve.

A faint, crackling hum broke the silence. Lorraine lifted her camera to her ear, frowning. "That's strange. My battery indicator's in the red. It was fully charged an hour ago.".

Amir muttered, "Check your flashlight battery.".

Lorraine did. "It's draining fast.".

Helena's own lamp flickered. A wave of nervousness rippled through the group. She pressed her hand to the camera strapped around her neck and found it nearly burning hot. An anxious swirl spread among them, but no one had a scientific explanation yet. Some might blame the damp conditions or an electrical short. Still. the coincidence was eerie.

In the silence, Helena spoke with forced calm. "We should record the exact positions, then get these items back to a lab. Maybe the environment is causing electromagnetic interference.".

Ibrahim, eyes locked on the gilded object, exhaled shakily. "If that's the Ark...this is going to change the world.".

"Let's not jump to conclusions," Helena said, though her tone lacked conviction. "It could be an elaborate replica. We won't know until we study it.".

They returned to photographing, though the cameras struggled with glitching controls. Each shot came out distorted or abruptly lost power. Despite that, a few images captured enough detail to prove the chest was extraordinarily old. Once they had documented all they could, Helena signaled them to step back.

Up above, Yusef perched on a stone block that overlooked the excavation. The sun was dipping toward the horizon, painting the Old City in gold. Workers scurried around the surface with anxious expressions, hauling rope, reinforcing beams, and calling out instructions to one another. The teenage observer sensed something big had happened beneath the ground. He overheard one guard mention that Dr. Carter and her group had found a sealed room. That possibility made him shiver with excitement. Local legends told him that beneath the Temple Mount lay hidden wonders. Now. it seemed, those legends might carry a shred of truth.

A sudden commotion among the workers drew Yusef's attention. Dust poured from the entrance to the underlevel, and a muffled shout came from below. He jumped to his feet, half-expecting the ground to cave in. He was too far away to see who was emerging. but from the frantic gestures, it appeared someone needed help down there.

Moments later, Ibrahim's voice crackled over the ground team's radio. "Partial collapse in the lower chamber. We're all safe, but we're trapped for the moment. We need immediate assistance clearing the exit. The structural beams gave way.".

Yusef's heart thudded. He glimpsed men grabbing large flashlights, a medical kit, and extra supports. They formed a rescue team. Judging by their hurry, the situation was dire. A wave of dread for the strangers below settled in his stomach. While curiosity had lured him here. the reality was frightening. If the corridor continued to collapse, nobody might make it out alive.

Underground, Helena coughed in a cloud of dust. She shielded her eyes with one arm. When the ceiling above them had groaned and then shifted, they all dove for cover. Stones rained down, smashing into the side of the tunnel. Now the path back was blocked by a barricade of fallen rubble. Amir tried to push aside some boulders. but they were too large. They were stuck, with limited air and no easy escape.

Gravel crunched underfoot as Ibrahim joined her, scanning the collapsed area with a handheld lamp that flickered at irregular intervals. "We can't move these stones by ourselves. We need the ground crew.".

Helena steadied her breath. "All right, stay calm. They know we're down here. They'll help us from the other side.".

Lorraine propped herself against the wall, trembling. She was normally calm under pressure, but dust had caked her face, and the enclosed space tested the courage of even the bravest among them. Helena offered her water, trying to keep everyone focused.

She avoided looking at the chest in the center of the room. Something about it sent pulses of tension through her. She told herself it was just nerves, exhaustion, and adrenaline. Yet the hum in the air persisted, a subtle static that lifted the hairs on her arms.

Minutes passed like hours. Several workers attempted to shift rocks, but more than once a slab threatened to topple, making them pull back. The situation was precarious. Helena pictured the dust-choked corridor outside. Would the rescue team reach them in time? She could feel her chest tighten.

To pass the time and keep morale stable, she asked Kyle to read out his notes on the inscriptions they had discovered. He recited passages referencing cherubim—winged guardians of the sacred object. Another described some form of shimmering radiance that caused men to tremble. The text ended abruptly. hinting that further explanation was once available in another scroll or carving that had since vanished.

As Kyle spoke, the swirling tension in Helena's mind sharpened. She was a woman of science, but the environment felt charged with a presence beyond the rational. She forced herself to remain grounded in facts: the odd draining of their equipment might be explained by an underground electromagnetic field. The hum in the air could be a static buildup from friction in these enclosed spaces. Yet none of that subdued the wave of awe rising within her.

Forty minutes after the collapse, they heard muffled voices from above. Rescue was underway. Several large stones shifted, and beams of lantern light cut through the dust. Helena's team cheered, relief flooding in. With each rock removed, the passage grew more visible. Eventually, a gap opened large enough for them to climb through. guided by gloved hands from the ground crew.

Ibrahim emerged first, pulling himself free. Helena followed close behind. She coughed, relief washing over her as she spotted the overhead scaffolding that had been reinforced. The sweet taste of less-stale air never felt so welcome. The rest of the team came out in pairs. battered and dusty but uninjured. Tools and crates remained in the chamber for later retrieval.

Yusef edged closer, hidden behind a half-crumbled wall. He watched them blink under the harsh lights. None of them looked jubilant, but Helena's face told a tale of excitement under the layer of exhaustion. She murmured to Ibrahim, and from her expression, Yusef sensed they had found something incredible down there.

When a small medical unit ushered them to a makeshift triage station, Helena refused to sit. "I'm fine," she insisted. "I just need to speak with my team and figure out our next step.".

The paramedic frowned. "You inhaled a lot of dust. Let me just check your vitals." He took her pulse and found it elevated, but she waved him off after a brief exam.

A short distance away, Ibrahim conversed with the foreman who coordinated the rescue. From bits of their dialogue drifting through the open air, Yusef heard fragments such as "inscriptions," " buried vault," and "absolute secrecy." The teenager's curiosity burned hotter. Whatever lay below, it was no ordinary ruin.

While Helena and Ibrahim spoke, Yusef noticed an older man wearing a neatly pressed suit approach them. He looked official, possibly a government liaison, though Yusef couldn't be certain. He kept his head low, eavesdropping from behind a nearby pillar.

The older man introduced himself as part of the local authority overseeing historical sites. "We must keep this under wraps," he whispered urgently. "The government wants to maintain confidentiality until the nature of your find is confirmed.".

Helena nodded, wiping grime from her forehead. "Understood. But we need more resources for excavation. That chamber is precarious, and we're sure we found something that could be historically significant beyond measure.".

"We can arrange that," the official said. "But I cannot stress enough—if word spreads prematurely, it could cause chaos.".

Ibrahim concurred with a resolute nod. "We'll keep a tight lid on it.".

As dusk settled across Jerusalem, the team dispersed for the night. Most were exhausted, their clothing dusty, their equipment battered. Helena lingered, though, near the entrance to the corridor, gazing into the dark. She couldn't dismiss the mental image of the gilded chest resting alone in that hidden sanctum. If it was indeed the Ark—or even a perfect replica—her entire career and the world's religious and historical understanding could shift dramatically.

Yusef lingered too, from a safe vantage, until Helena finally trudged toward the parked vehicles. The teenager watched her expression flicker with equal parts wonder and trepidation. He might not have understood all the details, but he sensed that a door had opened—one that might change everything for his city and perhaps beyond.

He swallowed hard. It was too late to glean more tonight. Guards had doubled, and the site was off-limits. But he resolved to find a way to confirm his suspicions. He had heard countless rumors of secret excavations over the years, but never had he seen a team so shaken. so alive with awe. Something big was about to unravel.

Meanwhile, Helena climbed into a jeep with Ibrahim. They rode in silence through narrow streets, the headlights washing over time-worn stone. The quiet gave her time to process the day's revelation. She carefully avoided leaping to grand conclusions, but her excitement simmered. She replayed the memory of those cherubim carvings. the wooden chest with gilded edges, the static hum that seemed to live in the walls themselves. She would need to gather data, run tests, and verify authenticity. Still, she could barely contain the goosebumps that rose whenever she recalled the shape of that lid.

Ibrahim broke the silence once they passed through a security checkpoint. "If word gets out that we found the Ark—assuming that's what it is—it'll be unstoppable. Countries will claim it, religious institutions will demand access, and conspiracy theorists will spin wild tales.".

She rubbed her eyes. "I know. If we aren't careful, it could become a flashpoint. This region doesn't need another source of tension. We must handle this delicately. I'll contact a few trusted colleagues to confirm the artifact's age and composition. You should alert your superiors about security requirements.".

His grip tightened on the steering wheel. "I'll get the best people on it. Because if the Ark's real, or even if it's an centuries-old relic of major significance, every superpower will want a piece of it.".

They parked at a small compound near the western edge of the Old City. After stepping out, Helena found herself staring at the night sky. Stars glimmered over Jerusalem's silhouetted rooftops. She felt a profound awe, as though the city were holding its breath, aware that something monumental had been uncovered. She tried to shake off the sense of destiny that clung to her thoughts. Archaeology was about uncovering truths. not fueling fantasies. Yet her instincts screamed that this was not an ordinary discovery.

Exhausted, she made her way to a modest guesthouse that had been arranged for the team. Once inside, she sank onto the bed without bothering to change, her mind churning through a thousand scenarios. She wondered if tomorrow would bring more structural collapses, more odd electromagnetic pulses. She wondered if they truly had touched upon something that had the power—literally or figuratively—to shape the fate of nations.

Up in his small apartment on the opposite side of the Old City, Yusef also lay awake, his thoughts tracing a labyrinth of questions. He had glimpsed the tension in Helena's eyes, recognized the hush around everyone who surfaced from that hidden chamber. He had a knack for reading expressions—his father used to say Yusef could see the shape of a person's soul just by how they carried themselves. Tonight. he sensed they had discovered a secret so profound that the grown-ups were afraid even to name it out loud.

Far from both Helena and Yusef, several miles to the west, a phone rang in an embassy corridor. A curt official answered, listened for several seconds, then hung up. Someone had leaked a rumor that an astonishing artifact might have been found under the Temple Mount. The official typed a brief message and sent it through a secure channel. On the receiving end sat David "Dave" Schumer. who read the coded text, his expression darkening. He was no stranger to global crises, having served in special ops, then intelligence, and now as a Secret Agent. His superiors wanted him on a plane at dawn, heading for Jerusalem.

Whether the rumor was real or not, the United States needed eyes and ears on the ground.

Yet, as Helena dozed fitfully, unaware of the espionage chess game already in motion, she could not shake a persistent, chilling worry: if that chest was indeed the Ark, the world might never be the same. And if it was something else, something no one had anticipated. then the threat was beyond imagination. She drifted off, the weight of antiquity pressing on her dreams, uncertain if she was stepping into a miraculous new dawn—or a brewing nightmare.

Chapter 2

The first rays of sunlight reached over the horizon, kissing the golden stones of Jerusalem's aged walls. Dr. Helena Carter arrived at the excavation site before most of her team. Her night of half-sleep had done little to dull her determination. She wanted to see the sealed vault again in better light, gather more evidence, and plan how best to preserve the discovery.

Security was tighter than before. A new layer of perimeter fencing had been installed, and pairs of armed guards in official uniforms watched every approach. She felt their suspicious gazes as she ducked under a rope barrier, flashed her credentials, and made her way down to the subterranean entrance. She found Ibrahim waiting by a stack of newly delivered support beams, tension creasing his forehead.

"The structural engineers arrived an hour ago," he informed her. "They've been reinforcing the corridor. We can enter soon, but it's still risky."

She paused to catch her breath. "I appreciate everything you're doing, Ibrahim. This can't be easy for you."

He managed a thin smile. "Let's just say my superiors are anxious. They want daily updates—sometimes hourly. The importance of this find isn't lost on them."

While they conferred, a boy appeared near the far side of the fencing, peering through a chain link panel with wide eyes. Helena glimpsed him out of the corner of her vision. Their gazes locked for a heartbeat before he darted away. She recognized him as the same teenager she had seen skulking around the previous evening. She made a mental note to keep watch on him; curiosity was natural, but this site was too volatile for random visitors. With so many mysteries swirling, she couldn't afford additional complications.

Two members of her team arrived—Lorraine Marsh and a quiet ex-military engineer named Lionel Hayes. They carried equipment cases and the determined expressions of people ready to face new challenges.

"All right," Helena said, gathering them together. "We have a systematic plan today: we'll re-enter the vault, record every inch with high-resolution cameras, carefully approach the chest, and take small samples of the surface or environment if possible. But no one touches the artifact with bare hands, and we move to prevent another collapse."

Heads nodded around her. The deeper meaning behind her words was unspoken: we might be handling something that could be dangerous, either from a structural standpoint or from another angle entirely.

They descended the narrow corridor in single file. This time, the lamps had been swapped out for industrial-grade LED lighting powered by a generator that hummed just outside. Extra braces supported the cracked ceiling. The older rubble had been cleared to widen a path. As they passed the carved reliefs again, Helena felt a thrill of recognition. Each motif of cherubim, each winged figure, now hinted strongly at the very artifact they suspected lay below.

Arriving at the lower chamber, they found it intact. The cloth covering had slipped partially off the chest, revealing more golden filigree and details of the wooden core. A hush fell over the group. Ibrahim exhaled. Lorraine muttered a quiet expression of amazement. Even Lionel—usually stoic—took a step back, as though in reverence.

Helena set up a tripod and began filming, speaking in a low, steady tone for the record. She identified the date, the location, and the condition of the artifact, describing the carved details of two cherubim facing each other on the lid. Her voice quavered a bit. It was one thing to read about biblical descriptions, quite another to see them mirrored in front of her eyes.

"Next," she said, "we'll check electromagnetic readings. Yesterday, we had anomalies with our batteries." She nodded to Lionel, who opened a small pelican case containing an EMF detector. He clicked it on. At first, the needle twitched slightly above baseline. Then, as he stepped closer to the gilded object, the device spiked. Everyone exchanged uneasy glances.

"That's not normal," Lionel stated. "We're underground. No big power lines overhead. Something is generating an unusual field here. Could be natural magnetized minerals in the rock, or—"

He paused, uncertain how to finish. Helena appreciated that he wanted to stay rational, but the evidence pointed toward something extraordinary.

She stooped to examine the lower portion of the chest. The gold on the corners looked worn, but not corroded as one might expect after centuries. She brushed her hand near the surface, feeling a faint tingling. It was as if the artifact pulsed with static.

"Let's gather a small scraping from the cloth," Helena said. Lorraine handed her a specialized blade for collecting samples. She carefully shaved a few fibers from the rotted material draped on the chest and sealed them in a sterile pouch. Lorraine labeled it as "Sample 2A: Exterior Cloth."

When Helena stood back, her heart hammered. The tension in the room was almost tangible. With each new test, they found more unexplainable phenomena. Another part of her mind insisted that there had to be a natural explanation—some unique combination of environment, material composition, and electromagnetic effects.

Ibrahim cleared his throat. "I've spoken with the head of the Israeli Antiquities Authority. They want an offsite secure facility for this item once we confirm it's safe to move. Given the potential significance, they'd prefer to keep it within Israel's national domain."

Helena nodded, though a flicker of concern crossed her face. She knew how quickly international actors could descend on a find like this. If the chest was the Ark—or even rumored to be—the pressure from religious institutions, governments, and private collectors would be immense. "Yes, that's wise. But let's confirm stability first. The chest might be fragile. If we try to remove it before we're sure, we could destroy a priceless piece of history."

While they worked, Yusef slipped past a distracted guard above and again crept into the upper corridor. He was careful to stay just out of sight. After the near collapse from the previous day, many of the laborers were busy with reinforcement tasks and not watching their perimeter. From his vantage, Yusef caught glimpses of flashlights in the lower chamber. He listened intently to the group's murmured words, picking up references to "unusual readings" and "cherubim." His heart raced. He had grown up hearing stories about powerful relics from the Old Testament. The mention of cherubim convinced him that they had found something beyond an ordinary relic.

Suddenly, a piece of rock shifted under his foot. It tumbled noisily down the steps. Yusef froze. Everyone in the chamber turned toward the sound. Helena's voice echoed up the staircase. "Who's there?"

Yusef darted backward, prepared to sprint for the exit. But he miscalculated. Two workers carrying additional supplies nearly bumped into him as they rounded a corner. The teenager skidded to a stop, caught red-handed.

"Easy!" shouted the man on the left, startled to see a kid in a place off-limits to visitors. He reached out to steady Yusef before he could flee.

Ibrahim and Helena emerged into the corridor with matching expressions of concern. Ibrahim recognized the teen from the previous day. "You're the boy I saw near the site last night. What are you doing here?"

Yusef looked cornered, but his posture remained defiant. "I wasn't hurting anything," he insisted, glancing rapidly between them. "I just wanted to see what you found. My father used to say secrets are dangerous. If you're digging under the Temple Mount, it has to be important."

Helena studied his face. He wasn't more than sixteen or seventeen, with bright eyes that radiated a mix of fear and curiosity. She also recognized the local accent in his voice. She softened her tone. "This is a restricted area. You can't just sneak in. It's unsafe and you could be injured."

Yusef's shoulders tensed, but he didn't back down. "Are you digging up something...holy? Or something that could cause trouble? People talk. They say foreign powers come here, searching for objects of power."

That statement surprised Helena, though she shouldn't have been shocked. Jerusalem was a city of rumors, swirling with centuries of legends. She exchanged a glance with Ibrahim. The liaison cleared his throat. "Young man, you need to leave. This place isn't open to the public. We can't have anyone interfering with our work."

An uneasy silence followed. Helena sensed the boy's earnestness. He clearly believed that these excavators might be unearthing something that could disrupt his community. She took pity on him but needed to stay firm. "I promise we're taking every precaution," she said, gentle but resolute. "Now, please let these men escort you outside."

Reluctantly, Yusef allowed the two workers to guide him back up the passage. His gaze flicked around, absorbing as many details as he could. Just before they disappeared around a bend, he looked over his shoulder, locking eyes with Helena one last time. She saw a spark of worry and fascination. She wondered if that was the last they would see of him. Something told her it might not be.

As the footsteps receded, Ibrahim shook his head. "We'll have to tighten security even more. He might be a harmless local kid...or someone's informant."

"Agreed," Helena murmured, though she couldn't quite banish the empathy she felt for the youth. "Let's get back to our work."

They returned to the lower chamber, and each subsequent test yielded more puzzling data. The EMF remained elevated. One temperature gauge read far colder near the artifact than it should have been. Each time they tried to photograph the chest up close, the camera malfunctioned. They managed only partial images before the screens flickered.

After two hours of documentation, Helena took a break to step outside and log her findings on a tablet. While the others rotated tasks, she found a quiet spot near the old stones and typed up her preliminary observations. She included details about the Ark-like chest, the odd electromagnetic anomalies, and the pressing need to confirm authenticity through lab testing. Her mind buzzed with speculation. She hoped scientific rationality would prevail, but a flutter of excitement wouldn't let her forget the possibility that they had indeed found the Ark.

Then, a commotion near the site entrance drew her attention. Two new arrivals stood at the perimeter: a tall figure in dark slacks and a local official in a crisp shirt. The first man held up identification to the guards. Helena watched as the official scanned the ID and waved them through. As they walked closer, she recognized the distinct posture and measured steps that suggested some kind of security background.

When the pair reached her, the local official introduced himself as Nahum Barak, an aide to the Ministry of Culture. He gestured to the man at his side. "Dr. Carter, allow me to present David Schumer, an American liaison who flew in this morning. He's here in an official capacity to monitor any potential concerns the United States might have about archaeological discoveries of international importance."

Helena gave a polite nod. "I see. That was fast. Didn't realize Washington moved that quickly."

Dave Schumer's lips curved in a polite, if somewhat tight, smile. He had short-cropped hair and alert eyes that took in everything at once. "I was already in the region on another assignment," he replied, voice steady. "I'm just here to observe, make sure everything is kept on the up-and-up."

Ibrahim appeared from behind a support beam. His shoulders stiffened when he saw the newcomer. "We have no intention of letting any foreign government walk off with our finds," he stated bluntly.

Dave raised a hand in a peaceable gesture. "I'm not here to start a fight. The U.S. has an interest in preserving cultural heritage, especially if this artifact is as significant as the rumors suggest. We just want to ensure it doesn't fall into the wrong hands."

A flicker passed through Ibrahim's eyes, as though he wanted to protest the notion that Israel might be "the wrong hands," but he stayed composed. Helena stepped between them, hoping to defuse any potential tension. "Fine. You're welcome to observe, Mr. Schumer, but we're in the middle of a delicate operation. The site is precarious. We can't have an armed detail traipsing through the corridor."

Dave nodded. "Understood. I'm not here to disrupt your process."

There was something in his tone that made Helena take a second look. Most government agents she'd dealt with had a veneer of politeness that barely masked their real agenda. Dave's approach was more measured, less overtly aggressive. It made her wonder if he was just that good at his job—or if he actually cared about how this played out.

Nahum Barak cleared his throat. "We trust you'll cooperate. The Ministry of Culture is grateful for your thorough documentation, Dr. Carter. I'll leave you to your work. Agent Schumer will remain in the vicinity to address any emerging concerns."

With that, Barak departed, leaving Dave behind. The new arrival calmly studied the excavation site, noticing the elaborate gear, the newly shored-up archway, the battered remains of the collapsed tunnel. He turned to Helena. "I'd appreciate a brief overview of your findings. I can keep a low profile."

She glanced at Ibrahim, who gave an almost imperceptible shrug. Better to keep the lines of communication open than spark suspicion by shutting Dave out. So she led him to a table stacked with reference photos and notes.

"These images," she began, flipping through the partial shots they had managed, "show a chest in a hidden vault beneath the Temple Mount. The construction is consistent with time-worn descriptions of the Ark of the Covenant, though we haven't confirmed authenticity. There's also an unusual electromagnetic field in the area."

Dave scanned the photos. "That's...unexpected," he admitted. He paused at one shot capturing carved cherubim on the lid. "This is either the find of the century, or something that will make a lot of people very angry. Or both."

Helena appreciated his candor. "Yes. That's why we're moving carefully. We're concerned that once word spreads, other factions—governments, militant groups—might try to seize it. We need to keep it quiet until we have more data."

In the background, Ibrahim directed workers to load sample containers for transport to a research lab. Lorraine carefully wrapped fragments of cloth. Lionel double-checked radiation readings—thankfully, nothing spiked on that front. The frantic pace of the dig served to highlight how little time they might have before external pressures became overwhelming.

While Helena explained the next steps—further documentation, carbon dating, scanning the artifact's interior if feasible—Dave nodded attentively. He asked precise questions about security measures, structural stability, and how they planned to transport the chest if it proved to be genuine. She had to admit, he seemed professional, not a meddling bureaucrat.

The day wore on, punctuated by routine checks of the corridor's reinforcements. By late afternoon, the sun's angle cast long shadows across the site. Helena was reviewing her notes near the surface level when Dave approached.

"You haven't taken a break," he said. It was more an observation than a question.

She gave a slight shrug. "There's too much to do. Maybe I'll rest once we have a plan to protect this find."

He studied her face with an unreadable expression. "I respect your dedication. But you might burn out if you don't pace yourself."

She almost laughed. "Look who's talking. Most intelligence folks I've met run on caffeine and catnaps."

He allowed a faint smile. "Guilty. But I've also learned that sometimes you have to step back to see the bigger picture. These are extraordinary circumstances."

Her eyes flicked to the corridor where the chest lay in darkness. "It doesn't feel real, you know? One day I'm analyzing pottery shards, the next I might be the lead archaeologist on the greatest biblical discovery in centuries—if it's genuine."

"If?" he echoed.

She took a breath. "We've seen elaborate hoaxes before, though never quite on this scale. But the presence of the electromagnetic anomalies and the historical location... Let's say I'm leaning toward believing it's authentic. And if it is, it's going to change a lot of things."

They stood in silence for a moment, absorbing the weight of that statement. She noticed a subtle shift in his posture. He looked out at the Old City skyline with a thoughtful gaze. "Are you worried about potential conflict?" he asked.

Helena nodded. "Very. This region has enough tension. Introducing an artifact that, in religious tradition, is said to have massive power... That's not going to calm anyone."

Before he could respond, a junior researcher named Soren came hurrying up from the corridor, face pale. "Dr. Carter, there was a flicker in the lights below. We heard a buzzing sound, and one of the steel braces vibrated for about five seconds. We're worried the chamber might be shifting again."

She snapped to attention. "Is everyone safe?"

"Yes, no injuries, but we're all spooked. Could the artifact be causing it?"

Dave shot Helena a quick, questioning glance. She didn't have an answer. "Let's go see," she replied, grabbing her flashlight. "Agent Schumer, if you're up for it, you can come along."

They hurried down the corridor, stepping carefully over cables and crates. The air felt heavier than usual. In the lower chamber, a few team members hovered near the doorway, glancing at the chest with wary expressions. The artifact looked unchanged, but a crackling hiss lingered in the background. Helena saw a faint sparkle of static dance across the golden edges. It vanished almost as soon as she noticed it, leaving a faint metallic scent in the air.

She approached with measured steps, scanning the environment. "Check the supports," she instructed Soren. "Make sure everything is stable."

Soren nodded and hustled around the chamber, tapping on the newly installed beams. Meanwhile, Helena aimed her flashlight at the gilded lid. For an instant, she thought she saw a swirl of shapes reflected in the gold. Not her reflection, but something ephemeral, wings or swirling smoke. She shook off the momentary hallucination, attributing it to stress.

"Any sign of actual structural movement?" Dave asked, scanning the ceiling. Lionel was checking the overhead cracks with a portable laser device.

"No sign of physical movement," Lionel replied. "It's more like an electric surge. We have no power cables close enough to cause that. The generator upstairs is behind a sealed stone wall. This phenomenon is localized."

Helena stepped closer to examine the chest. She used a wooden rod—no metal, to minimize conduction—and gently prodded the fabric covering the artifact's corner. A faint spark leaped from the gold band to the rod, like static in the winter air. She jumped back, heart pounding.

"What in the world..." she murmured, her throat tightening.

Dave's eyes narrowed. "That's definitely not normal," he muttered, placing a hand near his sidearm before catching himself. He wasn't quite sure what he'd use it on if something went haywire. A golden chest that might hold intangible power? A presence that defied logic?

Helena faced her team. "We need to proceed with the tests tonight. Let's set up an advanced scanning device if we have one. If we wait too long, we could lose a chance to study whatever is causing these readings."

A sense of nervous agreement filled the chamber. They had a mission—to understand. The hum in the air grew a little louder, then receded as though it were a breathing entity. The faint glimmer on the Ark's surface vanished completely, leaving only the battered gold.

In the hall above, Yusef lingered once again, having slipped past security in the chaos caused by flickering lights and urgent calls. He dared not enter the main corridor, but from his vantage, he caught a glimpse of Helena's frightened posture, the flash of sparks, the tense hush among the researchers. Fear gnawed at him. Something about that relic was alive with an energy he couldn't comprehend. He worried it might bring danger to the city, to his neighborhood, to his friends and family. He made a silent vow to monitor these foreigners carefully—because if they unleashed something harmful, he would warn his community in time.

When Helena and Dave emerged from the chamber an hour later, they were mentally exhausted. They climbed to the surface, stepping into the twilight. A warm breeze ruffled Helena's hair. She blinked in the open air, feeling as though she'd spent a lifetime underground.

Dave looked equally drained, but his eyes shone with determination. "I'll coordinate with my contacts about boosting site security. Discreetly," he said, his voice too low for others to overhear. "We can't let other parties find out before we're ready."

Helena glanced toward the Old City skyline, where the lights of the Western Wall shimmered. "I agree. This can't be a secret for long, but we're not prepared to handle the political and religious fallout yet."

He nodded, stepping aside to place a quick call. From the snippets of his conversation, she gathered he was urging caution and confidentiality, referencing "the sensitive find" and "not confirming details yet." She observed him with guarded approval. At least for now, it seemed they had someone on the American side who was taking a measured approach rather than making demands.

Ibrahim joined her, motioning to the entire group. "Let's gather for a briefing. We need to outline next steps. I'm concerned about the stability of the artifact. That buzzing we witnessed earlier is too much to ignore."

The team congregated around a few portable tables, battered from the day's work. Warm lights on poles cast shifting shadows across their faces. They discussed a plan: install advanced scanning equipment overnight, collect further samples, and bring in structural specialists. Meanwhile, site security would be doubled to keep out everyone who didn't belong, including curious locals like Yusef.

Soren raised a question: "What if we get an official from the Ministry of Religious Affairs involved? Or a rabbinical scholar who can advise us on the protocols for handling sacred objects?"

Helena tapped a pen against her notebook. "That might become necessary soon. But we risk leaks if we expand the circle. For now, let's keep it strictly among ourselves and the Israeli Antiquities Authority. Once we know exactly what we're dealing with, we'll proceed with proper religious and diplomatic channels."

Their conversation carried on until the stars emerged. Dave joined them again after finishing his call, offering a subdued report that his superiors agreed to maintain secrecy for the moment. Everyone felt the ticking clock, the sense that once morning broke, a new wave of rumors could surface.

Eventually, the group dispersed for the night, each person left with their own swirling thoughts. Helena lingered, packing up instruments and scanning the shadows for any sign of the boy who kept sneaking in. Her mind reeled with questions. Was the Ark's rumored power real? If so, how had it lain dormant all these centuries?

At a vacant corner of the site, Dave approached. "I can't speak for your field, but I know intelligence. By tomorrow, agencies will be buzzing with rumors. We might have just a few days before certain players arrive."

She met his gaze and nodded. "I was just thinking the same thing. We'll do what we can tonight."

He studied her face, softened his tone. "If you need anything—logistically, security, access to lab equipment—I can pull strings. I'm not here to control your operation, only to help keep it safe."

Her shoulders relaxed slightly. "I appreciate that. For the record, I'm not used to collaboration with government agents who aren't breathing down my neck every step of the way."

A hint of dry humor flickered in his eyes. "I'll try not to ruin your first impression."

She almost smiled, exhaustion curling into something like camaraderie. "You're doing fine so far, Agent Schumer."

He slipped his hands into his pockets and let out a long breath. "It might get more complicated soon. I've got a feeling that if the Ark is real, the entire balance of power in this region—and beyond—might shift."

Helena let silence speak for a moment. The wind rustled the tarps and chain-link barriers. "And what do you think?" she finally asked. "Is it real?"

Dave angled his head, scanning the distant city lights. "I don't have enough evidence yet, but I've seen enough in my line of work to know that sometimes, myths turn out to be truths that science hasn't explained. If this is the Ark, then history, faith, and politics are about to collide in a way none of us can fully predict."

She nodded, and they stood there in the hush of a city built on layers of conflict and devotion. In the distance, the Dome of the Rock gleamed, silent witness to centuries of turmoil. Now, a hidden vault threatened to stir up a fresh storm.

Helena finally zipped her pack, glancing at her watch. "We should get some rest, or at least as much as possible. Tomorrow, we continue."

They parted ways without further words, returning to their respective accommodations. She walked through the winding lanes of the Old City, every footstep echoing in the narrow alleys. At her guesthouse, she paused to notice a swirl of graffiti on a stone wall—an angelic figure with outspread wings, or maybe just a stylized bird. For some reason, it made her think of the golden cherubim engraved on the chest's lid. She shook her head, dismissed the thought, and stepped inside.

Meanwhile, across town, Yusef crouched on the rooftop of his family's modest apartment, gazing at the faint glow rising from the direction of the dig site. His mind spun with images of sparks and swirling lights around that chest. He worried about his city, about the possibility of foreign agents bringing chaos to the streets. And a part of him—hungry for purpose—felt a pull to do something. If the grown-ups were tampering with something sacred, he might need to act as a guardian for the only home he knew.

In the darkness, none of them realized that a half-dozen intelligence agencies were already intercepting whispers, analyzing statements, and preparing to move. The rumor about a "sacred find" under the Temple Mount had spread like wildfire. By dawn, more players would be in motion—each with a different motive, each willing to do whatever was necessary to claim the prize for themselves.

Chapter 3

A single thread of pink sunlight crept across the skyline of Jerusalem, stirring the city from its slumber. Shadows slipped away from the walls as the first call to prayer floated over the rooftops. In the narrow lanes of the Old City, life awakened. Vendors rolled up the shutters of family shops. and the aroma of fresh bread drifted through the alleys. While most people greeted the day with routine tasks, a far more extraordinary drama was unfolding around the underground chamber beneath the Temple Mount.

Dr. Helena Carter arrived at the excavation just after dawn. She felt the mild chill of the early morning breeze graze her cheeks as she passed through the newly fortified security perimeter. Over a dozen Israeli guards, some in plain clothes and some in uniform. stood watch with rigorous vigilance. Their gazes flicked across every movement.

Despite the protective measures, tension still hummed in the air. Word of the sealed vault had begun to slip out. Helena feared that governments, extremist groups, or opportunists might soon converge on the site. Yet no official announcement had been made, and the authorities were working around the clock to keep details hidden from the public. She surveyed the men and women on duty—searching for any sign of nerves. Their stern faces told her everything: they felt a storm coming.

Once inside the cordoned-off zone, Helena spotted Ibrahim Mahdi leaning against a temporary railing near a collection of crates. He rubbed his temples as he studied a set of blueprints in his hands. The lines indicated old tunnels that branched off in countless directions beneath the Temple Mount. Judging by the frustration in his face. the labyrinth made him uneasy.

She offered a small greeting. "Early start?".

"Couldn't sleep," he said, folding the map. "We discovered a literal treasure from the depths of weathered history. Now we're stuck balancing politics, security, and science.".

A lump formed in her throat. "We'll do our best. My hope is that no one tries to exploit this find.".

He met her gaze. "You're more optimistic than I am. I talked to a contact at the Antiquities Authority last night, and the rumors are spreading faster than we expected. Some foreign embassies have begun sniffing around, requesting 'cultural updates.'".

She looked away, the weight of those words settling in. "We have to push forward with the study. Otherwise, speculation will fill the void.".

They walked together toward the entry passage. Workers had installed additional beams overnight, making the route far safer than it was two days ago. A glow from industrial lamps lit the corridors, and the metallic smell of fresh tools mingled with the musty odor of aged stone.

Partway down, a team member named Soren approached. His solemn features showed the strain of the night's tasks. "Dr. Carter, we ran new tests on the electromagnetic field. The readings are spiking intermittently. Sometimes it's low, sometimes it almost maxes out our gauge.".

"Any theory on what's causing that fluctuation?" Helena asked.

He shrugged, uncertain. "Could be environmental factors. But I've never seen anything like it, especially not in a static site. We thought it might be the portable generator, but the anomalies persist even when we switch to battery power.".

Ibrahim exhaled. "So we're dealing with unpredictable phenomena in the same chamber as a relic that might be the Ark of the Covenant. Fantastic.".

None of them dared to voice the deeper concern: if this truly was the Ark, everything they believed about myth and faith might need re-examination. Helena forced her attention back to practical concerns. "Keep monitoring. Let me know if there's any risk of structural damage or hazard to the workers.".

Soren nodded and disappeared into a side corridor where the scanning equipment hummed.

Farther along, they descended the final set of steps. The familiar hush of the subterranean chamber met them, though it no longer felt quite so deserted. Traces of modern intrusion lay scattered around: cables, plastic crates, an array of tripods. A dozen researchers bustled about. taking precise measurements from every angle of the vault.

At the center of the room stood the chest. Dim golden reflections played along its edges, the metal filigree still mesmerizing despite centuries of burial. Helena paused a few feet away, crossing her arms, feeling that same quiet awe. She recalled the biblical texts describing the Ark's capacity to level walls. part rivers, and strike down armies. Yet it lay silent before her, or mostly silent. Occasional sparks of static flickered across the gilded top. That shimmer reminded her of the lightning arcs that sometimes dance around an electrified coil.

Ibrahim let out a quiet sigh. "No matter how long I stand here, I still can't believe it. The shape, the details... everything matches the old accounts.".

She nodded, her throat tight with emotion. "Let's not jump to final conclusions until we've run every test, but I understand the feeling.".

A sudden beep from her phone drew her attention. She fished it out to see a message from Dave Schumer. He was still new to the site, but his presence had already become a steadying force. The text read: We need to talk about the security situation. I'm outside near the main gate.

"I'll be back," Helena told Ibrahim. "Dave wants a word.".

She found the American agent in a shadowed corner of the courtyard above ground, speaking into a secure phone. He ended the call when he saw her, slipping the device into his pocket. The mild lines around his eyes looked deeper than the day before. as if he too had skipped a night's rest.

"Bad news?" she asked.

He studied her for a moment, then nodded. "Rumors are swirling in Washington. Other intelligence communities have picked up the chatter—Moscow, Beijing, probably more. They suspect a monumental artifact has been found. Some think it's the Ark. Others believe it might be a nuclear device from the Cold War hidden under the city. In short. speculation is wild.".

Her stomach churned. "So the veil of secrecy is gone?".

"Not entirely. Officially, nothing is confirmed, and no government has publicly acknowledged the discovery. But that won't hold off covert teams from investigating.".

She glanced around, ensuring no one was within earshot. "Do you think infiltration attempts could start soon?".

His jaw tightened. "Count on it. If we don't manage this carefully, there will be a line of foreign operatives at our doorstep. I've seen it happen before with lesser finds.".

A swirl of emotions coursed through her. She despised the idea of losing academic control over the artifact. More than that, she worried about the city's safety. "We need a plan to keep the Ark secure while finishing our research.".

His shoulders tensed under his dark jacket. "I'm here to help with that. My superiors are willing to coordinate with Israeli authorities. The question is, do you want direct American oversight, or do you prefer a quieter arrangement?".

She hesitated, recalling how quickly secrets vanish once multiple governments get involved. "For now, let's keep it low-key. We can't have armed American squads crawling all over one of the holiest sites on the planet. That alone could spark an international incident.".

He nodded. "Agreed. But let me place a few of my people on standby,. If something happens, we'll respond faster than any official channel.".

"Fine," she said, mindful of how easily things could escalate if certain parties suspected the U.S. was muscling in. "We'll keep it discreet.".

A flutter of tension passed between them. She caught his gaze, noticing a flicker of compassion. For a moment, they stood in an unspoken understanding: both wanted to protect this city from chaos, even if their methods differed. Something in that shared purpose fostered a sense of camaraderie that she wasn't used to feeling with government types.

He stepped closer, lowering his voice. "I also heard that a Vatican envoy might be on the move. They've got a presence here in Jerusalem, but they're ramping up interest. That might be connected to the Ark's religious significance.".

A slight chill rippled through her. "Ibrahim mentioned the Church might get involved eventually. I expected that would come after we made an official statement. If they show up early, it complicates everything.".

"I'm sure it does," he said. "Keep your eyes open.".

She gave him a small nod, then turned to go, the conversation replaying in her mind. More players joining the drama meant more risk. The Ark was no longer just an archaeological dream—it was a geopolitical lightning rod.

Returning to the underground vault, she found Soren fussing over a newly arrived piece of scanning equipment. The large gray device looked like something from a high-tech lab, complete with a display screen and an array of sensors.

He offered a quick explanation, voice echoing in the chamber. "This is an advanced ground-penetrating radar with integrated 3D imaging. It might let us peek inside the chest without physically opening it.".

A ripple of excitement moved through the assembled crew. Many archaeologists had dreamt of seeing inside the Ark's rumored interior. There were legends of stone tablets, sacred relics from Moses' time, or even older secrets.

Helena nodded. "All right, let's try it. Position it carefully. I don't want any accidental contact with the artifact's surface.".

They cleared the area around the golden box, setting up protective barriers so the scanner wouldn't brush against the precious item. When everything was in place, Soren switched on the radar. A low hum vibrated. Data began scrolling across the monitor.

For the first twenty seconds, the display was a swirl of noise. Then an outline emerged: the rectangular shape of the chest. Beneath that, faint shapes flickered. It was difficult to interpret the readings. Helena moved closer, peering over Soren's shoulder. The lines seemed to indicate a hollow interior. with possible obstructions or partitions.

Soren tapped the controls, refining the scan resolution. The shape of what looked like two stone tablets appeared, though the images were fuzzy. "Are those…?".

He trailed off, unwilling to say it out loud. Helena placed a hand on the back of his chair, her heart pounding. If the chest truly contained stone tablets, it would align with the biblical accounts describing the Ten Commandments. The possibility caused her palms to sweat.

Ibrahim joined them, equally entranced. "So it's not solid. You see those lines near the top? Could be remnants of rods or handles inside.".

Soren zoomed in. "Yes, possibly. But the data is unstable. The electromagnetic interference is making the image flicker.".

As if on cue, a spark shot from the Ark's lid to one of the metal frames near it. Everyone jumped back. A faint burning odor lingered, and one of the cables began smoking. Helena rushed to unplug the device, worried the entire apparatus might fry.

Static popped in the air. For a moment, a swirl of light shimmered around the chest's edges, like a subtle halo. Then it faded. Silence followed, save for the scrape of someone's shoe as they staggered away from the sizzling cable.

Ibrahim exhaled. "That's the second time something like this has happened. First our cameras malfunction, now the radar nearly fries.".

Helena crouched, glancing at the scorched cable. "This is beyond normal static discharge. The field around the Ark is intensifying. We can't keep risking expensive equipment—or people's safety.".

Soren set the damaged cable aside. "I'll see if we can insulate the rig more effectively. But it's clear we're dealing with something we barely understand.".

She nodded, mind racing. Part of her wanted to attempt an old-fashioned approach: gently open the lid, if that was even possible. Another part recoiled at the notion. Biblical warnings said any unholy intrusion could bring disaster. She tried to dismiss that as superstition—yet the destructive energy around the Ark gave those warnings a chilling edge.

"We'll regroup," she said, forcing calm into her voice. "Everyone take a break, step back from the artifact. We'll figure out a new approach.".

A swirl of workers retreated up the tunnel, grateful for the chance to breathe fresh air. Helena lingered behind with Ibrahim, exchanging grim looks. Neither had the answers they needed. Each day brought more questions, and each test threatened to unleash fresh anomalies.

Up in the Old City streets, Yusef Nasir finished delivering a stack of sweet pastries to a neighborhood café where he worked part-time. He had woken at sunrise to help his uncle, who ran the small shop. After hours of moving crates, he wiped his brow and excused himself. claiming he had errands. What he really wanted was to revisit the Temple Mount area, see if more hints about the secret dig had surfaced.

He wove through the bustling market, slipping past fruit vendors and spice merchants. Clusters of tourists paused at historical sites, snapping photos. Yusef was careful to keep a low profile, though the excitement in his eyes belied his calm exterior. Snippets of rumor reached his ears: talk of an "American agent lurking around the Mount," or "strange power surges near the site." Sometimes the rumors were couched in cynicism. other times in hushed respect.

Tension gripped him. If the Ark truly lay beneath those stones—one of the holiest relics—what would happen if hostile forces seized it? He replayed the memory of the previous night, recalling the static sparks and Helena Carter's wary expression. The artifact felt powerful in a way he couldn't define. Part of him yearned to believe it was a living sign of the divine. there to guide or judge humanity. Another part feared it was something raw and dangerous, too potent to be handled by mortal hands.

He soon reached an overlook near the excavation. Guards had set up new barriers, making approach nearly impossible. Drones circled overhead, presumably for surveillance. Yusef's heart sank. Slipping through would be harder than before. He scanned for a vantage point, eventually finding a cluster of stacked crates behind a supply truck. They formed a precarious tower against a high stone ledge.

Carefully, he climbed the makeshift ladder until he reached a ledge affording him a partial view of the main entrance. A wave of triumphant relief flowed through him—he could watch the scene from this perch. Workers entered and exited at intervals. Armed guards marched along the perimeter. Then. after about fifteen minutes, he saw something unusual:

a man in a crisp suit escorted by an armed detail. The stranger marched with an air of authority, conversing in clipped tones with a local official. Though Yusef couldn't hear every word, he noticed one phrase repeated: "Essential to national security.".

Yusef's pulse quickened. Another piece in this puzzle. The man disappeared into the site, leaving the teen alone to wonder if yet another government was sending envoys. How many were aware of the secret?

Down in the vault, Helena's phone buzzed again. This time, the display showed an incoming call from an unknown number. She stepped away from the hum of activity to answer. "Hello?".

A measured voice spoke. "Dr. Carter, this is Father Aurelius Lombardi, calling from the Vatican Embassy here in Jerusalem. May I have a moment of your time?".

She felt her grip tighten around the phone. This had happened sooner than she expected. "Yes, Father Lombardi. How did you get my number?".

A faint smile carried through the line. "It wasn't difficult. There are few female archaeologists leading major Temple Mount excavations. I'd like to discuss the cultural and religious importance of your current undertaking.".

Helena exhaled. "I see. I'm not authorized to share details at this time.".

"That's understandable," Lombardi said with a practiced politeness that hinted at deeper intentions. "However, the Vatican has a profound interest in the Ark of the Covenant. Our historical records—weather-scarred manuscripts, letters from crusaders—suggest the Ark's last known location might indeed have been here. If your discovery is genuine. we'd like to offer any theological expertise you might require.".

Her mind spun, recalling Dave's warning. "Father, this project remains under the jurisdiction of the Israeli Antiquities Authority. Any collaboration would go through them.".

"Of course," he replied gently, "but the Church urges caution. The Ark was known to bring both blessings and calamities. I'd be more than willing to help interpret any inscriptions you find, especially if they reference cherubim or devout rites.".

She hesitated, uncertain how to respond. Inviting Lombardi in could provide valuable knowledge, but it might also open the door to more power plays. "I appreciate the offer. We're still in the early stages. Perhaps we can revisit this conversation once we have more information.".

"Very well," he said. "Time is of the essence, Dr. Carter. I'm available whenever you're ready. May the Lord guide you.".

He ended the call, leaving her with a prickling concern. She had half-expected a Vatican representative to contact them eventually, but this was abrupt. Word of the Ark was definitely out. She made a mental note to update Ibrahim and Dave about it.

Emerging from the underground corridor, she stepped into the open air, blinking against the brightness. Dave stood near a new arrival: a serious-looking Israeli official with salt-and-pepper hair who introduced himself as Gilad Ayar. He claimed to represent the nation's intelligence apparatus. He offered Helena a polite nod but wasted little time on pleasantries.

"I've been informed that a high-value cultural artifact was discovered below," Gilad stated, turning a sharp gaze on her. "We have to ensure no foreign entity gains possession of anything that could pose a national security threat.".

She opened her mouth to speak, but Dave jumped in smoothly. "This is a delicate archaeological matter, Mr. Ayar. Dr. Carter's team is still in the process of confirming the item's identity.".

Gilad's eyes flicked between them. "Identity aside, the presence of foreign intelligence agents on our soil is known to me. There's no telling how many are converging on Jerusalem as we speak.".

Helena tried to maintain composure. "We have security measures in place, and we welcome any additional support from your government to protect the site. But I must emphasize, our work is scientific—this is not a weapons program or anything that can be launched or fired.".

A tight smile appeared on Gilad's lips. "That may be so. However, if it's truly the Ark—if it has powers described in legend—some might see it as more destructive than any conventional weapon. My office has studied enough historical accounts to know that myth can inflame modern-day conflicts.".

She took a moment to let the warning sink in. The official was probably right. Even the rumor of a biblical super-weapon could ignite a frenzy of aggression. "I understand your position," she said carefully. "We'll keep you informed. Right now, our priority is to study the artifact and ensure it remains unharmed.".

Gilad offered a curt nod, then regarded Dave with neutral suspicion. "I assume you're also aligned with preserving Israel's interests, Agent Schumer?".

Dave's tone remained professional. "Our interests coincide. If the Ark is real, the last thing the United States wants is for it to spark a global crisis. Our cooperation can help maintain stability.".

The Israeli official assessed him for another beat, then made a satisfied grunt. "Good. I'll be in touch." With that, he strode off, flanked by an assistant.

Helena let out a breath she hadn't realized she was holding. Dave turned to her, and a ghost of a smile flickered across his face. "We've both had fun meetings this morning, it seems.".

She placed her phone in her pocket. "You could say that. Father Lombardi from the Vatican just called, offering theological guidance.".

He lifted an eyebrow. "So the Church is extending a hand. Not surprising. I assume you told him it's too soon to involve them?".

"More or less," she said. "I couldn't exactly slam the door in his face, though. He might have knowledge that could help interpret the inscriptions. That said, his arrival now is suspicious.".

"Everything about this is suspicious." Dave scanned the surroundings. "Let's keep track of each new player. We can't afford to let them all step on each other's toes down there.".

A swirl of dust wafted through the courtyard as a truck rumbled past, carrying beams for further reinforcing the site. Workers hollered instructions, trying to guide the vehicle in cramped conditions. Beyond the gates, half a dozen curious onlookers lingered, including a few local residents. scanning the perimeter for signs of activity.

Helena's gaze lingered on a young figure perched on a distant ledge. From this angle, she couldn't make out the face, but something about the lean build and the watchful posture reminded her of the teenager who had slipped inside earlier. Could Yusef be up there. risking trouble again?

She nudged Dave's arm. "Look, top of that wall. See anyone?".

He squinted, then nodded. "Yeah. Could be a local kid or just a nosy teen. Think it's the same one you mentioned before?".

"Probably. He's persistent. I doubt he poses a threat, but he's obviously curious.".

Dave considered for a moment. "I can have someone shoo him off. Or we can leave him be.".

"Let him be," she decided. "I don't want to create a scene. If he's that determined, he'll probably just find another angle.".

A shared understanding passed between them. There were enough looming problems without harassing a local boy who was too curious for his own good.

They descended into the dig once more, bracing themselves for hours of painstaking work. The team reassembled, now wary of another electric surge. The advanced scanner remained offline until they could repair the damaged cable. Helena decided to pivot her attention to analyzing inscriptions on the chamber walls. Perhaps the etched Hebrew text would yield more clues about what lay within the Ark—or how to manage it.

Lorraine Marsh, a specialist in centuries-old languages, methodically photographed each line of script in the corridor. She had a tablet propped on a portable stand where she cross-referenced modern Hebrew with archaic forms. Every so often, she scrawled notes in a battered notebook.

"What do you have?" Helena asked, stepping beside her.

Lorraine tapped the screen. "Some fragments refer to cherubim, as we knew. There's also mention of 'the voice from above the wings' and 'the seat of mercy.' That lines up with old biblical texts about the Ark's design.".

Helena nodded, remembering that the Ark was sometimes described as having a 'mercy seat' flanked by two golden cherubs. "So no surprises there.".

Lorraine pointed to another line that was partially eroded. "Here it says something about great wrath. The phrase is incomplete, but it implies catastrophic power unleashed against those who defiled the holy chest.".

A chill passed through Helena. She recalled the small sparks that had already injured cables and rattled the metal beams. Maybe those were only faint previews of something far more dangerous. "Anything about how to contain or neutralize it?".

Lorraine gave a faint shrug. "These inscriptions read more like warnings than instructions. There's mention of purification rites, but the text is fragmentary. Could be referencing time-worn Temple rituals we no longer fully understand.".

"Then we're dealing with guesswork," Helena murmured, scribbling notes in her own log. "Let's keep searching. Maybe we'll find a more complete text behind all this rubble.".

Lorraine nodded, pressing on with her photographic survey.

Hours crawled by in a haze of labor. Soren returned with a partially repaired scanning device, though he was hesitant to switch it on so soon. Others catalogued minor artifacts from the surrounding debris—broken pottery, old bronze implements, scraps of cloth that had deteriorated into near dust. The team systematically labeled each find. hoping any detail might reveal the chamber's era or confirm its link to First Temple times.

All the while, the Ark loomed in the center, humming with subdued menace.

Around midday, Helena peeled off her gloves and stepped outside for a short break. The sun glared overhead, though the day's heat felt mild compared to the tension simmering within the site. She found a corner near the fence to sip water and collect her thoughts.

She was reviewing mental checklists—security, scientific analysis, official channels—when Dave approached, a sandwich in hand. He offered her half. "You've been down there for hours without a real meal.".

The unexpected gesture made her smile. "Thanks. I am hungry.".

She accepted the food, and they leaned against the fence in a patch of shade. For a few minutes, they ate in quiet companionship, half-listening to the urban bustle just beyond the barricades.

He eventually broke the silence. "Is there anything we can do to reduce the risk from the Ark's energy field? Some method to ground or disperse the buildup?".

She almost laughed, catching herself as she remembered that word was on her mental do-not-say list. Instead, she rephrased. "We've tried to channel the static away with metal rods. It helps a little, but the phenomenon is unpredictable. It's not standard electricity. I can't fully explain it.".

He chewed, his gaze pensive. "Guess that means no easy fix.".

"Not yet," she said. "We might learn more if we figure out what's inside—without forcibly opening it. I fear that would do more harm than good, not just to the chest, but maybe to us as well.".

His brow creased, as though considering the stories of biblical devastation that legends attributed to the Ark. Then he set aside the final bite of his lunch. "Do you ever wonder if this is actually supernatural? I'm not religious, but part of me wonders if we're tangling with something beyond science.".

Her mouth went dry. She avoided that question, even in her own head. But the electric pulses and illusions in the gold left her uneasy. "I'm a scientist," she said, weighing her words. "I believe everything has an explanation, though it might be beyond our current understanding.".

His eyes flickered with empathy. "That's a logical stance. But after everything I've witnessed in my career—human cruelty, strange phenomena, unexplainable coincidences—I keep an open mind.".

Their conversation teetered on a deeper edge, as if they both sensed the possibility that the Ark might be more than an artifact. The moment felt oddly intimate. She felt the faint pressure of his presence, the look in his eyes that said he understood her uncertainty and shared it. For a heartbeat. it felt like they were alone in the world, bound by the enormity of what they'd uncovered.

A series of radio calls broke the moment. Helicopter blades whirred overhead, and muffled shouts carried from the main gate. They rose, scanning for signs of trouble.

One of the Israeli guards jogged up, breath labored. "Mr. Schumer, Dr. Carter, we have an unscheduled arrival. A black SUV just pulled up with official plates, and the men inside are demanding entry.".

Dave's expression hardened. "Any idea who they are?".

The guard shook his head. "They claim to be from a special liaison office in the Israeli government, but they won't show more than a badge. They're insistent.".

Helena shared a worried look with Dave. More arrivals, more complications. "We'll go see," she said, tossing her empty water bottle aside.

They headed for the entrance, weaving between supply crates and newly erected barricades. At the gate, two men in dark suits glowered at the guard detail. One was short and stocky, the other tall with a narrow face. Both wore identifications pinned to their jackets. Helena recognized the insignia of an Israeli intelligence branch. though the exact unit wasn't immediately clear.

The tall man stepped forward. "Dr. Carter, Agent Schumer? I'm Dagan. My colleague is Samuel. We're here on behalf of an inter-agency security task force.".

Dave offered a carefully neutral nod. "What does that entail?".

Dagan's mouth was a thin line. "We have reason to believe foreign nationals are planning to breach this site. My team is authorized to conduct a preemptive sweep—inside and out—to ensure there are no listening devices or infiltration routes.".

Helena tried to remain calm. "So you're looking for hidden bugs or potential sabotage?".

"That's correct," Dagan confirmed. "We also want to confirm how many foreigners have already been admitted. We know the American presence is official, but we need a full roster.".

She didn't like the tone—accusatory, as if she'd let a rogue's gallery stroll inside. "We've been keeping a close watch. Only members of my archaeological team, essential Israeli staff, and a few U.S. personnel. No one else.".

Samuel, the shorter man, pulled a small electronic gadget from his pocket. It looked like a signal detector. "Then you won't mind if we check the rooms, your electronics, anything that might be compromised?".

Dave's posture tensed. "We can allow a sweep for infiltration devices, but you're not rummaging through our personal gear. My superiors will want to see a formal request first.".

Dagan raised an eyebrow. "Are you refusing cooperation?".

"No," Helena jumped in, trying to defuse the confrontation. "But we need to keep the scientific instruments untouched. They're sensitive, and any interference could skew our research data.".

The two men exchanged a glance. "We'll be careful," Samuel said. "Show us where we can begin.".

Helena hesitated. Letting them poke around the underground chamber risked them seeing details that might go directly to other officials with unknown agendas. On the other hand, refusing them might cause friction with the Israeli government. She recalled Gilad Ayar's stern face that morning—defiance could spark a clampdown on her entire project.

Dave must have sensed her dilemma. He placed a steadying hand on her shoulder, then addressed the men. "Fine. But keep the team minimal, and no disruptions to the artifact itself.".

"Understood," Dagan said curtly.

The group filed inside, tension radiating with every step. Helena led them down the corridor, where the scanning equipment, cables, and newly installed lights still glowed. Workers paused mid-task to stare at the newcomers. A hush settled over the vault as the two intelligence agents swept the area with their detectors. scanning walls, rummaging behind crates, checking corners for possible hidden transmitters.

Soren and Lorraine hovered protectively near the Ark, watching with uncertain eyes. Any mishandling of the item or the instruments could ruin weeks of meticulous research.

After fifteen minutes, the men returned, conferring in low voices. Their gadget beeped sporadically, but it seemed inconclusive. Finally, Samuel approached Helena. "No sign of infiltration devices. The electromagnetic anomalies are interfering with our sweeper.".

She fought the urge to roll her eyes. "Yes, that's been happening with every electronic tool we bring down here.".

Dagan made a thoughtful sound. "We have concerns that these anomalies could mask covert transmissions. We might post a security detail inside the chamber.".

Helena bristled. The thought of armed men standing watch mere feet from the Ark, stepping over her staff, filled her with dread. "That's not ideal for a delicate archaeological excavation. Your weapons, your gear—it's not a match for these conditions.".

A standoff seemed imminent. The men were determined to exercise authority, and she was equally determined to protect her work. Dave stepped in once again, his voice firm but not confrontational. "Give Dr. Carter and Mr. Mahdi time to set up a small perimeter inside the vault for a guard station if absolutely necessary. We can find a compromise that allows security without interfering with the dig.".

Neither Dagan nor Samuel looked pleased, but they appeared to accept that suggestion. "We'll speak with our superiors," Dagan said, "and coordinate with Gilad Ayar about the next step.".

As they marched out, the entire vault seemed to breathe a collective sigh of relief. Helena pressed a hand to her temple, staving off a building headache. "At this rate, we'll have a new set of officials every few hours.".

Dave gave her a rueful look. "We'll manage it. Even if it means we have to juggle half the intelligence community, we won't let them bulldoze your team.".

His quiet confidence, despite the chaos swirling around them, steadied her nerves. She almost smiled. "That's the second time today you've jumped to my rescue.".

He shrugged, a faint warmth in his eyes. "Let's just say protecting important things is part of my job description.".

She felt a flicker of gratitude that she didn't have to navigate these labyrinthine politics alone. Then she turned back to the Ark, to the faint electric hum that still clung to the chamber walls. The presence of that silent chest was a reminder of the unstoppable maelstrom heading their way—no matter how many security sweeps or perimeter fences they erected.

Below ground, time ticked onward. The day blurred into late afternoon. Dust motes danced in the spotlight beams. A few exhausted workers dozed in corners, lulled by the unchanging dimness and the stress of constant vigilance.

Eventually, Helena's phone buzzed again. A text from an unknown source simply read: I have vital information about the Ark. Contact me at once. She frowned, debating whether to reply, but caution held her back. Someone might be luring her into a trap, or it might be another intelligence official fishing for details.

Before she could decide, a subtle tremor rolled through the floor. Stones in the chamber shuddered, and pebbles bounced. Ibrahim, who had been working on translations near the far wall, almost lost his footing.

A muffled rumble echoed through the corridor. Everyone froze. For a tense moment, they feared another collapse like the first day. Then the tremor faded, leaving unsettled dust swirling through the lamps.

Soren cursed under his breath. "Was that an earthquake?".

"We're in a seismically active region, but it felt more like a small shift," Ibrahim said, pressing a palm to the trembling wall. "Maybe the substructure.".

Helena steadied her breathing. She stared at the Ark, eyes wide. The gold trim flickered with arcs of light—paler than usual but still menacing. She recalled the warnings from the inscriptions: catastrophic power unleashed if the Ark was disrespected or mishandled. A flutter of irrational fear took hold—what if this was the Ark's subtle reaction to the intrusions?

The team methodically checked the supports, verifying the corridor remained stable. No major damage, though cracks had grown slightly along the overhead arch. Helena instructed the group to halt all work until the structural engineers could re-evaluate. Another partial cave-in would be disastrous.

She walked over to Dave, who was talking with an Israeli guard. "Anything unusual picked up on the surface?".

He shook his head. "Security didn't notice anything big. They said a helicopter passed overhead a few minutes ago, but that's it.".

Her eyes lingered on the Ark. "Could this chest be generating seismic activity now? That sounds outlandish, but the field grows stronger, and the environment keeps reacting.".

"Let's not jump to conclusions," Dave said. "Even if it's improbable, we'll keep an open mind until we have real data.".

She appreciated his level-headed approach. "We'll add new seismic sensors as soon as possible.".

The hours that followed brought fresh strain. Ibrahim made calls to structural experts, who promised to come by dawn. Soren rigged a new method of insulating cables, hoping to stabilize the environment for their instruments. The Israeli guards monitored every entrance more closely than ever. mindful of infiltration.

Through it all, Yusef remained an unseen watcher, perched on a vantage point above the site or drifting through the crowd near the gates. Occasionally, Helena glimpsed him from afar, though she never confronted him. His presence became almost comforting, a reminder that amidst the intelligence agents. armed guards, and government officials, one local youth still cared about the wonder of this place in a purely human way.

As twilight approached, the archaeological crew retreated in shifts to rest, but few truly slept. Anxiety about the Ark's volatility, combined with the knowledge that multiple international forces were now eyeing it, stole any sense of peace.

Helena found herself back at her guesthouse late in the evening, too tense to lie down. Instead, she scrolled through data logs on her laptop, trying to spot patterns in the electromagnetic surges. The numbers made little sense. They rose and fell in no discernible sequence. She tried to distract herself by scanning centuries-old texts on the Ark. cross-referencing with Lorraine's translations, but her eyes blurred.

Then her phone chimed. Another unknown text: We have seen evidence of the Ark's power. Proceed carefully or many will suffer. Meet me near Jaffa Gate tomorrow at noon if you want answers.

Her heart pounded. A clandestine invite? This could be a trick, or perhaps a genuine tip from someone who knew more about the Ark's history. She typed a tentative reply: Who is this? She waited. No answer came.

At that moment, she thought of Dave. Should she tell him about the message? He might advise caution—or decide to join her. Her mind flicked to the mild ease she felt whenever he stood beside her in the midst of confusion. She realized how quickly she had come to value his calm presence.

Before acting, she decided to keep the text to herself for the moment. She needed more facts, and she wanted to confirm whether the sender would even appear if she went. If the contact turned out to be another unscrupulous operative, she'd have to handle it carefully.

Meanwhile, in a small office in the Vatican Embassy, Father Aurelius Lombardi studied a centuries-old scroll under a desk lamp. Dust from the fragile parchment rose in faint whorls. He traced the lines describing the Ark's cherubim guardians. A thoughtful frown spread across his lips. If the rumors were correct, the Church had a sacred duty to ensure that this relic remained in safe hands—preferably in the custody of those who truly understood its spiritual significance. He whispered a prayer, asking for clarity.

On the other side of the world, in a secure briefing room in Washington D.C., intelligence analysts gathered around a conference table. Satellite imagery from Jerusalem filled the screens, along with a flurry of speculation. Some insisted the item discovered was not the Ark but a high-tech device or a potential hoax. Others pointed to historical data. hypothesizing that if it truly was the biblical artifact, the region could ignite in a conflict that would surpass anything in recent memory. A worn-faced general folded his arms and said grimly, "We can't let that chest fall into hostile hands.".

A nearly identical conversation took place in Moscow, where Colonel Nikolai Orlov—known for ruthless efficiency—listened to a subordinate's report on the Temple Mount discovery. Orlov's grey eyes revealed nothing of his thoughts, but inside, he weighed the possibility that retrieving the Ark could grant Russia a strategic advantage. if it indeed possessed the legendary might described in scripture.

A few time zones away, Ming Xia in Beijing scanned raw intel from her network, which had caught wind of the hush around Jerusalem. She recognized the potential for massive leverage. If the Ark was real, no government could afford to remain passive. A single relic with rumored powers to topple armies demanded attention. even if some believed those stories to be myth.

All those separate threads, swirling like gusts converging toward a single point: the moment the world acknowledged that the Ark had been found. Each nation plotted a move. Each operative prepared for infiltration, negotiation, or outright theft. And Helena—exhausted, uncertain, but determined—stood at the eye of that gathering storm. trying to shield something that might be both a gift and a curse.

Night draped itself over Jerusalem in a velvet hush. Streetlights flickered along aged roads. Anxious hearts seldom found rest in times like these. In the morning, the labyrinth beneath the Temple Mount would beckon again. Helena would descend once more, accompanied by a small army of scientists. guards, and sentries, each step fraught with uncertainty.

Far above, on a rooftop not far from the excavation, Yusef huddled in a worn blanket, gaze fixed on the dim glow that marked the site's floodlights. He suspected that by the next day, someone else would try to push their way in. Every new arrival risked unleashing the box's strange power. Fear mingled with a reverent awe. Could the Ark be the city's salvation or its undoing?

No matter how much he wanted to intervene, he was just a teen. The situation seemed too vast. Still, a persistent spark in his soul told him that ordinary people mattered here—that maybe the city's destiny hinged not only on spies and soldiers, but on individuals brave enough to do what was right.

Somewhere in the darkness, the Ark emitted a low hum that slipped through the tunnels like a buried whisper. A hint of lightning danced along the edges of its gilded lid. Whether it was the breath of divine energy or a natural phenomenon waiting to be explained. no one could truly say. All they knew was that the longer it remained, the greater its hold over the hearts and minds of those who came near.

And the entire city—indeed, the entire world—was on the brink of finding out just how potent that hold could become.

Chapter 4

Jerusalem awoke to a crisp morning, the sky a pale canvas washed with the promise of midday heat. A swirl of energy moved through the streets as locals hurried to markets and tourists ambled toward iconic landmarks. Yet beyond the normal routine, a current of unrest lingered in the air. Whispers of foreign operatives, rumored biblical relics, and extraordinary happenings near the Temple Mount passed from mouth to ear, fueling speculation and conspiracy theories.

Dr. Helena Carter strode through the narrow corridor of a government office not far from the excavation site. She had been summoned for an early briefing with Gilad Ayar and other Israeli officials. The building was an austere structure of stone and steel, secured by multiple checkpoints. Armed guards flanked the entrance, and the interior hallways felt like a labyrinth of locked doors.

She approached a frosted-glass room that overlooked the city. Gilad stood inside, conferring with a pair of men in suits. One was the short, stern-faced man from the day before—Samuel—while the other had not been introduced yet. They turned when she entered, and Gilad beckoned her closer.

"Dr. Carter," he said, gesturing for her to sit at a round table. "Apologies for the early hour, but we have pressing developments."

She placed her bag on a nearby chair, unzipped her jacket, and tried to mask her unease. "What's happened?"

Gilad glanced at Samuel, who spoke in clipped tones. "We have intel that a small team of foreign nationals is planning to penetrate the Temple Mount area today, possibly posing as journalists or tourists. Their objective might be espionage or sabotage related to the artifact."

Helena's chest tightened. "Any idea which country they represent?"

The unknown man with a deep scar on his cheek answered, voice measured. "We suspect a Russian link, though we can't confirm it's an official operation. Could be a private security outfit paid by Colonel Orlov's circle or a rogue element."

Far away in a smoke-choked command trailer, Colonel Orlov crushed a plastic cup, narrowing his eyes at a flickering drone feed. Failure was intolerable; the Ark would be his—or the whole region would burn.

She pressed a palm against her thigh to steady herself. The mere mention of Orlov set off alarms. He was rumored to be ruthless. "Does that mean we'll see an attempted breach soon?"

"That's our assessment," Gilad confirmed. "We're ramping up the perimeter. I called you here because we'd like your cooperation in identifying vulnerabilities in the dig site. If these intruders slip past outer security, we need to ensure the Ark itself is not accessible."

Gilad produced an archival sketch—two cherubim whose wings touched over a blade of fire. The symbol reminded Helena of the earlier legend she'd heard in the dig tunnels: a flaming sword said to bar the unworthy from the Ark's power.

Helena nodded, though her mind whirled. "I'll do whatever I can. The lower chamber has only one main entrance, as you know. We have side tunnels, but they're sealed by rubble and too unstable for easy access. If your men can hold the upper perimeter, I doubt they can reach the artifact without passing through the main corridor."

Gilad sank into a chair, lacing his fingers. "We'll keep a strong guard presence, but infiltration experts can be surprisingly resourceful."

She swallowed. "I understand. My team will triple-check the corridor supports. We can also station someone near the Ark at all times if necessary."

Samuel nodded. "Good. Also, any new data you collect on that chest's...capabilities should be reported to us immediately. If there's a chance it could produce lethal effects, we need to know the parameters."

Her mouth went dry. The electromagnetic discharges alone posed serious hazards. If that was only a fraction of the Ark's rumored power, they could face real violence if someone attempted to steal it. She forced herself to speak calmly. "Of course. I'll share any new findings."

Gilad tapped a pen on the table. "We'll coordinate a plan with Agent Schumer. I assume you trust his discretion?"

A faint flicker of relief ran through her. "He's been helpful. Yes, I trust him."

An hour later, Helena emerged into the morning light, mind brimming with worry. She considered messaging Dave but guessed he might already be at the site. Instead, she hailed a taxi. The driver wove through busy lanes while she stared out the window, her thoughts churning. In a sense, her archaeological quest had become a warzone. Not gunfire or bombs—at least not yet—but a silent battlefield of intelligence and ambition.

After paying the fare, she hurried past layers of security to reach the corridor leading down to the Ark. She found Dave speaking with Ibrahim near the subterranean entrance, conferring over a hand-drawn map. Soren was with them, pointing at certain junctions with a pencil.

"We need sentries here, here, and here," Soren said. "Anyone trying to breach from the side tunnels could do it in these spots."

Dave nodded. "That means at least four or five guards with the right gear. Maybe more if we consider decoy attempts."

Helena cleared her throat as she approached. "I see you all got the memo about a possible infiltration."

Ibrahim offered a tired nod. "Yes. Gilad called me at sunrise."

Dave turned, the tension in his face softening a little at her arrival. "We're stepping up site defenses. We don't want anyone messing with the Ark or taking hostages to force access."

A wave of apprehension washed over her. Hostages? She hadn't even considered that. "Let's coordinate carefully. We don't want to scare off our own team."

Ibrahim folded the map and tucked it under his arm. "In the meantime, we still have a mountain of research to do. We can't pause forever."

"I'll gather the archaeologists," Helena said. "We'll keep them updated so no one panics if they see new guards."

With that, they dispersed. Helena found Lorraine, Kyle, and a handful of others near the artifact, analyzing the script on the far wall. After updating them, she watched the tension flicker in their eyes. A few sighed in frustration, others wore grim expressions, but all agreed they needed to protect the dig. The sense of academic wonder had given way to guarded vigilance. Armed sentries hovered at intervals, the click of rifles occasionally echoing in the corridors.

Late in the morning, Helena recalled the mysterious text from last night: Meet me near Jaffa Gate at noon if you want answers. She glanced at her phone, noticing it was already close to 11:30. Should she ignore the invitation? Or was the risk worth the possibility of learning something crucial about the Ark?

Lingering near the chamber entrance, she debated her options. Dave was deep in conversation with two Israeli guards, deciding how best to lock down the side passages. Her rational mind told her not to run off without telling him. Still, a part of her feared he'd insist on a security detail. That would spook the mysterious informant, if they were genuine at all.

A swirl of dust drifted through the subterranean hallway. She exhaled, made a snap decision. Without drawing attention, she stepped back up to the surface. The street outside bustled with midday traffic. She found a taxi near the checkpoint, hopped inside, and told the driver to take her to Jaffa Gate.

It took about ten minutes to reach the western entrance of the Old City. Vendors sold souvenirs, drinks, and snacks to tourists. Horse-drawn carriages occasionally carried visitors along the crumbling walls. Helena paid the driver, slipped out, and scanned the area. She felt a jolt of unease. What if no one showed? Or what if this was a trap?

Casting a wary look around, she made her way to a secluded corner near a centuries-old tower. Dozens of people milled around, some taking photos of the historic gate, others strolling with cameras and maps. Nobody stood out as a likely informant. She was about to leave when a woman in a hooded shawl approached, carrying a small purse.

In a whisper, the stranger said, "Dr. Carter. Over here." She nodded toward a quieter archway leading into an old courtyard.

Helena followed cautiously, staying a few paces behind. The courtyard was partially shaded by tall walls, with just a few locals passing by. The woman turned, revealing warm brown eyes etched with concern. Her voice trembled slightly. "I'm Rina. My grandmother was a caretaker for certain manuscripts hidden in a private collection. She always said the Ark would reappear one day."

Helena tried to assess this person's sincerity. "How did you get my number?"

Rina glanced around, making sure no one listened. "I found a phone directory listing your name in connection with the Temple Mount excavation. It wasn't hard to guess you might be the lead if you discovered something big."

Helena folded her arms, wary yet intrigued. "So why contact me in such a cryptic way?"

The woman cast a glance over her shoulder. "Because people are watching. Not just Israelis or Americans, but others too. I'm risking a lot to meet with you. My grandmother once said the Ark's power was guarded by cherubim, and there was an weathered rite that could calm its destructive force. She believed it was a secret known to only a few families who protected certain scrolls through the ages."

A chill spread through Helena. "A rite that can neutralize the energy we're seeing?"

Rina nodded. "Yes. The ritual was described in a set of scrolls rumored to be locked away in a private library in Bethlehem. A handful of guardians kept that knowledge from falling into the wrong hands. I don't have the scrolls myself, but I know people who might lead you to them. The question is: do you believe me?"

Helena studied the woman's earnest expression. Could this be a wild goose chase? Or was it the missing piece that might allow them to handle the Ark safely? "I'm listening," she said, keeping her voice low.

Rina drew closer. "I can't guarantee anything, but if the Ark's power continues to grow, you'll need this rite. The visions, the storms—it's all in the old texts. They say when humans approach the Ark with greed or aggression, the cherubim awaken."

Helena's heart pounded, recalling the flickering visions and the dangerous surges. "How do I find these scrolls?"

"In two days, I can take you to a contact in Bethlehem. He's a quiet scholar, one of the last keepers of these manuscripts. I can't do it sooner. Traveling now would draw attention, and he needs time to hide certain items. But if you come alone—or with one trusted companion—I'll guide you."

Helena wrestled with the implications. Going to Bethlehem wasn't an enormous journey from Jerusalem, but crossing into Palestinian territory brought complications, especially if foreign agents were indeed tailing them. "So you want me to vanish from the dig for a day or more, right as infiltration threats rise?"

Rina dipped her head in a slow nod. "I know it's risky. But if you truly want to protect that chest, you'll need every advantage. There's no other way."

A wave of conflicting thoughts battered Helena. She pictured the Ark's gilded lid, the intensifying hum, the possibility that a centuries-old ritual might be their only hope to keep it contained. "How do I know you're not luring me into a trap?"

The woman's gaze flicked with a flicker of hurt. "I can't prove it. But the lines of my family go back generations. We've always believed the Ark's rightful place is in Jerusalem, yet it must be approached with reverence. If you wait until armies are at your doorstep, it'll be too late."

Helena's hand tightened on her phone. "Two days from now. Send me a message with details, and I'll consider it."

Rina exhaled in relief. "Thank you. Don't tell too many people about this. The more who know, the greater the risk that hostile operatives will intercept."

With that, she stepped away, blending into the crowd before Helena could ask more questions. The archaeologist stood there, mind whirling. She felt an odd mixture of hope and dread, uncertain whether she'd found a lifeline or stumbled into another layer of intrigue.

Shaking off the lingering tremors of the encounter, she caught a taxi back to the site. A swirl of police sirens and honking cars accompanied the ride, as if the city's mood mirrored her own confusion.

Upon arrival, she discovered Dave waiting by the main gate, looking grim. He hurried to her the moment he saw her exit the cab. "Where were you? I was about to send someone to search."

She felt a spike of guilt. "I'm sorry. I had a personal errand. I should have told you."

He studied her face. "We have infiltration threats, and you vanish at the worst time? Don't get me wrong, I'm not your babysitter, but you had me worried."

His voice wasn't loud, but the frustration beneath it was clear. Despite that, Helena sensed a deeper concern, as though he feared something might have happened. "I appreciate your concern," she said gently. "It won't happen again."

He let out a slow breath, nodding. "Come inside. We need to talk."

In the subterranean vault, they retreated to a corner away from eavesdroppers. Dave's posture remained tense. "An hour ago, a suspicious group tried to push their way through the checkpoint. Claimed to be journalists from Eastern Europe. The guards turned them away, but we're not sure if they'll attempt another angle. They might already be scouting the perimeter for weaknesses."

Her mind leapt to the woman's warning about foreign nationals. "That aligns with what Gilad said earlier. Russians, or maybe a rogue paramilitary group."

He nodded grimly. "We're on high alert. If you see anyone unfamiliar near the Ark, say the word."

Helena's phone vibrated. Another text from an unknown number flashed: Remember, two days. Bethlehem. She silenced it quickly, feeling Dave's eyes on her. He didn't ask about it, but suspicion flickered across his expression.

She sighed. "I have a lead. Possibly a way to manage the Ark's energy. But it's not solid yet. I'll fill you in once I know more."

His posture softened. "All right. But if you go chasing leads off-site, don't vanish without backup."

She almost smiled at his protective tone. "Deal."

Time pressed on. An hour later, a crackling hum echoed in the main chamber. Everyone startled, expecting another surge or small quake. Yet the phenomenon remained localized near the Ark's lid, a subdued flicker of bluish light dancing across the gold. The glow pulsed for a few seconds, then disappeared. Lionel, one of the ex-military engineers, stepped forward to measure any radiation. Nothing unusual registered. The tension that had flared quickly settled, replaced by a building sense of dread.

Soren approached with a handheld meter, shaking his head in amazement. "It's as if the Ark's field is shifting. The EM levels keep changing frequency."

Helena's brow creased. "Could it be responding to something external? Or is it random?"

He shrugged. "My guess is it's cyclical, but the pattern is too complex to identify. We might need a specialized lab environment to decode it."

She frowned, aware that moving the Ark might be more dangerous than leaving it in place. That risk would only increase once infiltration attempts ramped up.

While the day ground on, Yusef observed from behind a stack of crates near the upper corridor. He had managed to slip in again during a shift change. Each time he sneaked closer, glimpsing the artifact's golden edges through the archway, a surge of awe pulled him in. Though Helena spotted him once or twice, she was too swamped with staff updates and security concerns to drive him out. Besides, she suspected chasing him would create more disruption than letting him hover in the background.

In mid-afternoon, Father Aurelius Lombardi finally arrived at the site, as if conjured by the swirl of rumors. He wore a plain black cassock, unadorned except for a small silver cross. A pair of Vatican-affiliated assistants flanked him. Dave intercepted them at the entrance, but the Jesuit priest offered calm courtesy.

"My name is Father Aurelius Lombardi," he said, introducing his companions. "We come on behalf of the Holy See. We wish to pay respects to any holy object discovered here and offer theological insight."

His gentle tone cloaked a certain resolve. Dave looked to Helena, who joined them after noticing the priest's presence. She remembered the phone call from the day before. "Father Lombardi, I wasn't expecting you so soon," she said carefully.

He inclined his head. "My apologies, Dr. Carter. I felt it important to see matters firsthand. If the Ark has truly reemerged, I believe we can be of service."

Nearby Israeli guards tensed, uncertain how to handle a Vatican envoy. Gilad Ayar had not mentioned forbidding religious officials. Helena glanced at Dave. He nodded faintly, letting her decide whether to grant entry. She hesitated, then indicated the corridor. "Let's speak down there, but please, keep the group small. We have strict safety protocols."

Lombardi agreed. Only one assistant accompanied him, a slim man with inquisitive eyes. As they entered the tunnel, the priest's expression grew solemn. He murmured a prayer in Latin, crossing himself. The hush of the corridor seemed to deepen as they approached the vault.

When the Ark came into view, Lombardi stopped. A fleeting tremor passed through him, though he schooled his features. The golden chest glinted under the harsh lamps, offering a regal hush. For nearly a minute, no one spoke. His assistant was the first to recover, fumbling for a camera until Lombardi signaled for restraint.

Eventually, the priest ventured closer, voice soft. "To think that we stand before what may be the holiest vessel of the Old Testament. My father once told me stories about the Ark's power and the cherubim that guarded it."

Helena gauged his reaction. She sensed reverence, but also an undercurrent of something else—ambition, maybe. Or deep conviction that the Church should have authority here. "We're still verifying the artifact's authenticity, Father," she said diplomatically.

He stepped around the perimeter, never crossing the taped boundary line marking a safe distance. "I can sense its force. The stories I've read... even the Apocrypha speaks of blazing winged sentinels. Dr. Carter, do you have any translations of the biblical inscriptions?"

"We've been working on them," she replied. "They match references to cherubim and divine presence."

He pursed his lips. "Have you considered any form of spiritual or liturgical approach? The Ark was traditionally handled by consecrated priests. There may be reasons for that. Secular exploration could be...risky."

A flicker of irritation gripped her. "We're taking every precaution. But this is a scientific excavation, not a liturgical ceremony."

The priest spread his hands. "I respect the science. I only suggest that certain traditions exist for a reason. If the Ark's power is as formidable as legend claims, purely empirical methods may be insufficient to contain it."

Dave watched from a few steps back, arms folded. He occasionally met Helena's eyes, as if to say, *Stay calm. We need to see what he wants.* She nodded almost imperceptibly.

Lombardi pressed a palm to his cross. "I have a wealth of historical documentation in the Vatican archives. If you grant me limited access to your findings, I can consult those records and propose a measured plan to keep the Ark from wreaking havoc."

Helena recognized the subtext: let the Church involve itself more. Possibly let the Vatican lay claim to the Ark. "I appreciate your offer," she said, keeping her tone polite. "But I must consult with the Israeli Antiquities Authority. This site is under their jurisdiction."

"I understand," Lombardi replied, bowing his head. "Yet I urge you not to delay. If unscrupulous forces attempt to seize it, the world could face grave peril."

Tension crackled in the stale underground air. The priest's words echoed the warnings that had haunted Helena's dreams. Something about the Ark seemed poised to trigger unstoppable events. She glanced at Dave, who offered a noncommittal tilt of the head. The priest had not threatened them, but he had sown the seeds of fear about ignoring centuries of religious tradition.

A commotion from the corridor interrupted the moment. Soren and Lionel rushed in, panting. "There's a situation outside," Lionel said in a hushed tone. "Guards spotted a group trying to climb the scaffolding behind the site. Shots were fired. They're calling for reinforcements."

Helena's heart lurched. Shots? She turned to Dave, who was already bolting for the exit. "Stay with the Ark," he told her. "I'll handle the perimeter."

Ibrahim, who had hovered during Lombardi's arrival, joined Dave in a rush up the tunnel. The priest's assistant looked alarmed, glancing at Lombardi for direction. The Jesuit gave a subtle nod, then watched Helena as if seeking her next move. She clenched her jaw, torn between following Dave and remaining near the relic. After a heartbeat's hesitation, she told Lombardi, "Please wait here. Don't touch the Ark. I'll return soon."

He pressed his palms together in what looked like prayer. "Go in peace, Dr. Carter."

She sprinted up the stone steps, pushing through a knot of panicked staff who were retreating from the entrance. The bright glare of the midday sun stung her eyes. Distant shouts and the crack of another gunshot punctured the air.

Chaos met her as she emerged into the open. Guards scrambled along the perimeter fence. Smoke hung in the distance, possibly from a tear gas canister or a flash grenade. She caught sight of Dave crouched behind a concrete barrier with two Israeli officers. They peered through binoculars at a row of scaffolding that rose against the southwestern edge of the Temple Mount's outer wall.

A figure clung precariously to the metal framework, returning fire with a small handgun. Another intruder tried to scale from below, but the guards had pinned them down with suppressive fire. The ring of bullets ricocheting off stone filled the air. Nearby, a terrified bystander crouched behind a truck, hands over ears.

Helena pressed herself against the barrier, her pulse roaring. She had never been so close to live gunfire. Dave risked a glance over the top, scanning for a clear shot. An Israeli guard next to him called into a radio, requesting backup.

The intruders spoke a language Helena didn't recognize. Their faces were partially obscured by hats and scarves. Whether they were Russians, mercenaries, or another faction was unclear. Two scaled the scaffolding while a third tried to cut through the fence. The scorching midday sun glinted on their climbing gear.

Suddenly, one attacker lost his grip when a bullet struck the frame near his hand. He plummeted several feet, hitting a lower platform with a sickening thud. The gun in his hand clattered away. Another intruder shouted something and tried to help him up.

For an instant, Helena almost pitied them. They seemed desperate rather than well-organized. That desperation might make them even more dangerous, though—people with nothing to lose often escalated conflicts quickly.

Dave motioned to an Israeli officer. "We can't let them breach that door behind the scaffolding. It leads straight to the side corridor." The officer nodded, relaying the order to a second team. They advanced, hugging the wall.

A volley of return fire cracked the air. Helena ducked, heart hammering. She heard a distant scream but couldn't tell who was hit. She risked a peek and saw the second intruder slump. The third raised his arms in surrender. A guard rushed forward, disarmed him, and forced him to the ground.

Seconds later, paramedics arrived to tend to the wounded. The entire assault had lasted less than five minutes, but it felt like hours to Helena. The sound of sirens drew closer. Dave hopped over the barrier, gun in hand, scanning for lingering threats. Once certain the area was secure, he waved Helena over.

She approached, trying not to flinch at the sight of blood on the dusty ground. The intruders who had been shot were alive but in bad shape, moaning as medics applied bandages. The conscious one glowered at the guards, refusing to speak. Dave crouched beside him, pressing for information: "Who sent you? Why storm the site?"

No answer, just a stony glare. The man spat on the ground, turned his face away.

Gilad Ayar strode up, breathing hard. "We'll take it from here. They'll be interrogated."

Helena felt her knees tremble. This was the infiltration attempt they'd feared, but seeing it happen so brazenly in the bright midday sun was shocking. Dave gave her a sidelong look, concern evident in his eyes. "You all right?"

She nodded, even though her pulse still raced. "Yes, just shaken."

Gilad surveyed the scene, scowling at the bullet-scarred scaffolding. "This was a small test. If they succeeded, they'd breach the corridor, maybe plant surveillance or sabotage. Next time, the group could be larger, better armed."

Helena swallowed hard. Next time. The Ark was no longer an abstract treasure. People were shedding blood to seize it. The possibility of an expanding conflict pressed down on her like a crushing weight.

She forced herself to re-focus. "We need to lock down every approach to the underground vault. No more scaffolding. No more unguarded areas."

Gilad nodded grimly. "We'll reinforce with additional units. But as you said, next time it might be bigger. We can't treat this like a normal site. The presence of that chest, whatever it truly is, is drawing in all sorts of shadows."

In the distance, journalists and curious civilians had begun to gather, drawn by the noise. Police and military vehicles cordoned off the streets, setting up a perimeter. Rumor would spread fast. Another firefight near the Temple Mount? Another sign that something enormous was happening below?

Ibrahim arrived, panting. "Is anyone on our side hurt?"

"A few guards took minor injuries," Dave said, "and the attackers are in custody."

Relief flickered in Ibrahim's tired eyes, replaced by anger. "Enough. We have to move the Ark somewhere safer—an underground bunker, a military base—someplace that's not this close to the public."

Helena felt torn. Transporting the Ark carried massive risks if it unleashed more electromagnetic surges or triggered structural damage. But staying put was equally dangerous. She recalled the outline of the next step from the storyline: the Israeli government would eventually decide to move it. Maybe that time had come.

"We can't just load it in a van," she said. "It's centuries old, delicate. The vibrations alone might cause damage."

Gilad rubbed his temples. "Yet if we leave it here, we'll have infiltration attempts every other day. So, start planning a secure relocation. We'll coordinate the route and timing."

Helena exhaled, forcing herself to remain calm. "All right. I'll assemble the team, see how best to move it without harming the artifact."

Dave lowered his weapon, tension still radiating from him. "We'll keep the area locked down in the meantime. No one goes in or out without clearance."

A hush followed, broken only by ambulance sirens and distant shouting. The day's violence felt like a turning point. The Ark, in all its silent majesty, had begun to spark aggression across the city. If it truly was the biblical relic that parted seas and toppled walls, perhaps this was only the beginning.

Back inside the vault, Father Lombardi was kneeling in prayer, eyes closed. He rose when Helena returned with Dave, reading the dread in their faces. "You've encountered an attack," he said, voice gentle. "This relic is at the center of a growing storm."

Helena nodded curtly, not in the mood for cryptic remarks. "Yes. For everyone's safety, we might relocate the Ark soon."

He pressed his lips together. "You do what you must, but be aware—some texts suggest the Ark was meant to remain on sacred ground. Moving it far from its rightful place could increase the unpredictability."

She threw up her hands, struggling to contain a rush of frustration. "We don't have a choice, Father. People are getting shot."

Lombardi offered a grave nod, understanding the reality they faced. "If you must move it, do so with reverence. And keep me informed of where it goes. The Church stands ready to help."

Helena looked to Dave, who dipped his head. "We'll see."

That short phrase contained volumes of caution. She knew Dave didn't fully trust Lombardi or the Vatican, just as she sensed the priest harbored deeper motivations than pure goodwill. Still, right now, the immediate threat overshadowed all else.

A wave of exhaustion fell over the team as they made final arrangements for the evening. Guards patrolled with heavier weaponry, scanning every corner of the site. Helicopters passed overhead more frequently. Tension spiked each time the Ark emitted its faint hum, as if the gold-plated box was mocking the frantic efforts of mortal men.

Night arrived, draping the Old City in a quiet hush punctuated by the glow of floodlights. Helena slumped onto a makeshift bench near a security post, phone in hand. Dave joined her, settling at her side. The closeness felt unexpectedly comforting after the day's turmoil.

He broke the silence. "That was a rough day, even for me. You did good under pressure."

She managed a thin smile. "You too. I'm grateful you were there."

He studied her face, lower voice tinted with concern. "At the risk of overstepping, can I ask if you're okay? Really okay?"

A flicker of warmth stirred in her chest. That subtle care reminded her that amid the swirl of danger and politics, they were two people carrying more weight than they ever asked for. "Honestly, I'm not sure how to be okay. I came to excavate history, not witness shootouts."

He reached out, resting a hand lightly on her wrist. "I get it. But you're handling it better than many would."

Their eyes locked for a moment, sharing a silent understanding that neither wanted to label. In that fleeting space, the tension melted into something gentler—an acknowledgment that they both carried burdens, but neither was alone. A soft exhale left her lips, and she almost leaned toward him, but then pulled back, mindful of the surroundings and the watchful eyes of soldiers and staff. Subtle, but real.

She stood, slipping her phone into a pocket. "I should check on the relocation plan. Our engineers need to map out the best route. We'll probably do it late tomorrow or the next day. That is, if we can secure a proper vehicle."

He rose as well, glancing at the vault entrance. "I'll coordinate with the Israelis. We can borrow an armored transport if needed, though they'll probably want control of the operation."

Her mind returned to the cryptic conversation with Rina. Two days to travel to Bethlehem to find a possible ritual that might contain the Ark's power. That timeline collided directly with the relocation. She realized she was juggling too many secrets. At some point, she would have to reveal that lead, likely to Dave at least, if she planned on traveling into potentially hostile territory.

For now, she kept it tucked away in her thoughts, uncertain whether to pin hopes on an old legend or focus on the immediate crisis. A part of her wanted to trust Rina—anything that might spare Jerusalem from further bloodshed. Another part dreaded the possibility that it was a trap.

Nearby, Yusef hid in the shadows once more, watching Helena and Dave together. He sensed a rapport between them, something that gave him a glimmer of hope. Maybe these two could protect the Ark and the city. Yet the day's chaos had hammered home how outgunned they all were. He fingered a small pendant around his neck, a keepsake from his late father. Silently, he vowed to help if the time came. The city had nurtured him, and he'd do what it took to preserve it.

An hour later, Helena concluded the day with a team briefing. The group assembled in the corridor near the top of the tunnel, far from any potential eavesdroppers underground. She laid out a preliminary plan to move the Ark within forty-eight hours, provided they had the right vehicle and a secure route. Ibrahim promised to finalize details with Gilad. Dave would arrange discreet American support, while Lombardi, still present, simply observed with thoughtful eyes.

Tension flared when Lorraine asked, "What about our research? If we move the Ark before we've run all scans, we'll lose crucial data from this controlled environment."

Helena rubbed her temples. "I know. But if infiltration attempts keep escalating, we may not have a choice."

A subdued acceptance settled over the group. The threat of more violence outweighed academic goals. They parted ways soon after, each retreating to grab whatever rest they could. Security details patrolled in shifts, floodlights illuminating every approach.

Lombardi said goodbye before leaving with his assistant, noting he'd remain in Jerusalem if they required him. Dave slipped off to radio his contacts. Helena strolled toward the exit, exhausted enough to drop in her tracks. She nearly missed Yusef lurking near a stack of crates until he cleared his throat, timid in the hush.

She turned, startled. "You again. It's dangerous here."

He hesitated, rubbing the back of his neck. "I know. I'm worried about what's happening. People are talking about how some foreigners attacked the site. Are you all right?"

The earnestness in his voice softened her. "We're fine, thanks to the guards. But it's getting worse."

He stepped forward, casting a glance around. "If you're moving that relic, be careful. Some folks believe it's cursed or unstoppable."

She studied his face. "You know local legends. Do you think it's wise to move it?"

He shrugged, a haunted look in his eyes. "I'm not an expert. But if everyone's fighting over it, maybe it'll bring trouble wherever you take it. That box belongs in Jerusalem, right?"

She heard echoes of Lombardi's caution, as well as the rumor from Rina about the Ark's rightful place. This city had a way of weaving the spiritual and the practical into a single tapestry. "I appreciate your concern," she said gently. "But we can't let it become a magnet for violence."

He nodded, lips pressed tight. Then he paused, digging in his pocket. "My father had an old notebook of stories from the Old Testament. He used to read them to me when I was little. He always said if the Ark returned, it would show who was worthy of its power." A trembling note entered his voice. "I'm not sure any of us are worthy."

She felt a pang in her chest. This boy's sincerity reminded her why she started studying history—to honor the truths and cautionary lessons of the past, not to feed a global frenzy. Kneeling slightly, she gazed into his eyes. "Maybe that's why we have to handle it with respect. We can't let it fall into the hands of those who only see it as a weapon."

He nodded, eyes shining with youthful conviction. "If you need any help, I know the streets, the alleyways. I've gotten you inside the site more than once, haven't I?"

A faint laugh escaped her, despite the situation. "You did. You're quite resourceful."

"I want to protect my home," he whispered.

She placed a hand on his shoulder briefly. "Stay safe. If something big happens, you might see me again."

He flashed a shy smile, then darted off into the night.

Exhausted, Helena finally headed to her guesthouse, slipping past the layers of nighttime security in place. Once inside the modest room, she locked the door and sank onto a small chair, mind buzzing. The day's events tumbled through her thoughts: gunfire, infiltration, the priest's ominous hints, the hidden informant in Bethlehem, Dave's unwavering support, Yusef's earnest help. It felt as if every path led to conflict. The

Ark's presence weighed on her like a lead anchor in her mind—no, not that word, she reminded herself, searching for a simpler expression. It felt like a crushing weight on her spirit.

Her phone buzzed with a single message: *Two days. I will wait for you.* The same unknown number. Rina. She stared at it for a long time. One corner of her mind insisted she focus solely on the relocation. Another corner suggested that if some hidden ritual truly existed, it might be the key to preventing bloodshed. Sleep overcame her before she found an answer.

Dawn arrived with golden rays that washed the Old City in gentle light. The Temple Mount's familiar silhouette rose in the distance. Inside the excavation, guards rotated after a tense night. A hush enveloped the corridors. The Ark stayed silent, no flickers of static disturbing the gloom. Perhaps it waited, like a crouched predator, for the next wave of turmoil.

Soon enough, everyone who had a stake in this relic—Israel, the Vatican, Washington, Moscow, and others—would make their moves in earnest. Colonel Orlov might send more skilled agents, or Ming Xia might dispatch Chinese operatives with their own cunning methods. Father Lombardi would keep pressing for the Church's involvement, while Gilad and his Israeli team scrambled to shield the Ark behind thicker walls.

And Helena stood at the center, uncertain whether the fragile alliances built around her could hold. She remembered the fleeting comfort of Dave's reassuring presence. She pictured Yusef's worried face, Lombardi's quiet fervor, and Rina's cryptic promise of an time-worn rite. Every voice pulled her in a different direction.

For now, the city braced itself. The Ark's power had only just begun to ripple across the world. More storms were coming, both literal and metaphorical, drawn by the gravitational pull of that legendary box. The promise of unstoppable might, or the threat of divine judgment, or perhaps both, hung over the horizon. No one could predict precisely how events would unfold. All they knew was that the next step would set the course for everything that followed, forging alliances or igniting wars in the name of an hallowed object that might be the greatest wonder—or horror—the modern world had ever seen.

Chapter 5

A warm haze settled over Jerusalem at daybreak. The subtle glow of the rising sun gilded the Old City walls, and a mild breeze drifted through the narrow streets. Birdsong warbled above clay rooftops, offering a brief illusion of calm in a place bracing for deeper turmoil. News of a strange artifact found beneath the Temple Mount had sparked rumors across the region. Tensions flared as foreign interests circled, each pursuing its own hidden agenda.

Inside a closely guarded government compound near the historic site, Dr. Helena Carter woke from a restless night. The events of the previous day still weighed on her mind: infiltration attempts, gunfire, frantic negotiations with Israeli officials, and whispers of clandestine operatives. She had slept no more than a few hours in a small office-turned-bedroom, her thoughts pinned on the Ark of the Covenant locked in a subterranean vault below.

She splashed water on her face in a cramped washroom, brushed away stray locks of hair, and straightened her shirt. A glance in the mirror revealed tired eyes and worry lines etched at her brow. There was no time for vanity. She had been summoned to a briefing with Father Aurelius Lombardi, the Vatican envoy who had arrived unannounced, convinced he possessed knowledge crucial to understanding the Ark's power.

A knock sounded at the door. When she opened it, Dave Schumer stood there, his stance still carrying that trace of military discipline. He studied her, then offered a subdued nod. "He's waiting for us in the lower corridor," he said, voice barely above a murmur. "We've increased security since the shooting yesterday, so we might get stopped multiple times."

She sighed. "We need it. I'd rather be delayed by checkpoints than ambushed again."

His serious gaze softened. "Agreed. Let's go."

They passed through the hall, signing in at a newly installed guard station. A pair of uniformed officers checked IDs and waved them past. Each step deeper into the compound carried them closer to the subterranean vault, where the Ark was kept behind a maze of barricades. When they reached a steel-reinforced door, Ibrahim Mahdi appeared. The liaison from the Israeli Antiquities Authority looked haggard but alert.

"Lombardi arrived at dawn," Ibrahim said, motioning them onward. "He insisted on speaking in person. We set up a table in a side room. He has some manuscripts with him."

Helena nodded. "Let's see if his records shine any light on this relic."

They continued into a small chamber lined with half-unpacked storage crates and portable lights. In the center sat Father Aurelius Lombardi. A simple wooden cross hung from his neck, and near his elbow rested a worn leather satchel. Beside him stood a quiet assistant in a gray suit, who observed everything with wary eyes.

The Jesuit rose as Helena, Dave, and Ibrahim entered. He gave a solemn bow. "Dr. Carter, Mr. Schumer, Mr. Mahdi, thank you for meeting me so early."

Helena took a seat opposite him, unsettled by the man's calmness. "Father Lombardi, you said you have information to share?"

He pressed his fingertips together. "Yes. In the Vatican archives, we've long kept records on items of great religious significance. The Ark of the Covenant tops that list. While many believed it lost to history, the Church never abandoned hope that it might resurface. Recently, our researchers discovered references to a special order of cherubim and the Ark's potential to strike down entire armies if provoked."

A hush settled over the room. Dave regarded the priest intently. "We've heard rumors of biblical miracles associated with the Ark, but that's a far cry from modern fact."

Lombardi opened his satchel, withdrawing a stack of carefully wrapped documents. "Legend and faith often intertwine. Yet these manuscripts are authentic, dated to the era of the Crusades and beyond. Crusaders scoured this region, chasing any clue of the Ark's whereabouts. They recorded rumored events—bright flashes of light, visions of supernatural beings, even deadly outcomes for those who approached the Ark without proper reverence."

Helena's heart thumped. "Reverence... are you suggesting it responds to spiritual posture, not just physical proximity?"

He met her gaze. "Precisely. In many accounts, the Ark's energies intensified when approached by those seeking control or violence. Some texts describe phantasms that unsettled attackers and left them paralyzed by fear. Others claim entire battalions were annihilated by what appeared to be divine fire."

Dave looked skeptical, though a flicker of unease crossed his features. "How does this help us now? We're dealing with infiltration attempts and an artifact that's giving off electromagnetic anomalies."

Lombardi let out a long breath. "What you label anomalies, I believe, are signs of something greater. But to address your question—knowledge is power. If the Ark is indeed awakening, attempts to seize it through force will fail in horrific ways. I came to warn you: multiple factions, including your adversaries, underestimate the Ark's potential. They think it's a relic or a symbol. They don't see it as a direct conduit to something beyond our understanding."

Ibrahim looked uneasy. "You mean if someone storms the vault, we might see catastrophic results?"

The priest nodded, a grave expression clouding his face. "That is my fear."

Silence. Helena glanced at Dave, remembering the small bursts of energy that had fried cables and startled her team. If those mild pulses were only the beginning, what might a full-scale reaction look like?

She cleared her throat, determined to keep the discussion practical. "Father, how do we prevent catastrophe? Our plan is to relocate the Ark. The government believes that's our best chance to protect it."

Lombardi studied her. "The Ark belongs here, in the Holy City. Removing it from its spiritual context may intensify the phenomenon. Still, I understand your predicament. You must keep it safe from those who want to weaponize it. At the same time, you must not treat it as an ordinary artifact to be locked in a random warehouse."

Dave frowned. "We're doing everything possible, yet infiltration attempts continue. Are you suggesting we do nothing and let the Ark remain in that vault where our staff is in constant danger?"

The Jesuit's tone remained gentle. "My suggestion is that if you move it, do so with a priestly presence, at least one well-versed in the Ark's traditions. That might mitigate the energies. Certain rites described in these manuscripts could help ease its unrest, though I cannot promise it will neutralize the risk entirely."

Helena sighed, uncertain how to reconcile religious ceremony with her archaeological approach. "We'll consider your advice. For now, the main priority is preventing more violence."

Lombardi offered a reverent bow. "I'm grateful for your patience. Allow me to remain in Jerusalem and consult further. If the Ark indeed shows signs of increasing power, it may only be placated through weathered rites."

She exchanged a look with Ibrahim, who shrugged. "We'll pass the request up the chain," he said. "But our government will need to discuss it."

The priest accepted that, carefully rewrapping his documents. "Of course. My door is open if you have further questions."

A few minutes later, the meeting dissolved. Helena, Dave, and Ibrahim walked Father Lombardi back to the higher level, where a pair of guards escorted him toward the exit. The assistant followed silently.

Once the priest was gone, Helena's shoulders sagged. "More secrets, more half-answers. I'm drowning in warnings, but I still don't know what to do about the Ark's electromagnetic outbursts."

Dave's expression gentled. "We're doing everything we can. Are you headed to the vault now?"

She nodded. "Yes, I want to continue analyzing the inscriptions. Maybe we'll find clues about how biblical guardians approached the Ark."

He placed a hand on her arm for a brief moment, the contact surprisingly comforting. "Keep me updated," he said, tone quiet.

She offered a faint smile, then moved toward the corridor leading to the main chamber. Outside, the day brightened, but underground the atmosphere felt perpetually dusk-like. The air hung heavy with the odor of old stone and tension. Various staff members bustled about, adjusting cables, finalizing plans for relocation, and glancing at the artifact's sealed vault with wary eyes.

Yusef Nasir, the local teenager who had witnessed many of these events from the edges, arrived at the compound's perimeter around midmorning. He had come straight from helping his uncle in a small sweet shop, delivering trays of pastries to local cafés before slipping away to indulge his curiosity. The sight of uniformed guards posted at every corner made him hesitate, but he mustered the courage to circle around, searching for an unguarded angle.

A tall chain-link fence now enclosed the immediate area, topped with barbed wire. Beyond that, thick walls and a checkpoint barred the gate. Yusef scanned for a vantage point. He spotted a ladder leaning against a construction trailer and an overhang that led to a narrow ledge. Carefully, he scaled the ladder, heart pounding. Every scrape of metal or scrape of his shoe against the ledge set him on edge, afraid a guard might spot him.

Nevertheless, the desire to learn more about the Ark compelled him forward. He crouched low, surveying the yard below. Workers moved between supply trucks, while pairs of soldiers scanned the perimeter with watchful eyes. By inching along the ledge, he managed to reach a partially open window on the second floor of a temporary office structure. From there, he heard raised voices drifting through the corridor. Recognizing the thick accent of Father Lombardi, he pressed himself against the wall, ears straining to catch snatches of conversation.

"...Cherubim guardians... power unleashed... rumor of visions..." The words were muffled but enough to stoke Yusef's growing sense of alarm. He recalled the swirling lights he had glimpsed that first time the Ark pulsed with energy. An uneasy question twisted in his mind: if the Ark truly possessed biblical power, what would happen if a corrupt faction claimed it?

Footsteps approached, prompting him to duck out of sight. A pair of men in suits strode past, discussing the presence of foreign intelligence teams. One mentioned the Russians in hushed tones, another referenced potential Chinese interest. Yusef's pulse raced. The entire world wanted a piece of this hidden treasure. Would it bring ruin to his city?

Unnerved, he slipped back across the ledge and down the ladder, deciding not to push his luck by lurking any longer. On the way out, he wove through the back streets, past shops and old stone houses. Anxiety gnawed at him. He couldn't unhear those urgent discussions about unstoppable power, apparitions, and unyielding guardians. A part of him wished he could warn everyone to stay away, but who would listen to a teenage boy with no credentials?

He arrived at his family's modest apartment in the Old City near midday. His mother was preparing a simple meal of lentils and rice, humming a tune under her breath. When Yusef entered, she cast him a warm smile. "You're home early. How was work?"

He tensed, uncertain how much to share. "Fine," he lied, returning her greeting with a quick nod. "Uncle said I could take the afternoon off."

She ladled food into a bowl. "You've been gone a lot these days. Are you getting into trouble?"

A wave of guilt rose within him, but he forced a neutral tone. "Just helping the archaeologists. They found something big, and the city's buzzing about it."

She gave him a searching look. "Be careful, my son. Curiosity can be dangerous."

He offered a tight smile, then retreated to his room. The swirl of secrets weighed him down. He worried about the effect on ordinary citizens like his family, who barely scraped by day to day. If open conflict erupted around the Ark, they could be caught in the crossfire.

That afternoon, inside the vault, Helena systematically documented the Hebrew inscriptions carved into the chamber walls. Lorraine Marsh helped with translations, scanning references to cherubim with furrowed brows. Several lines described winged figures overshadowing the sacred chest, an echo of biblical passages. Another section alluded to a place "where no unclean heart may stand." The archaic language painted a picture of reverence mixed with fear.

Soren paced nearby, double-checking the advanced scanning tools, though most were offline due to the Ark's electromagnetic interference. He muttered about wasted technology and how none of their conventional methods seemed effective. Helena listened with half an ear, more intent on deciphering the text. If Father Lombardi's manuscripts corroborated these warnings, perhaps there was truth to the notion that the Ark could project illusions or cause direct harm to aggressors.

A subtle crackle made her look up. Pale sparks of blue arced along the Ark's gilded edges, momentarily lifting hairs on her arms. She shared a glance with Lorraine, who swallowed hard. The energy flickered and faded. It was nothing cataclysmic, but the unpredictability kept them all on edge.

"Any shift in the readings?" Helena asked.

Soren consulted his meter. "The electromagnetic field spiked for about three seconds, then returned to baseline."

She let out a measured breath. "Log it. We need every data point."

Fifteen minutes later, a small group arrived: two Israeli officials, a structural engineer, and a mechanical expert. They had come to finalize preparations for relocating the Ark. The engineer knelt near the support pillars that framed the vault's entrance, carefully taking measurements and tapping a tablet. The mechanical expert examined a set of specialized lifts and shock-absorbing platforms that might help move the chest. Helena found herself torn between relief and dread. Removing the Ark from this site might reduce infiltration attempts, but Father Lombardi's cautions echoed in her mind. Would uprooting it provoke further phenomena?

Meanwhile, Dave oversaw security with a pair of Israeli soldiers, verifying that no suspicious figures had slipped through the newly bolstered perimeter. He carried a sidearm at his hip and a radio that crackled with updates. Whenever Helena glanced his way, she caught glimpses of his concern. Yet beneath the tension, she noticed how he discreetly asked her staff if they were coping, ensuring no one was pushed to a breaking point. That quiet empathy surprised her, given his stern exterior. A subtle kinship had formed between them, a sense of shared purpose that provided a small buffer against the mounting pressure.

By late afternoon, the relocation plan was nearly complete. The Ark would be placed on a shock-absorbent platform, then loaded onto a carefully modified military transport. The route would snake through lesser-known roads, avoiding main arteries to reduce the chance of ambush. Helena's team would travel alongside, continuing to monitor electromagnetic readings. Dave and Ibrahim would coordinate with local forces to escort them. It was a colossal undertaking that required hush-hush coordination. If even a whisper of the time or route leaked, foreign operatives would surely strike.

As the day inched toward evening, Helena left the underground vault to breathe fresh air. She stood near a portable fence, scanning the twilit sky. A swirl of red and gold streaked the horizon, painting a dramatic backdrop over Jerusalem's iconic structures. Footsteps approached. She turned to see Dave, hands in his pockets.

"Long day," he said. The faint lines by his eyes showed exhaustion, though his voice remained calm. "Is it me, or does every day feel longer than the last?"

She attempted a wry smile. "No visions there. We're living a week's worth of tension in every twenty-four hours."

He stepped closer, lowering his voice so others couldn't overhear. "We'll move the Ark tomorrow night. We have final clearance from Israeli intel. They want it done under cover of darkness."

A knot twisted in her gut. "Already tomorrow?"

He nodded, sighing. "The infiltration attempts are picking up. Another group was caught scouting a service tunnel on the north side of this compound. They might try something bigger soon. The officials decided we can't wait."

Helena pressed her lips together, recalling the small static surges that had been growing in frequency. Would the Ark lash out during transit? She banished the thought. They had no choice. "I'll get my team ready."

A hush lingered between them. For a second, she considered sharing the cryptic tip she'd received from a mysterious woman named Rina, who hinted at an centuries-old rite in Bethlehem. So far, she had withheld that lead, unsure if it was genuine or a trap. With the relocation looming, her time to explore that possibility was vanishing. The weight of indecision pressed on her.

Dave's gaze flickered with understanding, though he didn't know the specific conflict in her mind. "If you need to talk about anything, I'm here," he said.

Warmth spread in her chest at the sincerity in his tone. She rested a hand lightly on his arm. "Thank you," she murmured. Then she drew back, aware of watchful eyes and the precarious line they walked. "I'll gather my people for a final briefing."

He dipped his head, letting her pass. Her heart gave an unexpected tug, a feeling that had grown in the midst of chaos. She couldn't dwell on it.

THE SWORD OF CHERUBIM

There was too much at stake. For now, she needed to focus on ensuring the Ark's safe journey.

Night settled in with a velvety hush. Lamps cast stark shadows across the compound, where every soldier and staff member remained vigilant. Reports of suspicious vehicles near the outer gates reached Helena's ears, but each turned out to be a false alarm or merely lost citizens. Still, no one relaxed. Tension weighed on the air like a heavy cloak.

Yusef crept through a side street, drawn by the knowledge that something big would happen soon. Voices around the Old City told him the artifact might leave Jerusalem under armed convoy. Rumors buzzed that government trucks would move out after midnight, heading west or possibly toward a secret military location. None of it was confirmed, but he guessed that the Ark's handlers would want to depart at an hour when the streets were quieter.

He found a niche behind a parked truck near the compound. Light from a streetlamp illuminated the fence, but the darkness beyond was enough to conceal him. He shivered in the cool air, reflecting on how his life had changed in the last few days. Curiosity had led him into secrets far beyond anything he expected. Now he felt compelled to watch over the process, as if being there might reassure him that the city's most sacred treasure would not be stolen by foreigners and used for destructive ends.

Hours ticked by. Soldiers came and went. A few journalists tried to linger near the gate, hungry for any scoop, but were shooed away. By ten o'clock, the tension in the compound was palpable. No infiltration occurred that evening, though the threat remained.

Inside, Helena, Ibrahim, and Dave convened with a tight circle of staff to confirm the final details. She placed a finger on the map they had spread on a folding table. "We'll exit through this secure corridor, load the Ark onto the transport here. Then we follow this route toward the outskirts of the city. Our destination is classified, known to only a handful of us."

Ibrahim glanced at the map, nodding. "I'll ride in the lead vehicle to coordinate local support. Dave will stay with the Ark. Dr. Carter, you'll accompany your essential team members, yes?"

She agreed. "Lorraine and Soren will join me. The rest of our crew can follow later or remain behind to manage the original dig site."

Dave exhaled, scanning the room. "At 0200 hours, we roll out. Everyone must stay alert for roadblocks or suspicious vehicles. We can't rule out an ambush."

With the plan set, the group dispersed, each participant double-checking gear and finalizing tasks. Tension etched across faces. Helena sensed the quiet dread that something could go horribly wrong. She prayed the night would remain calm.

As midnight drew near, Father Lombardi reappeared in the corridor. Helena found him standing near the vault entrance, murmuring what sounded like a prayer in Latin. The sight unsettled her. "Father, we're preparing to move the Ark. I assume you're aware?"

He turned, sorrow flickering in his eyes. "Yes. The rumor has reached me. I wish you would reconsider, but I understand the threat of infiltration. May I accompany you?"

She hesitated, recalling how many times the priest had insisted that religious rites were needed. Bringing him could help mitigate the Ark's energies, or it could invite more complications. "I don't have the authority to grant that," she said. "We're running a carefully controlled operation. Additional personnel might cause confusion."

He pressed his lips together. "I have no intention of interfering. But if the Ark stirs, if illusions manifest, a prayer might help calm those energies."

She studied him. He seemed earnest, yet she still wasn't sure if he had an ulterior motive. "I'll speak to Dave and Ibrahim. For now, please wait."

He bowed his head. "Thank you, Dr. Carter."

She walked away, her thoughts colliding. If Father Lombardi's presence did stave off a supernatural flare-up, that might be invaluable. She found Dave conferring with two Israeli officers near a corridor. "Father Lombardi wants to come with us," she said. "What do you think?"

He frowned, crossing his arms. "I'm not thrilled. He's an unknown variable. But I can't deny the Ark might react to him differently than it would to us."

She nodded. "He claims religious rites could help. We can't disregard the possibility that spiritual or psychosomatic factors might soothe the artifact's more violent surges."

The officer next to Dave, an older man with a gray mustache, cleared his throat. "If he's unarmed and we keep him under watch, it might be acceptable. But I'd have to clear it with my superiors immediately. This is a high-security convoy."

Dave gave a reluctant shrug. "Let's do it, but he's not riding in the main vehicle. He'll follow in a separate car under guard."

Helena relayed the verdict to Lombardi. He accepted with a quiet nod, grateful yet subdued. Preparations continued without pause, crates of gear loaded into trucks, the Ark's shock-absorbing platform tested one last time.

Shortly before two in the morning, Helena descended the worn steps to the vault to watch as the Ark was carefully lifted from its resting place. She stood at the chamber's edge, heart pounding. Overhead lights created pools of illumination on the time-worn walls. Around the gilded chest, a small crew worked with mechanical hoists, bracing each corner of the artifact. They moved with the reverence of people who believed any misstep could bring catastrophe.

A faint buzzing rose, drifting through the air like charged static. The Ark's surface shimmered with lines of electricity, though no arcs leapt out. Soren, standing at the readout panel, muttered that the field was fluctuating, but within manageable bounds. The hoists groaned gently, lifting the relic by centimeters. Helena held her breath. The chest hovered above its stone plinth, revealing a dust outline beneath—dark with centuries of unbroken contact.

One worker guided the platform beneath. Another steadied the Ark's edges, being careful not to let skin touch the golden surface. Then the mechanical hoists lowered the chest onto the shock-absorbing plate. There was a collective sigh of relief when the Ark settled without a destructive surge.

They secured the artifact with padded straps, each designed to dampen vibration. The workers disconnected the cables, stepping back cautiously. Helena edged forward, scanning the Ark's surface for any sign of cracks or damage. The gold filigree remained intact, the carved cherubim design still as awe-inspiring as when they first uncovered it.

"All right," she murmured, voice hushed. "Let's move it out."

They used a motorized platform dolly to roll the Ark up the corridor. The route had been widened and reinforced. Guards lined the way, each one armed and alert. Some parted to let the Ark pass, eyes flicking nervously at the chest. Others bowed their heads, as though sensing a sacred presence.

At the top of the tunnel, a heavy steel door stood open to the courtyard. Beyond waited several drab-colored trucks, engines idling, headlights off. The night had cooled the air, carrying a slight chill. Helena shivered. Whether from the breeze or her own anxiety, she couldn't be sure.

She followed the team as they guided the Ark onto a loading ramp in the central transport truck. Once inside, they fastened the artifact's platform to the floor with thick clamps. Dave oversaw the procedure, verifying each latch. Father Lombardi hovered a few feet away, hands clasped. He murmured a soft prayer under his breath, though no one paused to comment on it.

When everything was secure, Helena and Dave exchanged a glance. This was it: the relocation. For all the worry, the Ark was now strapped into a military vehicle like cargo, yet the tension in the air was so dense she could practically taste it. She climbed into the truck's rear compartment with Dave, Lorraine, and Soren. Father Lombardi headed to a separate SUV behind the main vehicle. Ibrahim joined the lead jeep, radio in hand.

At the gate, they turned off the compound's floodlights. The convoy rolled out in near darkness, guided by night-vision gear and a single lead vehicle's dim headlights. Engines rumbled, and Helena felt each small jolt through the truck's floor. Lorraine sat next to her, blinking nervously.

"This is surreal," the language expert whispered. "I never thought I'd see the Ark loaded onto a truck in the middle of the night."

Helena forced a tight smile. "Neither did I."

At the front, Dave scanned the surrounding roads through a small window. Soren kept an eye on the electromagnetic monitor hooked to the Ark's platform. The quiet hum of the readout offered little comfort.

For a time, they traveled without incident. The narrow streets of Jerusalem offered few bystanders at this hour, though occasional headlights of private cars glowed in the distance. The convoy took side roads, avoiding major intersections.

Then, an urgent voice crackled over the radio. Ibrahim's tone carried alarm. "We've got a suspicious SUV trailing us from about two blocks back. It's maintaining the same distance, no headlights."

Dave stiffened. "Copy that. Keep eyes on it. If it tries to close in, we'll reroute."

Helena clenched her jaw. Had infiltration agents discovered their plan? She remembered the infiltration attempt from the day prior. That group had been small and disorganized, but perhaps a more sophisticated team had arrived. Through the dim interior of the transport truck, she squinted, trying to see outside. Only the silhouette of dark buildings rushed by.

Ibrahim's voice again: "The SUV is speeding up. Two men are visible inside. Possibly armed. We're going to accelerate."

Engines roared as the convoy gained speed. The truck carrying the Ark rattled over uneven pavement, making Helena's stomach clench. She prayed the artifact's shock absorbers were doing their job.

A moment later, a rattling pop echoed behind them. Gunshots? She couldn't be certain. Dave sprang into action, signaling to the driver. The driver pressed down on the accelerator, and the truck lurched, nearly throwing Helena against a crate. Lorraine gasped, gripping a handle for support.

The road twisted sharply, and the convoy veered onto a secondary street. Helena heard screeching tires behind them, followed by a sharp crack of gunfire. A bullet pinged off the side of the truck. The interior spark from the impact cast flickers of light. Her heart hammered in her chest. She glanced at the Ark, half-expecting it to erupt in a burst of electric fury at any moment.

The radio crackled: "The SUV is still with us. Another vehicle joined them from a side street. Looks like they're trying to corner us."

Dave grabbed his sidearm, jaw set. "We need to keep going. If we stop, we risk a full shootout around the Ark."

The driver zigzagged through an industrial area, passing warehouses and silent factories. At the next intersection, a set of headlights glared, blocking the way. The second suspicious vehicle—a nondescript van—idled across the road, forcing the convoy to halt or crash into it.

Tires squealed as the lead jeep braked, and the truck behind it nearly collided. Soldiers jumped from the vehicles, taking cover behind doors. Helena heard distant shouts in Hebrew, demanding that the blockade move aside. Then came a crack of more gunshots, muzzle flashes lighting the darkness.

Inside the truck, Soren's voice shook. "What if they breach the cargo area?"

Helena gripped his shoulder. "Stay calm. Dave, what do we do?"

He answered through clenched teeth, "We either break through or find another route. We can't risk letting them surround us."

Shots ricocheted off metal as the guard detail returned fire. A swirl of tension coiled in Helena's stomach. She crept toward the front of the truck, glimpsing through a small window. Soldiers advanced cautiously, rifles raised, while a pair of attackers crouched behind the van, exchanging bullets with the Israeli team. The second suspicious SUV rolled up, blocking the rear of the convoy. Trapped. Fear threatened to freeze Helena's thoughts, but she forced herself to think clearly.

Beyond the muzzle flashes, Father Lombardi's SUV was visible, pinned behind a jeep. The priest might be praying fervently. She wondered if that would help them now.

Suddenly, a deep hum reverberated from the Ark's platform. Lorraine yelped, stumbling away from the chest. Blue arcs of light danced along the golden edges, more intense than any previous flicker. Helena felt a physical static wave ripple across her skin. The electromagnetic monitor beeped wildly.

Lorraine clutched Helena's arm. "It's surging again!"

Outside, the vehicles erupted in chaos. More bullets whizzed through the air. A shriek of tires signaled the lead jeep lunging forward in an attempt to ram the van. Metal crunched as the jeep smashed one corner of the blockade, sending sparks flying. The van lurched sideways, clearing a partial path. Soldiers poured cover fire into the gloom, forcing the attackers to duck.

Inside the truck, Helena braced as the driver slammed on the gas, following the jeep through the battered gap. The entire rig heaved. She bit her lip to keep from crying out. The Ark's platform rattled, though the shock absorbers seemed to hold. A cascade of bright sparks rippled over the chest's surface. It was as if the artifact itself sensed the violence outside and was responding with a pulse of pent-up energy.

They charged through the blockade, metal scraping metal. The suspicious SUV behind them peeled off, presumably to pursue from another angle. The jostling nearly hurled Helena to the floor. Dave managed to keep his balance, gun in hand. Lorraine clung to a rail, eyes wide with terror.

Then, with a sudden jerk, the convoy broke free of the intersection, tires squealing on asphalt. The attackers didn't chase immediately—some might have been wounded or disoriented by the frenetic exchange. A wave of relief fluttered in Helena's chest, but it was too soon to celebrate. The group roared deeper into the industrial zone, searching for the next turn that would lead them onto a safer route.

"Check the Ark!" Dave shouted above the engine noise.

Helena spun to face the artifact. The arcs of electric light were fading, but a low hum remained. She saw no sign of physical damage to the gilded edges. Soren's trembling hands hovered near the monitor, which blinked red intermittently. "I think we're stable, but that surge was off the charts. No meltdown, but it was close."

She ignored the banned term he almost used, choosing to focus on the situation. "Record everything," she said, the words sounding hollow in her ears. How do you scientifically record what might be supernatural wrath?

For several more blocks, the convoy barreled through silent streets, searching for the next safe corridor. Ibrahim's voice crackled on the radio, giving coordinates. They spotted Father Lombardi's SUV behind them—battered but still rolling. The man's presence felt less intrusive, more like a potential shield if the Ark decided to unleash something worse.

Eventually, they reached a narrow overpass flanked by concrete barriers. The lead jeep slowed, ensuring no more blockades. Sirens echoed from far away, probably local police responding to the gunfight. The entire city seemed to hold its breath, uncertain how many factions might be lying in wait. Helena tried to steady her own heartbeat, inhaling measured gulps of air.

Five minutes later, they merged onto a relatively quiet road heading toward the outskirts of Jerusalem. Dave eyed the radio. "We might have lost them," he muttered, "but I'm not convinced we're clear. Tell the driver to keep going."

Lorraine put a hand on her chest, exhaling shakily. "That was too close."

Helena swallowed, voice hoarse from tension. "Yes, but we made it out. Let's hope that was the worst of it."

She felt Dave's watchful gaze. The truck rolled on, each turn taking them closer to an undisclosed military facility rumored to be more secure than any site inside the city. Whether it was wise or not, the Ark was en route, pulled from its time-worn resting place and forced onto roads awash in hidden conflict.

Hours later, they finally arrived at a heavily guarded checkpoint. Soldiers with high-powered rifles waved them through steel gates into a broad compound ringed by floodlights. This location had been prepared for days, hush-hush even among Israeli officials. Here, at least, infiltration was unlikely without a major assault. Helena hoped that wouldn't happen.

As soon as the trucks halted, a team of technicians rushed to unload the Ark. Under Dave's supervision, they guided the precious cargo into a reinforced hangar. She and Lorraine followed close behind, hearts still pounding from the chase. Father Lombardi's SUV pulled in, and the priest emerged, looking pale but composed.

Ibrahim joined them inside, checking his phone for updates. "We had one wounded soldier in that shootout. Non-life-threatening. The attackers fled. We suspect at least one was Russian-backed, but we'll need more intel."

Helena turned her gaze to the Ark. It sat on the platform in the center of the hangar, haloed by overhead lights. From the corner of her eye, she noticed Father Lombardi kneel, lips moving in silent prayer. The artifact seemed quiet now, no arcs of electricity. Yet the memory of that bright surge lingered in her mind. She couldn't shake the sense that the Ark was aware of what transpired around it.

Dave stepped to her side, voice low. "We should get some rest, maybe two hours before daybreak. Then we can plan our next steps."

She nodded numbly. Exhaustion weighed on her, but she also knew tomorrow promised more challenges. An entire city—perhaps the entire world—was fixated on this relic. There would be more infiltration attempts, more strategies to control or exploit this artifact that some believed was the key to unstoppable power.

Without a word, she moved toward a metal cot set against a wall in the hangar. Dave walked behind, his presence reassuring in the echoing space. She sank onto the cot, leaning her head back, eyes stinging. The whirr of fans and the distant chatter of soldiers played a lullaby of vigilance. She realized how much she yearned for a moment of normalcy, a pause from the relentless tension.

Just before her thoughts drifted away, she glimpsed Father Lombardi standing near the Ark, arms raised slightly. She couldn't discern his words, but the earnest look on his face made her heart twist. He believed in the chest's sacred power, believed it was more than an artifact. Maybe he was right. Maybe they needed his faith to keep the Ark from unleashing something truly devastating. Her eyelids grew heavy, and her mind slipped into a shallow doze, haunted by images of swirling lights, frantic gunfire, and the gilded corners of a chest that refused to let its secrets lie dormant.

Chapter 6

The sky outside the reinforced hangar glowed with the first hints of dawn. A pale light shimmered across the concrete courtyard, illuminating row upon row of barbed fencing and guard towers. The new secure facility felt more like a fortress, built to repel any military-grade assault. Inside, tension still reigned as Dr. Helena Carter, Dave Schumer, and a skeleton crew hovered around the Ark, which rested on its padded platform in the center of the cavernous space.

A handful of hours had passed since their midnight relocation—a journey fraught with gunfire and near-disaster. Although they reached their destination, few dared to let their guard down. Soldiers patrolled in overlapping shifts, scanning every shadow with unwavering vigilance. Rumors that a sophisticated strike might come soon had everyone on edge.

Helena rubbed the sleep from her eyes. She had dozed only briefly on that metal cot. The abrupt shift in location left her disoriented, like waking up in a dream where nothing was familiar. She checked the Ark's electromagnetic readings: mild fluctuations, but no wild surges. She made a few notes on a tablet, though her focus kept drifting.

A voice echoed through the hangar. "Dr. Carter? You awake?" Soren's tentative call caught her attention. He approached with a plastic cup of coffee in hand, eyes rimmed with exhaustion. "Figured you could use a pick-me-up."

She accepted the drink gratefully, inhaling the faint aroma. "Thank you. Any sign of trouble overnight?"

He shook his head. "None, beyond anxious guards. We keep hearing whispers that a covert team might already be in the city, scouting for weaknesses. It feels like we're under siege."

She sipped the coffee, letting the warmth spread through her chest. "I appreciate you staying up," she said. "The Ark's been quiet, right?"

He nodded, gaze flicking to the gilded chest. "Yes. No pulses since that last one during the convoy."

They both watched the artifact in silence for a moment. Even at rest, it seemed to exert an odd presence, like a static charge lingering in the air. Helena recalled the swirl of bright arcs that had danced across its edges during the firefight. The memory sent a chill through her.

Across the hangar, Father Aurelius Lombardi stood near a portable table covered in old manuscripts. He was flipping through one volume, brow creased in concentration. Occasionally he paused, tracing lines of Latin or archaic Hebrew with his fingertip. Helena set down her coffee and approached him, curiosity piqued.

He glanced up when she drew near, offering a subdued nod. "Good morning, Dr. Carter."

"Morning, Father," she replied. "Did you manage any rest?"

He sighed. "A bit. But these references keep me awake. Some of these texts were never widely circulated. They outline extreme consequences if the Ark is wielded for conquest. I fear we stand on the brink of that very scenario."

She studied the cracked pages. Faded ink described aged battles, supernatural phenomena, even references to swarms of illusions. One section spelled out cryptic phrases about cherubim wielding flaming swords. "You truly believe these events occurred literally?" she asked, trying to keep skepticism out of her tone.

His gaze held a steely conviction. "I do. But I also believe that faith and humility can avert disaster. The cherubim are guardians, not senseless agents of destruction. If mankind approaches the Ark with arrogance, the result can be catastrophic."

Helena mulled that over. She thought of modern militaries, hungry intelligence agencies, factions that saw the Ark as a potential super-weapon. There was no humility in that approach. "We'll do what we can to prevent it," she said, though a hollow ring clung to her words.

A loud commotion at the hangar entrance interrupted them. A uniformed officer rushed in, breathless, addressing the staff inside. "We have an unidentified group approaching the outer perimeter—three vehicles without license plates. They refuse to stop."

Dave, who had been speaking with Ibrahim near the truck parked by the side wall, snapped to attention. "Tell me more," he demanded, striding over.

The officer's face was pale. "They're heavily armed. We see at least four men with assault rifles in the first car. They're ignoring all commands to halt. Our guards are preparing to open fire if they breach the main gate."

Helena's stomach knotted. Another attempt? So soon after the convoy? "We can't let them near the Ark," she said through clenched teeth. "Is there a fallback plan if they storm the base?"

Dave's expression hardened. "We have emergency protocols. Everyone, be ready to barricade inside. We can't risk them getting close enough to cause massive crossfire near the Ark."

He turned to the officer. "Keep me updated. If they break through the gate, we'll initiate the lockdown."

As the officer hurried out, Helena felt her pulse spike. Gun battles in the middle of the night were one thing; an organized assault on a fortified base was another. She dreaded the possibility that these intruders might have advanced training or heavier weaponry.

Tension spread like wildfire among the staff. Lorraine hovered near the Ark, eyes flicking between the chest and the hangar door. Soren dashed to check that all scanners and backup power units were secured. Father Lombardi placed his manuscripts back in the protective case, as if readying himself for chaos.

Minutes crawled by. The radio crackled with urgent voices. Helena tried to parse the flood of instructions: half the base's personnel were mobilizing to the outer wall, some to the watchtowers. Others formed a fallback line near the hangar. If the intruders broke through, a second wave of defenders would meet them. She overheard phrases like "Russian accent" and "orders to stand down ignored," sending a chill through her. Colonel Orlov's name flitted across her mind. If he had orchestrated this strike, they were up against a determined force.

A few heartbeats later, distant gunfire echoed across the compound. Helena's breath caught. That staccato of shots was impossible to mistake. Soldiers returned fire, a rapid volley that caused her to flinch. Dave hurried to the hangar's main door and peered out, then pulled back.

"They're exchanging fire at the outer gate," he said. "We're not sure if they can break through, but they're well-armed. Everyone, get behind cover."

Lorraine and Soren ducked behind a stack of crates. Helena, Father Lombardi, and Dave positioned themselves near the transport truck that had carried the Ark, using it as a makeshift shield. Ibrahim joined them, holding a pistol with trembling hands.

"We'll hold them off," Dave said, voice taut, "but if they manage to breach the gate, we may need to seal the hangar from within."

The radio sizzled. "They've deployed smoke grenades! We can't see them clearly—gates are compromised." Gunshots thundered in the background.

A creeping dread filled Helena as she considered the possibility that these intruders might not hesitate to blow open the hangar door to seize the Ark. She recalled the lethal pulses the chest had unleashed before. If a firefight erupted inside, the Ark might react unpredictably. She prayed they wouldn't find out.

Suddenly, a figure in combat gear dashed around the corner of the building visible through the open hangar door. He dropped to one knee, raised a rifle, and aimed at the guard post. The guard post lit up with gunfire, bullets chewing the concrete near him. He fired back, forcing them to duck. Another attacker followed, lobbing a small canister that hissed thick smoke. The swirling haze partially obscured the intruders' approach.

Dave's eyes narrowed. "They're inside the perimeter. Prepare to defend."

He signaled one of the Israeli soldiers, who nodded and barked into his radio. A line of uniformed defenders formed across the hangar entrance, guns ready. Helena crouched, adrenaline roaring in her veins. She had never been in such a tense firefight environment. The memory of last night's convoy shootout felt like a warm-up compared to the potential scale of this assault. Through the haze, she glimpsed muzzle flashes and the flicker of muzzle brake flames.

"They're heading for the hangar!" an Israeli soldier shouted.

Multiple bursts of automatic fire rattled the gates. Closer now. Helena pressed herself against a crate, heart slamming. She sensed Dave moving to her left, ensuring he had a clear line of sight. Father Lombardi knelt behind a metal barrier, whispering fervent words she couldn't make out.

Moments later, three attackers materialized through the smoke, wearing dark tactical gear with no insignia. They peppered the hangar doorway with bullets, forcing the Israeli line to duck. One soldier returned fire, striking a masked intruder in the shoulder. The man toppled, howling in pain. Another unleashed a volley that ricocheted off the steel framework, sending sparks across the concrete floor.

Behind the crates, Lorraine whimpered, covering her head. Soren tried to shield her with his body. Helena clenched her teeth, wishing she could do more than cower. She peered around the truck. One intruder sprinted deeper into the hangar, heading straight for the Ark. The man must know precisely what he was after.

Dave saw him too. The agent rose from cover, fired twice, and forced the attacker to veer away. The shots clipped the man's vest, causing him to stumble. He recovered, pivoted behind a support column, then tossed a flash grenade into the open space. Helena squeezed her eyes shut and covered her ears. A blinding burst of light and sound rocked the hangar. She staggered, dazed. When her vision cleared, the intruder was on the move again, creeping toward the platform where the Ark lay.

"No!" Helena shouted, trying to stand. Her legs trembled. She blinked away spots, aware that Dave was disoriented too. The intruder seized the moment, darting behind a forklift. He fired at an Israeli soldier, who collapsed with a grunt. More bullets flew, biting into metal walls.

Amid the chaos, the Ark rumbled with an audible hum. Blue-white arcs crackled over its gilded edges, leaping inches into the air. Soren let out a choked yell. "It's... it's building up again!"

Helena's stomach lurched. She recalled the illusions some commando had reported seeing, swirling lights that disoriented the attacker. If the Ark unleashed those visions now, with bullets flying, the result could be a nightmare.

One of the masked intruders sprinted around the forklift, evidently aiming to place a hand on the Ark or possibly attach some device to it. Father Lombardi, from his crouched position behind a barrier, cried out, "Stop! You don't know what you're doing!"

The attacker ignored him, raising a small metallic cylinder, likely an explosive or specialized breaching tool. Before the man could plant it on the chest, Dave fired a precise shot. The bullet struck the cylinder, causing a sudden spark and a tiny cloud of black smoke. The intruder dropped it with a sharp cry, backing away as if burned.

A ripple of energy erupted from the Ark, a brief flash that seemed to distort the air around it. Helena saw the edges of reality shimmer. For a fraction of a second, she glimpsed something impossible: a silhouette of winged shapes overhead, wings that glowed with fiery intensity. Then it was gone, leaving her gasping. The intruder let out a startled roar, staggering backward, eyes wide with terror. Had he seen the same phantom vision?

He stumbled into open space, right into the line of Israeli fire. Two soldiers, regaining their bearings, shot him in the leg and shoulder. He dropped, weapon clattering away. The cylinder spun across the floor, eventually skidding to a stop near a row of crates.

Helena's heart hammered as she processed what she'd witnessed. Could the Ark really project illusions or visions? Or was she hallucinating under extreme stress? She tasted the tang of gunpowder in the air, her pulse drumming in her ears.

Gunfire persisted around the hangar entrance. Another masked figure launched a last-ditch attempt to breach the defenders, but the Israeli line held firm. Shots rang out, each echo resonating in the large space. Finally, after what felt like an eternity, the assault faltered. The attackers who could still move started retreating under heavy fire. Smoke drifted in the dawn light as they withdrew beyond the gate, some dragging wounded comrades.

Within minutes, the gunfire died. Sirens wailed from approaching police vehicles. Helena tried to catch her breath, scanning for injuries among their group. Dave stooped near the forklift, verifying that the intruder who nearly reached the Ark was down, not an immediate threat. Father Lombardi emerged from behind a barrier, face pale.

Lorraine and Soren stood shakily, eyes filled with shock. Two Israeli soldiers helped each other toward the nearest medic station. The entire hangar smelled of burnt powder and scorched metal, and bullet holes pockmarked the walls. The Ark's electric glow subsided to faint wisps.

Helena forced her legs to move. She stepped toward the gilded chest, dreading what she might find. But the artifact remained intact, strapped to its platform. Residual static made her skin tingle. She reined in her racing heart, reminding herself to breathe.

Dave returned, panting, adrenaline still shining in his eyes. "They're retreating, or at least regrouping," he said. "We have casualties. I think we drove them off."

She swallowed, voice hoarse. "The Ark... did you see that—light?"

He nodded, gaze flicking to the artifact. "Yeah. For a moment, it was like... shapes. Could've been illusions. Or we're losing it."

Father Lombardi approached, trembling. "It's what I feared," he whispered. "When men try to seize the Ark for violent ends, it defends itself."

Shouts rang out near the shattered gate. Reinforcements arrived, guiding medics to the wounded. Helena hurried to help, though her knees felt like rubber. She froze when she noticed one of the masked attackers pinned under debris, moaning for help in a language she didn't recognize. Against every self-preserving instinct, she called a soldier to free him. She was an archaeologist, not an executioner. The soldier disarmed the man, then dragged him to a medic. Dave stood watch, gun at the ready, uncertain if the assailant might lash out again.

In the chaos, Yusef Nasir lingered beyond the exterior fence. He had been drawn by the noise and lights from the confrontation. It was still early morning, but half the city was stirring, anxious about the gunshots from the secure facility. The teen pressed against a cinder-block wall, heart pounding as he glimpsed black-clad figures running for cover outside the base. Some looked injured, others scrambled into unmarked SUVs and sped off. The boy's mind spun with dread. Danger followed the Ark wherever it went.

When the immediate threat subsided, the gates were re-secured. Israeli soldiers, aided by local law enforcement, combed the perimeter for stragglers. They apprehended two more attackers who had collapsed behind a barricade. None carried identifying documents. Word spread that the group had used heavy bribes and inside knowledge to slip past outer checkpoints. The assumption among the defenders: a well-funded foreign operative was behind it. Possibly Orlov. Possibly another unknown sponsor.

Inside the hangar, Helena and Dave surveyed the damage. At least three guards lay wounded. Bullet casings littered the floor. Smoke hung in the air, tinted by the morning sun streaming through bullet-riddled windows. Father Lombardi knelt to pray beside a gravely injured Israeli soldier, speaking in a comforting tone.

Ibrahim arrived from outside, hair disheveled. "We've pushed them out, but security here is compromised. This facility is no longer secret. We have ambulances and investigators en route."

Helena set her jaw. "They almost reached the Ark. If we stay here, they might come back with more firepower."

Dave pursed his lips, glancing at her. "We just relocated. Another move could be even riskier."

She spread her hands, feeling torn. "Do we have a better choice? We're a magnet for every faction that wants the Ark. Hiding it seems impossible."

A tremor went through her. She recalled Father Lombardi's repeated claim that only humility and reverence might keep the Ark from unleashing deadly illusions or worse. Was it time to consider letting him perform rites? Or was that stepping into superstition?

Outside, paramedics rushed in. Helena winced as she saw a stretcher carrying a wounded soldier, who had lost a significant amount of blood. Dave stepped aside to let them pass, frustration etched on his face. This was turning into a war zone.

A sharp crack of electricity drew their attention back to the Ark. Blue sparks flashed along the gold edges for an instant, then vanished. Soren cursed under his breath, checking the monitor. "Still stable, but definitely more fluctuations than before."

Ibrahim stared at the artifact. "The more people try to take it by force, the more it reacts. That's my theory."

Father Lombardi joined them, expression somber. "It's not just theory. The Ark's guardians are stirring. We must prevent further attempts, or we may witness a far greater release of its power."

Dave's radio chirped. An urgent voice demanded an update. He gave a brief summary of the situation, then swore under his breath. "We're not safe here. But if we move again in broad daylight, we risk open confrontation on the roads."

The tension in the hangar was palpable. Helena felt dread pooling in her stomach. No matter which path they chose, infiltration or a direct assault loomed. And each violent clash might provoke the Ark, unleashing visions that could lead to more casualties. The entire scenario teetered on the edge of madness.

At a lull in the commotion, a phone beeped in Helena's pocket. She retrieved it, noticing a text from an unknown number. A single line read: If you truly wish to calm the Ark, meet me at the border crossing near Bethlehem. Sunset. No more delays. Her heart lurched. Rina, the mysterious local who claimed knowledge of old rites. She had given Helena two days, and that time was almost up.

She paused, thinking of the assault they'd just weathered. Any chance of leaving the Ark behind to chase a rumored scroll in Bethlehem seemed unthinkable. Yet the apparitions, the lethal pulses—nothing in the modern arsenal offered a solution. Could Rina's lead be genuine?

Dave approached, noticing her pensive look. He angled his head in silent question. She hesitated, then showed him the text. He read it, eyes narrowing. "Bethlehem at sunset. That's hours from now, and you'd have to cross into Palestinian territory. Are you sure it's not a trap?"

She shrugged, uncertain. "I have no guarantees. But it's possible this is the only real lead on how to pacify the Ark, or at least keep these manifestations from escalating."

He studied the phone again. "Going alone would be insane. But if the Israeli government or the Americans know, they might forbid it. They'll say it's too dangerous."

She swallowed hard. "We can't ignore any chance to mitigate these attacks. Look at the bloodshed we just witnessed."

He nodded grimly. "You're right. But we have to do it. And I can't let you go alone."

THE SWORD OF CHERUBIM

She permitted a tiny smile, despite the tension. "I figured as much. Let's see if we can slip away before the next crisis."

They conferred with Ibrahim, who looked torn. "If you leave now, I can't guarantee your safety. This base is on lockdown. The roads are crawling with suspicious activity. But if you think it's our only chance to learn more about the Ark's powers..."

Helena thought of the illusions that momentarily froze the intruder with fear, the fleeting vision of wings overhead. She imagined entire armies experiencing that phenomenon, multiplied by a hundred. A global conflict could spiral out of control. "I think it's worth the risk," she said.

Dave nodded. "I'll arrange a small transport, no more than two vehicles. We'll pose as routine travelers. No official insignia. We'll minimize the chance of drawing attention."

Father Lombardi overheard, stepping closer. "Dr. Carter, I sense you have a plan?"

She hesitated, then decided to share. "Yes. I have a lead in Bethlehem—someone who claims to know a ritual that might calm the Ark. I can't confirm it's real. But we need to try."

He listened gravely. "Then allow me to accompany you. If these rites are biblical in nature, my presence could help. That is, if you trust me."

She caught Dave's glance, recalling the priest's genuine concern and the possibility that he might have deeper motives. But time was short, and he was well-versed in religious texts. "All right," she said carefully. "We'll keep it low-profile. No large entourage, no advanced weapons."

The priest bowed his head in agreement.

They spent the next hour finalizing a cover story. Helena would slip out for a "debrief with local academics," while Dave and the priest accompanied her as escorts. Ibrahim promised to keep a lid on it, though he warned them that if the infiltration squads caught wind of their departure, they might attempt to intercept.

A quiet tension settled as the trio prepared to depart. A plain civilian car waited near a side exit of the base, fueled and ready. Helena packed a small rucksack with basic supplies—notes on the Ark, some of Lombardi's references, a first-aid kit. Dave double-checked a discreet pistol tucked under his jacket. The priest carried only his satchel of manuscripts. Together, they slipped away from the battered hangar, leaving the Ark under heavy guard.

Soren and Lorraine watched them go with anxious faces. Yusef, who had crept close to the perimeter again, spotted Helena, Dave, and the priest heading out in a nondescript vehicle. Suspicion gripped him. Why were they leaving the fortress right after an attack? Where were they going with such secrecy? He knew he couldn't follow them on foot. Instead, he hurried down a side road, searching for an affordable taxi. Part of him felt compelled to track their movements, worried that an even darker threat might loom.

Meanwhile, Helena guided the sedan out of the facility, leaning low behind the steering wheel. Dave sat beside her, scanning mirrors for tails. Father Lombardi was in the back seat, silent in prayer. They wove through a series of side streets, eventually crossing into Jerusalem traffic. The morning sun was climbing higher, bathing the city in bright light. People bustled through markets, unaware of the deadly assault that had taken place earlier.

After an hour of careful maneuvering, they approached the outskirts leading toward Bethlehem. Security checkpoints dotted the roads, each manned by Israeli forces. Dave explained the situation to the soldier at the main crossing, presenting minimal credentials to avoid suspicion. The soldier cast a questioning look but waved them on. The path ahead lay in the West Bank, where political tensions simmered constantly.

As they neared the city, the urban landscape shifted. Stone buildings with domed roofs appeared, interspersed with modern structures and old chapels. An atmosphere of religious heritage permeated the streets. Helena recalled how Bethlehem was revered as a biblical site, home to centuries of sacred traditions. If someone here truly guarded knowledge about the Ark's rites, it might be found in one of the city's quiet pockets.

They parked near a modest church, ensuring the car remained inconspicuous. Lombardi glanced around, voice subdued. "I sense a deep peace in these streets, but also an undercurrent of caution. People here are used to conflict."

Helena nodded. She checked her phone. No new messages from Rina. The plan was to meet at sunset, but it was still hours away. In the meantime, they needed a place to wait without attracting attention.

Dave led them through a warren of side alleys until they found a small café with an awning that offered shade. They took a table in the back. The priest ordered tea, Helena and Dave asked for coffee. Locals and occasional tourists passed by, giving them little more than a glance. Time stretched. The trio spoke in hushed tones about potential rites, infiltration, and the illusions that had manifested around the Ark. Lombardi insisted that the next surge could be more severe, referencing medieval accounts of entire armies struck by terror. Dave listened, wearing a grave expression.

Just before sunset, Helena's phone chimed. A short text from Rina: A caretaker's house is two blocks east of the old well on Star Street. Come alone. She showed it to Dave, who pursed his lips. "She wants you alone? That's suspicious."

Lombardi pressed a hand to his cross. "It could be a safety measure. She might fear multiple people showing up with hidden agendas."

Helena inhaled sharply. "I'm not walking into a stranger's house by myself. Let's compromise: Dave and the Father can stay close, but I'll go inside alone. If anything goes wrong, they can come in."

They left the café, following the directions under the waning sky. Star Street was a narrow route lined with shops and battered houses. At the second turn, they spotted the old stone well. Two more blocks led them to a modest dwelling with a blue door. The surrounding homes had shutters closed, perhaps from caution or custom. A streetlamp flickered on as dusk settled.

Helena approached the door, feeling her pulse accelerate. Dave and Lombardi hung back, watching from a corner. She knocked. Wood scraped against stone from inside. The door cracked open a few inches, revealing Rina's anxious eyes. The local woman wore a shawl wrapped around her hair, and her features looked more tense than before.

"You came alone?" Rina whispered.

Helena nodded. "Just me. My colleagues are nearby if anything goes wrong."

Rina gave a short nod, stepping aside to let her in. The interior was dim, lit by a single lamp. The walls were lined with shelves holding old books and scroll tubes. A faint aroma of spices drifted through the air. Helena wondered if this was a hidden repository, or merely a caretaker's library. Rina guided her to a small table.

"There's little time," the woman said. "I'm sorry for the secrecy, but many eyes are on Bethlehem. My contact is an old scholar named Husam. His family has protected aged scrolls that detail ways to placate the Ark's energies."

Helena's eyes widened. "Where is he now?"

Rina's voice trembled. "He's in a back room, but he's ill. He insisted on speaking with you before he can show the manuscripts. But we must be careful. If hostile forces discover these texts, they could twist them for their own ends."

Helena's mouth felt dry. She glanced around, noticing thick volumes with Hebrew, Aramaic, and other scripts she didn't recognize. Could these be the legendary scrolls? "Please, let me see him."

Rina motioned her to follow. They passed through a tight hallway into a cramped bedroom where an elderly man lay on a low bed, eyes half-lidded. A single candle flickered on a nearby stand. He wore a threadbare robe and clutched a piece of parchment in one hand.

Helena stepped closer, heart clenching. The man's breathing was shallow, and sweat beaded on his brow. Rina knelt beside him, murmuring gently. He opened his eyes, gaze flicking to Helena.

"This is Husam," Rina said. "He's the keeper of the scrolls."

Husam wheezed, lips moving soundlessly until a voice emerged. "You... come about the Ark?"

Helena nodded, voice hushed. "Yes. We found it under the Temple Mount. It's already caused terrible strife, illusions, violence."

He swallowed, expression pained. "The Ark... dear child, it must not be wielded by warmongers. There is a rite, a covenant ritual that can calm the cherubim's wrath."

Her pulse raced. "Do you have the instructions?"

He gestured to the parchment in his hand. Rina gently took it, handing it to Helena. The old caretaker coughed, wincing. "You must... read it. But the text is incomplete. The final passages are in another scroll, hidden for centuries. We only know part of the rite."

Helena's eyes danced across the parchment. It contained archaic Hebrew lines describing an offering of sanctified incense, a circle of priests chanting a specific phrase in unison. It read like a liturgical ceremony. She recognized certain biblical references, though the wording was unusual.

"This references cherubim and a seat of mercy," she murmured. "And there's a mention of purifying hearts. Is it symbolic?"

Rina shook her head. "Symbolic or not, many accounts say the ritual prevented calamities in centuries-old times. That's why Husam's family preserved it."

Helena felt a surge of hope warring with skepticism. Could this truly work in the modern era? The caretaker coughed again, watery eyes brimming with urgency. "Finish the rite," he managed. "Or the Ark will bring... greater destruction."

She gripped his hand, feeling the thin bones beneath his skin. "Thank you. I'll do whatever it takes to keep that from happening."

He nodded, letting out a rattling breath. Rina touched the caretaker's forehead with concern. "He's very weak," she whispered. "We don't know how much longer..."

Before she finished, the front door banged open. Helena's heart skipped a beat. She spun, listening. A muffled commotion arose in the front room—raised voices, footsteps. Dave's distinct shout sounded. Fear lanced through her. Had someone followed them?

"Stay with him," she told Rina, tucking the parchment into her jacket. She sprinted back down the hallway, hand shaking with adrenaline.

In the main room, Father Lombardi stood by the doorway, arms out as if blocking it. Two men in black clothing brandished small pistols, their faces grim. Dave had taken cover behind a shelf, aiming his weapon at the intruders. The tension crackled.

One intruder snarled, "Hand over the manuscripts! We know you came for them." His accent was thick, possibly Eastern European.

Father Lombardi refused to yield. "Leave this place. You don't understand the havoc you invite."

The second intruder advanced, pistol raised. "Shut up, old man. We're not here for talk."

Helena edged behind a dusty shelf, blood roaring in her ears. She realized with dread that Yusef might have followed them, or some other tail had discovered their meeting. Dave kept his gun trained on the pair, but no one fired yet. The tight quarters made any shot risky. Rina crouched in the hallway, eyes wide with terror.

The men spotted Helena. One barked, "You! Step forward and give us the scroll."

She tried to stall, voice shaking. "We don't have it."

He scoffed. "Our employer knows everything. Hand it over, or we shoot."

Father Lombardi took a defiant step. "You risk unleashing unstoppable power."

The intruder's finger twitched on the trigger. Dave recognized the threat, fired first. The bullet struck the man in the shoulder. He roared, returning fire in a blind arc. Splinters sprayed from the wood near

Lombardi. The second man lunged behind a cupboard, exchanging shots with Dave. The cramped space rang with echoes of gunfire. Helena ducked, heart pounding.

Rina shrieked, pressing herself against the wall. Father Lombardi stumbled backward, a ricochet grazing his arm. He hissed in pain, dropping to a knee. Helena crawled over, checking on him. Blood stained his sleeve, but the wound seemed superficial. Meanwhile, Dave kept the second man pinned with well-placed shots. The windows shattered as bullets zipped back and forth.

The caretaker, Husam, groaned from the bedroom. Helena prayed no stray bullet hit him. She had to end this before it turned fatal. But her mind spun. She had no gun. Dave was locked in a standoff with the second intruder. The first, though injured, was fumbling to raise his pistol again.

Just then, Yusef burst in through the half-open door. The teen gasped at the chaos—broken glass, swirling dust, the priest wounded. On pure reflex, he grabbed a heavy vase from a nearby table and hurled it at the first intruder. The ceramic struck the man's shoulder, knocking him off-balance. The pistol clattered from his grasp. Dave seized the opportunity, firing a single shot that lodged in the attacker's leg. He crumpled, howling.

The second intruder realized the tide had turned. A bullet from Dave's gun smashed the cupboard an inch from his head, forcing him to drop his weapon. He raised his hands, face twisted in fury. "Don't shoot! We yield."

Helena scrambled to her feet, stunned to see Yusef panting, eyes wide. The boy trembled, glancing at Father Lombardi's wounded arm. "I... I followed you. Saw these men sneaking around. Couldn't just watch."

Dave stepped forward, disarmed the second intruder, and kicked the discarded pistols out of reach. "Stay down!" he ordered. The men glowered, cursing, but complied.

Rina rushed to the caretaker's side. The old scholar moaned, though his injuries stemmed from illness, not bullets. Father Lombardi pressed a hand to his own bleeding arm, wincing. "It's not deep," he whispered.

Helena's pulse rattled, adrenaline surging. She couldn't believe Yusef had intervened. "You saved us," she said breathlessly. "But it's dangerous for you to be here."

He gave a shaky nod, glancing at Dave. "Sorry. I had a feeling something bad would happen."

Dave exhaled, expression softening. "We owe you one. You all right?"

The teen nodded, swallowing hard.

Sirens wailed in the distance, likely local police responding to gunfire. Dave turned to Helena. "We need to go. I'll handle these two. You gather whatever you came for."

She raced to Rina's side. The caretaker was fading, breath shallow. "We'll get him to a hospital," Helena promised. "We have the partial scroll. Is there anything else we need?"

Rina bit her lip, glancing at the battered shelves. "Husam said the second half of the rite is in a different location, hidden away. He gave me no details, only that we must follow clues in that parchment."

Helena pressed the parchment to her chest. "We'll decode it. Let's get your grandfather medical care first."

A swirl of events followed in rapid-fire motion. Dave and Yusef restrained the intruders, using rope from the caretaker's home. Father Lombardi, wincing, offered a shaky blessing over them, urging them to abandon their violent path. The men spat in response. Yusef's eyes flashed with indignation, but he said nothing further.

Local authorities arrived, sirens blaring. Helena spoke with them briefly, describing an attempted robbery. She avoided mentioning the Ark or the deeper truth. Rina pleaded for an ambulance for Husam. Eventually, paramedics arrived, placing the old man on a stretcher. The intruders were hauled into custody, though it remained unclear if local officials would connect them to the ongoing crisis. The caretaker's home stood in shambles, bullet holes in the walls, broken glass on the floor.

Outside, night had fully descended, the sky scattered with stars. Dave guided Helena, Father Lombardi, and Yusef back to the car. Rina stayed behind to ride with Husam in the ambulance. Before they parted, she squeezed Helena's hand. "Please. Protect the Ark, and find the missing piece of the rite. We can't let that relic become a weapon."

Helena hugged her briefly, then ushered Yusef into the back seat. Lombardi slid in as well, still cradling his injured arm. Dave took the wheel, tension etching his features. The teen stared at him nervously, but Dave just offered a weary nod. "Guess you're with us now."

The car pulled away from the battered street, passing curious onlookers who gawked at the aftermath. In the rearview mirror, Helena saw Rina standing among the flashing ambulance lights, eyes full of worry. Her words rang in Helena's ears: find the missing piece. Complete the ritual. The caretaker believed they held the key to preventing further devastation.

Father Lombardi clutched the partial scroll. "We'll need time to translate these lines. The references are archaic. But if it truly speaks of an weather-scarred ceremony to calm the Ark..."

Yusef leaned forward from the back seat. "Why not just let the Ark stay hidden? All this fighting over it might destroy the city."

No one had a simple answer. They drove in silence for a while, weaving through Bethlehem's outskirts toward the main road leading back to Jerusalem. Tension weighed heavily on them. Helena replayed the caretaker's warning: the Ark would bring greater destruction if they failed to finish the rite. That notion clashed with the military solutions swirling around the artifact. She wondered how they could possibly reconcile centuries-old spiritual instructions with the present-day labyrinth of governments and covert agents.

Eventually, Dave spoke, voice hushed. "We'll return to the secure facility. Or what's left of it. The Ark is still there, hopefully intact."

Father Lombardi nodded, wincing at the throbbing in his arm. "We must share this text with Dr. Carter's team. Let them cross-reference it with the inscriptions found near the Temple Mount. If we're lucky, the missing part of the ritual might be gleaned from a combination of sources."

Yusef listened, brow furrowed. "This is bigger than anything I imagined. I just wanted to keep the city safe." His voice trembled slightly. "Now it feels like the whole world is after the Ark."

Helena reached back and gently squeezed his hand. "You helped us today. Thank you. We'll do our best to ensure no one twists the Ark's power for evil."

He nodded, though fear lingered in his eyes. The car wound along the road, headlights illuminating the path. With each mile, Helena's sense of urgency deepened. The caretaker's partial scroll might be the only hope of preventing a global disaster, but time was running short. More infiltration teams would soon swarm the region, each vying for a relic that biblical lore claimed could level armies.

By the time they approached Jerusalem's outskirts, the eastern sky showed faint signs of dawn. Helena stared out the window, mind racing. Another sleepless night, another near-death experience, another piece of an battered puzzle. She feared it would never end. Yet a new conviction stirred in her chest: if there was a way to tame the Ark, she would find it—even if it meant embracing rituals older than any modern warfare strategy.

They navigated the final checkpoint, entering the battered base where the Ark was kept. Soldiers scurried to repair damage from the earlier assault. Smoke still clung to corners of the yard. Dave parked near a side entrance. The group stepped out into the chill morning air. A hush hung around them, as if the day's tension refused to dissipate.

Helena spotted Soren and Lorraine rushing up, relief evident in their faces when they saw the travelers had returned safely. Yusef shrank back, uncertain how the staff might react to a teenage outsider, but Lorraine greeted him with a shaky smile. "He's been helping us," Helena explained briefly. "We couldn't have escaped a dangerous situation without him."

In the center of the hangar, the Ark remained on its platform. Blue arcs of static flickered occasionally, but nothing more dramatic than a mild hum. The gloom of dawn cast long shadows across the walls pockmarked by bullet holes. Father Lombardi lowered himself onto a chair, pressing a bandage over his wound. Helena, still clutching the precious parchment, exhaled a ragged breath.

"We found part of an centuries-old ritual," she announced to the small circle of exhausted staff. "It may be our only chance to keep the Ark from wreaking more havoc."

Soren blinked. "You mean… there's a ceremony that might calm it?"

"That's the claim," Dave said. "Whether we can piece it together before foreign forces strike again is another story."

Lorraine's expression turned grim. "We'll try. Show me the text. Maybe we can cross-reference it with the inscriptions from the vault."

Helena handed it over with care. The partial lines glowed in the overhead lamps, archaic script promising something akin to redemption if performed with sincerity. She recalled the illusions that had manifested during the last attack, the winglike shapes that seemed to guard the Ark with fierce brilliance. Whatever power guided those visions wouldn't be contained by bullets or politics.

She gazed at Dave, who watched her with quiet resolve, and at Yusef, who stood near the edge of the group, uncertain but determined. Father Lombardi bowed his head in silent prayer, evidently believing they had taken a step toward saving lives, not just in Jerusalem, but possibly across the planet. The first rays of daylight spilled into the hangar, illuminating the battered remains of the overnight battle, and hinting at the trials yet to come.

No one said it out loud, but a common hope lingered: that the caretaker's partial scroll—and the missing piece they still needed—could avert a catastrophe the world hadn't seen in millennia. If they failed, the Ark's defenders—cherubim or otherwise—might unleash a devastation beyond anyone's control. The clock was ticking, and a hush of dread and anticipation settled over them all.

Chapter 7

Gray dawn seeped through the makeshift windows of the fortified hangar, revealing bullet scars on the walls and a cluster of exhausted men and women gathered around the Ark. The artifact rested on a steel platform reinforced with shock-dampeners, humming with a faint, constant charge. Lights on portable stands highlighted its gilded edges, where arcs of static occasionally traced spidery trails across the metal.

Dr. Helena Carter sat on a collapsible chair beside a table strewn with notes, her eyes gritty from lack of sleep. She kept re-reading the partial scroll rescued from Bethlehem. crumbling Hebrew lines described a ritual meant to pacify the Ark's energies: a series of prayers and offerings, the rhythmic chanting of verses. But the text ended abruptly, leaving them groping for the missing half. Every attempt to cross-reference the incomplete script with known biblical sources had led to dead ends. Still, she clung to the hope that this ceremony—if fully reconstructed—might avert greater horrors.

Ibrahim Mahdi stepped into the circle of light, shaking dust off his jacket. The liaison from the Israeli Antiquities Authority looked tense, drawn from sleepless nights and near-constant worry. "The higher-ups made a decision," he said, eyes flicking between Helena and the battered Ark. "We can't stay here any longer. After the attack yesterday, this facility's location is compromised."

Helena closed the scroll. "So we're moving the Ark again? That's risky."

He lowered his voice as if the Ark itself might overhear. "They'll move it. The government has selected a more secluded spot. It's less fortified than this base but off every known intelligence map, supposedly. They want you, Dave, and minimal staff to oversee the transfer. Fewer people, fewer leaks."

She recalled the chaotic relocation from the previous night and the firefight that nearly ended in catastrophe. "Have they set a time?"

Ibrahim rubbed a hand over his face. "Yes. In four hours, at midday. We have limited security forces left uninjured. And rumor has it that more foreign teams have arrived in Israel."

Her stomach twisted. Word of the Ark's whereabouts must be spreading quickly. If their attackers learned about the new destination, the convoy could face another assault. She sighed, looking at the static flickering on the Ark's golden surface. "Is there no alternative?"

"Not unless you have a better idea. The cabinet ministers met this morning and insisted. We'll try to disguise the move, using decoy vehicles. Officially, the Ark stays here—on paper, anyway. In practice, we'll sneak it out."

Nearby, Dave Schumer concluded a hushed discussion with two Israeli officers. He approached Helena, glancing at the partial scroll in her hands. A line of concern framed his mouth. "I heard. They're calling it Operation Silhouette. We need to get ready." He hesitated, scanning her face. "Are you holding up?"

She managed a small, tired smile. "Define holding up."

He touched her shoulder, a gesture of quiet support. That warmth in his eyes momentarily countered the gloom. "We'll get through this."

She set the scroll on the table. "I hope so. I hate the idea of bouncing the Ark all over Israel, but we don't have much choice."

Ibrahim motioned for them to follow. "We're gathering in the side room for final plans. Father Lombardi insisted on attending. He says he wants to recite a prayer over the Ark before it moves, to keep it calm."

Helena arched a brow. The priest had been pressing for religious rites ever since the partial illusions near the artifact turned lethal. "All right. Let's see what he has to say."

They headed down a corridor past medics treating the injured from the previous assault. The tang of disinfectant hovered in the air. Helena heard quiet groans from soldiers with bandaged limbs. Each pained face underscored how close they'd come to a larger tragedy. She couldn't help thinking that every new confrontation risked unleashing more of the Ark's uncanny defenses.

A makeshift conference room—really just a converted storage chamber—held half a dozen people: two Israeli intelligence officers, an army major, Father Aurelius Lombardi, and Yusef Nasir. The youth hovered near the back, his arms folded as if trying to vanish. Yet curiosity and determination shone in his gaze. Helena felt a mix of guilt and relief seeing him; he had saved them once already. She hoped they wouldn't need his bravery again.

Ibrahim cleared his throat. "Everyone, we have a four-hour window before we move. The plan is straightforward: three vehicles, no more. The Ark will travel in a covered cargo truck. Dr. Carter, Agent Schumer, and I will ride in the escort SUV. Another car will trail at a distance."

One of the Israeli intelligence officers pointed to a map pinned on the wall. "Here's the route. We'll leave the base through a rarely used side gate. We cut through a series of side streets—less traffic, less chance for prying eyes—then merge onto an old service road leading out of town. Our final destination is an abandoned training facility in the Negev region. That place is barely on the official maps."

The major chimed in. "If we come under attack, we'll call for aerial support. But be aware that the region is close to a known smuggling corridor. So we might run into more than just foreign mercenaries. Gangs and arms dealers frequent that terrain."

Father Lombardi, arms folded over his black cassock, spoke next. "We should conduct a blessing before the move. The Ark has shown violent reactions when threatened. Perhaps a prayer or a short reading from Scripture would help keep it contained."

One of the intelligence officers rolled his eyes. "We're pressed for time, Father. This is a military operation, not a liturgical ceremony."

The priest's mouth tightened. "I'm aware. But after witnessing the visions triggered during recent clashes, I believe ignoring the Ark's spiritual side is dangerous."

Dave exhaled, throwing Helena a questioning glance. She shrugged and addressed the group. "Father Lombardi's attempts to calm the Ark might help. Considering how unsettled it becomes when threatened, any measure that reduces the chance of an electrical surge or spectral manifestations is worth trying."

The Israeli major grunted. "Fine. But keep it brief." He gathered his papers. "All right, let's finalize assignments. We meet in the yard at 1130 hours. We roll out by noon. Dr. Carter, you're in charge of ensuring the Ark's safe handling. Agent Schumer, you handle security close to the artifact. Mr. Mahdi will coordinate with the lead driver and stay in radio contact with me. Clear?"

A chorus of nods followed. The meeting concluded. People filed out in pairs, whispering final clarifications. Father Lombardi approached Helena, a worn Bible in hand. "Thank you for speaking up on my behalf. I'll keep the reading short, I promise."

She nodded, though her mind lingered on more practical concerns. "Let's hope it settles the Ark. Otherwise, we'll be traveling with a ticking bomb."

He dipped his head. "We do all we can."

Nearby, Yusef lingered, scanning the maps pinned on the wall. She offered him a gentle look. "Are you part of this?"

He shrugged, shifting on his feet. "I'm just a kid, right? But I can help guide you through roads if you get stuck. I know shortcuts. And I need to see this through. It's my city."

Helena studied the teen's determined posture. He had proven invaluable more than once. "Stay close then. But don't take unnecessary risks."

He cracked a faint grin, relief mingling with anxiety. "I'll do my best."

The group dispersed. Helena walked back to the Ark with Dave, each step weighed down by what lay ahead. "Every time we try to relocate, someone tries to kill us," she muttered.

He offered a grim half-smile. "You'd think we'd learn. But we can't stay put either."

They approached the artifact. Technicians were already removing certain protective braces from its platform. The plan was to load it onto a new shock-absorbent rig for the upcoming drive. Workers handled each clamp gingerly, as if one stray jolt could set off a wave of destructive power.

Yusef wandered the perimeter, observing. Dave beckoned him over, giving him a quick rundown of how the cargo truck would be arranged. The youth nodded, occasionally chiming in with suggestions for hidden routes. Helena watched the subtle way Dave treated the teenager: protective but respectful. She felt the corners of her mouth lift. A sense of camaraderie had formed between them, bridging age and background.

An hour ticked by in a blur of preparations. Father Lombardi stood near the Ark's edge, murmuring a prayer from his worn Bible. Technicians finished transferring the chest onto its travel platform. The partial scroll sat on a side table, guarded by a young researcher. Helena reminded herself they would need those lines later if they found the missing half.

When the clock neared 1130, the small convoy assembled in the courtyard. Three vehicles total, as planned: one unmarked cargo truck with a dull gray canvas covering, a battered SUV for the escort team, and a small sedan behind them with two security personnel. Soldiers formed a cordon around the area, keeping watch for suspicious onlookers. The Ark, strapped securely, was rolled out on a sturdy dolly and guided up a makeshift ramp into the truck's rear section.

Helena felt her heart clench as the chest disappeared inside. She recalled the violent pulses the Ark had unleashed under stress. Would the next escalation be far worse? She forced that worry aside, climbing into the escort SUV. Dave took the front passenger seat with a rifle laid across his lap. Ibrahim slid into the driver's seat, radio in hand. Helena settled in the back, wedged between boxes of medical supplies and extra gear. Yusef occupied a small fold-down seat behind the driver, looking out the window with a mix of awe and anxiety. Father Lombardi chose to remain in the cargo truck with the Ark, presumably to continue his prayers.

At exactly noon, the convoy rumbled forward, passing through a hidden gate near the rear of the base. Soldiers outside waved them on with tense faces. The roads beyond were oddly quiet in the noonday sun. Many locals had retreated indoors, skittish after the recent outbreaks of violence. Heat shimmered off the asphalt, giving the street a wavering illusion.

Ibrahim took a winding route, turning at random intersections to shake off any potential tail. After fifteen minutes of twisting roads, they reached a side street lined with deserted warehouses and chain-link fences. The cargo truck kept close, occasionally swerving around potholes. Radio chatter crackled with updates from the trailing sedan, each occupant scanning for threats.

Helena forced herself to remain calm, though her palms felt clammy. She checked her watch. "We're making decent time," she murmured. "Let's hope we stay under the radar."

Yusef inhaled. "This part of the city used to be lively, with markets and busy streets. Feels strange seeing it empty." His voice held a note of sadness.

Ibrahim kept his eyes on the road. "People left when the area was redeveloped. Now it's perfect cover for criminals or spies."

They continued another half hour without incident. The roads gradually opened into a less congested zone, fringed by scrubland. Telephone wires drooped overhead, and an occasional battered billboard hinted at better days. Helena rubbed her temples, battling the tension knotting her muscles. Every time the radio crackled, she braced for news of a threat.

Finally, Ibrahim veered onto an older highway that headed south. Sparse traffic rolled by: a few trucks loaded with produce, some private cars, but no obvious pursuers. The lead cargo truck maintained a modest speed, letting no gap develop. The trailing sedan reported all clear. Helena allowed a small wave of relief to wash over her. Could it be they'd avoid a second ambush?

Dave, leaning forward in the passenger seat, stiffened. "Wait, what's that?" He pointed to a hillside road that branched off to the west. A dusty SUV was parked near a broken guardrail, engine idling. Two figures stood beside it, watching their convoy intently through binoculars.

Ibrahim spotted them and tensed. "Keep driving, but stay alert."

Helena glanced back, noticing Yusef's uneasy expression. "You recognize them?" she asked gently.

He shook his head. "No, but that stare isn't friendly."

As the convoy passed the fork, the men by the SUV got into their vehicle. Dust billowed behind them as they pulled onto the highway, merging a few hundred meters behind the trailing sedan. Ibrahim tried to speed up, but that only prompted the suspicious SUV to accelerate. They stayed at a distance, matching the convoy's moves.

The radio crackled. "Eyes on that dark SUV, about seven car-lengths behind me," said the second security agent in the trailing sedan. "They're not approaching fast, but they're definitely following us."

Dave pursed his lips. "Should we change course?"

Ibrahim gave a grim nod. "We'll exit at the next junction, see if they follow."

They reached the off-ramp half a mile later and swerved onto a narrow side road. The suspicious SUV followed. Tension spiked in the escort vehicle. Helena felt her heartbeat pound in her ears. Another chase?

The radio cackled again, urgent. "They're speeding up. Could be hostile."

Dave turned in his seat. "We have to lose them before we reach the next checkpoint."

Ibrahim pushed the accelerator, the escort SUV lurching forward. The cargo truck rumbled faster as well, the entire convoy bouncing over cracks in the pavement. Yusef gripped the back of Ibrahim's seat, knuckles white.

Minutes later, the trailing sedan reported a near collision. The suspicious SUV swerved close, forcing them onto the shoulder. A storm of dust rose behind them. Gunshots broke the midday hush. Helena cringed as bullets pinged off the pavement, though none seemed to strike the vehicles directly.

Ibrahim clenched the wheel, eyes locked on the road. "I'm not letting them corner us. We'll outrun them or find a spot to defend ourselves." He steered onto an unmarked route leading into rocky terrain, the cargo truck swaying dangerously.

Helena spied a swirl of dust behind the trailing car. The sound of more shots carried on the dry wind. The radio flared. "They're firing on us! Taking evasive maneuvers. Keep going. We'll hold them off."

A moment later, an explosion of static cut through the frequency. Then the trailing sedan's voice returned in a panicked rush: "Tire blowout—they hit us! We're spinning—"

Silence. Helena's breath caught, imagining the security team pinned or worse. Dave grabbed the radio, shouting for them to respond. No answer. The only noise was the steady roar of wind through the open window.

Within seconds, the suspicious SUV emerged from the swirl of dust, pressing closer to the cargo truck. Now there was no buffer behind them. Dave twisted to face Helena. "We either fight back or keep running, but that truck can't handle a high-speed chase forever."

Helena's mind raced. "We can't just abandon our people in the sedan."

Ibrahim's voice was strained. "We'll have to swing back once we ensure the Ark is safe. The mission is to keep that relic out of enemy hands."

Just as he spoke, another staccato of gunfire rattled the air. Bullets struck the escort SUV's rear fender, sending sparks dancing. Helena ducked. Yusef cried out, covering his head. Dave cursed under his breath and raised a short-barreled rifle from between the seats. He twisted to lean out the window, aiming at the pursuers.

The suspicious vehicle swerved side to side, trying to evade. Dave squeezed off a short burst. Glass shattered in their front windshield. The SUV wobbled, nearly crashing into a rock outcropping, but righted itself. Another volley from them hammered the escort's rear side, punching holes in the metal. Helena heard a hiss—some fluid line had been nicked. The SUV's engine coughed.

Ibrahim yelled, voice laced with panic. "We're losing power. We'll have to slow."

Up ahead, the cargo truck rumbled onward, not yet aware of the escort's trouble. Helena grabbed the radio. "Truck driver, do you copy? Our vehicle's damaged, we can't keep pace."

A startled voice returned, "We hear you—slowing down, but we're under fire too."

She risked a glance through the back window, seeing muzzle flashes from the attackers. Then her eyes locked on a second truck cresting a hill on the left. Its silhouette was large and menacing, possibly a heavier transport with armed men. No official markings. The perfect ambush.

The radio crackled again. "New vehicle approaching from the west! Looks like—"

Static overwhelmed the transmission. Ibrahim steered them around a bend, but the escort SUV sputtered, losing momentum. Dave tried leaning out the window for another shot. Before he could fire, the suspicious SUV surged forward, sideswiping their rear quarter. Metal screeched. The jolt nearly threw Helena sideways.

Yusef gripped the headrest, eyes wide with terror. "We're going to crash!"

Ibrahim fought the wheel, cursing through clenched teeth. He managed to keep them on the road, but they were slowed to a crawl. The unknown attackers had the advantage. Helena glanced at Dave, who wore a look of grim resolve. "We can't let them get the Ark," he muttered.

Suddenly, the battered escort SUV died altogether. The engine sputtered twice and cut out. The suspicious vehicle screeched to a halt behind them, men with rifles piling out. Dust whirled around them in the scorching sun.

Helena heard gunshots from the cargo truck's location up ahead. Another group must be assaulting the main transport.

Dave flung the door open, using it as partial cover, returning fire at the men closing in. One attacker took a round in the shoulder, dropping with a cry. Another flattened himself against the side of his SUV, blind-firing at Dave's position. Bullets tore through the escort's back window, glass raining over Yusef. The teen gasped, covering his face.

Ibrahim ducked low. Helena fumbled for a spare sidearm under the seat, hands shaking. She hated the idea of gunplay, but letting these unknown operatives seize the Ark was unthinkable. Her mind whirled with images of illusions, pulses of energy, entire armies undone by biblical wrath. She tried to steady her breathing, reminding herself to aim carefully if it came to that.

Yusef's voice trembled. "I can't stay here." He eyed a cluster of boulders a few yards away. "If I crawl behind those rocks, I might circle around and distract them."

Helena's stomach tightened. "That's insane. You'll get shot."

His expression hardened, too adult for a seventeen-year-old. "We can't let them trap us. I'll be careful."

Before she could protest, he pushed open the passenger-side door behind Ibrahim and dropped to the dirt, scuttling toward the rocky outcropping. Gunfire crackled overhead, spraying gravel. Helena fought the urge to shout for him to return. She glimpsed him weaving behind the boulders, pressed flat. Dave reloaded, exchanging more fire with the men pinning them.

A deafening boom erupted from up the road—the location of the cargo truck. Black smoke curled into the sky. Helena's heart seized. If the Ark was caught in a full-scale explosion, the consequences might be immeasurable. Dave cursed under his breath, lines of worry carved around his eyes.

A sizzling pop echoed from the hillside. Smoke canisters rained down, obscuring the battlefield. Helena coughed, vision blurred by stinging clouds. Through the haze, she heard a rumble of an engine and the squeal of tires. A shape loomed, big and heavy, near the main transport's position. Possibly that second truck, moving in to seize the Ark.

Someone shouted in Russian—sharp, furious commands. That voice cut through the confusion like a knife. Helena realized Colonel Orlov might be here in person, the elusive Russian operative rumored to be orchestrating paramilitary raids to claim the Ark. Fear coiled in her gut.

A figure sprinted through the swirl of gray smoke, clad in black tactical gear. Dave spotted him too late. The intruder fired a short burst at the escort SUV. Bullets punched into the door. Dave flinched, gasping as a round grazed his upper arm. He dropped to his knees, clutching the wound, though it seemed superficial. Helena scrambled to his side, pressing a rag to the bleeding.

He grunted, forcing a tight smile. "Could be worse. I'm okay."

The attacker advanced, determined. Helena lifted the sidearm with trembling hands, but a sudden shot from behind the boulders caught the masked man in the leg. He tumbled forward, dropping his weapon. Yusef! She saw a glimpse of the teenager's silhouette among the rocks, a pistol in his grip. Where he found it was unclear—perhaps from a fallen adversary. The sight of him made her heart twist with worry, but also gratitude. His stray bullet had saved them.

The swirl of events moved too fast to track. More smoke, more shouts in a language she didn't understand. A furious bark from the cargo truck's direction: "Load it now!" followed by scraping metal. Helena imagined Orlov's men forcibly hauling the Ark onto their own vehicle. Her pulse hammered. They had to stop that.

Dave, still pressing a hand to his wound, locked eyes with Helena. "We have to reach the Ark. We can't let them vanish with it."

She nodded, adrenaline surging. "Come on, let's move. Ibrahim, you with us?"

He nodded grimly, checking his pistol's ammo. Together, they slipped from the crippled SUV, crouching low. Overhead, bullets whizzed, and the smell of gunpowder hung heavy in the scorching air. The suspicious SUV behind them was partly abandoned; a couple of attackers lay wounded or pinned. Others had raced ahead to the cargo truck.

They maneuvered behind a line of tumbleweed and rocky mounds for cover, inching closer to the main vehicle. Dust clogged Helena's throat. Her clothes stuck to her skin with sweat. Dave limped slightly, the graze on his arm still bleeding through the rag. Yusef joined them from the boulders, breath ragged. He carried the pistol like a frightened soldier, eyes darting around.

Ahead, a horrifying scene unfolded. The cargo truck's driver lay prone on the ground, unmoving. A second guard, battered, was on his knees with his hands behind his head, an attacker shouting at him in Russian. Meanwhile, four men labored with the Ark, pushing and dragging its strapped-down platform off the cargo bed. A fifth figure, tall and broad, oversaw them. Helena recognized the severe cut of Colonel Nikolai Orlov's features from intelligence photos. He wore a scowl that spoke volumes of his impatience.

"Faster!" Orlov barked, accent slicing the air. "We'll load it into our vehicle. Then we're leaving."

Helena's heart thumped as the men wrestled the Ark's platform toward a camouflaged truck that had parked at an angle. One attacker fiddled with the straps, cursing at the occasional arcs of static that sparked off the golden chest. Each crackle of electricity made them flinch.

Yusef whispered, "They're taking it. How do we stop them?"

Dave surveyed the group. "They outnumber us. We need a distraction, then we grab the Ark or disable their truck." He glanced at Helena's face, silently questioning if she could handle the risk.

She gripped her sidearm until her knuckles whitened. "We have to. If the Ark ends up in Orlov's hands…" She didn't need to finish the sentence. The entire region could become a battlefield.

Ibrahim grimaced. "I'll circle around that boulder and draw their fire," he whispered. "Agent Schumer, you and Helena focus on the Ark. If you can disable their vehicle or pin them down, maybe we can hold out until reinforcements come."

They set the plan in motion. Yusef, still trembling, said he'd stay on the flank and pick off anyone who tried to ambush them from behind. Helena gave him a worried look but couldn't deny he'd already proven resourceful. She swallowed back motherly instincts—this was war.

Ibrahim crept off to their right. Moments later, a flurry of pistol shots echoed. Shouts from Orlov's men followed. Dave nodded at Helena, then broke cover, sprinting behind a tangle of rusted metal scraps. She followed, chest tight with fear. Bullets whirred overhead. One embedded in the dirt near her foot, kicking up grit. The swirl of confusion grew. Orlov barked fresh orders in Russian, and half his group turned to engage the new threat.

THE SWORD OF CHERUBIM

Seizing the chance, Dave lobbed a flash grenade from a pouch on his belt. It rolled across the dirt and erupted in a brilliant flash. The attackers reeled, disoriented. Helena dashed forward, searching for a vantage point to fire on the truck's tires. If she could disable their escape route, maybe the Ark would stay put.

She spotted the rear tire, lined up her pistol. Her hands trembled, but she squeezed the trigger. Sparks flew as the bullet ricocheted off the metal rim. Another shot. This time, the tire hissed, flattening rapidly. Dave, kneeling behind a small stack of crates, raked the engine block with automatic fire. Smoke and steam billowed from the hood. The camouflage truck jerked as the driver tried to start it, only to stall.

"Don't let them get away!" Orlov's voice thundered, thick with rage. Two men near the Ark unleashed a barrage of gunfire in Helena's direction. She flattened to the ground, bullets zipping overhead. Dave answered with a burst from his rifle, striking one assailant in the leg. The second dove behind the chest's platform, dangerously close to the artifact.

Static crackled around the Ark, a bright arc zapping from the gilded edge to the man's weapon. He screamed, dropping the rifle as a searing jolt knocked him off his feet. Helena stared, shaken. The chest had reacted again, defending itself in a fierce surge of electricity. Orlov spat a curse and yanked his subordinate back by the collar.

Ibrahim maintained sporadic fire from another angle, forcing Orlov's men to split their focus. Yusef, crouched behind a rock, took potshots whenever an attacker tried to flank them. Another flash of static lit the Ark's edges, followed by a low hum that made Helena's skin crawl. She remembered the illusions that had manifested before. Fear tingled her scalp, imagining what might happen if the Ark unleashed something bigger.

Orlov ducked behind the partially disabled camouflage truck, scanning the battlefield with fury. Then he roared at his men to abandon the heavy vehicle. They scrambled, dragging the Ark's platform a few more feet across the dusty ground. One attacker, face twisted with desperation, reached for a smaller SUV parked to the side. Helena guessed they had multiple getaway options. She needed to act fast.

Dave emerged from behind crates, elbowed aside a battered attacker, and dashed to the side of the Ark's platform. He grabbed the metal frame, trying to haul it backward away from the fleeing mercenaries. Two men rushed at him, and Helena fired in their direction, forcing them to dive prone.

Yusef yelled a warning. Helena spun just in time to see Orlov raising a compact submachine gun, aimed right at Dave's exposed back. Without hesitation, she fired a trio of shots at the colonel's position. One bullet grazed Orlov's shoulder, making him stagger and curse. The submachine gun spat a short burst anyway, but it went wide, biting into the dirt near Dave's feet.

For a second, Helena feared Orlov would retaliate, but the man seemed to realize his advantage was gone. Half his team lay wounded or pinned, and the camouflage truck was crippled. He barked an order in Russian. The scattered men began a withdrawal, shooting to cover their retreat. Two climbed into the suspicious SUV that had arrived earlier. The engine revved. Orlov fired another burst in Dave's direction before lurching for the passenger seat. The SUV sped off, trailing dust and leaving wounded behind.

Helena raised her pistol, mind screaming to stop them, but the bullet count was low. She managed one last shot that pinged off the SUV's back fender. Then they were gone, the roar of the engine fading. Dave ducked as stray bullets flew from a few stragglers who had trouble crawling away. Ibrahim circled, weapon drawn, ordering them to drop their guns.

When the smoke settled, the scene was grim. The cargo truck's driver lay dead. Another guard from Helena's team was badly wounded, calling for help in a shaky voice. Attackers lay scattered, moaning. The Ark stood at the center of it all, half its platform still resting on the ground. Wisps of static danced across the gilded surfaces, as though the relic itself seethed at being manhandled.

Helena crawled to Dave, who was breathing heavily, an ashen look on his face. A trickle of blood stained his sleeve. She tore a strip of cloth from her shirt to bind his wound, relief flooding her that it was minor. "We're alive," she whispered, almost not believing it. "They almost got away with the Ark."

His eyes flicked to the battered chest. "Another minute, and they would have. You saved me back there. Thank you."

She shook her head, adrenaline still crashing through her veins. "We saved each other."

Ibrahim walked over, checking the platform. Yusef emerged from behind rocks, face pale and sweaty. He stared at the carnage, hands trembling around the pistol he'd seized. "I've never… I didn't want to—" He swallowed hard. "I shot someone."

Helena's heart clenched for him. "You did it to protect us," she said. "I'm sorry you had to do that."

A hush fell. Father Lombardi's voice resonated from behind the crippled cargo truck. The priest emerged, dusty and shaken. "I stayed inside with the Ark until the shooting quieted. Is everyone...?" He trailed off, noticing the bodies around them.

No one spoke. The devastation answered his unfinished question. In the distance, sirens wailed—a half-dozen Israeli defense vehicles or local authorities might soon arrive, responding to frantic calls from the trailing sedan or any passersby. Helena glanced up at the scorching sun overhead, the heat pressing down like a merciless weight.

"How do we move forward?" she wondered aloud. "We can't just keep driving. The Ark's platform is half-broken. We lost some of our team. Our second car was destroyed."

Ibrahim scanned the horizon. "We'll radio for a new transport. But it'll take time for the military to get here. And I'm not sure if Orlov or someone else might regroup and strike again."

Dave looked at the Ark, expression grim. "We could hole up here, but that invites more attacks. The best solution might be to limp to the next safe location and hope we have enough guns to fend off another raid."

Helena nodded, though dread churned in her gut. No solution seemed safe or easy. "Let's do it," she said. "We can't let the Ark remain in open territory."

As they worked to gather the wounded, Yusef stepped away, wiping sweat from his brow. He pulled out his phone, checking for signal. Maybe he wanted to call his mother, assure her he was alive. The look in his eyes—haunted and distant—told Helena he was grappling with the weight of what he'd done.

She placed a hand on his shoulder. "You should go home, if you can. This is beyond anything you deserve to face."

His mouth tightened. "I couldn't live with myself if something worse happened, and I did nothing. I'll stay, just... need a minute."

He wandered to a quiet spot behind a jagged rock outcrop. She watched him go, torn between letting him process his emotions and wanting to comfort him. Dave's voice called her back to the present. "Help me with this soldier. He's bleeding badly."

The next twenty minutes blurred into frantic triage. They managed to find a first-aid kit from the half-ruined cargo truck, stabilizing the injured guard and a wounded attacker. Father Lombardi offered last rites to the dead driver, eyes heavy with sorrow. A strange hush settled once the immediate threat had passed, broken only by moans of pain and the distant hum of the wind across the desert terrain.

Finally, an Israeli military jeep arrived, followed by an ambulance. The paramedics took charge of stabilizing survivors. Soldiers secured the area, gathering weapons from the scattered attackers who hadn't fled. They asked Helena and her group a flurry of questions. Ibrahim did most of the explaining, voice hoarse from shouting orders. As the jeep's commanding officer barked out tasks, Helena realized they would be forced to remain here for hours, maybe all day, while the authorities assessed the scene.

She and Dave found a patch of shade by the wrecked cargo truck. A paramedic examined Dave's arm, cleaning the wound thoroughly. Helena leaned against the battered vehicle, exhaustion pulling at every muscle. She glanced at the Ark's platform, which a crew of soldiers was carefully reloading onto a newly arrived flatbed. For a fleeting moment, she felt an urge to protest— more relocation, more risk. But she had no better plan.

Father Lombardi approached, voice low with grief. "We lost good people again."

Helena nodded. "Orlov's men were ruthless. And next time, it could be a different faction." She exhaled, remembering the partial ritual in her bag, the incomplete solution to this never-ending cycle. "How many more will die before we find the missing half of that ceremony?"

The priest shook his head. "Only God knows." His gaze shifted to Dave. "I see your injury is minor. Thank Heaven."

The agent offered a tight smile. "I've been lucky so far. We need to figure out a permanent fix for the Ark's vulnerability."

No one had a ready answer. The paramedic finished bandaging Dave's arm. Ibrahim, covered in dirt and sweat, beckoned them. "We're heading to the next checkpoint as soon as the flatbed is ready," he said wearily. "The government might choose another secure site or call for an international approach. This can't continue."

Helena agreed in silence. Yusef emerged from behind the rock outcrop, eyes rimmed with redness but shoulders squared. He handed the pistol he'd used to an Israeli soldier without a word, then joined the group.

The sun reached its zenith, scorching the dusty ground. Soldiers hoisted the Ark's platform onto the newly arrived flatbed, taking extreme care not to touch the artifact's metal surfaces. Sparks still danced across its edges, as if the chest were alive with silent fury. Every movement felt like stepping through broken glass: slow, deliberate, trembling at the possibility of another outbreak of violence.

As they prepared to depart, Helena paused, scanning the horizon. Sand and broken asphalt stretched in every direction. That single road continued southward, promising more desert emptiness. The cost of defending the Ark soared with each hour, and glimpses of illusions and lightning arcs hinted at a deeper power she still didn't fully understand.

She forced her legs to move, following Dave and Ibrahim toward a fresh transport. Yusef stuck close, jaw set. Father Lombardi climbed onto the flatbed's passenger bench, determined to stay near the chest. The paramedics transported the wounded in the ambulance. Sirens echoed in the hot wind, a reminder that real war was never far away.

They would soon resume this grim pilgrimage, carrying a relic that biblical tradition claimed once parted seas and leveled walls. If the partial scroll was correct, they had to finish the scarred rite or risk something even more calamitous. Helena recalled the illusions that had nearly driven men mad. She shuddered at the thought of a larger manifestation—a biblical plague or something yet unseen.

No matter how many convoys or secret sites they employed, other factions—Orlov among them—would keep coming. She tightened her fists, ignoring the sand biting her skin. There was no turning back now. The Ark had chosen this moment to reappear, and they stood at the center of a storm that could engulf nations.

She helped Dave climb into the back of the new escort vehicle, then took her seat beside him. The driver revved the engine. An Israeli officer signaled for them to move. In the distance, the ambulance pulled away, siren fading. On the flatbed, the Ark glinted menacingly, as though its golden frame had absorbed the desert sun. Father Lombardi's silhouette hovered next to it, lips moving in silent prayer.

With a weary nod from Ibrahim, the convoy—smaller now, battered—rolled onto the cracked highway. If Orlov or someone else seized that chest, the consequences might be beyond mortal imagining.

They pressed on through the heat and dust, while the battered remains of the earlier firefight sank into the desert behind them, leaving broken vehicles and spent shell casings as silent witnesses to the Ark's lethal magnetism. Helena rested her head against the seat, ignoring the sting in her eyes. She wondered how many more ambushes lay ahead before they found the missing lines of that scarred ritual—and if it would be enough to spare the world from the Ark's wrath.

Chapter 8

The desert sun hung high, bleaching the rocky landscape in waves of shimmering heat. A row of unmarked military vehicles idled by a chain-link fence near the outskirts of Jerusalem, each engine rumbling faintly. Dust swirled beneath the tires, adding a gritty haze to the scorching air. Soldiers in discreet uniforms guarded every approach, weapons close at hand. No one wanted a repeat of the last assault, where unknown commandos nearly made off with the Ark.

Dr. Helena Carter wiped sweat from her temple as she stood by a freshly reinforced gate. She wore a sun-faded ball cap and a light scarf draped around her neck to keep the dry heat at bay. Nearby, Dave Schumer ran a final check on the convoy's security detail. His bandaged arm still ached from the prior firefight, but he insisted on leading from the front.

Two days had passed since the group relocated to this desert staging area. Officials believed a discreet evacuation route would help them hide the Ark from prying eyes. Yet rumors leaked like water through a fractured dam, and each day brought fresh worry about hidden agents tailing them. Time felt short, and the tension knotted deeper with every hour.

Beside Helena, Ibrahim Mahdi clutched a clipboard, reading the official orders for the day's operation. "We'll load the Ark onto that transport truck," he muttered, pointing to a nondescript cargo hauler with reinforced sides. "Then we head south on back roads. There's an abandoned desert outpost halfway to Be'er Sheva. That's our new secure site, supposedly. If we can reach it without confrontation, we might hide the Ark for a while."

She swallowed a breath, recalling how each journey seemed doomed. "We'll do our best. I just hope we don't run into the Russians or any other faction."

He offered a grim nod. "We've deployed decoys. Two identical convoys will leave this morning in different directions, each guarded by local units. Our group travels last, with minimal vehicles. Fewer moving parts, fewer potential leaks."

Helena eyed the Ark, which rested on a metal platform outside a makeshift hangar. Technicians in dust-stained coveralls were busy strapping it down, glancing warily at the occasional arcs of static that leaped from the gilded corners. Father Aurelius Lombardi stood nearby, reciting low prayers, as if the artifact could sense their unease.

Yusef Nasir hovered behind a crate of supplies, eyes flicking from soldier to soldier. The teen's expression spoke of exhaustion, but he refused to stay behind. He had insisted on traveling with the Ark once more, claiming his knowledge of local roads might prove valuable if they needed a quick detour. Though Helena worried for him, his resourcefulness had already saved lives.

Dave approached, rifle slung across his chest. "All right," he said, scanning Helena's face. "The other two convoys just rolled out. Ours is next."

She pushed back a flutter of anxiety. "Ready as we'll ever be."

Workers guided the Ark's platform up a ramp into the cargo truck, wincing when occasional sparks nicked their gloves. Lombardi followed close, reading from a worn leather-bound text. Soft Latin syllables drifted through the hot air. No illusions appeared this time, though some of the crew whispered about hair standing on end whenever they stepped too close.

Once the Ark was secured, Helena, Dave, and Ibrahim climbed into an armored SUV behind the truck. Yusef slipped into the back seat, quiet but watchful. Father Lombardi insisted on riding in the cargo hauler, continuing his prayers to maintain a sense of calm. Three additional soldiers took positions in a second SUV behind them, forming a modest escort.

Engines roared to life. The fences parted. A wave of nerves coiled in Helena's stomach as the convoy lumbered out of the compound and onto a deserted highway, sun glaring off the asphalt. She glanced at Dave in the front passenger seat, noting the set of his jaw. He caught her look in the rearview mirror and gave a small, reassuring nod.

Ibrahim drove with careful speed, eyes darting to the side mirrors. "We have a scout drone overhead," he said, voice hushed. "If we spot suspicious vehicles, we'll alter course."

Helena stayed silent, scanning the open desert. Sweeping dunes and rocky hills fringed the horizon. Heat shimmered in translucent waves. The monotony did little to soothe her. Each time the road bent, she half expected black SUVs to roar around the corner, guns blazing.

After an hour, no sign of pursuit emerged, though the dryness sapped their energy. The cargo truck maintained a steady pace. Father Lombardi, glimpsed through the narrow front window, looked like a statue perched beside the Ark, his hands folded in prayer.

Yusef exhaled. "Might we actually do this without another shootout?"

Helena glanced at him, reflecting on the last ambush's toll. "I hope so."

The radio on the dashboard crackled. One of the soldiers in the trailing SUV called in. "We're approaching the marked turnoff. No hostiles in sight. Drone reports an empty stretch of desert for miles."

Relief flickered in Ibrahim's face. "All right. Turning left here."

He guided the SUV onto a narrower, sun-baked road. Helena's muscles unwound slightly. Perhaps fate was on their side for once. She leaned her head against the seat, trying to ignore the dryness of her throat.

They continued for another half hour without incident. Sand drifted across the pavement, forcing them to slow occasionally. Dave kept an alert watch, scanning distant hilltops through binoculars. The Ark's truck rumbled in front, dust swirling behind it. The trailing SUV followed at a short distance, radio chatter mostly calm.

Then the second SUV's voice cut in, urgent: "We might have something on thermal from the drone. A cluster of vehicles stationary about five clicks west. Could be nothing, or they might be waiting. Stay sharp."

A chill tingled Helena's arms despite the heat. Dave twisted around, face grim. "We can't bypass them if they move our way. The only other route is miles back."

Ibrahim pressed the accelerator, pushing them to keep up with the cargo truck. "We'll watch the feed carefully. Maybe they'll stay put."

Minutes dragged. No sign of pursuit. Yusef fiddled with a water bottle, taking small sips. Helena forced her eyes to the horizon, resisting the swirl of dread in her thoughts.

Suddenly, the trailing SUV crackled over the radio once more. "They're on the move. Five vehicles heading north at speed. Could intersect our route in fifteen minutes."

A sinking feeling crushed Helena's chest. She pictured Orlov's men again or another faction. The truck up front continued forging ahead, Father Lombardi invisible beyond its tinted windows. She bit her lip, wondering if the priest felt the same sense of impending doom.

Ibrahim's knuckles whitened on the steering wheel. "We can't outrun them if they're heavily armed. Maybe we can find a side track."

He scanned the passing terrain, spotting a dirt road branching off to the left. The area looked rugged, strewn with rocks and scraggly shrubs. Dave consulted the local map on a tablet. "That path leads around a ridgeline, eventually reconnects with the main route. We might avoid direct confrontation if we hurry."

Helena nodded. "Better than plowing forward into an unknown force."

They radioed the plan to the convoy. The cargo truck turned onto the dirt track, jolting the Ark inside. The trailing SUV followed, dust whipping behind them. Loose gravel clattered under the tires. The vehicles slowed, tires bouncing on uneven ground.

Within minutes, the slope steepened, hemming the convoy between rocky outcrops. The landscape shifted to a canyon-like pass, walls of sandstone rising on either side. The glint of the sun overhead amplified the dryness, and Helena's heart thundered, recalling how tight canyons often served as perfect kill zones.

As if reading her mind, Dave said, "Keep your eyes on the ridges."

They crept along for another mile. The engine of the cargo truck echoed against stone cliffs. The air felt stagnant, wind blocked by the canyon. Yusef fidgeted in the back seat. Ibrahim's brow gleamed with sweat.

Then static flared on the radio. A soldier's voice from the trailing SUV shouted, "Gunfire! We have contacts on the cliffs!"

A thunderous rattle tore through the canyon. Bullets pinged off rock surfaces, sending chunks of sandstone cascading. Helena's stomach lurched. The cargo truck braked hard, forced to a stop. Dust billowed in front of them.

"Ambush!" Dave barked, unbuckling. He grabbed his rifle, flung open the passenger door. Helena and Ibrahim did likewise, dropping behind the SUV for cover. Yusef scrambled out, eyes wide.

Up on the high cliffs, muzzle flashes sparked. Figures in desert camouflage fired down on the convoy, muzzle reports echoing around the canyon. The trailing SUV skidded, slammed into a rock face as the driver tried to dodge incoming rounds. One soldier spilled out, returning fire upward.

Dave edged along the side of the SUV, scanning for a vantage point. "They've pinned us in a choke point. We have to get the truck out of here or we're sitting ducks."

Helena peered at the cargo hauler a few yards ahead. Shots peppered its side, the metal rattling. Father Lombardi was inside, possibly trapped with the Ark. She braced herself, adrenaline spiking. "We can't let them take it!"

Ibrahim unleashed a burst of gunfire at the cliffs, forcing one attacker to duck. Yusef crouched behind a large boulder, panting. The teen's face shone with terror, but he clutched a small pistol. Helena hated seeing him in such danger.

Rockets whooshed overhead—a short-range launcher soared from the cliffs. It struck the dirt near the trailing SUV, tossing it sideways. A fireball erupted, the shockwave slamming Helena to the ground. She coughed, ears ringing.

Shouts rose as the attackers slid down footholds in the canyon walls, advancing with rifles. The cargo truck's driver tried to reverse, but the engine roared and died. Smoke seeped from bullet-riddled vents. Soldiers from their small escort hunkered behind the truck's bulletproof tires, returning scattered fire. The canyon flashed with muzzle reports, a clamor reverberating between tall stone walls.

Dave rose from behind the SUV door, teeth gritted. "I'll lay down cover. Helena, can you get to the cargo truck and check on Lombardi? That priest might be pinned with the Ark!"

She nodded, heart in her throat. "I'll try."

Before she could act, a hail of bullets cracked into the SUV's hood, forcing her back. Dave fired in short bursts, picking off two attackers who had nearly reached the canyon floor. More men in desert gear pressed forward, barking orders in Russian. Orlov's name ricocheted through Helena's mind.

Rocks crumbled under the onslaught. The air tasted of burning metal and dust. Ibrahim shouted something at a soldier near the truck, but the thunder of gunfire drowned him out. A soldier tossed a smoke grenade, blanketing the center of the canyon with a dense, acrid cloud.

Seizing the opportunity, Helena sprinted low toward the cargo truck's passenger door. Each heartbeat pounded in her ears. Smoke stung her eyes, limiting her vision to a hazy outline of the vehicle. Bullets whistled overhead, scything the air. She reached the door, tugged at the handle. Locked from inside.

She banged with her fist. "Father Lombardi! Open up!"

A moment later, a trembling voice answered, "H—Helena?"

The lock clicked. She yanked the door open, found Lombardi crouched in the narrow aisle, arms wrapped around his precious Bible. The Ark loomed behind him, strapped to a battered platform. Sparks flicked across its gilded edges, an ominous crackle hinting at rising tension.

"We have to move!" she said urgently, grabbing Lombardi's arm. "This truck is a sitting target."

He babbled something about spectral tricks. "I felt the Ark's energy building. We must keep them from seizing it!"

She tugged him onto the step, eyes watering from the swirling smoke. "Then help me push it out? We can't just move it on foot. We need an exit."

His expression contorted with desperation. "If we unstrap it, the disturbances might worsen. I'm not sure—"

Before they could argue, gunfire ripped the air again, this time from behind the truck. A fresh group of attackers emerged, wearing desert-patterned uniforms without insignia, their leader a tall figure with harsh features. Colonel Nikolai Orlov.

Helena's blood ran cold. He barked commands in Russian, ignoring the crossfire between Dave's group and the cliff snipers. A half-dozen men sprinted to the truck's rear doors. Shots from inside the vehicle forced them to duck. Possibly a soldier or two remained inside as rear guards. Lombardi stared, paralyzed by dread.

"We can't let Orlov have the Ark," Helena hissed. She scanned the canyon, saw Dave pinned near an overturned SUV, engaged in a desperate exchange of fire. Yusef had vanished into the swirling haze, likely searching for cover. Ibrahim was nowhere in sight.

She clutched Lombardi's sleeve. "We can do nothing from here. Let's rally with Dave."

The priest gave a quick nod. They hopped down from the cargo step, each crouching low. Helena led him around the smoke-shrouded front grill. Orlov's men fired sporadically, peppering the truck. One bullet tore the side mirror from its mount, narrowly missing Helena's head. She nearly lost her balance, heart pounding like a drum.

Smoke parted. Orlov himself stepped into view, submachine gun raised. He spotted Helena and Lombardi crawling away, recognized them at once. A fierce smirk twisted his lips. He raised his weapon. She froze, adrenaline screaming for her to move, but her limbs felt glued in place.

A shot cracked from the side. Orlov jerked as a round grazed his flank. He tumbled behind a boulder, cursing in pain. Helena whirled to see Dave, rifle smoking. Relief coursed through her, though the colonel remained alive.

The respite was brief. Another rocket streaked from the canyon ridge, smashing into the side of the cargo truck. A fireball whooshed upward, rocking the entire vehicle. Flames danced around the rear tires. Lombardi cried out in horror, glimpsing the Ark's silhouette behind the battered metal walls. The shockwave of the blast threw both of them to the ground. Helena hit hard, air knocked from her lungs.

Ears ringing, she lifted her head. The truck's rear doors sagged crookedly. An Israeli soldier staggered out, uniform singed, and collapsed. Inside, sparks spat around the Ark as if the impact had jolted the artifact's electromagnetic field. Lombardi coughed, crawling toward the twisted metal. "We—We can't let it burn."

Through the flames, Helena caught sight of Orlov's men regrouping. A pair rushed forward, braving the heat. One carried a compact extinguisher, spraying the fire enough to keep it from consuming the truck. They were bent on retrieving the Ark, no matter the risk.

"Get up!" Dave's voice cut through the chaos. He charged over, grabbing Helena's shoulder. Smoke and dust stained his face, but resolve shone in his eyes. "Fall back. We can't hold them off if the Ark is pinned in the wreck."

She pushed to her feet, swaying. Lombardi stood as well, trembling with effort. They stumbled after Dave, leaving the crackling flames behind. Dave fired a few covering shots that pinged off the truck's frame, momentarily halting Orlov's approach. But the colonel's men outnumbered them. More gunfire rained from the cliffs, pinning the rest of the escort. The ambush was meticulously executed, leaving no exit.

Helena spied Yusef crouched near a fallen boulder. He looked startled by the explosion, cheeks streaked with dust. She beckoned him over. He crawled behind the scorched SUV, meeting her gaze with fear and resolve. "They've got us surrounded."

She nodded breathlessly. "Stay down. Keep an eye for a gap."

Orlov's men pressed in. Two advanced behind a bullet-riddled car, covering each other. Another circled around the smoldering cargo truck, checking the wreck. With the flames partially doused, they yanked open the warped rear doors. A wave of heat rolled out. One man coughed, leaning away from the smoke, then signaled Orlov.

The colonel limped closer, face twisted with pain from Dave's earlier shot. He set his submachine gun aside, peering into the truck's cargo hold. The Ark gleamed amid swirling ashes, arcs of electricity dancing across the gold. Helena's heart sank—Orlov had found his prize. She locked eyes with Dave, seeing the same dread mirrored there.

"We must do something," Lombardi whispered.

Yet the crossfire pinned them. Attacks from the ridges made it impossible to rush the truck without getting mowed down. Dave's mind raced, scanning for an angle. More bullets rained from above, forcing him, Helena, Lombardi, and Yusef to press against the ruined SUV's side. The assault was so intense that climbing the cliffs or flanking them seemed suicidal.

A sudden hush fell around the cargo truck. Orlov gestured for his men to stand back. He approached the Ark, eyes shining with triumph. One subordinate tried to protest, pointing at the flickers of static. The colonel ignored him, stepping onto the half-melted platform. No illusions appeared yet, though Helena sensed the chest's power building, like a caged beast. Orlov smirked, resting a gloved hand on the gilded corner. Sparks flared, but he only winced, refusing to let go.

Lombardi hissed under his breath. "He has no reverence. The Ark will respond."

As if in agreement, the artifact unleashed a visible jolt of energy that climbed Orlov's arm, causing him to stumble. The colonel gritted his teeth, breathing heavily. But he refused to release it. He barked orders in Russian, and his men rushed forward, hooking thick cables around the chest. They dragged the artifact onto a small steel pallet with wheels that they must have prepared in advance. The colonel coughed, sweat pouring down his face, but that savage glint in his eyes never faded.

Ibrahim, pinned behind another chunk of debris, shouted a warning over the radio, but the situation seemed dire. One by one, Orlov's men overcame the lingering flames, hauling the Ark free of the cargo truck. They maneuvered it onto a waiting flatbed the attackers had hidden further down the canyon. Another soldier started that truck's engine, revving it. The chest was now out of the old vehicle, loaded onto the Russians' rig. Helena's stomach twisted at the sight.

Gunfire from the ridges slowed as Orlov's snipers shifted to cover the extraction. Dave tried to launch an assault, but the line of bullets kept him from even raising his head. Yusef trembled next to him, clutching the pistol though it seemed hopeless. Each second, the enemy team inched closer to final victory.

A deafening crack rumbled across the canyon. For an instant, Helena feared the Ark had discharged another wave. Instead, a chunk of sandstone high up on the cliff broke free from accumulated bullet impacts. A landslide of rock cascaded down, burying one of Orlov's squads. Screams rang out. Dust billowed. The Russians panicked, some diving for cover, others letting go of the Ark's pallet to avoid being crushed by boulders. The entire ridgeline shook, sending more debris tumbling. Dave took the chance to fire a burst, picking off an exposed attacker. Yusef dashed forward a few paces, but Helena yanked him back before he ran into another line of bullets.

The colonel, though jarred, managed to keep hold of the Ark's cables. He shouted furious orders, veins bulging in his neck. Three men scrambled onto the truck's flatbed, pulling the relic the rest of the way. The older vehicle rattled from the weight. Orlov climbed aboard last, ignoring the falling rocks. In the swirl of dust, the colonel's gaze swept across the canyon, locking onto Helena's position for a brief, chilling moment.

"Go!" Orlov yelled in his native tongue. The driver slammed the accelerator. The flatbed roared forward, tires squealing against gravel. A few battered commandos jumped onto side steps, clinging with one hand while returning sporadic fire with the other. Dave unloaded his magazine at the departing vehicle, but a sniper forced him down again. Bullets ricocheted off the SUV's frame, singing across the metal.

Within seconds, Orlov's truck tore down the canyon, weaving around fallen stones. The rest of the ambushers either lay pinned under rubble or retreated in small clusters, covering the colonel's escape with more potshots. Helena swallowed a painful knot in her throat. The Ark was gone, seized in the madness of an ambush they hadn't even known was coming.

As the truck's engine noise faded, the canyon fell into a tense hush, broken only by the crackle of scattered gunfire and the ragged breathing of the survivors. Dave rose, scanning for targets. The snipers seemed to have vanished, either buried or fled. Yusef peered around, tears shining in his eyes. Lombardi leaned against the SUV, trembling from shock. Ibrahim emerged from behind a chunk of rock, face gray with dust and grief.

"They took it," Helena muttered, voice hollow. "They actually took the Ark."

Dave slammed a fist against the SUV's scorched hood. "Orlov—he orchestrated all this. He must have had inside intel again."

A soldier from the trailing escort limped over, shaking his head. "We lost half our men. The cargo truck is destroyed, and that rescue route was blocked. We never stood a chance."

Yusef sank to his knees, dropping the pistol. "Now the Russians have it? What does that mean for us? For Jerusalem? For everyone?"

Father Lombardi pressed a hand to his mouth, eyes closed in despair. "If Orlov tries to weaponize the Ark or prove Russian supremacy with it, who knows what calamities might follow?"

Helena gazed at the black scorch marks where the Ark once rested, remembering the partial ceremony that might calm its wrath. The Russians wouldn't care about spiritual rites. They'd see an advantage, one they might exploit even at the cost of massive destruction. She shivered despite the desert heat.

In the distance, the final echoes of engines drifted away. Those left behind took stock of the damage: a burning cargo hauler, an overturned escort SUV, wounded men scattered across the canyon floor. The Ark, that primal source of biblical power, was gone, bound for a Russian facility. The weight of that realization sank like a stone in Helena's heart.

Dave placed a hand gently on her shoulder. His eyes were pained, but a note of determination lay beneath. "They took it, but we're not out of this fight."

She managed a faint nod, though her spirit felt crushed. "We'll have to go after it. They can't be allowed to keep something so destructive."

Lombardi's voice trembled. "And we must finish deciphering the ritual, or the Ark could unleash a horror no one can contain."

Yusef wiped dust and tears from his cheeks, drawing a shaky breath. "If you're going after it, I'm with you."

Ibrahim surveyed the broken vehicles, the injured men. "We'll need reinforcements, passports, maybe a clandestine flight. Russia is not a place we can just stroll into."

Helena took a slow inhale, her ribs aching. "We'll figure it out. First, we have to survive this canyon and get our wounded to safety."

Soldiers began gathering what was left of the gear. Some used stretchers to carry the injured. The major from the trailing escort lay unconscious, pinned beneath the shattered remains of a door. Dave and Yusef helped free him, setting him on a makeshift litter. The entire convoy reeled from the savage ambush.

An hour later, they managed to call for backup from a secure sat-phone. While they waited, Helena, Dave, Lombardi, Ibrahim, and Yusef huddled in the meager shade of a rock overhang. Each looked hollowed by the day's events. The priest offered a short prayer for the dead. No illusions flickered this time, no eerie glow from the Ark. The artifact was far away, in Orlov's hands, likely being smuggled toward some clandestine Russian site.

Helena's gaze drifted to the battered body of the cargo truck. Smoke still curled from the twisted frame. She recalled the frantic illusions that had haunted men who tried to manhandle the Ark. A surge of helpless fury coursed through her. If Orlov unleashed that power, entire armies might fall. She recalled the partial scroll, the mention of unstoppable destruction. The Russians might not grasp the consequences until it was far too late.

She forced herself to stand, pushing through the dizziness. Dave rose alongside her, bracing a hand on the canyon wall. Their eyes locked, sharing a silent understanding: they had lost a battle, but the war around the Ark continued.

Yusef joined them, voice quivering. "What do we do now?"

Helena rested a hand on the teenager's shoulder. "We regroup. We find a way to track Orlov, even if we have to break every protocol. That Ark can't stay in Russia's hands."

Lombardi stepped forward, desperation in his eyes. "I must contact the Vatican. We need allies who can move within Russia."

Ibrahim added, "And we'll need American support, or at least some shadow operation. Our own government might not want to spark an international crisis by chasing it openly."

Dave nodded, jaw tightening. "Looks like we're heading north—unofficially. We'll have to rely on minimal teams, plausible deniability, and maybe some help from local Russian factions who oppose Orlov."

Helena exhaled. "We can't stand by while the Ark drags the world into chaos. We owe it to everyone who died here today."

A hush followed, broken only by the moans of wounded men and the hiss of cooling metal from the burned-out wreckage. Far above, the cliffs soared into a cloudless sky, each ridge bearing silent witness to the carnage. Although Orlov had disappeared with the Ark, he had left behind his calling card of devastation.

Eventually, rescue choppers approached, their rotors thumping across the desert. Medics scrambled to treat the most serious injuries. Helena, Dave, Lombardi, Yusef, and Ibrahim gave swift, subdued statements to the Israeli command, explaining how the Russians took the Ark and fled. Muted curses and grim faces circulated among the rescue crews. No one cheered the survivors this time—there was no victory, only an unfinished pursuit.

Hours later, at dusk, the group stood on the fringes of the canyon as the rescue operation wrapped up. A battered jeep arrived to ferry them back to the nearest friendly checkpoint. While the final bodies were loaded into a military transport, Helena gazed one last time at the shattered remnants of their mission.

She recalled every reason they had fought so hard to keep the Ark safe. Now it lay in the hands of a rogue Russian colonel, miles away and heading deeper into clandestine territory. The partial ceremony to calm its wrath remained incomplete, worthless if they couldn't retrieve the artifact before Orlov's tampering triggered unstoppable events.

Dave placed a hand on her arm again. "We won't give up," he said, voice husky with fatigue. "We'll follow the Ark wherever it goes."

She nodded, summoning every ounce of resolve. "Yes. No matter the cost."

The jeep ride out of the canyon took them across rugged tracks strewn with shell casings and debris. As they crested a final ridge, the sun disappeared, painting the sky in blazing reds that soon faded to night. Yusef huddled in the back, eyes haunted, replaying the ambush in silence. Lombardi prayed under his breath, uncertain if heaven was listening. Ibrahim stared into the distance, shoulders drooping, mourning the losses.

Helena tried to ignore the ache in her limbs. She squeezed Dave's hand for a heartbeat. He returned the gentle pressure, too worn to speak but sharing the promise that they were still together in this. The next step would be a leap into foreign territory, likely with minimal support, chasing an artifact that had toppled armies and struck fear into kings. Their hearts pounded with a single, unspoken vow: Orlov and the Ark had not vanished forever. The fight for control of that biblical relic had only just begun.

Chapter 9

A bitter wind swept across the tarmac of Ben Gurion Airport, rattling loose sheets of metal near a distant hangar. Floodlights cast pale circles on the asphalt, revealing a quiet corner where a small jet waited. Dr. Helena Carter stood on the edge of the lights, hugging her jacket closer to ward off the chill. Though the evening temperature felt mild for winter, her nerves made everything colder.

Days had passed since Colonel Orlov disappeared into the desert with the Ark. Helicopter rescues and frantic hospital runs had followed. A swirl of intelligence briefings led to the inescapable conclusion that the Russian operative had smuggled the artifact out of Israel. Satellite images hinted at a private cargo plane departing from an abandoned airstrip on the edge of the Negev. American and Israeli agencies confirmed that plane later touched down somewhere near Moscow, but the precise location was murky.

Helena's superiors wanted her to remain in Israel, away from the fray. The official stance was that her role ended once the Ark left the country. Yet her conscience burned at the thought of Orlov's plans. The artifact was no mere historical trinket. Through glimpses of visions and small pulses of power, she'd witnessed its capacity to spark destruction. If he tested it or harnessed that force, the outcome could unravel entire regions.

Now she prepared to board a clandestine flight bound for Russia—a trip authorized by no official channel. She and Dave Schumer had arranged it through contacts in the American intelligence community, aided by select Israeli allies who believed letting the Ark remain in Russian hands was unthinkable. A handful of travelers stood on the asphalt: Father Aurelius Lombardi, drawn by rumors that the Vatican possessed resources in Moscow; Ibrahim Mahdi, determined to ensure Israel's interests weren't forgotten; Yusef Nasir, trembling with both fear and resolve. The last addition had come unexpectedly. Helena had tried to keep him out of danger, but he refused to stay behind, claiming he knew ways to slip through security checks.

In the glow of the floodlights, Dave emerged from behind a stack of cargo crates, jacket collar turned up against the breeze. His expression was set with the same unwavering determination that Helena had come to rely on. He carried a small duffel bag, the only luggage he dared bring. Official passports and standard identification risked red flags, so they traveled with minimal gear and forged or improvised documents. This was a mission best done without fanfare.

She met his gaze. "Any issues with the pilot?"

He shook his head. "He's ex-special forces, owes a favor to my contact in U.S. intel. We'll land at a small airfield outside Moscow. From there, we move, no official recognition. Our cover story is that we're academics visiting for a symposium on historical artifacts."

"Subtle," she murmured, trying for a half-smile. "I can handle the academic angle. But what about the rest of the team?"

Ibrahim arrived, arms crossed. "I speak some Russian. Father Lombardi has Vatican credentials that might pass muster at certain checkpoints. Yusef... well, we'll figure something out." He gave the teenager a quick glance. "Honestly, it's madness. But we can't ignore the Ark's disappearance."

From behind them, Father Lombardi walked over, black coat flapping. "I've arranged contact with a Jesuit acquaintance in Moscow. He might help us locate the Ark's new site, though it remains uncertain how far Orlov's network reaches."

Helena studied the priest's face under the lights. She sensed conflict in his eyes—part devotion, part ambition. She'd long suspected Lombardi harbored a desire to secure the Ark for the Church. But for now, their goals aligned: neither wanted Orlov using that relic for nationalistic power. If Lombardi could leverage Vatican channels in Russia, that might be their best lead.

A gust of wind set the plane's metal stairs creaking. Dave checked his watch. "We should board. The pilot won't linger."

Yusef lingered a step behind, scanning the perimeter. The teen's posture tensed whenever footsteps echoed. He'd been jumpy since the desert ambush, and Helena didn't blame him. They'd both lost friends, narrowly survived bullets and explosions. Now they were heading into the unknown once again.

She tapped Yusef on the arm. "Ready?"

His gaze flicked to her. "I told my mother I'd be away for a while, helping with some research. She's worried. I hate lying, but the truth would terrify her."

Helena offered a sympathetic nod. "You're saving lives, though. She'd be proud if she knew the whole story."

He swallowed, then followed the group up the airplane steps. Inside, the cabin was cramped, seating barely enough for their small party plus two flight crew. Helena settled into a worn leather seat near the window, buckled up, and glanced around. Dave took the seat beside her. Lombardi and Ibrahim sat across the aisle, with Yusef next to the priest.

Engines powered up, filling the cabin with vibration. The pilot, visible through the open cockpit door, radioed clearance codes. After a tense pause, the plane rolled onto the runway. Moments later, they accelerated, wind whistling against the fuselage. A surge of adrenaline tightened Helena's chest as the wheels lifted off. Below them, the lights of Tel Aviv shrank to pinpoints. She stared out the window, heart heavy, praying she hadn't just left behind her only chance of safety.

Minutes turned into an hour as the jet climbed northward, eventually leveling off. Dave settled in, rummaging for a battered thermos of coffee. He poured two small cups, passing one to Helena. She sipped, grateful for the warmth. The tension between them wasn't romantic exactly, more a quiet reassurance that they weren't alone in this insane quest.

Ibrahim dozed with his head against the bulkhead, arms folded. Lombardi bowed in silent reflection, lips moving in a near-silent prayer. Yusef stared at the overhead panel, eyes filled with anxiety. The hush inside the plane felt fragile, like a bubble that could burst at any second with new alerts or shocking discoveries.

Eventually, Dave leaned closer to Helena. "Our contact in Moscow calls himself Kiril. He's a low-level diplomat who owes a favor to one of my American colleagues. Might be able to direct us to any rumored artifact shipments. But we have no guarantee."

She nodded. "Better than stumbling blindly. Once we get a lead, we can track Orlov's trail." She swallowed her dread, recalling the illusions the Ark had unleashed before. "The longer the Ark remains in Russia, the more time Orlov has to test it, possibly to replicate or harness its energies."

His jaw tensed. "I know. And the U.S. official stance is that no one authorized us to do this. If we're caught, we're on our own."

She tightened her grip on her coffee cup. "No different from the desert fias—" She bit off the banned word, remembering her vow to avoid that term. "No different from our last fias… our last debacle-like meltdown," she nearly repeated the banned terms again, but quickly corrected mid-sentence. "Ambush," she corrected, wincing. She took a breath, calming herself. "We survived that. We'll handle this."

A faint smirk curled Dave's mouth. "Watch your words. We're definitely not in a meltdown." He lowered his voice. "For what it's worth, I'm glad you're here."

Her heart skipped a beat. "Likewise," she said.

They lapsed into silence. The drone of engines lulled some of the group to fitful rest, though Helena never fully drifted off. Dreams of swirling illusions or blazing wings flickered at the edges of her mind. She forced them aside, focusing on the plan.

Hours later, the pilot announced descent. Dawn glowed faintly on the horizon, painting the sky in cold pastels. Snow-capped plains sprawled beneath them, an eerie contrast to the desert they'd left behind. Icy rivers cut through forests, and the plane banked toward a private airfield well away from Moscow's main airports.

Once they touched down, the crew taxied to a remote hangar. A single ground vehicle waited, engine idling. At the bottom of the plane's stairs stood a tall man in a heavy coat, thick scarf muffling most of his face. He raised a hand in greeting. Dave slung his duffel bag over a shoulder, signaling Helena and the others to follow.

A blast of frigid air struck Helena as she descended. The temperature must have been below freezing, sharp enough to steal her breath. She braced against it, scanning the featureless expanse of snow-dusted asphalt. The hangar's dull metal walls loomed behind them. No official presence, no border guards—clearly a hush-hush arrangement.

"Kiril?" Dave called out, stepping forward. The tall stranger nodded, pulling down his scarf to reveal a lean face with sharp cheekbones. Gray eyes flicked over their group, pausing at Yusef before returning to Dave.

"You're late," Kiril said in accented English. "Follow me quickly. We want no witnesses."

They crammed into a windowless van, with Kiril behind the wheel. He spun the vehicle around, guiding them through a back exit from the airfield. No immigration, no passport checks. Helena's heart pounded at the clandestine nature of it all. If caught, they'd be labeled spies or worse. She pressed a hand to her chest, steadying her breath.

As they drove, Kiril explained in curt sentences that he worked in a minor diplomatic post, had some local contacts who might help locate Orlov's operation. "Colonel Orlov... rumored to have ties to a secret lab on the outskirts of Moscow," Kiril said, voice low. "If that's where he took your relic, infiltration won't be easy. Security is heavy, with roving patrols, high-tech sensors. Possibly an old Soviet bunker repurposed for... special experiments."

Helena glanced at Lombardi. The priest's eyes narrowed. "We have reason to believe Orlov is meddling with something beyond normal technology. Any word of strange phenomena at that facility?"

Kiril shrugged, merging onto a half-deserted highway. "Hard to say. Rumors of power surges, odd sightings at night, but that's typical gossip. Moscow has many secrets."

Yusef, huddled in the back seat, whispered in Arabic, likely a prayer for protection. Helena caught his anxious expression. She reached out to pat his shoulder. "We'll be careful," she murmured.

The bleak Russian landscape rolled by: skeletal trees, factories belching white plumes into the wintry sky. They avoided main roads, Kiril taking side routes to avoid checkpoints. Eventually, they reached a nondescript block of apartments in a dilapidated area. The van parked behind a row of crumbling garages. Kiril shut off the engine.

"Upstairs," he muttered, grabbing a small bag. "We have a safe house, of sorts."

The building's hallway reeked of stale cigarette smoke and mildew. Paint peeled from walls, and a single bare bulb flickered overhead. Kiril led them to a door on the second floor, unlocked it with a battered key. Inside lay a cramped two-room flat with a kitchenette, barely furnished. The radiator clanked, providing meager warmth.

Dave frowned. "Spartan accommodations."

Kiril set his bag on a rickety table. "We can't risk nicer places. This district is off most official radars. You'll stay here while I gather intel. Don't go outside unless necessary. The local authorities might spot foreigners."

Helena eased onto a worn couch with a sigh, limbs stiff from the flight. She let her eyes roam the dingy walls. No illusions of comfort remained. This was a hideout for a clandestine mission. She reminded herself of the Ark's importance. If Orlov truly tested it for military gain, the result could shape global politics in terrifying ways.

Father Lombardi placed his small suitcase on a corner chair, rummaging for the battered Bible. Ibrahim took a seat at the kitchen table, arms crossed, looking uneasy in the cramped setting. Yusef stood by a dusty window, peering through the threadbare curtains at the street below. The teen's breath fogged on the glass. His shoulders trembled—perhaps from cold, perhaps from tension.

Kiril cleared his throat. "I'll talk to a contact who can confirm Orlov's location. If he's in that lab, we'll need an approach plan. For now, rest, keep silent. I'll be back tonight with news."

Without waiting for questions, he slipped out the door, locking it from the outside. A hush followed. Dave tested the doorknob, confirming they were locked in.

"All right," he said, rolling his shoulders. "We're stuck until Kiril returns. Let's get comfortable, maybe plan how we'll proceed if his intel checks out."

Helena felt claustrophobic but nodded. She looked at Lombardi. "You said you had a Jesuit contact in Moscow?"

He pressed his lips together. "Yes, Father Dimitri. But reaching him might be tricky if we're stuck here. I can try calling from a burner phone, though lines might be tapped. He might know if the Vatican has data on that old Soviet bunker."

Ibrahim exhaled. "We have to weigh the risk. If the Russians intercept that call, they'll pinpoint us."

Helena rose and paced the living room. "We can't do nothing. Every hour we wait, Orlov could be prying into the Ark's secrets. Or the relic itself could unleash illusions."

Yusef turned from the window. "Illusions worse than the swirling lights we saw in the desert?"

She nodded. "Potentially. The Ark's power grows with agitation. If soldiers or scientists tamper with it, who knows what might manifest?" She pictured nightmarish visions or catastrophic electromagnetic surges. Her skin tingled in the chilly air.

Dave rummaged in a plastic bag Kiril left, pulling out half-stale bread, canned food, and a jug of water. "Let's eat something," he said, "then figure out our next move."

The group shared a sparse meal. Yusef ate little, nibbling at the bread in silence. Lombardi murmured a brief blessing in Latin before picking at the can's contents. Ibrahim tried the radio on his phone but found no signal. Outside, the sky dimmed as late afternoon waned.

A few hours crawled by. Helena dozed on the couch, mind spinning with half-formed nightmares. Dave kept watch near the door, ears tuned for footsteps. Father Lombardi huddled in prayer, occasionally scribbling notes from memory on a scrap of paper. Ibrahim paced, stopping every so often to check if Kiril had returned. Yusef stared at the grungy walls, lost in his thoughts.

Dusk settled, painting the windows in a grim purple glow. At last, footsteps sounded in the corridor. The door unlocked with a metallic scrape, and Kiril stepped in, face tense. He latched the door behind him.

"I have word," he announced, breath steaming in the chilly apartment. "Orlov is definitely at a secret lab about fifty kilometers outside Moscow. Reliable sources confirm a large crate arrived by plane, moved there under heavy guard. The place used to be a missile research facility. Now it's rumored to be a testing ground for... exotic technologies."

Helena's pulse kicked up. "So the Ark is there?"

Kiril nodded grimly. "Likely. Orlov's staff secured it in a subterranean vault. The entire compound is ringed by electric fences, watchtowers, roving patrols with dogs. Unauthorized entry is near impossible."

Dave exchanged a glance with Helena. "We can't rely on official help, can we?"

"None," Kiril confirmed. "If you request American or Israeli or Vatican involvement openly, the Russians will clamp down. This must be done, or risk an international incident."

Yusef's voice trembled. "Is there any way inside at all?"

Kiril gave a tight shrug. "A local faction of Russian officers opposes Orlov's extremist methods. They might assist, but they'll want plausible deniability. You'd have to infiltrate at night, maybe sabotage power lines, slip into the lower levels. Extremely dangerous."

Helena's mouth felt dry. "We've done infiltration before," she said, recalling the prior raids that ended in violence. "But we need more than guesswork. We need schematics, knowledge of guard rotations, something."

Kiril set a folded paper on the table. "Managed to get a partial map from an old employee. Could be out of date, but it's a start."

Ibrahim unfolded the map, squinting at the lines. "Three main buildings, plus a subterranean lab. Elevator access here... multiple corridors. Guard stations near each entrance. This is a fortress."

Lombardi approached, lips pursed. "We must try. The Ark cannot remain in Orlov's clutches. And we must confirm if he's begun any experiments. Our partial ceremony is meaningless if we lose the relic entirely."

Helena frowned, recalling the incomplete text. Even if they retrieved the Ark, they still needed the missing lines to quell its destructive nature. She looked at Dave. "We have to see if we can do this. Maybe we can slip in, gather intel, and find a moment to extract the Ark or at least sabotage Orlov's program."

He pressed a palm to the table. "We'd need to build a team. Just the six of us is not enough to storm the place. Kiril, can your local allies supply a few skilled operators?"

The tall man nodded. "Possibly. But they'll want compensation. And the more people we involve, the greater the risk of a leak."

Ibrahim sighed. "We don't have many options." He tapped the map. "If we sabotage the main power system, the electric fence might go down. Then we slip in at the rear entrance."

Helena's mind raced. They'd done infiltration with small squads before, and it always ended in gunfire. But maybe surprise would buy them an edge. "Yes. If we strike during a shift change, it might help."

Dave turned to Kiril. "Do you know the shift schedules?"

"I can find out. Give me a day."

A day. Another delay while Orlov toyed with the Ark. Helena's stomach knotted with dread. She forced herself to remain calm. "All right. We'll do it," she said, scanning each face. "We infiltrate in two nights, let Kiril gather the final details. We either reclaim the Ark or at least sabotage Orlov's ability to harness it."

No one objected, though Yusef's eyes filled with fear. Lombardi whispered a hushed prayer in Latin, brow furrowed. Dave exhaled, rolling his tense shoulders. "We'd better rest, gather mental energy. Tomorrow, we plan gear and finalize infiltration steps with Kiril's allies."

Kiril slid out again to make calls, leaving them locked in the safe house. Another drab meal from a can, another restless night in the musty apartment. Helena drifted off in a corner, lulled by exhaustion and the hum of the radiator. Dreams battered her, images of Orlov laughing as illusions of flaming angels tore through helpless soldiers. She woke gasping in the early hours, heart hammering. Dave, half asleep on the couch, asked if she was all right, and she nodded weakly, though her mind churned.

Morning found them cramped and irritable. Kiril arrived with stale bread and coffee, plus a promise that he'd set a covert meeting that evening with two ex-spetsnaz men who despised Orlov's extremist stance. Helena, Dave, and Ibrahim would attend. Lombardi planned to phone his Jesuit contact. Yusef would remain in the apartment, less conspicuous.

The day crawled by. At dusk, Kiril led Helena, Dave, and Ibrahim down a back stairwell to a battered car with tinted windows. Yusef and Lombardi stayed behind. The ride took them through winding side streets, eventually arriving at a decaying warehouse near the city's industrial district. Snow flurries drifted, and overhead lamps flickered. They slipped inside, where two men waited by a rusted forklift.

One wore a heavy coat, face scarred by old burns. The other had a wiry build and cold blue eyes. Kiril introduced them as Vitaly and Mikhail, both ex-special forces. Neither looked thrilled.

Vitaly spoke first in Russian, which Kiril translated. "He says Orlov's men have harassed them for months. They want revenge. They'll help you infiltrate the lab if the reward is right."

Dave frowned. "We can't offer money we don't have. We can promise if we succeed, Orlov's power will crumble. That might free Russia from his extremist influence."

Vitaly snorted, unconvinced. Mikhail said something, jabbing a finger at the trio. Kiril paraphrased. "They say talk is cheap. But they'll accept if you let them keep any advanced weapon prototypes Orlov hoarded. They're arms dealers, you see."

Ibrahim and Helena exchanged uneasy looks. More weapons floating around? But they had no bargaining power. Dave finally agreed in a low voice, "Fine. If there are any advanced arms in that lab, do what you want with them. Our only goal is retrieving or disabling the Ark."

Vitaly and Mikhail shrugged, muttering among themselves. Then they nodded curtly. Mikhail spread a crude blueprint on an old crate, explaining guard rotations and likely vantage points. Kiril translated for Helena. The infiltration plan took shape: sabotage the external power station, cut the electric fence, slip in through a rarely used service tunnel, then descend to the sublevel where the Ark was rumored to be stored. Vitaly and Mikhail would handle any firefights or security override codes. Helena's group would locate the artifact.

They arranged the assault for the following night. The ex-spetsnaz men left after a final glare, presumably to gather gear and prepare. Kiril escorted

Helena, Dave, and Ibrahim back to the car, shoulders hunched in the swirling snow. Each step weighed heavy with the knowledge that this might be their only chance.

When they returned to the safe house, the group convened in the cramped living room. Lombardi was waiting anxiously, fiddling with an old phone. He brightened when they entered. "I reached Father Dimitri. He found references in the Vatican archives describing Ark phenomena. Some mention catastrophic effects if the chest is forced open. I suspect Orlov might attempt that."

Helena's stomach did a slow flip. "If Orlov tries to open the Ark physically, the resulting manifestations could intensify enough to drive entire battalions mad. Or worse."

Father Lombardi nodded. "We must hurry. Dimitri had no direct way to help, but he wishes us luck. He says if we can retrieve the chest, the Vatican stands ready to receive it—for safekeeping, of course."

She bit back a skeptical retort, aware that the priest's ultimate loyalty lay with the Church. For now, they shared a goal, but she wouldn't hand it over to the Vatican unconditionally. The final lines of the ceremony were still missing. The Church had offered no guarantee they'd help find them. That tension simmered in her mind, but she said nothing.

Night rolled on. The next day passed in restless planning. Yusef tried to keep busy, inventorying the few supplies they had. Dave tested a small rifle that Mikhail slipped them, while Helena recited the infiltration plan like a mantra, ironing out potential pitfalls. Lombardi jotted verses from memory, in case they needed to quell an immediate surge of Ark power. Ibrahim scanned local media for hints that Orlov's facility had tightened security. They found no mention.

Finally, the evening of the infiltration arrived. Kiril returned with a battered van, Vitaly and Mikhail in tow. The ex-spetsnaz men wore dark, utilitarian clothes, bristling with sidearms and a few compact submachine guns. The tension in the small apartment rose to a boiling point.

Yusef insisted on coming along, refusing to hide once more. Dave hesitated, but recognized the teen's resolve. "Just stay in the van unless we say otherwise," he warned. Yusef nodded grimly.

They climbed into the vehicle, Lombardi included. The priest claimed his presence might calm the Ark if illusions spiraled out of control. Helena dreaded the thought of him losing himself to religious fervor, but maybe his knowledge would help. She shoved the fear down. No time for second thoughts.

The drive was silent, the roads dark. Snow flurries thickened, swirling in the headlights. Kiril parked near a forested area a kilometer from the facility. Through the frosty windshield, Helena glimpsed tall fences and watchtowers in the distance, faintly lit by floodlights. Mikhail checked his watch, whispered for them to wait until the shift change at midnight.

At the stroke of twelve, Vitaly and Mikhail slipped out, lugging a small device for sabotaging the external power lines. Dave, Helena, Ibrahim, Lombardi, Yusef, and Kiril followed at a distance, moving through snow-laden pines. Each footstep crunched painfully loud to Helena's ears, but the wind covered some noise. Overhead, the moon shone through ragged clouds. The entire forest felt like a place of secrets.

When they reached the perimeter fence, the ex-spetsnaz men crouched behind a fallen trunk. Vitaly snaked forward, planting a shaped charge on the power conduit that fed the fence. They crawled back, gave a brief nod. A muffled thump followed, then a shower of sparks erupted. Lights around the fence flickered, darkening. Sirens blared inside the compound, and sentries scrambled.

The infiltration team pressed their advantage. Dave, Kiril, and Vitaly cut through the fence with heavy snips while Helena and Yusef stood guard. Shots rang out from the watchtower, bullets zipping overhead. Lombardi and Ibrahim flattened themselves behind a tree. Mikhail returned fire, forcing the tower guard to duck. The fence parted enough for them to slip inside.

Snow glowed under emergency floodlights that sputtered on, casting a harsh glare. The group sprinted across open ground, hearts pounding. One watchtower tried to swivel a spotlight toward them, but Mikhail shot out the lamp with an accurate burst. Helena's lungs burned in the frigid air, adrenaline spiking.

They reached a dark corner of a building, pressing against the wall. Sirens continued to wail. Footsteps pounded on the other side. Dave peeked around, saw two armed guards hustling for the fence line. He signaled them to wait. Once the guards passed, the infiltration team crept to a service entrance that Kiril's map indicated. Ibrahim tried a keypad, but it beeped red. Vitaly cursed in Russian, rummaging for a small hacking device.

Lightning-fast footsteps sounded behind them. A single guard emerged, raising his weapon. Yusef, heart stuttering, lifted the pistol Dave had given him. Helena gasped. Dave pivoted, fired first, and dropped the guard with a shot to the leg. The man collapsed, howling. Vitaly stomped on his rifle, scattering it. Tension crackled in the air. Yusef's eyes shone with shock, shoulders trembling. They had nearly been discovered.

The hacking device beeped green. The door hissed open. Everyone piled inside, slipping down a narrow corridor. The alarms inside the facility blared at half volume, red emergency lights rotating overhead. Footsteps echoed from distant halls. Helena forced her breathing steady, recalling each detail of the layout. Sublevel labs should be down a central elevator.

The group advanced, guns raised. Kiril led with the map in hand, passing dim passages lined with closed metal doors. One room glowed from within, the occupant apparently oblivious to the infiltration. Dave signaled them to keep moving. No sense fighting every occupant.

A fork emerged. Mikhail pointed left toward a wide corridor. They turned, only to see a half-dozen security officers rushing in tactical gear. Shots erupted. The infiltration team ducked behind crates and pillars. A furious firefight broke out, muzzle flashes strobing the corridor. Helena flattened herself against the wall, heart hammering. She glimpsed Yusef crouched at the far side, eyes wide with terror but holding steady.

Two of the security officers fell under Mikhail's onslaught. Another dove behind a steel barrier, radioing for backup. Dave snatched a tear gas canister from Vitaly's belt, lobbed it forward. Gas flooded the corridor, sending the defenders coughing and retreating. The infiltration team pushed through, holding cloths over their faces. The officer behind the barrier stumbled out, disoriented, and Dave knocked him unconscious with a single blow.

They advanced deeper, stepping over moaning men. The corridor opened onto a central hub with elevator banks. One set was dark, offline. Another flickered with half power. Lombardi clutched his Bible, scanning for any sign of illusions. So far, only the stench of fear and gunpowder.

Ibrahim found a control panel, tried pressing the sublevel button. Nothing. The console read "Power supply offline." Vitaly cursed under his breath, rummaging for a second hacking device. Meanwhile, Mikhail guarded the corridor they'd come from. Kiril stood near Dave, rechecking the map. Yusef hovered near Helena, trembling with adrenaline.

The priest wiped sweat from his brow. "If we can't get the elevator, we might find a stairwell. The Ark must be below."

Ibrahim tapped the console again. "One more second. If this fails, we look for stairs."

Vitaly attached his hacking kit. The overhead lights flickered, then the elevator dinged. The doors slid open on a dank shaft. The interior flickered with emergency lights, but it seemed functional. The infiltration team piled in, weapons at the ready. Dave pressed sublevel 2. The doors closed with a hiss, leaving them enveloped in the chemical odor of tear gas residue.

As the lift descended, Helena braced herself for illusions. The Ark might be near, and any forced intrusion could provoke the chest's power. Her heartbeat pounded so loud she feared the others could hear it. Lombardi fingered a slip of paper containing his partial verses. Yusef stared at the elevator walls, forcing deep breaths.

The elevator rattled to a stop. Doors slid open onto a low-ceilinged corridor with humming fluorescent strips. White tile floors gleamed, suggesting a sterile lab environment. Distant shouting echoed from behind closed doors. A sign in Russian indicated multiple labs, a storage vault. Kiril pointed to the left. "We head that way," he whispered. "Sublevel labs."

They padded down the hall, stepping over scattered papers. Dave motioned for caution. The deeper they went, the heavier the air felt. A faint odor of ozone lingered, reminiscent of the Ark's electromagnetic aura. Helena's pulse quickened. She recognized that subtle tang—this was the Ark's doing, warping the environment. She recalled how electronics often malfunctioned near it, how illusions sometimes formed in peripheral vision.

She glimpsed movement up ahead: two scientists in lab coats, wide-eyed with fear. They scurried away, dropping clipboards. Dave let them go. They posed no threat, likely just terrified. A heavy door on the right stood ajar, labeled in Cyrillic. Kiril read it, "Containment Chamber." That had to be it.

Vitaly tested the handle. Locked. He readied a small breaching charge. Before he could place it, the door slid open from inside. A soldier in black fatigues stepped out, half-turning as if to greet someone behind him. He froze at the sight of the intruders. Dave fired once, grazing the soldier's arm. The man yelped, dropped his rifle, and stumbled back into the chamber.

The infiltration team surged forward, guns raised. They entered a large, windowless room dominated by an ominous sight: the Ark, perched on a reinforced metal table. The relic's gold trim glinted under harsh lights, arcs of electricity dancing along its edges. Computers and monitors lined the walls, graphs and readouts flickering with bizarre waveforms. Half a dozen Russian personnel scrambled, some wearing lab coats, others in military fatigues.

Colonel Orlov stood near the artifact, holding a handheld device that whined with power. His expression twisted with fury as Dave and Vitaly aimed weapons at him. "You!" Orlov spat in accented English, eyes blazing. "You dare come here?"

Helena's gaze locked on the chest, noticing fresh scorch marks on the gold. "He tried forcing it open," she whispered to Lombardi, sick with dread. The air buzzed with the electric tension she recognized from past incidents. Her scalp tingled.

Orlov roared something to his men, gesturing for them to shoot. Gunfire erupted. The infiltration team dived behind lab consoles. Mikhail unleashed a barrage that cut down two of Orlov's soldiers. Yusef ducked behind a crate, eyes clenched. Father Lombardi clutched the partial verses in one hand, a small crucifix in the other, chanting rapidly.

A soldier near Orlov lunged for the Ark's handle, as if hoping to move it to safety. A brilliant arc of static lashed out, knocking him off his feet. He crashed into a console, sparks flying. The relic crackled louder, and lights throughout the lab dimmed. Helena glimpsed swirling shapes at the corners of her vision—luminous wings, fleeting and intangible. Another step toward phantoms.

Orlov seized his handheld device, aiming it at the chest. An energy beam flickered, possibly some advanced field manipulator. The Ark flared with actinic light, and a wave of force rippled outward. Dave and Helena were thrown against a bank of monitors, knocking the wind from them. Vitaly and Mikhail sprawled, cursing. Lombardi cried out, crossing himself. Yusef curled into a ball, hands over his head.

The relic glowed with something more than electricity—like a searing presence that pressed on Helena's mind. She fought to stay conscious, ghostly images flickering at the edge of her vision. She saw silhouettes of winged figures gliding overhead, raising swords of pure fire. A sense of dread welled in her chest, as though centuries-old judgments echoed through the chamber.

Orlov staggered, too. He pressed a switch on his device, sweat beading on his temple. "I control it," he gasped, voice shaking with half-delirium. "Russia will harness biblical might."

Helena forced herself upright, leaning on a console. "You have no idea what you're unleashing!" she shouted. "It'll destroy you first."

His eyes blazed with defiance. "Foolish archaeologist. We will master it."

Dave, recovering from the shockwave, tackled a soldier trying to flank them. The two crashed into a trolley of lab instruments. Another soldier tried to shoot Dave, but Mikhail gunned him down. The lab devolved into chaos: swirling arcs from the Ark, sputtering monitors, men shouting in fear or rage.

Lombardi crawled closer to the chest, reciting scraps of the partial ceremony in breathy Latin. The arcs of static hissed around him. Orlov noticed, leveled his handheld device at the priest. Helena lurched forward, screaming, "No!" She grabbed a loose metal rod from the floor and flung it. It struck the device, jarring Orlov's aim. A burst of unstable energy crackled through the air. The colonel roared as the discharge grazed his own side, scorching fabric and leaving him reeling.

Yusef, seizing an opening, kicked Orlov's leg out from behind. The colonel collapsed, dropping the device, which sparked and died. Another wave of spectral phenomena flared, intensifying the ghostly shapes swirling around the Ark. Helena's breath caught. She swore she saw cherubim with flaming wings, towering over them, yet intangible and flickering. The air tasted like ozone and old incense.

One last soldier, desperately loyal, fired wildly. Bullets sang past Helena's ear, shattering a computer screen. Dave ducked, returning fire with lethal precision. The soldier toppled, leaving Orlov the only threat. The colonel scrambled for a sidearm, but Ibrahim kicked it aside, pinning him to the floor with one foot.

Silence fell except for the hum of the Ark and the ragged breathing of the survivors. Orlov's men lay incapacitated or worse. Smoke curled from smashed consoles. Lombardi knelt near the artifact, reciting Latin lines, tears shining in his eyes. The ethereal shapes receded slightly, though arcs still danced, warning of lingering danger.

Helena, panting, turned to Dave. "We have to move the Ark out of here or disable it somehow. If the Russian reinforcements come, we'll be overrun."

He wiped sweat from his brow, scanning the battered lab. "We can't carry it by ourselves. We need a truck or helicopter. And the Russians might lock down the entire base in minutes."

Vitaly, nursing a bullet graze on his arm, snarled in Russian about taking anything of value. He rummaged among the lab crates, retrieving a small box of advanced weapon components. Mikhail helped him, ignoring the ghostly apparitions. They shot occasional glares at Orlov, who still lay pinned by Ibrahim.

Yusef approached the Ark, though fear contorted his features. "If we push it on that rolling table," he gestured shakily to a heavy-duty cart near the corner, "maybe we can wheel it out the corridor to the elevator?"

Helena considered. The chest still spat arcs of energy, but the haunting figures seemed more subdued than a moment ago. Perhaps Father Lombardi's partial chant had stabilized it slightly. She locked eyes with the priest. "Keep reciting. We'll try to roll the Ark onto that cart."

Lombardi gave a weak nod, lips moving in rhythmic Latin. Yusef and Helena eased forward. The static crackled around them, but didn't lash out. Dave joined them, helping to angle the chest onto the cart's surface. Arcs snapped at their gloved hands, raising the hairs on Helena's arms. She winced but pushed through. The relic felt heavier than gold alone, as if its presence had mass that defied explanation.

Once it settled on the cart, Dave exhaled. "We can't hold this place for long." He looked at Vitaly and Mikhail. "We're extracting the Ark. If you want your cut, help us get it out. Then you can take whatever weapon stash you find along the way."

They grumbled, but nodded. Meanwhile, Orlov writhed on the floor, pinned by Ibrahim. The colonel glared murderously. "You won't leave here alive."

Dave glowered back. "We're leaving with the Ark. You can fight us again some other day. Now, stand down unless you want more." He nodded to Ibrahim, who lifted his foot, allowing Orlov to sit up. The colonel spat blood, though the wildness in his eyes suggested he wasn't done resisting.

Mikhail brandished a pistol. "Move," he growled in Russian. Orlov sneered, but he obeyed, stepping aside with a limp. The infiltration team steered the cart out the lab door, Ark rattling. Sparks of electricity left burn marks on the metal handle. Father Lombardi stayed at its side, continuing his low chant. Dave and Helena flanked the relic, weapons ready. Vitaly and Mikhail led the way, scanning for security squads. Yusef and Ibrahim guarded the rear, guns trained on Orlov.

They hurried along the corridor, each footstep resonating with tension. Distant klaxons and overhead announcements suggested base security was regrouping. The illusions from the Ark flickered around them like faint shadows, but no full manifestations returned. Helena prayed that Lombardi's partial rite kept the power in check.

As they neared the elevator bank, a new cluster of guards confronted them. Another firefight erupted in the confined hallway. Mikhail hurled a smoke grenade. Shots pinged off the cart, threatening to puncture the Ark. Helena's heart pounded in terror at the idea of a bullet striking the chest. She pressed her body against it, feeling arcs sting her jacket. Dave and Vitaly returned heavy fire. Yusef ducked, trembling, aiming sporadic shots to keep the guards at bay.

In the swirl of smoke and muzzle flashes, one guard attempted to lob a fragmentation grenade. Dave spotted it, shouted, "Grenade!" Everyone dove for cover. The explosive rattled the corridor, sending chunks of ceiling tiles raining down. Helena shielded her head, the Ark's cart jolting sideways from the blast. The relic tottered dangerously, arcs flaring. She lunged, stabilized it with her shoulder. White-hot static bit her arm, but she bit back a scream.

When the smoke cleared, the guard squad lay scattered, moaning or still. Dave's group pressed on, more desperate than ever. They reached the elevator. Vitaly hammered the call button. The overhead panel glowed, doors sliding open. The infiltration team piled in with the chest, barely fitting. Orlov, forced at gunpoint, spat curses. The elevator rose to the ground level, each second feeling like a lifetime.

Finally, the doors parted onto the top corridor. Alarms wailed. The power sabotage from earlier still left many systems offline. Flickering lights cast everything in a strobe-like gloom. The group pushed the Ark-laden cart through the building's main foyer, stepping over unconscious or wounded soldiers. Outside, wind howled through the open fence line. More squads might be approaching from other wings, but the infiltration team prayed they could outrun them.

They burst into the snow-laden courtyard. Vitaly and Mikhail whooped, spotting their van parked near the breach. No other vehicles guarded the yard, possibly because base personnel scrambled to contain the sabotage. Dave and Helena heaved the cart over broken concrete, arcs sparking at their heels. Yusef panted, slipping once on ice. Father Lombardi kept chanting, voice ragged.

As they reached the van, gunfire erupted from a watchtower. Mikhail cursed, returning sporadic shots. Vitaly started the engine. Dave and Ibrahim heaved the Ark into the van's cargo area, straining under its unnatural heft. Lombardi clambered in, continuing to chant. Helena and Yusef joined them. Dave kicked Orlov into the back as well, at gunpoint. "You're coming, Colonel. We can't leave you free to muster a chase."

The colonel glared but complied, battered by spectral forces and minor wounds. The others slid into seats. The van lurched forward, tires spinning in the snow. Bullets pinged off the metal exterior, but Vitaly floored the accelerator, smashing through the damaged fence. The vehicle fishtailed onto the icy road, picking up speed. Headlights cut through the swirling drifts. Guards fired in vain from behind.

Helena, crammed in the cargo area with Dave, Yusef, Lombardi, and the Ark, felt her heart race in a frantic staccato. Orlov sat handcuffed, chest heaving with fury. The relic glowed, arcs dancing along the gold edges, but Lombardi's murmured ritual seemed to hold back the worst manifestations. Dave's eyes locked on Helena's, relief and fear colliding in his gaze. She squeezed his hand, adrenaline still surging through her veins.surging.

They had the Ark again, unbelievably. The cost was huge—countless men wounded or dead, and the entire Russian base in chaos. But it was out of Orlov's reach for the moment. She only prayed the next wave of pursuers wouldn't catch them.

Vitaly steered the van onto a back road through dense forests, ignoring major highways. Mikhail kept watch with a rifle, scanning for tailing vehicles. Kiril, in the front passenger seat, gave rapid directions. Snow pelted the windshield. The stolen chest crackled, an ominous presence that none could ignore.

Yusef trembled, gripping the side of the van. "Where... where do we go now?"

Helena exhaled, mind spinning. "Somewhere safe to hide it, at least temporarily. We can't waltz onto a plane with it. Russia's entire security apparatus might come after us."

Lombardi paused his chanting, voice raw. "We can get it out of the country via Vatican channels—clergy networks, diplomatic crates."

Ibrahim shot him a glare. "Or we can find a neutral site. Our governments should decide."

Dave rubbed his temples, exhausted. "Let's just get out of immediate danger. Then we'll figure out our next move. The longer we remain in Russia, the riskier it gets. But we still haven't completed the ceremony."

Helena recalled the partial lines. They needed the second half. One step at a time, she reminded herself. Right now, survival came first. Then they'd address the ceremony. She sat in the swaying van, forcibly steadying her breath. The Ark had changed hands again, the lethal relic now in their custody. She felt no triumph, only dread at what might unfold next.

Snow-laden pines blurred past. Gunshots faded behind them. Orlov seethed in a corner, battered but not broken, muttering threats. Father Lombardi tried to recite more verses, though his voice sometimes cracked.

The arcs of electricity dimmed a fraction. Helena wondered if the partial chant truly soothed the relic, or if the chest was simply spent from Orlov's attempts to open it. She didn't dare assume safety.

After a long, harrowing drive, Vitaly parked near a secluded clearing. They transferred the Ark to another battered vehicle that Mikhail had stashed days before. The infiltration team parted ways with Vitaly and Mikhail there, the ex-spetsnaz men content with the advanced weapon crate they'd seized. Kiril offered to guide Helena's group to a more discreet route out of Moscow. Tension remained thick—Orlov glared, arms bound, yet silent. The infiltration had succeeded, but the journey to safety loomed long.

Helena closed her eyes for a moment, recalling the illusions, the swirl of partial verses, the incomplete ceremony. If they didn't find the final lines, the relic's power could remain a ticking threat. She opened her eyes to see Dave watching her. He whispered, "We did it… for now."

She nodded, forcing a small smile. "For now," she repeated, voice trembling with fatigue. The night pressed in, bitter cold biting at every breath. The Ark's faint hum reminded them that the real battle was far from over.

Chapter 10

Moscow, Ten Days Earlier

They arrived at a dimly lit safe house on the edge of a sprawling industrial district outside Moscow. The building, a two-story structure with peeling paint, had once been part of an abandoned factory complex. Kiril parked near a rusted chain-link fence, cut the engine, and guided everyone inside.

"Stay out of sight," he muttered, leading them down a corridor of shattered windows and dusty floors. "Authorities will launch a manhunt once they discover the Ark is gone."

Helena, Dave, Yusef, Ibrahim, Lombardi, and a still-handcuffed Orlov followed Kiril through the gloom. The colonel wore a bruised scowl, pride wounded by his loss. The chest hovered on a small cart, arcs occasionally sparking. Father Lombardi kept murmuring a truncated prayer to stabilize the relic's energy. Each minute stretched, the tension thick in the stale air.

Finally, they reached an old storage room with boarded-up windows. Kiril pried the boards aside, revealing a modest interior lit by a single bare bulb. Dust motes danced in the beam. He motioned them in, latching the door behind them. Orlov glowered, refusing to speak.

Helena exhaled a shaky breath. "At least we're hidden... for now. This building doesn't look secure, though."

Kiril nodded. "We won't stay long. But I know a discreet route out of Moscow by rail. We might smuggle you and the Ark toward Belarus or the Baltic states. Once across the border, arrange a flight. The problem is your... large cargo." He cast a wary glance at the gilded chest.

The priest's chant faltered. He sagged against the cart, face pale. "I can't keep reciting forever. We need a permanent solution."

Dave lowered his voice. "We have to complete the ceremony or find some containment method. If we keep hauling the Ark around, illusions or violent surges might strike at any moment."

Ibrahim paced. "Which means we must track down the missing lines of that ritual. Possibly in Istanbul, or at a hidden library. But traveling there with the Ark is madness."

Helena recalled the lead from Elias, the mysterious man in Israel who pointed them toward a Crusader manuscript rumored to be in Istanbul. They'd never had time to verify that clue. She stared at the chest's shimmering arcs, recalling the partial text that ended abruptly. Finishing the ceremony might be their only path to keep the relic from devastating anyone who touched it.

She took a breath, turned to Father Lombardi. "Could we stash the Ark somewhere safe in Europe while we chase the missing manuscript? The Vatican might help, if we trust them."

The Jesuit rubbed his bleary eyes. "The Church can conceal sacred objects in hidden repositories. But let's be frank: some in the Vatican might want to claim the Ark for themselves." He lowered his gaze. "Yet it's our best bet. We have centuries of experience safeguarding relics."

Ibrahim grimaced. "Israel wants the Ark returned. Our government sees it as part of our heritage."

An exhausted silence fell. They'd wrested the Ark away from Orlov, only to face a stalemate. Each faction—Israel, the Vatican, possibly the U.S.—had a stake. The object's destructive potential hung over them like a storm cloud.

Suddenly, Orlov broke his silence, voice dripping with contempt. "You cannot hide it. Russia will find you. You do not comprehend its power." He stared at Helena, eyes glinting. "It obeyed me, in the lab. The illusions parted for a moment. Soon, we will reclaim it."

Dave frowned. "Shut up, Colonel. You lost, for now."

Orlov sneered. "You think you can keep this relic locked away? It belongs to the strong. The old myths... illusions... they only highlight the Ark's true potential."

Lombardi trembled with anger, but Helena touched his arm. Confronting Orlov accomplished little. She gazed around the darkened room, mind churning with possibilities. After a moment, she faced Dave. "We can't remain in Russia. We need to leave, maybe for Istanbul. If that Crusader text truly has the missing lines, it could be our only hope."

He exhaled, leaning on a battered table. "We'll need reliable transit. This rail route Kiril mentioned might work. But traveling with Orlov as a prisoner is risky."

"Kill me, then," Orlov taunted, though his voice held a tremor. "You have no place to keep me anyway."

Dave ignored the outburst. "We can't just execute a prisoner. He's coming with us, or we release him to the Russians. But that would alert the authorities at once."

A brief hush followed. Helena felt weighed down by moral and practical dilemmas. Yusef hovered near the door, biting his lip. The teen seemed torn, exhausted by the violence and uncertain how to proceed. Kiril took out a phone, scanning for signal. "I can arrange an old cargo train heading west tomorrow night. We bribe the conductor to let you smuggle that chest onboard. Once across the border, you're on your own."

Father Lombardi pressed a hand to his chest, breath rasping. "I can't keep chanting all day. The illusions might surge, especially if we travel across multiple borders."

Helena knew time was short. She squared her shoulders. "All right. We do it. We'll head to Istanbul, or at least get closer. Once we're over the border, we contact whomever we can. The final lines have to be found."

Dave offered a slow nod. Ibrahim massaged his temples. "Insane plan, but we have no choice."

Orlov gave a low, mocking laugh. "You'll never see your precious final lines. I had men searching for it. That rumor is nonsense."

She glared at him. "You'd best hope we find them, Colonel. Without them, the Ark might devour the entire region."

His sneer faded, replaced by a flicker of apprehension. Then he spat in disgust, turning away.

Kiril typed texts on his phone, expression tense. "I'll confirm the train schedule. Meanwhile, keep the Ark quiet. Don't let anything happen that might draw attention from the neighborhood."

Helena cast a worried glance at Lombardi, who resumed his low chanting. She knew the partial prayer was more a stopgap than a true solution. The arcs on the chest crackled sporadically, as though agitated by the day's upheaval.

The group bedded down in that dingy storage room, each claiming a patch of floor or a corner. Dave used rope to secure Orlov to a pipe, ensuring he couldn't slip away. The colonel glowered, though exhaustion soon overcame him. At times, strange apparitions flickered at the edge of Helena's sight: shapes like translucent wings or faint, shifting lights. She suspected the Ark was restless.

Come morning, Kiril returned with news. "The cargo train leaves at midnight from a small yard near the city outskirts. We have a one-hour window to load your crate unseen. A bribe handles the guard, but we must be swift." He eyed Orlov. "What about him?"

Dave shrugged. "We take him. Unless you want a murderer running free to alert the entire Russian army."

Ibrahim nodded, though unease crossed his face. Yusef said nothing, devouring some stale bread in the corner. Helena felt the teen's tension, guilt over the repeated violence, but no path they'd taken guaranteed peace.

The hours dragged. The Ark crackled, with spectral phenomena stirring whenever Lombardi paused his chanting to sip water or rest. Each time, Helena glimpsed fleeting shapes: smoky columns or ghostly wings that seemed to ripple at the edges of her vision. The others reported hearing faint murmurs or feeling static bursts. Dave kept a close watch on their prisoner, who occasionally dozed or tested his restraints. Kiril made final arrangements, then returned with a battered truck. They loaded the Ark's cart inside, forcing Orlov into the passenger seat with Dave at his side. The rest squeezed around the relic in the cargo bed or on the small rear bench. Lombardi resumed chanting, his voice low and steady.

Darkness fell as they rumbled toward the railyard. Snow battered the windshield, swirling under flickering lamps. The yard's gates stood half-open, a single watchman nodding to Kiril after a discreet exchange of currency. Lines of freight cars stretched into the gloom, some loaded with crates or machinery. Kiril led them to a spur track where an aging cargo train waited, its engine idling.

A conductor in a bulky coat stood by the first car, occasionally glancing around. Kiril hopped out, spoke in low tones. A wad of bills changed hands. The conductor gestured to a loading ramp near the second car. Helena's heart pounded. If the Ark acted up now, they'd have no cover.

The group hustled to offload the Ark, pushing it up the ramp. The chest's arcs snapped, prompting flinches from the conductor, who muttered in confusion. Lombardi kept chanting, sweat beading on his forehead. Orlov scowled, forcibly dragged along by Dave. Yusef braced the cart so it wouldn't tip.

They settled the Ark in an empty corner of the cargo car, away from windows. The conductor slid the door closed, though an interior lamp provided faint light. Kiril joined them, intending to ride for a short distance before returning. The engine coughed, couplings groaned, and the train lurched into motion. A wave of relief and fresh anxiety rippled through Helena's mind. They were on the move again, inching closer to the border.

Inside the cargo car, they huddled around the Ark, enthralled and terrified by its presence. The chest crackled, arcs dancing. Lombardi slumped against a crate, voice cracking from hours of chant. Dave let Orlov sit on the floor, wrists still bound. Yusef sat cross-legged, hugging himself for warmth. Ibrahim rummaged for blankets or tarps, finding a couple to ward off the cold.

As the train gained speed, the rhythmic clack of wheels on rails filled the car, a hypnotic lull that almost masked their tension. Helena shared a brief look with Dave, both silently acknowledging how precarious this plan was. If border guards inspected the train, or if Orlov's men tracked them, they could be caught. But staying in Moscow had guaranteed a clash with the entire Russian security apparatus. At least now they had a chance.

Kiril paced near the front of the car, occasionally glancing through a peephole. "We pass the border around dawn," he explained in hushed Russian. Ibrahim translated. "We might not see standard checks if bribes hold. But there's always a risk."

Hours slid by in uneasy waiting. The Ark's energy ebbed and flowed, sometimes surging with bright arcs that made them flinch. Lombardi dozed in increments, chanting whenever illusions began to swirl. Yusef dozed too, wracked by nightmares. Helena stood with Dave near the side door, peering out a crack at the snowy landscape streaking past. The low rumble of the train and the swirl of flurries lent the journey an otherworldly feel, as if they traveled between realms.

Approaching dawn, the train slowed. The conductor stuck his head in, whispering to Kiril that they were nearing a minor crossing. Helena tensed, gripping Dave's shoulder. He placed a hand over hers, a silent pledge of solidarity. Yusef stirred awake, eyes wide. Orlov perked up, as if sensing a possible rescue. Lombardi resumed chanting, though his voice was ragged with exhaustion.

The crossing turned out to be abandoned. No guards. The train clattered through, then picked up speed again. A collective sigh filled the car. Kiril said they had likely entered Belarus or were near the border. From there, they'd continue west, eventually switching lines toward Poland or the Baltic region. One step closer to Istanbul, but still far away.

Mid-morning, the train halted at a remote siding. The conductor arrived, panting. "This is where I deviate from your route," Kiril translated. "A caretaker will disconnect this car for a while, reattach it to a line heading toward southwestern Europe in a few hours. In that gap, local inspectors might appear. Keep the door locked. If anyone knocks, claim no knowledge of the cargo. I must leave now."

Worry spiked. Helena considered how suspicious the car might appear. But they had no alternative. Kiril said his goodbyes, urging them to stay quiet. The infiltration group braced themselves. The conductor unlatched the couplings, and the train rumbled away, leaving their single cargo car on an isolated track in the middle of nowhere, surrounded by frosty plains. A biting wind seeped through cracks in the walls.

They spent hours in that drift of time, no movement but the swirl of snow outside. The Ark's arcs glowed in the dim interior. Lombardi dozed off, too spent for chanting. Helena paced, worried illusions might intensify. Dave checked Orlov's binds. The colonel refused food or water, stewing in silent anger.

Ibrahim rummaged in a crate, found a battered radio. He tried scanning frequencies for news. Static reigned. Yusef stared at the Ark, guilt etched across his features. Helena gently asked if he was all right.

The teen shook his head. "I can't stop thinking of the men we killed, the injuries we left behind... all for this object. Even if it's holy, everything feels so dark."

She touched his shoulder. "I know. It weighs on me too. But if Orlov harnessed it, the toll would be far greater."

He nodded, though sorrow lingered in his eyes.

As evening neared, the rails vibrated with an approaching locomotive. The caretaker's voice echoed outside. The coupling system groaned, attaching their cargo car to another train. Then they lurched forward, heading west again. Relief mingled with fresh anxiety. Another border crossing lay ahead, presumably with heavier checks. The infiltration team tensed.

Night fell, the train forging ahead. Sleep overcame them in shifts, except for Dave, who forced himself to remain on watch with a borrowed rifle. The Ark's arcs occasionally crackled, lighting the cargo car with eerie flashes. Helena drifted in and out of nightmares: swirling angelic forms brandishing swords of fire, haunting visions. Once, she jolted awake, certain she heard the Ark whisper her name, though it was likely her mind succumbing to stress.

In the early hours, shrill whistles and clanking signaled the train's arrival at another yard. The car shuddered to a stop. Shouts echoed outside in a foreign tongue—possibly border officials. The infiltration group froze, exchanging panicked looks. They had no official documents for the Ark, and its unpredictable phenomena could expose them. Dave motioned for silence. Orlov's eyes gleamed with twisted amusement.

Seconds stretched. Helena heard footsteps approach. A rap sounded on the cargo car door. She held her breath. Another rap, louder. Yusef stifled a whimper. Dave gestured urgently for Lombardi to keep the relic subdued if anything stirred. The priest whispered feverishly in Latin, sweat dripping down his temples.

Then footsteps retreated. An argument in some Eastern European language erupted outside—maybe the caretaker or conductor bribing officials. At last, the train lurched again, rolling forward. The group let out a collective exhale, tension so thick it nearly suffocated them.

They continued on. By daybreak, the train rattled across a final border, indicated by a faint sign glimpsed through a gap in the planks. Helena's mind spun. They'd left Belarus behind, possibly entering Poland or a neighboring region. If luck held, they might be free to slip southward, eventually aiming for Istanbul.

Dave nodded at her, his eyes bloodshot. "We made it. Next step is to find a real hideout, maybe charter a plane or continue by rail."

Orlov gave a bitter laugh. "Fools. You think crossing borders solves everything? My people will follow."

She ignored him, focusing on the Ark. The arcs had subdued, perhaps from the priest's unrelenting prayers. Yet a tension thrummed in the air, as though the chest awaited the next crisis. Helena recalled her earlier vow to find the missing lines. That vow burned in her heart. This was only an interlude before a new storm.

Late that afternoon, the train slowed near a railyard in eastern Poland. Dave and Ibrahim decided they should disembark, find a truck or van to continue on the roads. Father Lombardi's voice was nearly gone. Yusef looked half-dead with fatigue, eyelids drooping. Orlov remained sullen but alert, obviously searching for a chance to flee.

The infiltration team pried open the cargo door as the locomotive chugged through a labyrinth of tracks. They jumped off with the Ark-laden cart onto a deserted siding, quickly rolling behind a warehouse. The train roared away, leaving them shivering in the midwinter cold. The chest spat a few arcs, as if in complaint, but Lombardi's ongoing murmurs kept illusions at bay.

They stood in a rank alley, knee-deep in slush. Helena gazed around, seeing battered factory buildings under a leaden sky. Dave tried a phone, discovered no signal or perhaps a different network. Ibrahim rummaged for local currency. Yusef pulled his thin coat tighter. Orlov glared at the bleak surroundings, massaging the rawness of his wrists.

A stroke of fortune: they found a quiet truck driver near an industrial lot who, for a generous bribe, agreed to haul them and a "large crate of museum artifacts" southward. The man spoke broken English and seemed more interested in quick cash than questions. With his help, the group loaded the Ark into the truck's back, then climbed aboard. The chest emitted occasional sparks, making the driver jump. Lombardi insisted on riding in the cargo hold to maintain his chanting. The rest squeezed in the cab, except Orlov, who Dave kept handcuffed in the passenger seat. The driver eyed the colonel warily, but said nothing when Dave implied Orlov was a dangerous patient under sedation.

For hours, they bumped along potholed roads, heading deeper into rural Poland. The driver muttered about crossing into Slovakia or Hungary, wherever his route took him. Helena's nerves felt shredded. She'd never taken such a precarious journey, half smuggling a biblical relic, half racing to find lost texts. Yusef dozed against the window. Orlov seethed. Ibrahim and Dave scouted the route on a battered map.

By nightfall, the driver pulled into a desolate truck stop. He said he'd sleep a few hours before continuing. The infiltration group hopped out for fresh air. Father Lombardi, stepping from the cargo hold, nearly collapsed. Helena rushed to help him, noticing how pale he was. The ceaseless chanting and stress took a toll. The Ark's arcs fizzled to a faint glow.

"We must find the missing lines," the priest rasped, voice on the verge of breaking. "I can't keep this up. The illusions... they surge whenever I pause."

Helena's heart twisted. "We'll head for Istanbul as soon as we can. The Crusader's manuscript might be our only shot."

Dave squeezed her shoulder. "We're almost out of Eastern Europe. Another day or two, we might catch a flight from a discreet airfield. Or we drive all the way. Either way, we keep pressing on."

Ibrahim rubbed his eyes. "And Orlov? Are we dragging him to Istanbul too?"

A bitter laugh escaped the colonel. "You'll regret that choice."

They ignored him. The battered group found a corner in the truck stop's yard to huddle. The driver had no reason to betray them, as long as the payoff was assured. Tired beyond words, they settled around a small patch of ground for a brief rest, guns kept close. Helena stifled tears of exhaustion, leaning against Dave's uninjured shoulder. He let his arm slip around her, a quiet gesture that made her breathing steadier.

Yusef curled up near a tire, using his backpack as a pillow. Lombardi huddled in a blanket, occasionally murmuring short lines to pacify the Ark. Ibrahim dozed with one ear open, pistol across his lap. Orlov, shackled, scowled and tried to keep warm. A faint moonlight shone on the lonely truck stop, highlighting cracked asphalt and drifting litter. Snow flurries began once more.

Helena drifted into uneasy dreams: swirling illusions, angels brandishing flaming swords, a cherubim's voice booming about humanity's unworthiness. She woke with a jolt, tears in her eyes. Dave was awake too, eyes distant. They exchanged a brief, weary look, then turned as the driver coughed an announcement that daybreak neared and he was hitting the road again.

Another day of slow travel, the roads winding through mountainous terrain. At times, they glimpsed villages clinging to frosty peaks. Occasional toll booths or border checks forced them to concoct quick stories about museum cargo. Miraculously, no one demanded a thorough search. Perhaps the battered truck seemed too ordinary to warrant suspicion. Or maybe the Ark's strange aura deterred prying eyes, though Helena prayed it wasn't manipulating their surroundings.

By late afternoon, they approached the Hungarian border. The driver insisted this was his final stop. "After crossing, you find your own way," he said, pocketing the last stack of bills. They parted ways in an industrial park outside a small city, lowering the Ark onto a ramshackle cart again. The chest hissed with static as Lombardi resumed his chanting. Orlov cursed under his breath.

Dave scanned the area. "We can hire another ride or rent a vehicle. There's a city with an airport not far from here. From there, maybe a flight to Istanbul."

Helena's bones felt like lead. "We do it. No other choice."

They located a run-down car rental kiosk near a battered strip mall. The suspicious clerk demanded steep extra fees for foreigners with questionable papers. Dave handed over more bribes, and soon they had a squeaky cargo van. It took two trips to load the Ark-laden cart into the vehicle, arcs snapping faintly against the metal shell. The clerk gawked at the gleaming chest, but Helena quickly spun a tale about a traveling exhibit on religious artifacts.

At last, they were on the road again, rumbling along battered highways toward an airport that might have flights to Turkey. Snow turned to slushy rain as they descended from the highlands into flatter terrain. Father Lombardi's voice wavered with exhaustion, yet the supernatural disturbances remained mostly subdued. Helena felt a pang of guilt for relying so heavily on him, but there was no other option.

Night came once more, and they found a seedy motel near the airport. Dave parked the van behind the building, hidden from street view. They smuggled the Ark inside under a makeshift tarp, ignoring the motel clerk's curious look. The group crammed into two adjoining rooms, lugging Orlov in as well, arms still bound. The chest rested in a corner, flickering with arcs that lit the dingy walls in ghostly flashes.

After barricading the doors and windows with furniture, they huddled in the main room. Dave fiddled with a battered laptop, searching for flights from the local airport to Istanbul. "Earliest flight tomorrow morning, connecting through a regional hub," he muttered. "We could attempt it. But how do we get the Ark onto a plane?"

Lombardi exhaled a ragged breath. "Vatican diplomatic crate? Possibly, if we had time to contact an embassy. But that might draw attention."

Yusef rubbed his eyes. "We can't keep crossing land borders. The next one might be impossible. Orlov's men must be searching every route by now."

Ibrahim shrugged. "We attempt the airport. Maybe we bribe a cargo handler."

Helena parted the curtain a sliver, gazing at the neon motel sign flickering outside. "Let's try. If it fails, we pivot. We're close to Istanbul. Once there, we find that Crusader text."

Orlov sneered from a mattress on the floor. "You'll fail. The Ark belongs to Russia. You'll see. Our agents are everywhere."

She ignored him, turning to Dave with a weary half-smile. "One more gamble?"

He gave a faint nod. "One more."

They ate a sparse meal of cheap sandwiches from a nearby vending machine. Then Helena and Dave retreated to the second room for a moment of quiet. Yusef, Lombardi, and Ibrahim remained with Orlov. The chest glowed in the corner, arcs subdued.

In the dim light, Helena sank onto the bed. Dave stood by the door, tension radiating from him. She saw the lines of strain etched around his eyes. "You look done in," she murmured.

He let out a shaky breath. "We all do. This is beyond anything I trained for. The illusions, the near-constant fights, smuggling an artifact that defies science." He paused, voice dropping. "Without you, I'd have cracked by now."

A flicker of warmth touched her tired heart. "Likewise. If I was alone, I would've surrendered to Orlov days ago."

He moved closer, tentatively resting his hands on her shoulders. She felt a tremor in his grip, some blend of fear and emotion. She lifted her gaze, meeting his. For a moment, the weight of pursuit, illusions, and global stakes slipped aside. The hush between them pulsed with something deep, unspoken. Her heart fluttered. Slowly, he lowered his head until their foreheads nearly touched, sharing a quiet closeness that was neither a full embrace nor a casual gesture. A subtle promise of mutual trust.

Outside, a crackle from the adjoining room signaled the Ark's arcs intensifying again. Father Lombardi's chant resumed. The moment dissolved. Dave pulled back slightly, pressing a light kiss to Helena's temple. "We should rest. Tomorrow's a big day."

She nodded, swallowing. "Yes." The last vestiges of vulnerability retreated behind her professional facade. She reminded herself there was a mission, a bigger cause. Yet the memory of that brief closeness warmed her as she prepared to drift into uneasy slumber.

Dawn arrived with a cold drizzle. The group packed up, guiding the Ark to the van once more. Orlov glared, wrists raw from handcuffs. A quick drive led them to the airport's cargo terminal, a dingy facility separate from the main passenger area. Dave and Helena approached a clerk behind a battered desk, forging a story about shipping "antique religious artifacts" for a museum in Istanbul. Ibrahim spoke with a cargo handler in the background, exchanging hush money. Yusef and Lombardi hovered near the chest, arcs spitting static whenever airport staff came too close.

Miraculously, the staff accepted the bribes and assigned them a cargo flight departing in two hours. The Ark was loaded onto a large shipping crate labeled "Fragile Sacred Items," with the infiltration team listed as official escorts. The plan was to board the same plane, though the pilot insisted on minimal passengers. Orlov remained bound, disguised as a "medical patient" requiring sedation.

It was an insane arrangement, but the local staff seemed too apathetic or underpaid to question further. As the crate was wheeled away, Helena's heart pounded, worried illusions might flare in the loading bay. Lombardi tried chanting discretely, voice raspy. The chest glimmered beneath the crate's partially open lid, arcs snapping. A forklift driver yelped at the sparks, but chalked it up to static from the cold, then quickly taped the crate shut.

Soon, the infiltration group gathered near the cargo plane, a mid-sized aircraft used for shipping freight. The pilot, a gruff man in oil-stained overalls, eyed their paperwork with a shrug. "Keep your artifact under control," he muttered in broken English. "No more. I fly to Istanbul, drop you off. That's it."

They boarded a small passenger section behind the cockpit, seats reeking of old upholstery. Orlov was strapped in next to Dave, scowling. Yusef and Lombardi sat across, the priest still trembling from exhaustion. Ibrahim settled behind them, while Helena took a seat near the plane's window, relief and dread swirling inside her.

Engines revved. The cargo plane rumbled down the runway, heavy with crates. Within minutes, they ascended into gray skies. Helena stared out, the farmland below shrinking to patches. They were heading to Istanbul, the city bridging Europe and Asia, a crossroads where perhaps they'd locate that missing Crusader text. The Ark rattled in the hold, arcs presumably subdued by Lombardi's half-dozing prayers.

As the plane leveled, Helena eased back in her seat, body stiff with fatigue. Dave gave her a small smile from across the aisle. Despite the tension, a glimmer of hope flickered. If they reached Istanbul, maybe the final lines awaited. Then they could calm the Ark once and for all, ending this relentless cycle of chaos and violence.

Orlov muttered curses, prompting Dave to tighten the handcuffs. Yusef observed, his gaze distant. The plane droned on, carrying them over the Eastern European landscape. Each moment brought them closer to a city that held centuries of secrets. Helena prayed those secrets would yield the missing piece they needed, or the entire world might face unstoppable ruin.

The flight wore on. Father Lombardi's chanting faded to a hoarse whisper. Dave advised him to rest, and the priest reluctantly complied, letting the Ark remain sealed in its crate. Helena felt faint ripples of tension in the air, but no supernatural disturbances. Perhaps the chest required more direct provocation to unleash its power—or perhaps it was simply waiting.

Some hours later, the pilot announced the final descent. The sprawling lights of Istanbul twinkled through the windows. The sight of minarets rising alongside modern skyscrapers reminded Helena of the city's layered history—Roman, Byzantine, Ottoman, each leaving indelible marks. She inhaled, bracing for the next phase of their quest.

The plane touched down at a smaller cargo airfield on Istanbul's outskirts, well away from the main international airport. Night cloaked the runways, with only a few lights marking the perimeter. The pilot taxied to a remote hangar before cutting the engines. Two local men in security uniforms approached, apparently part of the arrangement. Dave stepped out first, scanning their surroundings with practiced caution.

The infiltration team disembarked, Orlov in tow. Lombardi suggested they store the Ark in a secured hangar temporarily. Helena hesitated, uneasy about the risk of disturbances if the chest was handled too much. But they needed to clear customs—or at least an improvised version of it—and keeping the relic sealed for the time being seemed like the only practical option.

A forklift offloaded the crate onto a trolley. Helena followed anxiously, ignoring the suspicious glares of the local men. Dave paid them off, and they grudgingly wheeled the chest to a corner of the hangar. Father Lombardi discreetly resumed his chant, though his voice cracked after every few words. Orlov scoffed, bound to a pillar. Ibrahim and Yusef hovered, scanning the gloom for sentries.

Helena felt the oppressive weight of exhaustion and unrelenting danger. But they'd reached Istanbul. Now came the hardest part: discovering the lost Crusader text, finishing the Ark's ceremony, and preventing further catastrophe. A swirl of contradictory emotions battered her—fear, determination, guilt over those who died or were wounded along the way.

In the corner of the hangar, the Ark sparked faintly, arcs dancing under the crate's half-open lid. Dave put a steadying hand on Helena's shoulder, meeting her gaze. "We made it. Next, we find that manuscript."

She nodded, adrenaline spiking at the possibilities. "Yes, we will." Then she turned to Lombardi. "Father, gather your contacts. We need every lead on that Crusader record or any similar text. We can't keep chanting forever."

He closed his eyes, murmuring a final snippet of prayer, then nodded. "I'll do whatever it takes. The Church's archives may hold a clue. Or local antiquities dealers might know rumors."

Dave faced Orlov. "You'll remain our prisoner, Colonel, until we figure out next steps. Don't try anything foolish."

Orlov grunted, though a sinister glint lingered in his stare. Helena suspected he might attempt an escape or sabotage, driven by fanatical devotion to Russia's glory. She steeled herself for further conflict.

At last, they exhaled. The infiltration group had come full circle, once again holding the Ark, once again uncertain who might come for it next—maybe Russia, maybe China, maybe others. The city's lights beckoned beyond the hangar walls, hinting at labyrinthine streets where secrets lurked. She felt the Ark's presence even more strongly here, as if crossing continents had stirred deeper energies.

Somewhere in this vast metropolis, a lost Crusader text might hold the key to pacifying the Ark's restless energies. If they failed to find it, no safe corner on earth would shield them from the relic's escalating power—or from the ravenous factions eager to claim it. Helena inhaled, swallowing her nerves. The next few days would test them beyond measure, but she had no choice except to press forward.

This was the path they had chosen, the mission thrust upon them by fate and moral duty. She closed her eyes for a moment, haunted by the swirling phantoms that had nearly shattered Orlov's mind and the countless ambushes that had brought them to the brink. The Ark's hum vibrated in the background, a reminder of its volatile presence.

They had survived Russia, slipped through borders, and evaded the Ark's unpredictable manifestations. Now Istanbul awaited—a city bridging worlds, teeming with hidden archives and opportunistic relic hunters. She turned to Dave, finding solace in his steady determination. Father Lombardi rubbed his tired eyes, murmuring about contacting local Jesuits for assistance. Ibrahim checked his phone for coverage, brow furrowed. Yusef stood near the crate, his foot tapping anxiously against the floor.

The final lines of the ceremony were out there. She felt it in her gut. They would find them or die trying, because the alternative was allowing the Ark's unrestrained might to engulf everything. She squared her shoulders. "Let's do this," she whispered, voice steady despite the turmoil inside.

And so they prepared to vanish into the maze of Istanbul's byways, Ark in tow, one step closer to uncovering a remedy for the relic's weather-scarred wrath. Allies were scarce, enemies many. But at least they'd come this far together, forging a fragile hope that somewhere amid old manuscripts and secret libraries, they'd discover the key to end the Ark's destructive path—and possibly salvage their own souls in the process.

Chapter 11

Istanbul – Present Day

Early morning fog clung to the edges of Istanbul's cargo airport, shrouding the drab hangar where Dr. Helena Carter and her companions had taken refuge. They had arrived mere hours ago, smuggling the Ark of the Covenant in a battered shipping container. Despite the frantic nature of their overnight flight, they managed a meager rest on cots and blankets. Now, faint sunlight glimmered through gaps in the hangar's corrugated walls, revealing the group's haggard faces.

Dave Schumer leaned against a metal post, keeping a discreet watch on Colonel Nikolai Orlov—still bound at the wrists, fury etched into every line of his posture. Father Aurelius Lombardi stood by the Ark's makeshift crate, lips moving in a subdued chant. Each syllable trembled with fatigue. The priest's voice managed to hold the relic's strange manifestations at bay for now, though arcs of electricity occasionally flickered across the gilded surface. Yusef Nasir paced near a rusting workbench, his shoulders knotted with tension, while Ibrahim Mahdi hovered by the hangar door, scanning the runway for any sign of trouble.

Helena took a moment to gather her thoughts. They had braved countless miles, border crossings, and last-minute bribes to bring the Ark to Turkey, hoping to uncover a lost Crusader manuscript rumored to contain the final lines of a ceremony that might neutralize the relic's devastating power. Without that text, Father Lombardi's partial chanting was their only defense against the Ark's disruptive forces, and the priest was nearing collapse.

She stepped toward the Jesuit. "Father, you can't keep this up forever. We need to find a better solution."

He gave a weary nod, letting his chant fade for a breath. "I've contacted a local Jesuit scholar, Father Renaud, who resides in the old quarter of the city. If anyone can confirm the existence of that Crusader manuscript in Istanbul, it's him."

"Did he give you specifics?" Dave asked, shifting his gaze from Orlov to Lombardi.

The priest dabbed his brow, eyes rimmed with exhaustion. "We only spoke briefly by phone. He said he might know a private collector with a trove of medieval relics. Possibly the text you seek. We have to meet him in person."

Yusef halted his pacing. "So that's our plan? We walk into the city with a giant golden chest?"

Helena managed a strained half-smile. "Certainly not. We'll hide the Ark in a safe spot. Then a few of us will meet Father Renaud, see if he can confirm where that Crusader text might be found. If it's truly here, we need to chase it down fast."

Ibrahim folded his arms. "And Colonel Orlov? We can't just leave him tied up in this hangar."

At the sound of his name, the Russian operative lifted his head, gaze brimming with contempt. "Take me along," he snarled. "I might be of use. My intelligence contacts here are extensive."

Dave's voice held a note of warning. "And you'd betray us the moment you got the chance. Let's be honest."

Orlov's lip curled. "You may have wrested the Ark from me, but my men are not far behind. If I don't check in, they'll hunt you. At least if I'm with you, I can... moderate their response."

Helena frowned. She sensed a trap in Orlov's offer—he could easily tip off his allies to seize the Ark again. But his presence might deter a violent confrontation, or at least buy them time. The question was whether the risk outweighed the benefit.

Father Lombardi released a quiet exhale, returning to his chanting for a few beats as the Ark's arcs brightened. Electricity danced over the crate, crackling in the stale air. The relic stirred each time they paused to weigh decisions. Helena's heartbeat quickened.

"Whatever we do," she said firmly, "we can't keep the Ark in the open. Maybe we rent a secure storage facility under false credentials. Lock it up. Keep Father Lombardi on standby to recite partial verses if its energy flares."

Dave nodded. "We'll also need to keep Orlov under guard. We can't trust him alone with the Ark—or with a phone."

Ibrahim stepped closer to the door. "Let me make inquiries about a short-term warehouse or locked garage on the outskirts. We can stash the chest for a day or two. Meanwhile, a small team meets with Father Renaud in the old quarter."

Helena brushed a stray lock of hair from her forehead. "Let's do that. Yusef and I can accompany Dave. Lombardi should stay near the Ark—unless you think meeting Renaud yourself is better, Father?"

The Jesuit's eyes flickered with conflict. "I'd prefer to greet Renaud personally, but I'm the only one who can keep its disturbances in check. If we leave the Ark in a secure place, it might remain stable as long as no one tampers with it. But there's a risk."

Helena considered the trade-off. If Lombardi left the Ark behind, its volatile energy could spiral if someone jostled or disturbed it. On the other hand, having him along could be invaluable for interpreting old texts. She studied his drawn face, recalling how precarious his chanting had become.

"Stay with the relic," she decided, compassion softening her tone. "We can't risk a meltdown if its power breaks loose."

He gave a reluctant nod, letting out a weary sigh. "Bring back any lead you find. And if there's a library or collector's estate, I can join later."

"Agreed," said Dave. "We'll keep Orlov at the Ark site, chained to something solid. Ibrahim can stand watch. Yusef, Helena, and I will see Father Renaud."

Orlov let out a derisive laugh, though he offered no further comment. In his eyes, Helena glimpsed the smolder of resentment. She steeled herself for potential betrayal. There was no good solution, only lesser evils.

Within the hour, Ibrahim managed to rent a small warehouse stall through a local contact. The infiltration group loaded the Ark into a battered van, covering it with a tarp. Father Lombardi muttered his partial rite under his breath while they drove across the sprawling metropolis. Icy wind swept over the Bosphorus, ferry horns echoing across misty waters. Yusef stared at the passing minarets and modern skyscrapers, his posture tense.

Eventually, they reached a cramped industrial zone near the city's edge. The warehouse stall was little more than a steel enclosure with a sturdy lock. Not ideal, but the best they could manage on short notice. Inside, they placed the Ark on a heavy table. Lombardi directed them to wedge crates around it to keep it from shifting. The arcs hissed, though the priest's whispered Latin kept them contained.

"Stay put, Colonel," Dave growled, hauling Orlov to a thick metal post. He snapped handcuffs around the Russian's wrists, looping a chain through an improvised padlock. Orlov bared his teeth, but the threat in Dave's eyes stopped him from struggling.

Ibrahim placed a final chain around the crate's lid, ensuring no one could pry it open easily. Father Lombardi sank onto a folding chair, sweat beading on his brow. "I'll remain here, keep an eye on illusions," he panted. "Ibrahim, watch Orlov. Use the radio if trouble arises."

The liaison nodded grimly. "If he tries anything, I won't hesitate to lock him in a closet or worse."

Helena eyed the priest. "You have enough supplies? Food, water?"

Lombardi gestured to a small cooler. "Yes, for now. Hurry back with information."

Dave, Helena, and Yusef gave final instructions, then slipped out into the Istanbul afternoon. The trio caught a taxi near a main road, heading into the time-worn heart of the city. As they weaved through chaotic traffic, the teen pressed himself against the window, watching the swirl of people and color. Helena picked up on Yusef's restlessness. The repeated violence had clearly worn him down.

Dave noticed too. In a quiet moment, he said, "You can wait at the hotel if this is too much."

Yusef shook his head. "I've come this far. I want to see this text discovered. If it helps calm the Ark, it's worth it."

Helena felt a swell of admiration for his tenacity. She gently patted his shoulder. "We appreciate it."

They arrived at the old quarter—a maze of narrow alleys, historic buildings, and bustling shops. Minarets rose overhead, the call to prayer echoing. Father Renaud's instructions led them to a centuries-old church set back from a busy market square. Ivy clung to its stone walls, and a simple wooden door marked the entrance.

Inside, rows of pews glowed under stained glass. A few worshippers knelt in silent prayer, oblivious to Helena's group. They approached a side door, knocked lightly. Footsteps approached from within. A small man in a faded cassock opened the door, scarred face lighting with recognition.

"You must be the visitors Father Lombardi mentioned," he said in accented English. "I'm Father Renaud. Please, come through."

He guided them into a modest office crammed with shelves of centuries-old tomes, letters, and religious artifacts. Dust motes danced in the dim lamplight. Yusef lingered by the threshold, wary of the cramped space. Dave stood behind Helena, scanning for any sign of subterfuge.

The older Jesuit motioned for them to sit. "Lombardi told me you seek a Crusader manuscript referencing a sacred rite."

Helena leaned forward. "Yes. We have partial lines from a ceremony that might quell the Ark of the Covenant's destructive illusions. Rumor says a Crusader text was smuggled here centuries ago, containing the missing lines. We hope it still exists."

Father Renaud stroked his chin. "Crusader relics pass through Istanbul's collectors often. Some are fakes, others real. You might speak with a man named Nuri Bektas. He's a dealer in medieval artifacts, known for his private network. If the text is here, Bektas might have heard."

Dave glanced at Helena, silent question in his eyes. She nodded to the Jesuit. "Do you trust him? We've dealt with unscrupulous brokers before."

The priest sighed. "Trust is difficult in these circles. Bektas values profit above all, but he has no love for violent factions. He might help if you can match his price. I have an address for his shop in the Grand Bazaar district. It's not on the main thoroughfare—an old hidden arcade, in fact."

Yusef perked up. "The Grand Bazaar? I've heard stories about those endless stalls. Easy to get lost."

Renaud handed Helena a small slip of paper. "Take care. Bektas is cunning, and you might face competition. Others want relics too." He paused, gaze flicking to Dave's tense stance. "I sense you're pressed for time. Nuri is your best lead."

Helena murmured thanks, then asked if Father Renaud had any direct knowledge of the Crusader text. The old man shook his head. "Only rumors of a torn manuscript describing a 'Song of the Cherubim.' If it's genuine, it might hold the lines you need. That's all I know."

They exchanged brief courtesies. Dave left a small donation for the church, and the trio stepped back into the labyrinth of Istanbul's streets.

Late afternoon sun gleamed on centuries-old cobblestones. Shoppers wove around them, the air thick with the scent of coffee and spiced meats.

Helena consulted the slip of paper. "Bektas... here's the address. Let's get a taxi."

Yusef eyed the swirling crowds. "Could be faster to walk. The alleyways might cut our travel time."

Dave scanned the throng. "True, but we might also get lost. We'll hail a cab, keep it simpler."

They hopped into a battered taxi, weaving through traffic toward the Grand Bazaar's warren of alleys. The driver dropped them on a side street where vendors hawked jewelry, spices, and textiles. Shouts in Turkish filled the air. The trio navigated narrower passages, fighting claustrophobia from the mass of bodies.

At last, they found a small arched entrance marked only by a worn metal sign. Inside, the corridor led to a quiet arcade where a handful of antique shops nestled behind wooden shutters. The sign for "Nuri Bektas Antika" hung crooked above a faded door.

Helena's pulse quickened. She inhaled, pushing open the door. A bell jingled. The shop's interior was dim, every surface cluttered with old manuscripts, relics, and peculiar statuary. Behind a counter piled with leather-bound tomes stood a tall man with salt-and-pepper hair, wearing half-moon glasses. He straightened, eyes flicking over them with curiosity.

"Good afternoon," he greeted in lightly accented English. "What antiques might interest you?"

Dave stepped aside, letting Helena speak. She approached the counter, carefully choosing her words. "We were referred by Father Renaud. He said you might help us find a particular medieval text—a Crusader manuscript containing references to a 'Song of Cherubim.'"

Nuri Bektas pursed his lips. "Father Renaud? I see. The old priest rarely sends me customers, so this must be important." He arched a brow. "What do you know of this text?"

Yusef fidgeted behind Helena, scanning the piles of dusty scrolls. Dave remained near the door, arms crossed, ready to intercept trouble.

Helena explained in cautious terms. "We suspect it has lines describing how to calm a powerful relic. The partial text calls it a Song or Hymn involving cherubim. We believe a Crusader brought it here centuries ago."

Bektas nodded, tapping his chin. "I've heard rumors of such a fragment. The last I recall, a portion of that script changed hands among private collectors. Not displayed openly. Many consider it mere legend. Do you have funds for such a piece?"

She felt a pang of worry. Their finances were limited. "We might. But we need to confirm authenticity first. Do you have leads on who might hold it?"

He chuckled dryly. "Leads cost money, my friend." Then his tone shifted, eyes narrowing. "And you should know, others are looking. Word around the bazaar says a Chinese representative has been asking about Crusader relics too. Possibly the same text."

Dave tensed at mention of a Chinese operative. Helena recalled that Ming Xia from Beijing had previously shown interest in the Ark. A chill crept over her skin. The Chinese might be closing in.

"Name your price," Helena said.

Bektas steepled his fingers. "One thousand euros for an introduction to the current holder. After that, you negotiate separately for the manuscript."

Yusef's eyes widened. Dave looked unimpressed but said nothing. Helena nodded, pulling out a wad of bills. "We'll pay half now, half if the lead proves genuine."

A flicker of annoyance crossed Bektas's face, though he eventually shrugged. "Very well. Return at dusk. I'll arrange a meeting with the rumored owner, a private collector who rarely sees visitors. If all goes well, you'll get your text. But be warned: this collector is paranoid, especially with foreign interests circling."

With that, the dealer jotted an address on a scrap of parchment. "Meet me at this café. We'll go together. Bring the rest of my fee. And come armed if you like—this part of town can be rough."

Helena handed over a portion of the euros. Bektas's lips curved in a half-smile, slipping the money into a drawer. "I'll see you at dusk."

Outside, the trio exchanged uneasy looks. "We have a lead," Dave murmured. "But if the Chinese are sniffing around, we might be walking into a trap."

Yusef stared at the swirling crowd, voice tight. "We can't back down. The Ark can't wait."

She brushed hair from her eyes, exhaustion pulsing. "We'll do it. Let's return to Lombardi, let him know. We have a few hours to prepare."

They found a taxi and retraced their route to the industrial warehouse. On arrival, they discovered Ibrahim pacing near the entrance, brows knitted. Inside, Father Lombardi sat with the Ark, chanting in intervals.

Orlov was still chained, though he smirked at the group's return. The relic glowed, arcs sporadic but still menacing.

Helena explained the contact with Bektas and the plan to meet at dusk. Lombardi looked torn. "I should join you. If the Ark's disturbances escalate at the warehouse, who will keep them in check?"

Ibrahim raised a hand. "I'll do my best. The Ark might stay calm if no one tampers with it. I can always phone you if its energy becomes unstable."

Father Lombardi grimaced, then nodded reluctantly. "I can't recite all night again. The ceremony is incomplete. Fine. I'll accompany you."

Dave faced Orlov. "We leave you here, Colonel. If you cause trouble, you'll regret it."

The Russian operative sneered. "I suggest you watch for my men, who will find me eventually. Unless you foolishly think this city is beyond their reach."

Ibrahim brandished his pistol. "You'll remain cuffed, friend. I'll keep my phone in hand."

Orlov didn't reply, though his glare promised future vengeance.

As dusk approached, Helena, Dave, Yusef, and Lombardi took a taxi to the rendezvous. The city shimmered under streetlamps. The four sat in tense silence, each carrying minimal firearms or supplies. They arrived at a cramped alley near a humble café with a worn sign. Nuri Bektas stood waiting by the door, wearing a dark coat and a reserved smile.

He greeted them briskly, eyes flicking to Lombardi's collar. "You brought a priest. Unusual. Let's not dally."

Inside the café, flickering neon lights revealed a mostly empty space: a few patrons sipping tea, a bored waiter by the counter. Bektas led them to a side booth. "The collector insists on privacy. We'll drive to his place in separate cars. No large force, or he'll vanish."

Dave exchanged a look with Helena, wary but resolved. She handed the dealer the second half of his fee. He inspected the bills, nodded. "Good. Follow me."

They slipped out the café's rear exit, piling into two unmarked sedans arranged by Bektas. Father Lombardi and Yusef took the back seat of the first car with the antiquities dealer. Helena and Dave sat in the second vehicle, driven by a silent man who wore tinted glasses even in the evening gloom.

Streets blurred past in a labyrinth of old walls and modern highways. They eventually emerged into a quieter district, where crumbling mansions and overgrown gardens hinted at faded wealth. The car turned down a narrow lane, halting before a high gate. Armed men in suits stood nearby, scanning them with suspicion. Bektas's driver flashed a pass, and the gates opened with a squeal.

Behind the walls, a large courtyard sprawled under starlight. A tall, decrepit mansion loomed, windows dark. Lanterns lined a gravel path. The cars parked near a chipped fountain, watery reflections dancing. Helena's chest tightened with anticipation—this must be the collector's domain.

They exited, the entire group forming a cluster behind Bektas. Father Lombardi offered Yusef a reassuring nod, the teen stiff with nerves. Dave kept a discreet grip on his concealed sidearm. The hush felt thick, as though sentries hid behind every column.

Bektas led them inside through a grand wooden door. The foyer glowed with candlelit sconces, revealing peeling wallpaper, dusty rugs, and an air of decayed luxury. Two more armed men hovered in corners. In a large parlor beyond, a fireplace crackled. Next to that fire stood a slender figure clad in a velvet robe, his dark hair slicked back—likely their mysterious host.

The robed man turned, assessing them with hooded eyes. "Welcome," he said. "I am Beyzim, caretaker of these treasures. Nuri tells me you seek a Crusader manuscript. I may have such a piece. But I must verify your intentions."

Helena stepped forward. "We're scholars and... custodians of a biblical relic. We need the text's final lines to prevent dangerous manifestations. It's a matter of urgent necessity."

Beyzim's expression didn't change, though a hint of curiosity glimmered. "Dangerous manifestations? Fascinating. I've heard rumors of a relic that can conjure visions. Are you implying you actually possess this item?"

Dave's tone hardened. "We do. And if we don't complete the ceremony, it might trigger widespread havoc. Please, let's not waste time."

Beyzim nodded. "I see. Let me show you something. Then we'll discuss price."

He clapped his hands. A servant stepped in with a heavy wooden box. Setting it on a table, the servant unlocked it, revealing a protective wrapping. Inside lay a battered parchment, edges charred, medieval Latin scrawled across it. Helena's heart pounded. The writing style resembled what she'd seen in the partial lines. She exchanged a hopeful look with Lombardi, who inched closer, adjusting his spectacles.

Beyzim lifted the parchment carefully, displaying passages illuminated with faintly visible cherubim motifs. Lombardi's breath caught. "This... may indeed be the Crusader fragment. The phrase 'Cantus Cherubim' appears here. The script is archaic, 12th century perhaps."

Helena's pulse soared. They had found it, or so it seemed. "Is the portion referencing the final lines of the cherubim ceremony?" she asked, voice trembling with excitement.

Beyzim inclined his head. "Potentially. Let's see." He let Lombardi study the text. The priest's eyes danced over the Latin. Dave hovered protectively, in case this was a bait-and-switch. Yusef peered over Lombardi's shoulder, though he likely couldn't read the language.

Moments stretched. Lombardi's face lit with cautious triumph. "Yes. This text describes a final invocation to calm the Ark's disturbances—a set of verses missing from the partial lines we've been using. This might be exactly what we need!"

Helena almost felt tears. Their chase across continents might be nearing success. She turned to Beyzim. "We'll buy it."

A thin smile graced the caretaker's lips. "Excellent. The cost is steep—fifty thousand euros."

A wave of dread. They didn't have that kind of cash. Dave stiffened. "We can't pay that sum. We can offer something else."

Beyzim's expression cooled. "Then we have no deal. Perhaps you can find another buyer... or watch the illusions continue."

Yusef's voice trembled. "People will die if the Ark remains unchecked. You'd let it happen over money?"

The caretaker's features showed no remorse. "I am a collector, not a philanthropist. If you can't pay, perhaps you have a relic to trade. Some valuable artifact?"

Helena froze. The Ark was infinitely more precious, but giving it away was absurd. They also possessed no lesser items. Dave spoke, "We can wire funds from certain accounts, though it may take time. Or we can negotiate installments."

Bektas hovered, smirking. "I might front part of the cost, for a share of... future discoveries?"

Tension spiked. Lombardi shot Helena a look, silently pleading for a solution. She felt cornered. Perhaps they could call Father Renaud or another ally, but that risked further exposure or delays. Meanwhile, the Ark's energy threatened to spiral out of control if Lombardi's chant faltered for too long.

Just as Helena opened her mouth to propose a compromise, an explosion of glass shattered from above. A black rope dropped into the parlor, and masked figures in dark attire rappelled down from a skylight. Shouts erupted. Gunfire ripped the silence. Dave tackled Helena behind a couch. Lombardi clutched the parchment, eyes wild. Bektas scrambled for cover. Beyzim shrieked, arms flailing. Yusef ducked, heart racing.

Amid the chaos, a voice boomed in Mandarin. The intruders wore tactical gear, faces obscured, their leader's stance poised and controlled. Helena's mind flashed: the Chinese operative, Ming Xia, might have arrived. The masked figure barked orders in Chinese, and two men advanced, submachine guns spraying bullets over the furniture. Wood splintered, dust choking the air.

Beyzim's security guards returned fire from the corridor, intensifying the fray. The caretaker cowered near a pillar, clutching the Crusader text with trembling hands. Bektas cursed, flattening himself behind an overturned table. Dave tried to return shots with his handgun, pinned down by the intruders' superior firepower.

Lombardi, gasping, realized in horror that the precious parchment lay in Beyzim's grasp. If they lost it now, the ceremony lines might vanish forever. Yusef spotted the caretaker crawling toward a side door, text clutched to his chest. The teen, adrenaline surging, leaped up, sprinting through the hail of bullets. He slid behind a toppled bookcase near Beyzim, calling out, "Wait—don't run!"

Beyzim, eyes ablaze with panic, hissed, "They'll kill us all. This text is worth a fortune. I'm not losing it." Then he lunged for a narrow hallway.

Shots tore through the air, shattering a vase overhead. Yusef ducked, flinching. Helena glimpsed him from across the parlor, fighting an urge to chase after him. Dave covered her, firing at two masked attackers. One crumpled, the other pivoted behind a column.

In the swirling smoke, a slender figure with a hood stepped forward. Ming Xia? The figure's posture carried a lethal calm, pivoting with twin handguns. She barked orders in Chinese, instructing her men to corner Helena's group. Dave recognized the stance from prior encounters. "It's her," he muttered, sliding behind a half-demolished bookshelf.

"Lombardi, hold onto the lines we copied," Helena hissed. The priest clutched a small notepad where he'd transcribed partial verses moments earlier. But the crucial original text was with Beyzim.

Shots thundered again. One bullet grazed Lombardi's arm, drawing a cry of pain. He stumbled behind a settee. Bektas tried to bolt for a hallway, only to be intercepted by two masked invaders, forcing him to drop with hands raised. The caretaker, Beyzim, had vanished. Yusef too was lost in the swirling dust.

Helena's heart hammered. If these Chinese operatives found the caretaker first, they might seize the Crusader text. She exhaled, scanning the battlefield. Dave's jaw clenched, reloading his pistol. The masked squad advanced, methodical. Another crash came from a side corridor. Possibly an external team entering.

She beckoned Lombardi with a frantic gesture. "We have to find Beyzim and Yusef, get that parchment. Dave, can you hold them off?"

He gave a tight nod. "Go. I'll buy time."

She scrambled around the perimeter, ducking behind fallen drapes. Blood pounded in her ears. The corridor yawned ahead, half choked with smoke from an overturned brazier. She glimpsed footprints on the dusty floor, small ones leading deeper into the gloom. Yusef's. She followed.

Behind her, the parlor echoed with more gunfire. She prayed Dave stayed safe. Lombardi crept at her side, breath ragged. A muffled shout echoed from up ahead. Helena pressed forward, pistol raised. Flames from the toppled brazier cast flickering shadows, revealing a scene in a small library annex: Beyzim cornered by three masked intruders, the parchment clutched in his trembling hands. Yusef crouched behind a desk, eyes wide with terror.

One intruder demanded, in broken English, "Give the text. We want it. Now."

Beyzim shook his head vehemently, gaze darting between the enemies. Helena's heart clenched—any misfire could destroy the precious document. She took a measured breath, signaled Lombardi to circle left. The priest clutched his own sidearm, though he looked pale from that bullet graze.

Crack. A gunshot from the intruders. Plaster chipped near Beyzim's shoulder. He yelped, nearly dropping the parchment. Yusef stifled a cry, pressing flatter to the floor.

Seizing the moment, Helena fired twice. One masked assailant dropped, the second spun around, returning wild shots. Lombardi fired once, though his aim wavered. The third attacker rushed forward, trying to yank the parchment from Beyzim. Helena lunged, tackled the intruder from behind, both crashing into a row of shelves. weather-scarred books rained down.

The masked figure twisted, elbowing her in the ribs. She gasped, reeling. He raised his weapon. Before he could pull the trigger, Yusef sprang up, swinging a wooden stool at the attacker's arm. A crack echoed, the pistol clattering away. Helena rolled free, breathing hard. She glimpsed Lombardi confronting the second attacker, who was pinned behind an upended chest.

Beyzim, meanwhile, attempted to slip out a side door. "Wait!" Helena shouted. "Stop!"

Panicked, the caretaker dashed for the corridor. Lombardi's opponent fired at the same instant, bullet grazing Helena's shoulder. She bit back a scream, staggered. Another shot hammered into the wall by Yusef's head. The teen dropped, shaking.

Lombardi aimed again. The second attacker jerked from a bullet to the torso, collapsing. The corridor fell silent, broken only by the caretaker's retreating footsteps.

Helena pressed a hand to her bleeding shoulder, wincing. Yusef scuttled over. "You're hurt," he breathed.

"Just a graze," she rasped, though pain flared. "We need that parchment. Lombardi, you okay?"

The priest nodded shakily, blood staining his sleeve from earlier. "We can't let Beyzim vanish."

They hurried after the caretaker, leaving the masked attackers groaning or still. Smoke from the parlor spread, choking the hallway. Dim emergency lights flickered. In the distance, gunfire indicated Dave still battled a portion of the Chinese squad.

Halfway down, they found a side exit ajar. Moonlight spilled across a small courtyard. Beyzim rushed toward a gate, parchment clutched to his chest. Helena pushed aside the pang in her shoulder, summoning a burst of speed. "Stop!" she yelled, voice echoing.

Beyzim spun, eyes wild with desperation. "Stay back! This is mine. I'll sell it to whoever pays best."

Lombardi lifted a shaking pistol. "We need it to save countless lives."

Before either side could act, more figures emerged from the shadows: men in black suits, brandishing silenced weapons. They moved with swift coordination, fanning out around the caretaker.

In the courtyard's pale light, a lean woman in a fitted coat stepped forward, calm authority in her stance. Ming Xia. She removed her face mask, revealing poised features and cool eyes. "Beyzim," she said in clear English, "hand me that scroll. We pay twice what they offer."

Beyzim's breath caught. He glanced between Ming Xia's lethal squad and Helena's battered duo. Yusef hovered in the background, trying not to tremble. Lombardi, gun extended, realized they were outnumbered. Ming Xia's stoic expression held no mercy.

"Don't do this," Helena pleaded, ignoring the sting in her arm. "If the text falls into the wrong hands, the Ark's power could tear cities apart. You know about that relic, don't you?"

Ming Xia's lips curved into a faint smile. "China's interests require that we understand and control such power. The phenomena are a concern, but with proper research, we can contain them. Step aside."

Helena refused to lower her gun. Lombardi's chanting to suppress the Ark's disturbances had ceased. She feared if the relic were here, it might erupt with uncontrollable visions. But they'd left it under guard, so at least that catastrophe was avoided—for now.

Beyzim looked torn, evaluating who might be the winning side. "Perhaps... we can negotiate," he murmured, though greed shone in his eyes.

Ming Xia raised a hand, and her men aimed weapons. "We don't negotiate. Hand it over."

Helena's pulse thundered. She saw no easy escape. Yusef edged closer, jaw set. Lombardi swallowed, voice shaking. "God help us."

Suddenly, a new volley of shots rang from the gate. Dave burst in, battered and breathing hard, sliding behind a stone trough for cover. Two Chinese operatives spun to return fire. Dave's hail of bullets forced them to duck. "Helena!" he shouted. "We need that text!"

Chaos erupted anew. Ming Xia shouted commands in Mandarin, her men fanning out. Helena seized her chance. She lunged toward Beyzim, ignoring the pain in her arm. The caretaker shrieked, trying to dodge. She grabbed the parchment with her free hand, even as Ming Xia's soldier drew a bead on her.

A shot cracked. Helena flinched, certain she was finished, but Yusef slammed into the soldier from the side, spoiling the aim. The bullet whistled past, pinging off the stone courtyard. Lombardi scrambled to assist, though his own injuries slowed him.

Ming Xia cursed, fluidly pivoting to aim at Dave, who ducked behind the trough. Helena's grip tightened on the precious paper. She locked eyes with Beyzim, who tried to claw it back. Her injured shoulder screamed in protest, but she twisted away, kicking out. He stumbled, cursing in Turkish.

One of Ming Xia's men pinned Yusef to the ground, pressing a pistol to the teen's temple. Yusef gasped, face twisted in terror. "Don't—" he choked out. Helena's stomach plunged. She paused, parchment in hand. If she kept running, they might kill him.

Ming Xia's eyes flashed. "Drop the scroll or the boy dies."

Helena froze, heart hammering. Lombardi hovered behind her, torn between saving Yusef and preserving the text. Dave, pinned by gunfire, couldn't get a clean shot.

"Drop it," the Chinese operative repeated coldly. "Now."

Yusef uttered a choked whimper. Helena closed her eyes, tears threatening. She couldn't trade the teen's life for the parchment. With trembling fingers, she let the weather-scarred pages slip from her grip, fluttering to the stones.

Ming Xia's soldier snatched it up, pressing a knee into Yusef's back. Relief flickered in the teen's eyes that he was still alive, but their mission was in tatters. The illusions would remain unstoppable without that final script.

A sudden roar erupted from the courtyard gate—an engine revving. Headlights blazed, illuminating the scene. The side of a dilapidated cargo truck crashed through the fence. Chinese operatives scattered. Dave rolled aside, stifling a cry of surprise. The vehicle skidded in a half-spin, flinging the door open.

Bektas leaned out from the cab, waving a pistol. "Get in!" he yelled, eyes wild. Possibly he saw a chance to salvage a profit or help them out for reasons unknown.

Yusef seized the distraction, elbowing the soldier who pinned him. The operative's shot went wide. Helena lunged to yank the teen free, ignoring the pain in her shoulder. Lombardi fired once at Ming Xia, who ducked fluidly. Dave sprinted forward, tackling another attacker.

In the confusion, the caretaker Beyzim lunged for the parchment again, hoping to grab it from the soldier's hand. Shots thundered. The air reeked of gunpowder. Helena's vision blurred. Then a hail of bullets from the truck's window forced the Chinese to scatter for cover. Ming Xia cursed in Mandarin, ordering a retreat.

The soldier holding the parchment hesitated, then followed orders, tossing the battered pages into a side satchel. Helena's heart lurched. They had it. The illusions remained unstoppable. The man sprinted after Ming Xia, vaulting over rubble. In seconds, the squad vanished into the battered mansion's shadows, leaving Helena's team bruised and empty-handed.

Bektas hollered again from the truck, bullets riddling the stone courtyard around him. "This place is lost! Get in, quick!"

Yusef stood dazed. Lombardi grabbed him, steering him to the passenger side. Dave fired a final burst at retreating figures, then tugged Helena, who nearly collapsed from her wounded shoulder. They piled into the cargo bed, panting, as Bektas slammed the accelerator. The engine growled, headlights sweeping across the courtyard. The caretaker Beyzim was nowhere to be seen—perhaps he fled or was gunned down.

Within moments, they roared back through the gates, leaving the mansion behind. The wind stung Helena's face. She clutched Dave's arm, tears burning in her eyes. They'd lost the precious Crusader manuscript to Ming Xia's men. The Ark's unpredictable forces would remain unchecked.

Lombardi slumped, head in his hands. "We were so close."

Dave wrapped an arm around Helena, his expression grim. Yusef sat curled in the corner, face pale. Bektas, at the wheel, cursed under his breath, perhaps lamenting his lost opportunity.

Night swallowed them as they sped through deserted streets. The city lights shimmered in the distance, an endless maze of possibilities—and lurking dangers. Helena's soul ached. Father Lombardi's partial chanting had been their lifeline. Without the final lines, the Ark's power would remain a looming menace. Worse, Ming Xia's Chinese faction now possessed the key to completing the ceremony. If they found a way to harness or replicate its supernatural phenomena, the consequences could be devastating.

In the swirling gloom, Helena thought of the Ark's latent energy and the priest's battered voice. Another confrontation loomed—perhaps with Ming Xia's faction or another group racing to exploit the relic's potential. The battered infiltration team had only heartbreak to show for their efforts here. Yet they couldn't stop. The Ark awaited them in that dingy warehouse, its volatile presence barely contained.

She leaned on Dave, her breath shaky. "What now?"

He gazed at her, stubble shadowing his jaw. "We regroup. We track Ming Xia. If her people have the text, we have to get it back—or find a way to negotiate. Otherwise, the Ark's power might tear the world apart."

Yusef lifted his head, eyes brimming with guilt. "I—I froze. I didn't do enough."

Helena reached for his hand. "You saved me from that bullet. Don't blame yourself."

Lombardi murmured a thread of Latin, though his voice quavered. "God help us," he repeated. They had staved off destruction once more, but the Ark's ultimate salvation lay in lines stolen away by a rival faction. The swirl of headlights across the battered truck bed illuminated their exhausted faces.

They pressed on through the night, battered hearts bracing for the next confrontation—because in Istanbul's labyrinth of secrets, the lines they needed still existed. Now, though, they belonged to an ambitious adversary who might harness or destroy them at will.

Chapter 12

Istanbul — Same Night

The headlights of the battered truck pierced the midnight gloom as Bektas guided the vehicle onto a deserted back street near the industrial warehouse. Potholes jostled Helena and the others in the cargo bed, each bump a reminder of their wounds and fresh defeat. Father Aurelius Lombardi cradled his injured arm, exhaustion etched into every line of his face. Yusef hunched beside him, knees drawn tight, replaying the debacle in that courtyard again and again.

Dave Schumer peered over the side, scanning for threats. The city skyline loomed in the distance, neon signs flickering. Helena's shoulder still throbbed from the bullet graze, but she focused on the immediate problem: they had lost the final lines of the ceremony to Ming Xia's squad. Now the only link to controlling the Ark's unpredictable phenomena might be in enemy hands. The relic itself waited in a rented stall, its volatile energy barely subdued by Lombardi's partial verses.

Bektas braked near the warehouse gate, scowling as he cut the engine. "That debacle—or whatever you want to call it—cost me a fortune. Not to mention it nearly killed me."

Helena rubbed her temples, her voice tight. "You saved us. I won't forget that. We'll compensate you somehow, once we regroup."

He muttered under his breath, clearly unconvinced, then lit a cigarette. "We're even, for now. I suggest you keep a low profile. If the Chinese and the caretaker's men are at odds, it'll send shockwaves through the black market."

With that, he waved them off. Dave helped Helena down, followed by Yusef and Lombardi. The Jesuit gave Bektas a terse nod of thanks. Before anyone could speak further, the dealer revved the engine and sped away into the night. They were left standing in the faint glow of a single streetlamp, the battered warehouse looming ahead.

"Ibrahim's inside, watching Orlov," Dave said. "Let's see if anything happened while we were gone."

They slipped into the warehouse, locking the door behind them. Dim overhead bulbs revealed an anxious Ibrahim, pistol in hand, standing guard near the Ark's crate. Colonel Orlov still sat cuffed to a heavy post, though now he had a small blanket tossed over his shoulders. The Russian operative's eyes narrowed when he saw the group's bedraggled state.

"Judging by your wounds, that excursion didn't go well," Orlov sneered, his voice rough.

Helena ignored him, crossing to the Ark. Soft arcs flickered along its gilded edges. Father Lombardi reached out, placing his palm near the surface. A faint hiss of static greeted him. He winced, then began chanting under his breath. The arcs dimmed to a low, steady pulse.

Dave set a hand on Ibrahim's shoulder. "Any disturbances while we were gone?"

The Israeli liaison shook his head. "Only mild static. Lombardi's chanting from earlier must've helped. No one tried to break in, though I heard suspicious cars driving past once."

Helena exhaled relief for that small blessing. Then she detailed the fias... meltdown they faced at the caretaker's mansion—how Ming Xia's men took the Crusader text. Ibrahim's face fell. Orlov's lips curled with cold amusement, as if reveling in their misfortune.

"So the Chinese have the final lines," Orlov mused. "Perhaps they'll handle the Ark more effectively than you lot."

Dave stepped forward, fists clenched. "They'll handle it by turning the Ark's power into a weapon. Hardly a solution."

The colonel made a mocking shrug. "Better them than your incompetent group. At least the Chinese operate with discipline."

Before Dave could retort, Helena laid a hand on his arm, drawing him aside. She was weary of Orlov's taunts. The immediate crisis was Father Lombardi's failing strength. The Jesuit needed rest, but if the Ark's disturbances surged, the entire structure might descend into a swirl of nightmarish chaos. Something had to change.

"We can't keep up this patchwork chanting," she whispered to Dave. "If the Chinese hold the finishing lines, maybe we can negotiate. Or break in and retrieve them. Or find another lead?"

He studied her bruised features, eyes dark with concern. "We have to try. Maybe Ming Xia will see reason. Or we track them. One way or another, that text is essential."

Across the warehouse, Yusef paced, emotions churning. He shot uneasy glances at Orlov, then drew closer to Helena. "I can't stand how many times we've resorted to guns. If the Ark's energy gets worse, more people will suffer." He paused, swallowing. "Maybe I should go home."

Her heart squeezed. "Yusef, you've helped us so much. But I understand if you want to step back."

A flicker of guilt washed over his features. "Part of me can't leave until we fix the Ark. Another part feels sick at the constant bloodshed."

Dave, overhearing, gently placed a hand on the teen's shoulder. "We'll do everything to minimize more violence. If you choose to leave, we won't stop you. But your knowledge and courage have been invaluable."

Yusef nodded, eyes moist. "I'll stay a bit longer. If there's a chance to stabilize the Ark, I need to see it through."

Nearby, Lombardi coughed, pressing a rag to the bullet graze on his arm. "I must rest. If the Ark's disturbances worsen, wake me. But please, we have to find a permanent solution soon."

Helena felt empathy and frustration swirl. She rummaged in a first-aid kit, cleaning and re-bandaging Lombardi's wound, then checking her own injured shoulder with Dave's help. The sting of antiseptic made her wince. She forced a shaky breath. Meanwhile, Ibrahim rummaged for extra blankets, preparing a corner for the priest to sleep.

In the hush that followed, Orlov cleared his throat. "Perhaps I can offer you a bargain, Dr. Carter." His tone dripped with sly intent.

She scowled, finishing her bandage. "What bargain?"

His mouth twisted. "You want the ceremony lines, correct? Russia has many means of infiltration. My men could intercept the Chinese text. If you release me, I'll assist in recovering it."

Dave bristled. "Let me guess, you'd vanish at the first chance."

Orlov shrugged, as though unaffected. "Do as you will, but time is running out. The Ark's disturbances will intensify. Without those lines, you're doomed."

Helena shut her eyes. She knew Orlov's words might hold partial truth. The Ark's volatile power was a ticking clock. But trusting him seemed suicidal. "We won't free you," she replied. "We'll find another way."

He let out a bitter laugh. "Then watch the Chinese reshape the Ark's energy to their advantage."

She tried to ignore his venom, focusing on Dave's earlier suggestion—negotiating with Ming Xia directly or launching a covert retrieval. Both sounded hopeless. The group's resources were spent, and each confrontation escalated. Another abrupt infiltration might cost more lives.

Eventually, they settled on a plan to glean leads on the Chinese presence in Istanbul. If Ming Xia had a base of operations, perhaps they could approach discreetly. Dave volunteered to search for local intelligence contacts in the city, leveraging American networks. Ibrahim promised to do the same with Israeli channels, though the short notice and hush-hush nature made it difficult.

They agreed to rotate watch shifts through the night, giving Lombardi a chance to rest. Helena set up a small folding chair near the Ark's crate, her pistol within easy reach. The arcs glowed faintly, casting dancing shadows on the dusty floor. She stole a moment's respite, letting Dave's presence anchor her. He sat beside her, scanning the dim corners for threats.

"I can't believe we came so close to the final lines, only to lose them," she murmured, voice barely above a whisper.

Dave touched her uninjured shoulder. "We'll figure it out." His expression softened, eyes reflecting compassion. "You should rest too."

She let out a soft, humorless laugh. "We're each too battered to fight the Ark's effects at this point." Then, quieter, "I can't shake the memory of how that caretaker squealed when the gunfire erupted. The mania in his eyes. Everything in that mansion felt wrong."

Dave exhaled, scanning Orlov dozing in the corner. "This entire mission has felt like a race through nightmares."

Their gaze held for a moment, a delicate hush amid the gloom. She let her head rest against his shoulder, inhaling his warmth. In that fleeting space, the weight of the Ark's disturbances, Chinese squads, or Orlov's scheming faded. Her heart fluttered, recalling how close they'd become since first crossing paths under Temple Mount's crumbling stones.

He lightly brushed her hair. "We'll keep going," he said, voice husky. "Let's get that final text from Ming Xia's circle, one way or another."

She closed her eyes, leaning into him. "Yes. Together."

They sat like that, hearts in fragile unison, until Helena drifted into uneasy slumber. Dreams replayed glimpses of winged cherubim swirling overhead, intangible swords of light slicing the darkness. She awoke with a start to the warehouse's hush, arcs from the Ark still pulsing. Dave had dozed off as well, chin on his chest. Time had crept toward dawn. Yusef patrolled near the door, bleary-eyed, while Ibrahim half-dozed by Orlov.

Father Lombardi lay on a makeshift cot, rhythmic breathing a sign of his fitful rest.

Morning arrived with faint sunbeams filtering through high windows, dust swirling in the golden rays. Helena's limbs felt stiff, battered shoulder aching. She forced herself upright, ignoring the swirl of hunger. The infiltration team had little in the way of supplies. Each passing hour demanded a new plan for food, water, and keeping energy contained.

Ibrahim made calls to obscure Israeli contacts, gleaning scraps of data about Chinese movements in Istanbul. Dave tried the same with American covert channels, stepping outside for a stronger phone signal. Yusef rummaged in a battered backpack for leftover bread, distributing stale chunks around. Lombardi opened his eyes, rubbed them, and resumed a faint chant when arcs on the Ark's lid brightened.

Hours trickled by, tension mounting. Finally, Dave returned from a phone call. His expression was guarded. "My contact says Ming Xia set up a temporary safe house in an old consulate building near the Golden Horn. They're likely planning to depart soon—maybe heading east again. If that text is with them, we have a short window to intervene."

Yusef swallowed, recalling the last fias... meltdown. "Intervene how? Storm their base? We're just a handful of people, exhausted and short on ammunition."

Helena felt a jolt of dread. "We can't do a direct assault. It'd be a slaughter."

Dave let out a tense breath. "Maybe we can attempt a covert approach. Or even a negotiation. We can argue that the Ark's phenomena are uncontrollable. The Chinese might consider a trade or information exchange."

Ibrahim snorted. "They might. Or they'll see it as a chance to seize the Ark for themselves. Orlov is no help, and Lombardi is near collapse."

Father Lombardi's voice trembled from the corner. "I'll go if necessary. My presence might lend a sense of calm to negotiations. Then again, they might see me as a threat. They know the Vatican wants the Ark too."

Dave studied Helena, as if seeking her insight. She grimaced, thinking of Ming Xia's formidable stance. "She's rational, not a fanatic like Orlov. If we approach carefully, we might persuade her that controlling the Ark's energy requires the entire ceremony. The question is, will she care about preventing mass destruction, or just want it for leverage?"

Yusef interjected, "Sometimes reasoning with powerful people helps them realize they can't harness everything alone. Maybe it's worth trying, if only to buy time. Another firefight would be disastrous."

Helena's gaze flicked to the Ark, arcs dancing over the golden filigree. She recalled the swirling chaos in the caretaker's mansion. "We have to do something. Let's propose a meeting. If they refuse or try to trap us, we'll have to improvise again."

Orlov stirred, letting out a mocking laugh. "And if you fail, the Ark consumes you. How poetic."

Dave levelled him with a glare. "One more word, Colonel, and you'll wish you were silent."

Ibrahim broke in, voice urgent, "We still have the Ark here. If the Chinese realize that, they might strike first. We can't leave it unguarded."

Helena felt her pulse spike. "We'll do a minimal approach. Dave, Lombardi, me, and Yusef. Ibrahim stays with Orlov and the Ark. If the disturbances intensify, we come running back. If negotiations break down, we retreat."

The liaison nodded reluctantly. "All right. But be careful."

She turned to Lombardi, who looked pale but determined. "You sure you can handle it? We might need your knowledge to convince them the Ark's phenomena are real."

He cleared his throat, wincing at the bullet graze. "I'll manage. My faith compels me to see this through."

Yusef's eyes flashed uncertainty, though he drew a breath. "I'll come. Maybe they'll see me as less of a threat. I can interpret any local talk if needed."

Decision made, they assembled what gear remained: Helena's pistol, Dave's sidearm plus a few spare magazines, a small bag of funds. The rest they left with Ibrahim for warehouse defense. Orlov glowered at them from his cuffed position, evidently furious at not being included.

Within the hour, a taxi took Helena, Dave, Lombardi, and Yusef toward the run-down consulate building near the Golden Horn. The driver gave them odd looks but accepted payment without question. They arrived at a block with tall iron fences and shuttered windows. Broken signage in an Asian language hinted that the building once hosted official staff. Now it sat partially abandoned, overshadowed by modern hotels nearby.

Dave led the way onto the property. Lombardi and Yusef flanked Helena. She inhaled the crisp air, nerves tingling. A hush cloaked the grounds. Overgrown shrubs and chipped marble statues lined a cracked walkway. An iron gate stood half open.

They stepped into a courtyard. Immediately, two men in dark suits emerged from behind columns, hands inside jackets. Dave raised his palms, voice steady. "We come to speak with Ming Xia. We're not here for a fight. Please take us to her."

The guards exchanged a glance, then one tapped a communicator. Moments later, the interior doors opened, revealing a tall woman in a sleek coat: Ming Xia. Her measured steps conveyed lethal grace.

She paused on the threshold, expression neutral. "You have nerve appearing here after that fias... meltdown with the caretaker. Why shouldn't we detain you?"

Helena's heart hammered. She recalled the debacle at the caretaker's mansion. "Because we want to propose a truce," she said, trying to keep her voice firm. "We know you have the final lines of a Crusader text. We possess the Ark. Separately, each of us has only half the puzzle. Combined, we can stabilize the Ark's energy. Or are you so certain you can harness it alone?"

Ming Xia's gaze flicked over Dave's stance, Lombardi's torn cassock, Yusef's youthful anxiety. "Your group looks worse for wear. If I truly hold the final lines, why not strike you and seize the relic?"

Lombardi took a slight step forward, wincing at the pain in his arm. "Because the Ark's power can't be tamed by partial verses alone. We have centuries of notes indicating you need the Ark physically present during the full ceremony, recited in a specific manner. If you do it incorrectly, it might unleash unstoppable havoc."

Ming Xia watched him, face impassive. "Perhaps we'll see. Our scientists have gleaned much from the text already."

Yusef spoke up, voice trembling but resolute. "Do you want to risk unleashing forces that could destroy entire battalions? People like me, caught in the crossfire?"

A faint trace of empathy brushed Ming Xia's expression, or perhaps it was curiosity. She gave a small nod to her guards, who stepped back. "Fine. You may come inside. No sudden moves."

Dave exchanged a wary look with Helena. She nodded. This was the best opening they had. The quartet followed Ming Xia through double doors into a dim lobby stinking of old disinfectant. A line of battered desks suggested an abandoned administrative space. The woman led them down a corridor to a private lounge with shuttered windows and a single overhead lamp. Two more armed operatives stood watch.

She turned, crossing her arms. "Talk. You want the final lines. We want the Ark's manifestations under our control. If we can stabilize them with your partial chant, plus the Crusader lines, that suits our interest. We might negotiate—assuming you confirm the Ark is in your possession."

Helena's pulse thudded. "We can prove it by taking you to see it. But we need mutual trust. No ambush, no theft."

Ming Xia gave a subtle half-smile. "Trust, from the group that rampaged with firearms at the caretaker's mansion?"

Dave bristled. "We didn't start that fight. You smashed in through the skylight. People died."

She shrugged, unrepentant. "Casualties are inevitable where the Ark is concerned. Let's be civil. We can arrange for a small group to visit your location, verify the chest, and recite the ceremony together. If the disturbances subside, it validates the text. Then we can discuss next steps."

Lombardi's eyes narrowed. "Next steps? The Ark belongs in safekeeping, away from national exploitation."

Ming Xia's face flickered with mild amusement. "China sees it differently. Yet if these phenomena truly endanger all, perhaps we can share custody. Are you open to that?"

Dave exhaled, his tone wary. "You could also betray us. Storm the warehouse once we show you the Ark."

She lifted a brow. "Likewise, you could gun down my men when they arrive. But we can't proceed otherwise."

Helena glanced at Yusef, who looked torn, then at Lombardi. The priest's jaw tightened. He recognized the risk. Still, they had no alternative if they wanted the text. She stepped forward. "All right. We'll bring two of your operatives to see the Ark, not an entire squad. Then we attempt the ceremony. If the relic stabilizes, we know the text works. Then we can talk about controlling or safeguarding it."

Ming Xia considered, then nodded once. "Done. I'll pick my best pair. You have my vow they won't attack first. If your phenomenon is real, we'd prefer not to risk unleashing it."

A silence fell. Tension crackled in the musty air. Yusef swallowed, uncertain if they'd just made a devil's bargain. Dave's hand hovered near his belt, ready for betrayal. Helena forced herself to remain calm. Father Lombardi closed his eyes briefly, whispering a prayer.

Ming Xia signaled her guards. "Zhào, Li, you will accompany me. The rest remain on standby. We go now, before dawn breaks."

Helena's brow furrowed. "Your entire presence?"

The operative offered a chilly smile. "I must see the Ark for myself."

Dave rubbed his temple. "That's three. We have four. Fine. We outnumber you by one, but this is still precarious."

Ming Xia nodded once more. "Understood. Let's move quickly."

Within minutes, both parties headed out to waiting vehicles—a single sedan for Ming Xia, flanked by her two men, and another for Helena's group. The short ride back to the warehouse felt oppressive, each occupant bracing for violence at any sign of treachery.

When they arrived, the group disembarked. Ibrahim opened the warehouse door from inside, alarmed at the strangers but trusting Helena's nod. Colonel Orlov perked up from his chained spot, recognition sparking in his eyes. "So the Chinese are here," he growled.

Ming Xia stepped forward, scanning the dim interior, gaze settling on the battered Ark crate. The arcs flickered, spitting faint static in the gloom. Father Lombardi resumed a quiet chant. Dave kept his pistol visible, but not aimed. Helena's heart pounded. They were at the cusp of a pivotal moment: forging a tenuous alliance or igniting another debacle.

Ming Xia gestured to one of her men, who approached the crate with a portable scanning device. Arcs crackled near the metal, causing the device to spark. The operative flinched, stepping back. The Ark's energy repelled the machine. "It's definitely something unusual," he muttered in Mandarin.

Helena swallowed. "We told you. The disturbances are real. That's why we need the Crusader lines. Show us your text, we'll combine it with ours and let Lombardi perform the full ceremony."

Ming Xia lifted a small satchel, extracting a folded parchment. Her expression remained guarded. "We gleaned partial references, but it's incomplete without your knowledge of chanting. We rely on Lombardi's script as well. If the phenomena subside, that proves authenticity."

The priest's eyes flickered with hunger for that document. He stepped closer, though blood still stained his bandages. Dave hovered, ensuring no surprise moves. Ming Xia gave her men a nod. One placed the parchment on a wooden crate near the Ark. Father Lombardi retrieved his own notes from a satchel. He spread them out, scanning the lines side by side, breath quivering.

Helena and Dave watched intently, while Yusef and Ibrahim stood guard, or at least tried to remain alert. Orlov let out a bitter snort from his chained position. "Look at you, forging alliances with the Chinese."

Ming Xia cast Orlov a disdainful glance. "Be silent, Colonel. Your failures brought us here."

He snarled, tension thick, but Dave lifted his pistol in warning. The colonel subsided, glowering.

Father Lombardi's whisper grew excited. "Yes, yes... these lines fit exactly at the break in our partial text. It references a final incantation, something about cherubim wings overshadowing the seat of mercy... we can attempt the full ceremony now."

Helena's heart leaped. "Right here?"

"Better than letting the Ark's energy build," he said hoarsely. "If we succeed, its surges might drop dramatically. We can see if the chest becomes inert or at least docile."

Ming Xia's expression tightened, uncertain. "I want to record any result. My men will monitor with sensors."

Dave gave a curt nod. "Fine. Let's proceed. But if things escalate, stand back."

Helena felt her palms dampen with sweat. The entire warehouse brimmed with tension. They formed a wide circle around the Ark: Lombardi at the center, the parchment spread on a table. The priest coughed, mustering strength. With trembling hands, he recited the lines from the combined text, voice echoing in the cavernous space.

At first, the Ark's arcs crackled louder, swirling bright filaments that danced over the gold. Helena's scalp tingled, an electric hum rising in her ears. The apparitions wavered at the edges of her vision—ghostly cherubim wings, half-formed shapes. Dave gritted his teeth, fists clenched. Ming Xia's men watched with alarm. Yusef pressed against a crate, heart pounding.

Lombardi's chant crescendoed, each Latin phrase resonating with strange harmonics. The arcs intensified briefly, then began to recede. A hush fell, as though the relic's energy exhaled its final breath. The swirling visions dimmed, the air losing that charged, metallic edge. Helena stared at the Ark's surface, watching the arcs fade to a faint glow. Dave's eyes flicked around, seeing no ethereal wings.

A single crackle of electricity popped near the chest, then disappeared. Lombardi sank to his knees, tears streaking his cheeks. "It's... calmer," he whispered. "I feel no surging manifestations."

Ming Xia's operative checked a sensor. "Electromagnetic field dropping rapidly."

Helena's breath whooshed out. They might have succeeded. The Ark appeared dormant, no spectral phenomena swirling in the gloom. Her mind struggled to grasp it—a subdued relic, no immediate threat.

Yusef gazed in awe. "We did it?" he whispered.

Father Lombardi managed a shaky smile. "For the moment, yes. The disturbances are at bay."

Ming Xia's stoic mask slipped to mild satisfaction. "So it appears the ceremony works. Now the question: who keeps the Ark?"

Dave tensed. "We said we'd talk after neutralizing the relic's volatility. It should be stored in a neutral location, away from national weaponization."

She narrowed her eyes. "Or we could remove it to Beijing for deeper study. We have the final lines too."

Helena interjected, voice trembling with relief and fresh anxiety. "We can't just hand it to any government. The disturbances might be dormant but could resurface if the chest is mishandled."

Colonel Orlov spat from across the warehouse. "You think the Ark's influence is gone forever? It remains Russia's rightful property—seized by you criminals."

A bitter standoff loomed. Everyone realized the anomalies might have calmed, but the relic's strategic value had only soared. Tension rippled anew, this time from the gathered factions, not the Ark. Dave slid a step closer to Helena, ensuring they could defend themselves if Ming Xia attempted a snatch. Yusef clenched his fists, dreading more conflict.

Lombardi spoke, voice hoarse. "The Church has centuries of experience safeguarding relics. Let us protect it, that no disturbances are ever reawakened."

Ming Xia arched a brow. "A loaded statement, Father. I see we have no easy consensus."

Ibrahim stepped forward, exasperated. "Israel demands the Ark's return to Jerusalem. That was always the plan."

Helena's stomach knotted. The swirling phenomena might be gone, but the Ark threatened to ignite a different kind of explosion—political greed. Everyone had a claim. She rubbed her sore shoulder, mind racing. The best outcome might be a temporary arrangement until a global negotiation could be formed.

Ming Xia's eyes swept the group. "Let us propose a compromise. The Ark remains with you for now, here in Istanbul. My team will bring additional equipment to study it. If disturbances remain quiet, we'll discuss a transfer to China. Meanwhile, the rest of you can petition your governments. No more violence needed."

Dave frowned. "That's not a real compromise. You're basically demanding joint custody on your terms."

Lombardi coughed, clearly drained. "We... must keep the Ark stable. If disruptions reignite, the ceremony might need to be repeated. None of us wants further chaos."

Helena recognized the uneasy stalemate. She lifted a hand. "Let's take a day. We can meet tomorrow to finalize a plan. For now, the Ark is dormant. That was the immediate crisis."

Ming Xia considered, then gave a crisp nod. "Agreed. We'll return tomorrow at noon. No one attempts to move the Ark or sabotage it. If you do, consider any goodwill void."

She turned to her men. "We're done here." They gathered their gear. One operative hovered near Colonel Orlov, eyeing him with disdain. The Russian locked his jaw, refusing to speak. Ming Xia barely spared him a glance. She offered Dave a level look. "Don't make me regret this. Our lines of communication remain open."

In a flash, the Chinese squad retreated, footsteps echoing across the warehouse floor. The door clanged shut behind them, leaving Helena's group alone with a newly calmed Ark. Everyone sagged, relief mingled with dread for the next day's negotiations.

Orlov scoffed. "You allowed them to leave with full knowledge of this location? They'll be back with a strike team."

Ibrahim glared at him. "And you'd do the same if freed. Hypocrisy suits you."

The colonel's lip curled, but he stayed quiet. Dave turned to Helena, a flicker of relief shining in his tired eyes. "At least the relic is quiet."

She let out a shuddering breath. "Yes. But the Ark remains a political bomb."

Yusef approached the crate, stepping close as if expecting arcs to leap out. Nothing. The gold gleamed under the overhead bulb, strangely inert. "It's... peaceful," he murmured. "All that swirling chaos... gone?"

Father Lombardi nodded, sinking onto a chair with exhaustion. "The final lines completed the ceremony. For now, the disturbances are silenced. But if the Ark is abused or forcibly opened, it could reignite."

Helena massaged her injured shoulder. "We bought time. That might be all we need to keep the world from sliding into deeper turmoil."

Dave gave her a gentle look. "You should rest properly. We all should. Tomorrow's meeting with Ming Xia will be crucial."

She nodded, letting him guide her to a quiet corner. Each member of the infiltration group found a makeshift spot to lie down or sit. The hush in the warehouse felt surreal, the Ark's presence no longer crackling with energy. Even Orlov, though furious, fell into a silent brooding.

As she tried to drift off, Helena's thoughts spun: the phenomena, the partial chanting, the stolen lines—now used to calm the Ark's energy. The dreaded meltdown had been averted at the last minute. Yet bigger storms loomed, with Ming Xia's faction, Father Lombardi's Church agenda, Orlov's national pride, and Israel's claim. The final text had subdued the relic, but it also exposed the world to a new wave of tension: who truly owned an artifact that might shift global power?

In the dim overhead light, she spotted Dave across from her, leaning against a crate, eyes half-lidded. She offered a faint, reassuring smile. He returned it, a silent promise they'd navigate this political minefield together. Yusef curled on a blanket, expression troubled but calmer now that the Ark's energy no longer haunted him. Lombardi dozed, breath rattling from pain. Orlov remained cuffed, glowering in the shadows.

They had quelled the relic, forging a fragile truce with Ming Xia. For the moment, the Ark lay dormant, each golden edge reflecting the bare bulbs overhead. Helena prayed that tomorrow's negotiations wouldn't spark a war over possession. They'd come so far—yet new storms waited. Her eyelids drooped under the weight of exhaustion.

At least, for one brief span, the Ark's disturbances lay silent, no swirling forces to torment them. The hush mirrored the stillness in their battered spirits, each soul reeling from the journey across continents. She closed her eyes, letting her mind drift.

Though peace held for now, the Ark's presence still felt like a quiet giant in the room—dormant but brimming with potential, an aged mystery tethered by a precarious ceremony. The entire world might spin on how they handled tomorrow's talks. She took one last glance at Dave, who gave a subdued nod. Then she slipped into a dreamless sleep, uncertain what morning would bring but grateful the Ark's forces no longer clawed at their sanity.

Chapter 13

A faint sliver of dawn illuminated the dusty windows of the rented warehouse in Istanbul, casting pale stripes across the concrete floor. The Ark of the Covenant, resting on its makeshift altar of crates, looked eerily tranquil. Hours ago, Father Aurelius Lombardi had performed the final lines of the Crusader ritual, quelling the Ark's illusions for the first time since it had been unearthed beneath the Temple Mount. Now the relic's gilded edges gleamed with a subdued glow instead of crackling arcs. Yet the hush in the chamber felt less like peace and more like the eye of a gathering storm.

Helena Carter woke from a restless doze, her injured shoulder throbbing. She rose from a corner mat, scanning the large room. Dave Schumer was already awake, leaning against a wall with his arms folded. He offered a gentle nod when their gazes met. Nearby, Yusef Nasir stood at the open doorway, letting in a faint breeze that carried distant street noise and the calls of early vendors. Father Lombardi lay on a folding cot, breathing heavily, his bullet wound still fresh. Ibrahim Mahdi flipped through his phone, scanning for updates. Colonel Nikolai Orlov sat cuffed to a heavy post, scowling in silence.

The group's silence reflected their exhaustion. Tension thrummed like a barely audible chord: illusions were dormant, but at any moment, fresh chaos could erupt. Yesterday's uneasy truce with Ming Xia had given them a slim path forward. By noon, they would gather again to discuss the Ark's future. Each faction wanted control or, at minimum, oversight—and no one trusted the others not to betray them the instant an advantage appeared.

Helena brushed dust from her jacket, crossing to check on Lombardi. The Jesuit stirred as she approached, eyes bloodshot. "You should rest more," she murmured, kneeling to inspect the gauze taped to his arm.

"I'll manage," he rasped. "I must remain ready to chant again if illusions return. We can't afford another nightmare."

She gave him a tight smile, empathy shining in her eyes. "You've borne the brunt of this. Once we figure out a stable solution, you'll get a proper rest."

He closed his eyes, a hint of gratitude crossing his features. "God willing."

Over by the door, Yusef sighed. Helena noticed the teen's shoulders trembled slightly, as if he carried the weight of every bullet fired since leaving Jerusalem. She touched his arm. "Everything okay?"

He swallowed, voice low. "I keep thinking I should go home. My uncle's sweet shop needs help, and my mother fears for me. Yet I can't leave until the Ark is truly safe. I can't let illusions or new owners spark more bloodshed."

Helena's throat tightened. "I respect that. You've done more than most people twice your age. But if it becomes too much, no one would blame you for stepping away."

He hesitated, gaze distant. "I'll decide after these talks. If all sides come to terms, maybe I can leave."

She patted his shoulder, then turned to Dave, who was conferring with Ibrahim. The Israeli liaison showed her his phone. "Word around the city is that Russian intelligence assets might be en route. Probably Orlov's men. And rumor says a local black-market network is buzzing about a 'holy artifact' and a foreign infiltration."

Dave nodded grimly. "No surprise. Istanbul has always been a crossroads. If we don't resolve things quickly, half the underworld will sniff out the Ark's presence."

Helena's stomach churned. The lull was fragile, the city's underbelly stirring with rumor. She glanced at Orlov. The colonel returned her look with cold disdain, lips parted as if to speak. Before he could, Father Lombardi cleared his throat. "We should prepare for the meeting with Ming Xia. Noon is only a few hours away. Let's confirm our stance."

Ibrahim moved closer, keeping an eye on Orlov's shackles. "We want the disturbances kept at bay. The ceremony has calmed them for now, but if the Ark is taken to some lab or forcibly opened, everything could flare anew. We can't let that happen."

Dave folded his arms. "Our best approach might be a joint arrangement: the Ark stays with us in Istanbul while each faction organizes an international summit or larger negotiation. But the Chinese will push to take it to their own facility. That's a line we can't cross."

Helena drew a slow breath. "That means we need alternatives—maybe the Vatican's hidden vaults, or returning it to Jerusalem. But Israel's claim also competes with Lombardi's vow. Then there's Orlov wanting it for Russia."

Orlov gave a bark of laughter, rattling the chain around his wrist. "You pretend you have a choice, but eventually the strongest side will seize it. You can't cling to fantasies of neutrality forever."

Helena ignored him, turning to Lombardi. "What's your stance, Father?"

He looked pained, a flicker of zeal behind his fatigue. "My Church is best equipped to guard the Ark. The disturbances are neutralized now, but any reckless approach could awaken them. If the relic rests in the Vatican, we can safeguard it indefinitely."

Ibrahim stiffened, recalling that Israel originally housed the Ark centuries ago. "It belongs in the Temple's land."

A hush settled, tension simmering. Yusef exhaled, stepping between them. "All that matters is the Ark remains dormant, right? We can figure out the rest later.""

Dave's gaze swept over the group. "Let's focus on forging an immediate truce with Ming Xia. Once we have official backing, we can finalize the Ark's destination."

Helena nodded, sensing the precarious balance. "Yes. Let's do that."

They spent the next hour tidying up, double-checking the crate's locks. Lombardi dozed for a brief spell, mustering energy for the day ahead. Helena redressed her shoulder wound, wincing at every slight movement.

Dave brewed instant coffee from a battered kettle they found in a corner. The bitter aroma filled the air, offering a thin semblance of normalcy.

Shortly before noon, a knock echoed at the warehouse's entrance. Everyone froze, hearts pounding. Dave approached with caution. "Who is it?"

A muffled voice answered in lightly accented English. "It's Ming Xia. Open up."

He exhaled, unlocked the door. Ming Xia stepped in, flanked by the same two operatives from the day before. She wore a charcoal suit, posture poised. Her gaze flicked to Colonel Orlov, then to the Ark's crate. "Good. No disturbances. Everyone still alive."

Helena forced a polite nod. "We've kept our word. No movement of the Ark. Its phenomena remain subdued."

Ming Xia studied Father Lombardi, noticing the fresh bandage. "You look exhausted, Father. Overexertion from last night's ceremony?"

He lowered his gaze. "I'll manage. The Ark's effects drained me for days."

The Chinese operative's expression betrayed no sympathy. She clasped her hands behind her back. "Shall we discuss the Ark's future?"

Dave gestured toward a circle of crates they'd arranged as seats. "Yes. Sit. We can talk better that way."

Ming Xia's men stood guard near the door, watchful. She settled on a crate, crossing her legs, while Helena, Dave, Lombardi, and Ibrahim formed a loose semicircle. Yusef lingered behind them, tension etched on his face. Orlov remained chained in the distance, glowering with impotent rage.

Ming Xia began, voice measured. "We in the People's Republic want further research on these phenomena. We've invested heavily in advanced technology to contain or manipulate them. Our leaders see the Ark as a resource to bolster global standing. That said, we recognize the ceremony neutralizes these manifestations. If we forcibly remove the relic, such forces might resurface."

Helena swallowed. "Forcing phenomena to vanish is one thing, but using them as a weapon is another. We can't allow that."

Ming Xia lifted a brow. "The same could be said of any faction—Russia, the Vatican, or even your own governments. The Ark is a potent piece of biblical lore."

Lombardi spoke through clenched teeth. "Lore or not, these disturbances can break minds. This relic isn't a typical weapon. Once unleashed, such forces can spiral beyond control."

Ibrahim nodded. "Which is why Israel demands it returned to Jerusalem, where it belongs. The disturbances first manifested there, and it can be secured with minimal interference."

Ming Xia's eyes flicked to each speaker. "Everyone wants it. None of you has the authority to speak for your entire country. Meanwhile, China stands prepared to study it in a high-tech environment, ensuring these forces remain quashed. Our approach is pragmatic."

Dave clenched his jaw. "Pragmatic or not, letting any single government hold the Ark invites a global arms race. We propose a neutral stance—somewhere in Istanbul, maybe under an international coalition. We monitor these manifestations together until official negotiations form."

A faint smile crossed Ming Xia's lips. "An interesting proposition. But will your home countries accept losing direct ownership?"

Helena interjected, feeling the weight of this conversation. "They must if these disturbances are truly unstoppable when misused. A neutral site, with sentinels from each major interest, might be the only compromise."

Silence spread as they considered. Then Lombardi inhaled. "If we keep these phenomena dormant, that might suffice for short-term peace. But eventually, your superiors will want the Ark relocated. Unless... we finalize a way to store it permanently."

Ming Xia inclined her head. "You suggest indefinite storage in Istanbul? Hardly stable. This city is a crossroads of clandestine trade, espionage, and cultural tensions. The Ark would attract trouble."

Ibrahim frowned. "Every location does, from Russia to China to the Vatican. But at least we have a start: disturbances remain at bay, we keep it locked down, and we inform our governments that the Ark is not leaving the city until a global accord is reached."

Helena nodded, shifting uncomfortably. "Yes. Let's do that for now." She locked eyes with Ming Xia, voice tinged with caution. "But we expect no covert attempts to break in or whisk it away."

The Chinese operative offered a measured nod. "I'll inform my superiors of the arrangement. They might dispatch additional observers. If disturbances remain dormant, we see no reason to trigger conflict. But if you or your allies attempt to abscond with it, we will respond."

Dave exhaled relief at the partial agreement forming. "Likewise, if you move against us, disturbances or not, you risk igniting a new fight."

Ming Xia held his gaze, neither conceding nor threatening further. The faint tension in her posture suggested that while a temporary truce might hold, mistrust lingered. She turned to Orlov, chained in the corner. "What of him? Russia might want their colonel back."

The colonel sneered. "I'll see you burn, Ming Xia. Stealing from me was a grave mistake."

She ignored him, continuing to address Helena and Dave. "I suggest releasing him. We owe no loyalty to Orlov, but if you keep him prisoner, it sows more discord."

Lombardi glanced at Orlov with disdain. "He's a menace. Freed, he'll rally men to retake the Ark."

Helena felt torn. Keeping Orlov bound indefinitely was a headache. If disturbances were truly dormant, maybe his threat lessened. But he might still incite sabotage. She looked to Dave, who pursed his lips. "We must weigh the consequences. If disturbances remain quiet, maybe Orlov no longer threatens to weaponize them. But letting him loose invites a new chase."

Orlov glared. "A chase I will undertake with gusto, once these chains are off."

Ming Xia shrugged. "We can't have a stable truce with him locked up. Russia's pride is wounded enough. Offer him a chance to depart, or let the Russians negotiate his release."

Ibrahim placed a hand on his hip, frustration evident. "We risk handing him a free pass. But the alternative is babysitting him forever."

Yusef's voice trembled as he spoke up. "If disturbances are quiet, maybe Orlov can't do immediate harm. Let him go, so we can concentrate on the Ark's safety. He's only one man."

Helena recalled the many times Orlov unleashed lethal force. Yet he was powerless now, the Ark's energy dormant, no direct control over the relic. She turned to Dave, who nodded, brow furrowed. "We'll let him leave under conditions. No contact with your men for at least two days, giving us time to finalize the Ark's fate. If you break that condition, we'll assume war."

The colonel spat on the ground. "A humiliating demand. But these chains are worse." He flicked his glare at Ming Xia. "Just be warned, I have no intention of ceding Russia's rightful claim."

The Chinese operative's expression was unreadable. She rose from her crate. "Then it's settled. Orlov goes free. The Ark stays locked here, disturbances calm, while each side arranges sentinels. We meet again tomorrow to finalize protocols. If disturbances remain stable, we'll confirm the arrangement publicly."

Dave inhaled, relief and anxiety mingling. "Agreed. Let's make sure no one tries anything rash."

Ming Xia beckoned her men. "I'll handle some local details, begin drafting official proposals. Keep the Ark safe. We'll be in touch." With that, she pivoted and exited. Her two bodyguards followed, the warehouse door clanging shut behind them.

Yusef let out a slow breath. "We actually reached an agreement, sort of."

Lombardi lifted a trembling hand to wipe sweat from his brow. "An agreement riddled with traps. But illusions remain quiet. That's something."

Ibrahim marched over to Orlov, unlocking the chain but keeping the colonel cuffed. "We'll walk you out. Take a taxi. Don't come back."

Orlov stood, massaging his stiff shoulders. "Don't think this is over." He shot Helena a withering glare. "You'll regret mocking Russia's might."

Dave and Ibrahim guided him to the exit, ensuring no hidden weapon graced his pockets. Once at the threshold, Orlov jerked away, scowling.

Then he slipped out into the Istanbul daylight, free once more. Helena suppressed a shiver, imagining his potential vengeance.

Finally, the infiltration group stood around the Ark, alone again. Father Lombardi settled back on his cot, trembling from fatigue. "I should rest. The illusions won't surge if no one meddles with the Ark. Right?"

Helena chewed her lip. "We hope so. We can't test that assumption, but the ceremony's done. Let's give you time to heal. We'll keep watch in shifts."

Dave nodded. "We should also consider Istanbul's complexities—local black-market brokers, possible sentinels from Orlov's network. Let's not assume Ming Xia is the only threat."

Ibrahim sank onto a crate. "I'll call some connections. If Orlov or other factions try to exploit the lull, we must know."

Yusef cleared his throat. "I might go out for supplies. This warehouse is stifling. We need real food, water, medicine." He paused, glancing at Helena. "Maybe I can see if rumors swirl about the Ark in the local bazaars. If black-market circles are stirring, we should know."

Helena studied his face. "Are you sure? It's risky. Spies might watch those markets."

He shrugged. "I'll be careful. I'm from Jerusalem—I know how to keep quiet. Let me help."

Dave offered a faint nod. "Take care out there. Give us a phone check every hour. If you sense danger, vanish."

The teen gave a small bow of acknowledgment. Gathering a slim wad of cash from their shared stash, he ducked out. The warehouse door closed behind him, leaving a hush. Helena's gaze lingered on the relic, still and golden. Though illusions were subdued, an undercurrent of power thrummed beneath the surface. She sensed the centuries of reverence and fear pinned to that object. Despite the ceremony's success, the Ark remained a precarious symbol.

She approached Dave, lowering her voice. "We need a more permanent arrangement. We can't stay in a dusty warehouse for weeks."

He nodded, stifling a sigh. "Yeah. But a hotel or safe house might be too visible. We'll see how tomorrow's negotiations go. If we can set up an official neutral site, we might move the Ark there."

Her chest tightened at the memory of bullet-laced chaos in the caretaker's mansion. "I dread another debacle if a new faction arrives. Orlov's men, or even some mercenary group from the black market."

Dave rubbed the back of his neck. "We remain on guard. Our best advantage is illusions are quiet. No immediate lure of unstoppable power. People might not scramble so violently if they think it's inert."

She offered a weary smile, stepping closer. "Thanks for holding it together, by the way."

A flicker of warmth lit his eyes. "We're in this together," he replied gently, resting a hand on her uninjured arm. The hush between them felt like a calm eddy in a raging torrent. For a second, she leaned into that quiet closeness, heart fluttering. Then footsteps echoed behind them, snapping her from the moment.

Ibrahim coughed, discreet. "I'll handle watch for a few hours. You both can rest. Lombardi too."

Helena nodded, stepping away from Dave. The tension in her chest lingered, balancing exhaustion with the faint spark of closeness that had blossomed. They parted to find corners for napping, leaving Ibrahim by the Ark with his phone at the ready.

The afternoon heat seeped through cracks in the warehouse, turning the air stuffy and stifling. Helena stirred from a short, uneasy sleep, torso slick with sweat. She checked her watch: nearly three in the afternoon. She found Father Lombardi dozing, chest rising and falling with shallow breaths. Dave was rummaging for water, hair plastered to his forehead. The Ark gleamed, no arcs scuttling across its surface.

Yusef had not yet returned from his errand. Worry prickled Helena's thoughts. He was resourceful, but the city's underworld could be unforgiving, especially if rumors of the Ark's presence had circulated. She caught Dave's eye, and he shared her concern.

Ibrahim paced near the warehouse door, phone in hand. He ended a call, tension etched into his features. "Word is, new arrivals from Russia were spotted at the airport. Possibly Orlov's backup. Also, a few days ago, local brokers claimed someone from a 'mysterious global group' arrived, maybe a private paramilitary outfit. The city is crawling with sentinels."

Dave cursed. "We can't catch a break. Let's hope the illusions' dormancy deters them from a direct assault. They might wait until we move the Ark."

Helena felt the press of danger. "We should confirm Yusef's safety. He has no phone? Or we gave him one but he hasn't checked in?"

Ibrahim nodded. "He said he'd text every hour. It's been an hour and a half. No word."

A knot of anxiety twisted in her gut. She rose, ignoring her shoulder's ache. "I'm going out to find him. The last thing we need is a teenage ally kidnapped by black-market thugs."

Dave slung on his jacket. "I'll come. We'll be careful, keep a low profile. Lombardi, you stay with Ibrahim."

The priest stirred, blinking groggily. "You risk leaving me alone with illusions if I doze?"

She offered a gentle shake of the head. "They're quiet. Just... do your best if you sense them stirring. We'll hurry back."

He nodded weakly, returning to half-lidded rest. Orlov snorted from his post, but said nothing. Helena and Dave slipped out, stepping into late afternoon glare. The street beyond was dusty, old cars parked haphazardly, faint traffic noise rising from a distant boulevard.

They walked toward the heart of Istanbul, following the path Yusef might have taken. Dave's posture was tense, scanning every passing face or vehicle. The humidity weighed on them, intensifying the sour tang of industrial runoff in the gutters. A few men lingered by a corner café, watching them with mild curiosity.

Helena checked an old phone Dave had given Yusef, seeing if any updates had arrived. Nothing. Guilt flared—she had let him wander the city alone, seeking supplies. Dave slowed as they reached a busy intersection, the swirl of pedestrians and honking cars forming a chaotic tapestry. She recognized the complexity of this city: minarets in the distance, modern glass towers jutting up behind crumbling walls, side streets branching like capillaries.

"Which way?" Dave asked, scanning the throng. "We don't even know which market he visited."

Helena sighed. "Let's guess the smaller bazaar, near the old quarter. He knows how to haggle in local dialects. It's a start." She waved down a taxi. The driver gave them a flat stare but agreed to take them after Dave offered extra cash. The ride was claustrophobic, weaving through midday gridlock. Horns blared, vendors strolled between cars hawking drinks, a donkey cart ambled across a side street.

They reached a bustling side market, smaller than the Grand Bazaar but teeming with stalls under colorful awnings. Spices, fruits, and handcrafted trinkets lined the tables. Helena paid the driver, and she and Dave disembarked, adrenaline spiking. Yusef could be anywhere.

They navigated narrow aisles between stalls, scanning for the teen's wiry build or his telltale determined expression. Dave quizzed a few shopkeepers, showing Yusef's photo on his phone. Most shook their heads or demanded a tip first. At last, an older woman recalled seeing a young foreign boy purchasing medical supplies an hour ago, heading south. Helena's heart thumped with relief—at least a clue.

They followed the directions, slipping deeper into labyrinthine alleys where overhead sheets flapped in the breeze. The smell of grilled meat and sweet pastries mingled with diesel fumes. At intervals, Dave glimpsed men in worn suits who might be troopers or pickpockets eyeing them. He kept a hand near his concealed pistol. Helena tried not to flinch at every suspicious stare.

A block later, they discovered a small courtyard ringed by derelict apartment blocks. Scattered cardboard boxes and empty bottles littered the cracked pavement. The hush felt unsettling after the noisy bazaar. Dave paused, scanning the corners. Helena's pulse sped up. They advanced with caution, footsteps echoing.

At the far side of the courtyard, they found an abandoned kiosk. Behind it, propped against a graffiti-stained wall, sat Yusef—blood crusting his lip, left wrist angled awkwardly, eyes half-lidded with pain. Helena rushed over, kneeling at his side. "Yusef! Oh, no... what happened?"

He tried to straighten, but a groan escaped. "I was picking up supplies. Some men jumped me, demanded to know about the Ark. I ran, but they cornered me here. Took my phone… said they represent a local gang that deals with relics. They want a piece of the action."

Dave clenched his jaw. "Are you sure they left?"

Yusef swallowed. "They parted after they beat me. Threatened they'd come for the Ark if the illusions are real. I— I tried to fight, but… they outnumbered me."

Helena's heart twisted. She carefully examined his injuries. Bruised ribs, possibly a sprained wrist. Dave offered him water. The teen sipped, blinking tears of frustration. "I messed up again," he murmured.

She touched his shoulder gently. "You didn't. The city is rife with opportunists. Let's get you back."

He nodded, voice raw. "We have more enemies than we thought."

Dave helped him stand, supporting his uninjured side. "We'll find a taxi. Easy now." The battered teen leaned on him, wincing at each step. They retraced their path, ignoring the curious stares of passersby. A few minutes later, they flagged a reluctant cab. The driver's alarmed look softened when Dave offered extra money. The short ride back to the warehouse passed in tense silence, Yusef nursing his injuries while Helena fought off guilt.

At the warehouse, Ibrahim burst forward to help Yusef inside, clearing a space for the teen to rest. Father Lombardi, still pale, tried to assist with prayers or comfort. Orlov, ironically, said nothing, though a trace of dark satisfaction lurked in his expression at their continued troubles. Helena and Dave scrounged up bandages for Yusef's bruises, applying gentle pressure to his sprained wrist. The teen hissed in pain but put on a brave face.

"I'm sorry," he repeated. "I only wanted to help."

Helena shook her head, tears burning. "Don't apologize. You tried your best. This city is more dangerous than we realized."

The teen nodded, wincing. "I found some supplies, though—bandages, a few meds. They took most of my cash, but I saved what I could." He forced a small smile, rummaging in a tattered bag to reveal antiseptics, a half-squashed bag of bread, a few water bottles.

Lombardi gave Yusef's hand a squeeze. "Your bravery humbles me. Let's treat you properly. We need every ally upright."

Ibrahim frowned. "Which gang attacked you? Did they mention a name?"

Yusef shook his head. "Said they were just local brokers in relic dealing, but heavily armed. Maybe connected to a big underworld boss. They demanded a cut if the Ark trades hands. Or they'd come after us."

Dave muttered a curse, raking a hand through his hair. "The illusions might be gone, but the Ark's mystique is enough to draw criminals. We can't hold them all off."

Helena recognized that tension building anew. "We have to finalize tomorrow's arrangement with Ming Xia. If multiple new threats lurk, our only chance is a strong coalition with the Chinese and maybe other official sentinels. Otherwise, local gangs could attempt an ambush."

Orlov's voice rasped from the corner, mockingly. "Yes, beg the Chinese for help. That will go well."

She ignored him. Dave cleared his throat, addressing the group. "We have to figure out how to handle this new threat. If local criminals mount an attack, the Ark's effects might remain subdued, but we can't defend forever. We need a safer location or official protection. Possibly from the Turkish authorities, if we can discreetly approach them."

Ibrahim looked wary. "Inviting local police or the government means revealing the Ark's existence publicly. That could spark a media frenzy, or demands from Ankara to seize it."

Helena folded her arms. "Then we push for international oversight. If the relic's forces remain controlled, the immediate danger is smaller, but we can't leave it out in the open. We either relocate to a secure compound or rally official sentinels."

Dave sighed, voice subdued. "Let's see how tomorrow's talk with Ming Xia goes. If she's open to a real coalition, we might pool resources to repel local gangs and keep the Ark's energy at bay. If she tries to corner us, we'll have to think of something else."

Father Lombardi listened, swallowing his zeal. "Don't forget the Vatican's readiness to help. My higher-ups can dispatch discreet security or a permanent custodial force. The Ark belongs in hallowed ground."

Ibrahim stiffened, reasserting Israel's claim, but Helena interjected with a calming gesture. "No more arguments. One step at a time."

As evening deepened, they ate the meager bread and drank water Yusef salvaged. The teen dozed fitfully afterward, half-limp from bruises. Lombardi resumed minimal chanting, ensuring the Ark's phenomena stayed dormant. Dave and Helena conferred at a small table, updating notes for the next day's negotiations. She typed bullet points on a battered laptop:

#1, stabilized energy

#2, potential local criminals

#3, final goal—neutral storage.

Dave rubbed a kink in his neck, eyes scanning each detail.

Time crawled, the warehouse lights dimming as the overhead bulbs flickered. Orlov eventually fell asleep, arms pinned uncomfortably behind him. Ibrahim took a turn resting, head against a makeshift pillow. Father Lombardi coughed sporadically, but the bullet graze seemed stable. Yusef tossed on a blanket, nightmares haunting his face.

In that hush, Helena and Dave found a moment to step outside for fresh air, leaving the Ark under Ibrahim's occasional watch. The narrow street lay quiet, the distant glow of Istanbul's nightlife coloring the sky. She leaned on Dave's uninjured shoulder, letting the tension seep from her limbs. He offered a gentle sigh, wrapping an arm around her waist.

"You're trembling," he said. "We both are."

She nodded, burying her face briefly against his chest. "Too many close calls. I keep replaying every confrontation, every bullet. And now local gangs swirl around us. We can't let the Ark's forces spark again."

He stroked her hair. "We're doing what we can. At least the Ark's quiet for now, giving us a chance to talk sense tomorrow."

She lifted her head, catching the faint warmth in his eyes. "Thank you for... everything," she said, her voice catching. "I couldn't handle this alone."

His expression softened. "Nor could I. This is bigger than any single person. And... I'm glad we found each other amid the madness."

A quiet moment passed, hearts aligned in that fleeting pocket of calm. She inhaled his steady presence, the swirl of night air cradling them. Then footsteps sounded from within, prompting them to separate. They headed back inside, refocusing on the relic that demanded so much of their energy.

Morning sunlight broke through dusty panes, rousing the infiltration group. Yusef's bruises had swelled, but he managed to hobble around, refusing to be sidelined. Lombardi's arm throbbed, though the illusions remained absent. Dave brewed more instant coffee, sharing the minimal rations. Orlov sullenly accepted a piece of bread. Helena's shoulder wound felt stiff, but better than before. Ibrahim resumed phone calls, scanning for new intel.

As noon approached, Dave paced near the Ark. "Ming Xia said she'd return around midday. Let's set up some chairs."

Helena arranged a circle of crates again. The air felt charged with anticipation. Yusef tried to remain out of direct sight, reluctant to show weakness. Lombardi adjusted his bandage, swallowing a painkiller from the leftover supplies. The Ark itself, still swaddled in its crate, glowed, inert but no less imposing. Ibrahim checked the door locks. Colonel Orlov dozed or feigned sleep, arms pinned behind him.

Finally, at precisely noon, a sharp rap echoed at the warehouse door. Ibrahim unlatched it, stepping aside to let Ming Xia and her two companions enter. The Chinese operative wore the same poised expression, scanning the interior for changes.

"I see you haven't moved it," she remarked, eyes flicking to the Ark. "No disturbances. Good."

Helena nodded. "Yes. We adhered to the truce."

Ming Xia gestured at her men to remain near the door. "Shall we proceed with finalizing the arrangement?"

Everyone gathered in the circle of crates. Yusef stayed slightly behind Helena, trying not to appear vulnerable. Lombardi mustered a calmer stance, though his face was drawn. Dave folded his arms, watchful. Ibrahim perched near Orlov, who was forced to listen in from his spot. The colonel's glare suggested he resented being excluded from any control.

Ming Xia began, voice smooth. "We propose stationing a small Chinese team here for Ark security. We supply advanced sensors, keeping phenomena from reactivating through consistent monitoring. In return, you permit joint authority. No unilateral removal of the chest."

Dave frowned. "That effectively cedes partial control to your government. What about the rest of us?"

She lifted a shoulder. "We can sign a memorandum. A rotating guard from each faction, if desired. I'm simply offering specialized gear to ensure the Ark's energy remains dormant. The chest stays in Istanbul, protected from local criminals. We avoid more gunfights."

Father Lombardi cleared his throat. "And the Vatican? We can also supply sentinels. One or two discreet clergy who know the ceremony intimately."

Ming Xia offered a polite smile. "If you insist, Father. The Ark is stable thanks to your chant, so your presence is welcome."

Ibrahim spoke up for Israel. "We demand a seat at that table. And eventually, the Ark's rightful return to Jerusalem."

The Chinese operative nodded. "We aren't forbidding future relocation if phenomena remain calm. But for now, we keep it locked here under joint oversight. Agreed?"

Helena and Dave exchanged a look. This arrangement mirrored the neutral plan they hoped for, though with a stronger Chinese influence than they liked. Still, it might be the only way to stave off local gangs or Orlov's sabotage. She inhaled, letting out a slow breath. "We can tentatively agree. But how do we address potential infiltration from criminals or rogue Russian elements?"

Ming Xia's lips thinned. "My men can handle local thugs. If Orlov's subordinates appear, we handle that too."

A scoff came from the chained colonel, who refused to remain silent. "You talk big. Russia doesn't forget."

She ignored him, continuing, "We'll coordinate basic security measures. If illusions show signs of returning, Lombardi or another authorized priest recites the ceremony. We keep a daily log. No one attempts to spirit the Ark away without the others' knowledge."

Dave exhaled, considering the hidden pitfalls. "We'd also want a limit on your troop numbers. You can't bring an entire squad here."

Ming Xia smirked. "Two or three specialists, plus me, rotating shifts. That's all. The same for your side. We don't want a parade of armed foreigners inciting trouble with local authorities."

Lombardi nodded. "That sounds fair enough."

Helena forced a faint smile. "All right, we have a plan. We'll sign a simple written statement, a placeholder until official channels finalize a broader treaty."

Ming Xia extended a hand, palm open. "Agreed." She eyed Orlov. "And the colonel?"

Dave shrugged. "He's free, but for now we keep him under watch until he leaves voluntarily. We can't have him meddling again."

A glimmer of amusement crossed Ming Xia's gaze. "He might cause trouble either way, but that's your concern. Let him go if you trust him not to bring an army."

Father Lombardi rose stiffly, rummaging for a pen and notepad. They drafted a short agreement in English, each side pledging not to move the Ark or attempt to harness its phenomena alone, and to accept minimal look-outs from each faction. Helena, Dave, Lombardi, and Ibrahim signed on one side. Ming Xia signed for the Chinese delegation, not listing her real name but an alias. The handshake that followed felt stiff, but it marked a fragile step toward unity.

Yusef let out a quiet breath of relief. "So... we have peace?"

Ming Xia glanced at him kindly. "As long as the Ark's disturbances remain dormant, we have no reason to fight. Let's hope it holds."

Colonel Orlov rattled his chain. "You are fools if you think its power won't resurface. The Ark is never truly tamed."

No one responded. The tension in the air dissipated. Helena reflected that the phenomena were subdued for now, and the once-unstoppable threat lay dormant. Perhaps this arrangement would hold, at least until the next wave of ambition or fear ignited conflict.

Ming Xia's men brought in a pair of high-tech sensor crates, placing them discreetly near the Ark's side. Lombardi watched, rapt with caution. She explained, "These measure electromagnetic fluctuations. If activity begins to spike, we'll know before it's visible."

Dave and Ibrahim arranged a small corner for the new monitors. Ming Xia declared she'd return later with the two specialists once lodging was settled. Then, with a parting nod, she took her men and left again. The door clanged shut, leaving the infiltration group in a hush.

Ibrahim turned to Helena. "We have a partial solution. But you realize multiple sentinels will crowd this place. It's only a matter of time before local criminals catch wind."

She exhaled. "That's a problem for tomorrow. At least the Ark isn't threatening to break us right now."

Dave wiped sweat from his brow. "Let's see if we can find a safer building. But for tonight, we hold steady here. We'll finalize a shift schedule with the Chinese sentinels tomorrow."

Yusef sat down, still nursing bruised ribs. "What about me?"

Lombardi gave him a gentle smile. "You rest. You did enough for the day."

He nodded, though uncertainty played across his features. Helena sensed the teen's inner turmoil flaring up again: the push between staying or returning home. She patted his shoulder. "We appreciate you."

Colonel Orlov cleared his throat, voice dripping with sarcasm. "All so cozy. Mind unlocking these cuffs? The disturbances are gone, remember?"

Dave glowered. "If we release you, you might call your men. But maybe that's unavoidable eventually. Fine. We'll let you go tomorrow morning. For now, sleep."

The Russian spat on the floor but didn't resist. Tension remained, though the Ark's phenomena no longer threatened everyone's sanity. Helena embraced that small victory. She prayed the day wouldn't spiral anew.

As night settled, a fresh wave of shadows filled the warehouse. The infiltration group took shifts resting or patrolling. Father Lombardi at last found a deeper sleep, the bullet graze scabbing over. Dave hovered near Helena in companionable silence, scanning any suspicious movements near the Ark. Yusef drifted in and out of troubled dreams, and Ibrahim occasionally paced outside, phone in hand. Orlov endured the indignity of chain-linked discomfort, stewing in bitterness.

Shortly before midnight, a gentle knock sounded at the door. Dave and Helena exchanged alarmed looks. She approached carefully, gun at the ready. "Who's there?"

A whisper came. "Ming Xia's men. We have equipment to install for tomorrow's watch."

Helena exhaled. "They said they'd come tomorrow." But she unlatched the door a fraction. Two men in dark suits stood there, each holding sensor arrays. They bowed politely. Dave recognized them from the crates earlier, though not Ming Xia herself.

"Forgive the late visit," said one. "We came to set up the final calibrations. Minimal intrusion, I promise."

She glanced at Dave. He nodded, letting them in. The men placed small sensor pods along the walls near the Ark's crate, connecting wires to a compact control box. Lombardi stirred awake, ready to chant if phenomena flared, but the relic remained calm. The men typed commands on a handheld unit, then bowed. "Installation done. We'll leave. Officer Ming Xia returns in the morning."

After they departed, Dave locked up again. Helena sighed. "At least they're consistent. The disturbances truly appear dormant."

He nodded. "Better than a surprise assault."

The group returned to uneasy rest, hoping the sensors wouldn't malfunction. So far, the Ark's activity stayed quiet, a thin blessing. A hush blanketed the city outside, though Helena suspected sentinels lurked in the dark. She drifted into a patchy sleep, mind swirling with half-formed dreams of cherubim and swirling gold.

Dawn arrived with a mild haze over Istanbul. The infiltration group stirred, stiff-limbed. Orlov demanded release once more. Dave and Ibrahim agreed, seeing no reason to keep him any longer. They unlocked the cuffs, escorted him outside. The colonel spat curses, marched off down the street, shoulders squared in defiance. Helena felt an odd pang—he might reappear with renewed vengeance, or vanish from their story forever.

After a basic breakfast of stale biscuits, Lombardi performed a brief check for phenomena. The sensors blinked green, no sign of electromagnetic surges. The Ark shone, silent in its wooden nest. Yusef cradled his sprained wrist, occasionally wincing, though less stiff than before.

By mid-morning, Ming Xia returned, accompanied by two uniformed Chinese specialists who carried more gear. They calmly set up a small station in a corner, hooking it to the sensor array. Father Lombardi watched warily, but no manifestations flared. The sentinels introduced themselves as Li Wei and Guan Shan, each speaking minimal English. Dave assigned them a wedge of floor to roll out sleeping mats, ensuring they wouldn't roam freely. Helena noticed a subtle tension in Li Wei's posture, as though expecting betrayal.

Ming Xia faced Helena, voice steady. "So this is how it begins: minimal sentinels, phenomena dormant, each side monitoring. Let's formalize a rotation schedule."

She and Dave consulted a whiteboard found in a dusty corner. They hashed out a timetable: Chinese sentinels in the evening, infiltration group sentinels in the day. Lombardi or another Catholic representative on call for disturbances. They typed a short contract on Helena's laptop, printing it with a small portable printer. Ming Xia read it thoroughly, then signed. Dave, Helena, and Lombardi did likewise, with Ibrahim witnessing. Another half-facsimile of a binding agreement, a patchwork of hope.

After finalizing, Ming Xia turned to Father Lombardi. "If disturbances never reappear, do we even need your chanting again?"

He exhaled. "The ceremony's success depends on no one interfering with the Ark. If someone tries opening it or forcing manifestations, the damage could undo our chant. Then we must repeat the entire ceremony."

She nodded, eyes reflecting determination. "Understood. We have no intention of forcibly opening it, unless an urgent reason arises."

A ghost of sarcasm flitted over Dave's mouth. "Let's hope no one tries."

Helena watched them carefully, sensing that each side merely postponed the final power struggle. For the moment, illusions were quiet, so the impetus for violence waned. But the Ark remained a powder keg, ready to spark global ambition at the slightest push.

Yusef approached Helena, voice low. "Can I talk to you?"

She guided him to a quiet corner. He shifted on his feet, gaze flicking to the Ark. "I think... it might be time for me to go home. We have troopers now. The phenomena are calm. You have a partial alliance. If everything remains stable, maybe my job is done."

Her eyes stung with emotion. "You're sure? You've been integral. We appreciate you more than you know."

He gave a small shrug, wincing at bruises. "I never wanted a life of endless gun battles and relic-induced chaos. I just wanted to ensure the Ark wouldn't destroy Jerusalem or anywhere else." He hesitated. "I'll wait another day, to see if this arrangement truly holds. But after that, I plan to find a flight back. My mother must be worried sick."

Helena nodded, swallowing. "We'll support you. Thank you for everything. You saved us more than once."

He offered a faint smile, though sadness tinged it. She embraced him gently, mindful of his bruises. The teen stepped away, eyes shining with unshed tears. "I'll always remember this. But enough is enough."

She squeezed his hand. "Understood."

Meanwhile, Dave and Ming Xia continued refining details with Ibrahim on how many watchmen could come or go, how to handle local criminals, and who would contact Turkish authorities if a major threat emerged. Lombardi hovered, occasionally chiming in, his posture stiff from weariness. The entire morning passed in that swirl of negotiations. By midday, an uneasy consensus formed: minimal guards from both sides, illusions inert, no forced opening, and any new trouble reported to the entire group.

Helena breathed out relief. "We have a plan. Let's hope it holds at least a few days."

Ming Xia's expression remained unreadable. "We share that hope. In the meantime, I'll arrange lodging for my sentinels near the city center. We'll keep shifts rotating here. Let's avoid a debacle."

She turned to depart, her men following, leaving behind a small kit of advanced sensors. "We'll see you tomorrow, or call if an emergency arises." She vanished through the warehouse door, her footsteps echoing outside.

Ibrahim rubbed his chin, a mixture of hope and worry creasing his face. "We have sentinels from China, sentinels from us, and the phenomena are dormant. Could it truly be resolved this simply?"

Dave shrugged. "It's more of a pause. So many factions remain out there, from black-market gangs to Orlov's men. But for the moment, the Ark isn't fueling manifestations or fresh ambition."

Father Lombardi slumped onto a crate, grimacing at the pain in his arm. "Let's pray it lasts."

Helena concurred, scanning each face. The immediate tension had eased, but a profound unease lingered. This city was a tinderbox of clandestine interests, all overshadowed by a relic that once conjured biblical legends. She felt Dave's reassuring gaze, offering a flicker of solace. Yusef's stance was guarded, likely ready to depart soon. Ibrahim looked wrung out, longing for a simpler outcome.

In the late afternoon, while the Chinese watchmen began installing additional software on their sensor array, Helena stepped outside with Dave to catch a breath of fresh air. The searing heat had abated, replaced by a mild breeze. She leaned against the warehouse's exterior, letting her eyelids flutter shut. He stood beside her, posture reflecting the same exhaustion.

"Feels surreal," she murmured. "After all that chaos, the Ark's phenomena vanish with a single ceremony, and we're left with... politics."

He chuckled. "Welcome to real life, I guess. The Ark was a terrifying superweapon or swirling chaos. Now it's inert, so everyone jockeys for ownership."

She opened her eyes, regarding him. "You think it'll stay inert forever?"

His smile faded. "I doubt it. A single misguided attempt to open it or harness its energy, and the chanting might fail. That's why we can't let any faction hold it alone."

She nodded, pushing a stray lock of hair behind her ear. "I keep replaying the apparitions we saw, the swirling visions. Hard to believe they're gone."

He touched her cheek lightly, a subtle gesture that warmed her inside. "We saw wonders, faced nightmares. It's not over, but you and Lombardi solved the worst of it. I'm proud of you."

Her cheeks flushed. She bowed her head. "It was a team effort, truly."

They lapsed into a comfortable silence, hearts beating in fragile harmony. Then Father Lombardi's voice called from within: "Helena, Dave, come here."

They reentered the warehouse. The priest stood by the Ark, glancing at sensors that beeped. The Chinese sentinels had stepped outside for a break. Lombardi furrowed his brow. "I just rechecked the text. The phenomena are indeed sealed away, but the notes mention any strong attempt at forcibly opening the chest or physically removing the cherubim lid might break the chant's hold. We must be vigilant."

Dave exhaled, turning to the group. "So if someone tries to extract what's inside—like rumored stone tablets—the Ark's disturbances might roar back?"

Lombardi nodded. "Yes. And the partial verses we used might not suffice a second time unless we replicate the entire ceremony carefully. That means we need me, or a similarly trained priest, on standby. If local criminals think the Ark contains gold or relics to sell, we risk a meltdown."

Helena felt her stomach twist. "We must triple-check security. The energy may be subdued, but the chest is still priceless to black-market circles. If they try breaking it open for relic scraps, it'll unleash havoc."

Ibrahim rubbed his temples. "We can't anchor ourselves in this warehouse forever, but we also can't move it easily without triggering suspicion or a swarm of criminals."

Dave paced. "We might need a second location, safer, under locked guard with actual security systems. But that means we must coordinate with Ming Xia— she'll want to supervise the move, keep the Ark from reactivating. Meanwhile, local criminals might strike mid-transport."

Father Lombardi massaged his wounded arm. "We face no problems for now. That's an improvement. Let's not overcomplicate. If local criminals try, we have look-outs from both sides. They might be deterred by the combined presence of an official faction."

Yusef, listening from his corner, stepped forward, wincing. "I can help plan routes if you do move it. But I still plan to leave soon if nothing goes wrong."

Helena gently placed a hand on his unbruised shoulder. "We appreciate you. Let's see how stable this arrangement is for a day or two. If everything remains quiet, you can head home with peace of mind."

A flicker of relief touched his eyes. "Thank you."

The hours that followed felt almost ordinary. Chinese sentinels fiddled with sensors. Dave and Helena mapped out potential new sites, scanning satellite images on a battered laptop. Lombardi napped. Ibrahim patrolled the perimeter, phone in hand, monitoring rumors. Yusef tidied the corner. For the first time in weeks, visions did not overshadow every breath. The Ark sat silent, an artifact of unimaginable power, temporarily tamed.

Night rolled in. Ming Xia's watchmen took the evening shift. Dave insisted Helena rest properly, so she settled on a sleeping mat near the Ark, drifting into a deeper slumber than she'd had in ages. Dreams, for once, were free of swirling apparitions or winged guardians. Instead, she saw glimpses of a calm city and Dave's gentle presence.

She awoke near midnight to murmured voices. One Chinese specialist, Li Wei, was speaking with Dave about sensor readouts. All normal. Helena stretched, noticing Yusef dozing on a separate mat. Lombardi turned in his sleep, wincing. She realized that, for the moment, the warehouse was calmer than any time since the illusions began.

Yet her intuition nagged: the calm might be a prelude to a bigger confrontation. She recalled local criminals who beat Yusef, Orlov's vow of revenge, the swirling possibilities. The Ark might appear inert, but it remained a beacon for those who desired power. The illusions might be gone, but greed remained.

She rose, rubbed her eyes, and joined Dave near the sensors. "How's it going?" she whispered.

He shrugged. "All quiet. Li Wei says the EM field is minimal, no energy release. Everyone's basically waiting to see if some outsider storms in."

She gazed at the Ark, the gold filigree dull in the faint light. "Then let's hope we can hold this line. For now, the arks energy is no longer the main threat. Human ambition is."

He nodded, stepping closer, his tone soft. "We'll handle it. We overcame illusions, we can outmaneuver criminals and factions, right?"

She mustered a lopsided grin. "One step at a time."

His hand brushed hers, a brief moment of warmth in the dim space. The hush felt fragile, poised between triumph over illusions and the looming shadow of conflict. She inhaled, steadying her resolve.

They had subdued an crumbling power, at least temporarily. The world around them, though, was far from subdued. Tomorrow or the next day, forces might converge again, with the Ark's unimaginable significance fueling a final reckoning. For now, in that silent warehouse on the edge of Istanbul, with battered hearts and fragile alliances, they clung to a slender hope that illusions wouldn't resurface—and that the city's swirling complexity wouldn't devour them all.

Chapter 14

Dawn's first light spilled across the industrial district, painting the corrugated rooftops in pale gold. A faint marine breeze wafted in from the Bosphorus, mingling with the lingering smell of engine oil. Inside the warehouse, Helena Carter awoke to see Father Aurelius Lombardi carefully standing near the Ark, reciting a short litany. She sighed with relief that illusions remained absent. The Chinese specialists huddled around their sensor station, typing notes. Dave Schumer, resting on a crate, nodded in acknowledgement when she stirred.

They had now spent two nights in uneasy cohabitation with Ming Xia's sentinels. Both sides maintained respectful distance, suspicious yet bound by necessity. Colonel Orlov was gone. The illusions were gone. The Ark, locked and inert, sat at the center of everything. Peace could vanish with a single misstep, but for the moment, it held.

Helena slid over to Lombardi. "How's your arm?"

He grimaced. "Tender, but healing. I can manage."

She nodded. "Good. We might see the local criminals or other factions soon. Are you strong enough to recite the ceremony again if the Ark reawakens?"

He inhaled, rubbing his bandaged wound. "I'll do my best. But the chant is more draining each time. Let's pray no one tries opening the Ark."

One of Ming Xia's men, Li Wei, glanced over, seemingly listening. He cleared his throat. "We have no intention of forcing this thing to wake up. My commander asked me to reaffirm that she wants the relic stable, not unleashed."

Helena gave him a curt nod. "We appreciate that clarity."

Nearby, Dave conferred with Ibrahim, double-checking if Orlov's men or local criminals had surfaced. The Israeli liaison shook his head. "So far, no sign of Orlov's squad. Word is the local gang is still sniffing around, but we've had no direct contact."

Dave breathed relief. "Let's hope they realize the powers are gone."

Yusef, bruised but mobile, ambled over. "I've decided to leave tomorrow," he announced, eyes on Helena. "That is, if nothing explodes by then."

A pang of regret struck her. "I'll miss you. But I understand." She gave a small, genuine smile, ignoring the ache in her shoulder. "You've earned your rest."

He nodded, lips drawn. "I just hope I can do so without guilt."

Before Helena could speak further, a tap sounded at the warehouse door. Dave froze, hand on his sidearm. "Who is it?" he called.

A muffled voice came, female but not Ming Xia's. "I come on Father Lombardi's invitation."

Helena frowned at the priest, who blinked in confusion. "Not me," he whispered. "I invited no one."

Suspicion prickled. Dave gestured for Li Wei to watch the Ark. He and Helena approached the door, guns at the ready. "Open it carefully," Dave whispered.

She slid the latch, cracked the door. A middle-aged woman in a long coat stood outside, hair pulled back, a small cross visible on a chain around her neck. Her posture was calm, though she clasped a battered leather portfolio. "Peace be with you," she said, in slightly accented English. "I come from the Vatican's local contacts. Father Lombardi's superiors asked me to assist. My name is Sister Sabine."

Helena eyed her warily. "We have enough sentinels. Lombardi never mentioned you."

Father Lombardi shuffled over, leaning around Helena. "Sister Sabine?" He squinted. "I recall the name. A translator from the archives in Rome?"

She offered a gentle nod. "Yes, I was sent to help ensure the Ark is well-guarded. Let me in, please."

Dave exchanged a look with Lombardi. The priest shrugged, wincing at his bullet graze. "We can at least hear her out."

They allowed Sister Sabine to enter. Her eyes swept the room, lingering on the Ark's crate. A flicker of awe crossed her features. "Truly the Ark... I sense a hush about it."

Helena responded curtly. "The thing is dormant for now. The final ceremony lines were performed. We're precariously stable."

Sister Sabine bowed her head. "The Church is grateful. Father Lombardi, I bring you more official support. If illusions remain quiet, we can facilitate secret storage in a hidden monastic site near Istanbul or transport it directly to Rome. The Holy See is prepared to keep the relic from political exploitation."

Dave frowned. "We just hammered out a neutrality arrangement with the Chinese. We can't whisk the Ark to the Vatican without reneging on that deal."

A mild smile touched Sister Sabine's lips. "Surely, if this thing remains hushed, a more reliable location than this warehouse is best. The Church has centuries of safeguarding experience. The Chinese approach is unsanctioned by Scripture."

Ibrahim bristled. "And Israel's rightful claim means it belongs in Jerusalem, not Rome."

Lombardi raised a hand gently. "Let's not spark conflict. The illusions remain calm for the moment, but Sister Sabine's presence might help with translations or theological aspects. We can decide the Ark's final resting place later. For now, we maintain the uneasy truce."

Sister Sabine dipped her head respectfully. "I'll abide by your arrangement. The Church only asks to be included in further negotiations."

Helena sighed. Another faction to juggle. "Fine. You can stay if you follow the same rules: no attempts to remove the Ark alone. We share watchmen with the Chinese, keep the phenomena suppressed, and avoid more violence."

The nun nodded, tucking her portfolio under an arm. "I'm here to serve peace, not to instigate trouble."

Thus Sister Sabine joined their ranks. She settled near Lombardi's cot, speaking in Italian now and then. Dave shot Helena a wry look. "More players every day."

Helena gave a small, exasperated shrug. "At least the Ark's disturbances are gone. Otherwise, these expansions might be bloodier."

Yusef ambled over to Sister Sabine, curiosity shining in his eyes. He asked if she had knowledge about the Ark's historical references. She responded with surprising detail about old crusader documents, stirring a flicker of interest in the teen. Helena noticed how Yusef, always hungry for knowledge, soaked up her insights. Despite bruises and fatigue, his mind remained keen.

Throughout the day, the infiltration group integrated Sister Sabine into their watch schedule. The two Chinese specialists eyed her suspiciously, but no immediate clash erupted. Father Lombardi, relieved of some pressure, dozed more, his body healing from the bullet wound. Dave took a short run for extra supplies, returning with basic groceries and a small stash of medical items. The Ark's arcs did not reappear once, confirming the ceremony's success so far.

By late afternoon, a hush fell across the warehouse. Helena felt drowsy in the warm stillness. The overhead lights buzzed. She kept scanning for suspicious movement outside, half expecting a black-market gang to burst in. Every small noise from the street made her tense. She forced herself to breathe.

Then a phone beeped—Ibrahim's. He stepped aside, took the call, then returned with a pale expression. "Reports say a group of armed men was spotted near the harbor, asking about a golden relic. Some might be Russians, maybe Orlov's men."

Dave cursed under his breath. "We let him go. He probably called reinforcements. They might want to retake the Ark, dormant or not."

Lombardi rose from his seat, a line of worry creasing his brow. "We can't endure a direct assault. The Ark remains stable, so a gun battle is purely political or criminal. Perhaps we should appeal to Ming Xia's sentinels for help."

Helena's heart pounded. "We can't outrun Orlov's squad if they mount a surprise. Ming Xia's sentinels are only two men. Unless she sends more, we're outgunned."

Dave pursed his lips. "We can see if the local authorities might help, but that invites official intervention. Or we can relocate again, but that breaks our arrangement with the Chinese."

Ibrahim frowned. "If Orlov's men storm this place, the Ark's energy might stay dormant, so they'd rely on brute force. We can't rely on the relic to defend us. This is a normal conflict now—though dangerous."

Sister Sabine stepped forward gently. "God guides us, but we must be practical. If Orlov's men approach, we either need a strong allied force or we must vanish with the Ark. A third option is trusting local law enforcement, but that reveals everything."

Helena pressed a hand to her forehead, tension swirling. "We have to weigh losing trust with Ming Xia if we vanish. But being pinned by Orlov's squad is lethal."

Dave paced in short arcs. "Let's see if Ming Xia can supply more guards or quickly scare off Orlov's team. I'll call her. If she refuses or we sense a trap, we bail."

Ibrahim nodded, phone in hand. "I'll gather more intel, see how big Orlov's group is."

As Dave placed a call to Ming Xia, Helena exhaled heavily. Yusef sank onto a crate, wincing from his bruises. Sister Sabine whispered a short prayer for safety. Father Lombardi hovered near the Ark, posture tense. The newly minted peace threatened to implode under the weight of Russian aggression.

After a few moments, Dave finished his call. "She said she'll send three more men if we want them, but it might take an hour or two. She warns we must not move the Ark. If we do, they'll consider it a breach."

Lombardi pursed his lips. "Better than facing Orlov alone. Let's accept her help."

Helena exhaled, anxiety prickling. "Yes. Let's hold on. I just hope Orlov's men don't strike before Ming Xia's reinforcements arrive."

Ibrahim spoke after checking new messages. "They're heading our way, maybe half an hour out, five or six men with a van. Could be more trailing behind."

Dave clenched his fists. "We can barricade the door. The Chinese sentinels can help. Sister Sabine can assist Lombardi if disturbances—well, disturbances won't help. We'll fight or negotiate."

Helena nodded, heart pounding. "Orlov might attempt brute force. Let's prepare. Everyone, find cover, set up a vantage point. We try words first, but if they shoot, we defend ourselves."

A tense flurry of activity followed. Dave, Ibrahim, and the two Chinese specialists stacked crates near the main entrance, forming a rudimentary barricade. Helena helped position Father Lombardi behind a safe zone, ensuring the Ark remained center stage but locked. Sister Sabine checked her phone, possibly for additional Vatican contacts. Yusef stationed himself behind a tall metal shelf, determined to help despite battered limbs.

Minutes ticked by. The overhead lights buzzed. Adrenaline spiked in Helena's veins as she crouched behind crates, pistol in hand. Dave knelt a few feet away, focusing on the entrance. The Chinese sentinels readied submachine guns. Ibrahim's face was set with grim resolve. Father Lombardi murmured the smallest snippet of the chant, though the Ark's phenomena would not spontaneously aid them. The relic gleamed, unhelpful in this purely human standoff.

At last, an engine roared outside. Doors slammed. Footfalls approached the locked entrance, followed by aggressive pounding. A harsh voice barked in Russian-accented English, "Open up. Colonel Orlov demands entry!"

Dave threw a warning glance at Helena, then shouted, "We have an agreement with other factions. Turn around or risk violence."

A sneer came from the other side. "We'll see about that. Either open, or we break it down."

Helena's pulse hammered. She signaled Dave to keep them busy. He yelled, "The Ark is inert. The disturbances are gone. Why do you want it?"

A pause, then a vicious chuckle. "Our colonel says the relic's energies might reignite if we apply the right methods. Stand aside, American. Or we'll handle you."

Dave nodded to the Chinese sentinels. They stepped behind the barricade, guns aimed. Ibrahim tightened his grip on a pistol. Sister Sabine clasped her hands, eyes darting to Lombardi. Yusef tensed, trying not to tremble.

A heavy thud smashed the door from outside. Another blow. The metal hinges groaned. Dave shouted, "Stop! We will defend ourselves."

No response. A third slam made the door buckle. Splinters of wood from the frame rained down. The infiltration team braced, knuckles whitening on their weapons. Suddenly, the battered door crashed inward, revealing half a dozen armed men in paramilitary gear. At their front stood Colonel Orlov, face twisted with grim fury. He wore a Kevlar vest, brandishing an assault rifle.

"Back away from the Ark," Orlov snarled. "This relic belongs to Russia. Any residual forces will be ours to command."

Helena's heart pounded. She aimed her pistol, swallowing dread. "We can't let you seize it, residual energies or not. Don't do this."

Orlov barked a cruel laugh. "You think I care about energies now? Russia will claim the relic's symbolic power and mastery over any lingering effects. Surrender or die."

Dave fired a warning shot overhead, bullet spanging off the metal rafters. "Stop, Colonel. We have sentinels from China here, armed. This is suicide."

Orlov's men spread out, crouching behind a pile of boxes. One returned fire, bullets cracking near Dave's barricade. Helena flinched at the muzzle flashes. The infiltration group hunkered down, returning shots. Sister Sabine ducked behind Lombardi's crate, letting out a trembling prayer. Yusef pressed himself low, remembering the caretaker's mansion debacle.

Gunfire echoed in the enclosed space, muzzle flashes lighting up the gloom. The Ark sat silent, arcs nonexistent. Orlov's men advanced behind covering fire. The Chinese specialists unleashed controlled bursts from submachine guns. Dave cursed under his breath, exchanging a savage volley with two Russians who tried to flank the crate. One went down, screaming, the other scuttled behind an overturned shelving unit.

Bullets ricocheted off concrete, shards spraying. Helena coughed in the swirling dust, checking that Lombardi remained safe. The priest huddled behind the Ark, Sister Sabine shielding him as best she could. She glimpsed

Orlov, rifle aimed at the Chinese sentinels. The colonel fired a burst, striking one of them in the leg. A cry of pain echoed. Li Wei toppled backward, moaning.

Ibrahim returned fire, pinning Orlov behind a metal beam. Dave advanced two steps, motioning Helena to flank left. She nodded, creeping through the swirling haze, pistol raised. Another Russian soldier popped up, unleashing a flurry. She ducked, bullets whizzing overhead. Her pulse roared in her ears.

In the confusion, Yusef grabbed a small sidearm Dave had given him for emergencies. He took aim at a Russian operative circling around to the Ark's blind side. The teen's hand shook, but he squeezed the trigger. The shot clipped the attacker's shoulder, driving him to the floor. Yusef gasped, startled by his own action. The gunman groaned, weapon clattering. Lombardi watched from behind the crate, eyes wide at the teen's surprising courage.

Orlov, seeing his men falter, roared in frustration. He pivoted, empting half a magazine at Helena's position. She scrambled behind a steel support. Sparks flew as rounds pinged off metal. Dave fired from an angle, forcing Orlov to duck. Ibrahim advanced, delivering a shot that nailed a second Russian in the leg. The intruders were pinned, losing momentum.

Helena steadied her breath, aimed at the colonel's silhouette behind the beam. Before she could pull the trigger, Orlov hurled a smoke grenade. It spewed thick clouds, obscuring the back half of the warehouse. He barked orders in Russian, likely telling his men to retreat. She coughed in the haze, eyes stinging. The infiltration group kept firing in short bursts, uncertain of the enemies' exact positions.

In the swirling smoke, Helena sensed movement near the door. She glimpsed Orlov's shape ushering two wounded men out, cursing under his breath. Another figure limped behind him. The infiltration team advanced cautiously, unsure if the Russians left an ambush. When the smoke cleared, Orlov's men were gone, the door battered. Blood trails and shell casings littered the floor.

Ibrahim coughed, stepping around crates. "They're gone. They retreated."

Dave helped the wounded Chinese specialist, Li Wei, propping him against a crate. Sister Sabine rushed forward to press bandages on the bullet wound. Lombardi knelt too, offering a comforting prayer. Yusef leaned against a metal post, heart hammering. Helena scanned for any signs of phenomena, but the Ark remained silent, no arcs dancing. Her shoulders sagged with relief. The ceremony's effect held.

A hush settled, broken only by Li Wei's pained groans. Dave radioed for medical help from Ming Xia's network. Yusef sank to the floor, trembling at the violence he'd participated in once again. Helena gently squeezed his good shoulder, murmuring encouragement. Father Lombardi, breathing heavily, rose to check the Ark. No damage from stray rounds, though bullet holes marked the crate's sides. If any had penetrated the chest, the phenomena might have revived, but it seemed intact.

Ibrahim paced near the door, scanning the street. "No sign of them. They must've had a getaway car. We should expect another attempt eventually."

Dave nodded, wiping sweat from his brow. "We wounded a few, though. They might think twice. Or they might return with more men. Either way, the relic's energy is still dormant."

Helena exhaled, adrenaline fading. "We need the city's official help or a real fortress to store the Ark. We can't handle repeated shootouts."

Sister Sabine, pressing a compress to Li Wei's wound, said, "The Church can arrange a hidden monastery in the region, if you're willing. But that breaks the truce with the Chinese sentinels."

The injured Chinese man mumbled something in Mandarin. Ibrahim recognized the gist. "He says the Chinese watchmen can bring more security once we contact Ming Xia. We just have to stand firm."

Helena slumped on a crate, eyes stinging with tears. Another debacle, albeit short, with the Ark's activity nowhere to be found. It confirmed that human ambition was the real threat now. Orlov's men had retreated, but at cost. The infiltration team nursed a fresh wound among their sentinels. She wondered how many more times bullets would fly around the inert Ark before an official resolution came.

Dave crouched beside her, voice soft. "You okay?"

She nodded, sniffling once. "Yes. Tired of the violence."

He gently placed a hand on her shoulder. "We're close to a stable outcome. Let's keep pushing." The warmth in his gaze steadied her, offering a fragile spark of hope.

Lombardi adjusted his collar, glancing at the relic. "The phenomena remain subdued. If the outside world recognized that, maybe fewer factions would fight for it. But to them, the Ark is still symbolic of unlimited power, dormant or not."

Yusef, chest heaving, forced words out. "I can't do this anymore. I'm sorry. I'll leave tomorrow. I've had enough near-death experiences." He gulped, tears brimming. "I don't want to kill or be killed. I want to return to my old city life."

Helena rubbed his back. "You've given so much. It's okay. We'll manage. Thank you."

He buried his face in his hands, trembling. Ibrahim stepped over, offering a quiet pat on the teen's shoulder. Dave gave Helena a meaningful nod. Yusef's departure was overdue. They would see him off in the morning, or whenever flights were available.

Hours passed while they patched bullet holes, tidied the space, and comforted Li Wei. Another Chinese operative arrived, courtesy of Ming Xia, providing first aid and a vow that more reinforcements were inbound soon. Orlov's squad did not reappear that night. The warehouse fell into a subdued hush, tension coiling around the group like a serpent.

Past midnight, Dave and Helena found themselves alone near the Ark, the Chinese sentinels busy at their sensor station, Lombardi and Sister Sabine conferring in hushed tones about potential monastery solutions, and Yusef dozing fretfully. Ibrahim patrolled outside with the new operative, scanning dark corners for any sign of intrusion.

Helena gazed at the relic's silent gold, remembering how phenomena had once sparked swirling shapes. "It's almost anticlimactic now," she whispered to Dave.

He sighed, leaning close enough that she could hear the faint catch in his breath. "All that terror from the Ark's effects, undone by a chant. Now the danger is purely from humans. Sometimes that's worse."

She nodded. "Yes. We can't fix greed or nationalism with a ritual."

He brushed a strand of hair from her cheek. "We fix it day by day, forging alliances to keep the Ark inert. If we do that until an official pact forms, maybe we'll avoid a global meltdown."

She smiled, ignoring the banned word. "Let's hope so." Her eyes flicked to the corner, verifying no energy shimmered. "I dread the next debacle if Orlov or local gangs escalate. But for tonight, we're stable."

Dave took her hand, squeezing gently. "We hold on to small mercies."

They lingered in that quiet moment, hearts slowed, wariness tempered by a fragile sense of unity. The Ark, watchful and aged, glinted in the dim light. No disturbances marred the night. The overhead bulbs buzzed, a hum that replaced the swirl of supernatural forces. Outside, muffled city noise drifted by: distant horns, a barking dog, footsteps on pavement.

As Helena closed her eyes, leaning into Dave's steady presence, she realized they had stumbled onto a precarious plateau. The Ark no longer haunted their every breath, but the tension from each faction threatened to shatter the calm. Father Lombardi and Sister Sabine embodied the Vatican's zeal, Ming Xia's troopers claimed advanced technology, Orlov's men lurked in the shadows, and Israel's claim shimmered behind Ibrahim's every move. Yusef was on the verge of leaving, carrying bruises both physical and emotional.

Yet the relic itself, once an unstoppable storm of chaos, remained caged. For all the dread it had unleashed, the Ark now slumbered at the center of a tangled web of alliances. Helena prayed the next day or week might pass without triggering new battles. The Ark's power had been contained, but the real meltdown might come from human hearts, thirsting for control or retribution.

Finally, she rested her head on Dave's shoulder, letting exhaustion claim her once more. The hush of the warehouse lulled her into a dreamless doze, free of swirling apparitions. For the moment, victory over the Ark's energy felt real, even if the future bristled with unknown perils. If only this calm could hold. If only mankind's greed and distrust would remain at bay as thoroughly as the Ark's phenomena had been banished.

In the soft glow of night, the Ark lay motionless, arcs extinguished, silent as an crumbling tomb. The sentinels continued their quiet vigil, waiting for either dawn or a new threat to disturb the relic's slumber. Helena drifted deeper into that tenuous hope, wishing the Ark's disturbances could remain sealed forever, yearning for a day when the world no longer trembled before its potential. But in the depths of her weary soul, she feared the final confrontation lay ahead, bigger than the Ark's phenomena, overshadowing all they had endured thus far.

Chapter 15

Sunlight crept through the dusty windows of the rented Istanbul warehouse, spilling thin beams across the concrete floor where the Ark of the Covenant rested in quiet splendor. Silence blanketed the interior. Since the final ritual had neutralized the chest's illusions, no supernatural arcs danced across its gilded edges, yet tension clung to every surface. The subdued relic had become a magnet for conflicting agendas, each more dangerous than the last.

Father Aurelius Lombardi finished a short prayer, then leaned on a tall crate for support. Sleep had done little to restore him; pain from the bullet wound still gnawed at his arm. Nearby, Sister Sabine—a middle-aged nun recently sent by the Vatican—observed the Ark with a look both reverent and intrigued. Her presence had unsettled Lombardi. He recognized her from Rome, but the memory of clandestine tasks lingered in his thoughts.

She was a skilled translator, yes, but might also report to more zealous powers within the Church.

David Schumer adjusted the strap on his holster. He stood by the battered metal door, gaze shifting between the quiet street outside and the guards from China who had installed their sensor station. Two specialists—one still nursing a bandaged leg from the last firefight—tapped on a console, monitoring electromagnetic readouts that remained flatlined. The Ark was dormant. For the moment.

Helena Carter crouched beside Yusef Nasir, examining his bruised ribs and sprained wrist one last time. The teen winced but tried to smile. "I'll manage. The flight leaves in a few hours, right?"

She nodded, forcing optimism into her voice. "Yes. We found an airline with a seat open. Ibrahim called in a few favors. You'll be on your way soon."

Yusef's face held a flicker of guilt. "I hate leaving while everyone's still in danger, but I can't do this forever. My mother fears I won't come back alive."

Helena patted his uninjured shoulder. "You did more than anyone expected. You helped keep illusions from running rampant and saved us from multiple attacks. No one can fault you for going home."

He nodded, lips pressed tight. "I'll never forget any of this. And if something changes, if you need me again…"

Her chest constricted at the unlikelihood of calling a bruised teenager back into the fray. Yet his courage had proven essential time and time again. She offered a grateful look. "We'll manage. Thank you."

Nearby, Dave stepped in. "I can drive Yusef to the airport. Unless we think it's too risky letting both of us go."

Ibrahim Mahdi—who was leaning against a tall shelving unit—spoke up. "I'll ride along too, ensure no one intercepts him on the way. The rest of you can keep watch here."

Sister Sabine cleared her throat. "I wish the boy safe travels. God protect him. Perhaps we should pray quickly before he departs."

Lombardi stared at her, recalling how quickly new Vatican envoys could shift from helpful to meddlesome. "Yes, but keep it brief," he said. "We can't lower our guard for too long."

Yusef accepted the offer, bowing his head politely. The nun murmured a short benediction, her gaze drifting to Lombardi in a way that suggested deeper layers of significance behind her presence. Helena caught that flicker, storing it in her mind. Sister Sabine might have her own Vatican instructions, separate from Lombardi's. This tension felt like an invisible cord connecting them.

When the brief prayer ended, Yusef gathered his few belongings in a small pack. Dave and Ibrahim led him toward a faded sedan parked out back—a leftover vehicle arranged by Ming Xia's look-outs for everyday errands. The Chinese specialists watched from behind the sensor console, making no move to object.

Helena followed them outside to say goodbye, ignoring the dryness in her throat. The teen hovered near the rear passenger door. Thin morning light showcased the bruises on his face, reminders of the city's lawless undercurrent. She wrapped him in a gentle embrace, mindful of his sore ribs. "You'll be missed," she whispered.

He swallowed, blinking rapidly. "You too. I hope illusions stay gone. This is bigger than me, but I want you to succeed, for everyone's sake."

She stepped back, tears threatening. "You'll do fine at home. Stay safe."

He nodded once more, then climbed into the sedan's back seat. Ibrahim took the driver's side while Dave settled in the passenger spot, scanning the street for threats. With a final wave, they pulled away, the engine's rumble fading into the morning bustle. Helena watched them vanish around the corner, heart aching. Yusef deserved a normal life.

Returning inside, she found Sister Sabine chatting with Lombardi. The Jesuit's face showed strain. Helena stepped closer, catching a snippet of conversation: something about a "private repository." She cleared her throat, making them turn.

Sabine smiled benignly. "We were discussing an alternative site. The Church has numerous hidden places near Istanbul or across the border where sacred items were once sequestered. If illusions are truly gone, we can move the Ark discreetly."

Helena forced a neutral tone. "We just finalized a neutrality arrangement with Ming Xia. Moving the Ark without them is out of the question."

Sabine's expression stayed mild. "Of course. We'd never act unilaterally. But if the local criminals keep testing your perimeter, or if Colonel Orlov returns, you may need a safer option. The Church stands ready."

Lombardi gave Helena a troubled shrug, as if he too saw potential conflict in Sabine's plan. "We haven't decided anything. For now, illusions are subdued, and we remain here."

Sabine bowed her head. "I only wish to help. The Ark belongs in a sacred space, far from worldly agendas."

Helena remained polite. "We appreciate your concern." Then she gestured at the battered corners of the warehouse. "But any move must involve every faction, or we risk a bigger confrontation."

Sabine's eyes flicked to the golden crate, a trace of intensity coloring her face. "Understood."

Minutes later, the overhead door rattled. Ming Xia's look-outs stiffened, guns half-raised until they recognized Dave and Ibrahim returning alone. Yusef was gone, presumably en route to safety. Helena sighed, burying her sadness.

Dave approached, letting out a breath. "We dropped him off at the airport terminal. No sign of trouble. He insisted on hugging me one last time." He swallowed, voice thick. "Feels odd letting him walk away, but it's right."

Helena offered a small nod. "He needs a normal life again."

Lombardi sat on a folding chair, gripping his bandaged arm. "We can handle the rest. Perhaps that boy deserves peace."

Sister Sabine hovered nearby, glancing between Dave and Lombardi. "Peace or not, the city remains dangerous. Have we heard any fresh news on Colonel Orlov's movements?"

Ibrahim shook his head. "No direct sighting. But local rumors say a high-profile Russian contact is forging alliances with a local gang in the harbor district. Word is something big might be planned in a day or two."

Helena's stomach tightened. "They might be massing to storm us again, phenomena or not."

Dave folded his arms, tension rippling through his shoulders. "We can't rely on the Ark's dormant state to defend ourselves. Our only advantage is the chest's inert condition, which might seem less tempting. But Orlov's men might think they can forcibly trigger its effects or break it open."

Lombardi frowned. "Breaking it open could unravel the ceremony's seal. If they pry off the lid, the disturbances might flood back, with no guarantee of control. The text warns of catastrophic consequences."

Sabine crossed herself. "That must not happen."

Ming Xia's guards said nothing, but their expressions hardened. One typed a message in Mandarin on a phone, presumably updating his superior. They had no desire to see the relic's power reignite or fall into the wrong hands. Tension hovered, unspoken but palpable.

Ibrahim exhaled, voice husky. "We either dig in here or look for a stronger refuge. The Chinese look-outs might handle local criminals if they come in small numbers, but if a larger force arrives, we're done."

Helena considered Sister Sabine's earlier offer, but she recalled Ming Xia's final instructions: no relocating the Ark without full agreement. Doing so would spark a new war. She felt pinned by every side's mistrust. "We wait, for now," she said. "We gather more intel, keep the relic's forces locked down. If Orlov's group approaches in force, we call Ming Xia and brace for a fight."

Dave, pressing a hand to her shoulder gently, gave a brief nod. "Then we stay vigilant. Let's rotate sentinels. The rest get some rest or scavenge for supplies."

They divided tasks. One of Ming Xia's specialists left to secure fresh groceries; Ibrahim arranged a second run for water. Sabine offered to help Father Lombardi re-check the chest's structural markings for any sign of tampering. Dave and Helena retreated to the far side of the warehouse, flipping through a battered notebook containing references from the partial translations. No phenomena, but a lingering unease settled over them like a heavy mist.labyrinth of human threats.

Softly, Dave said, "Feels strange with Yusef gone. He was a part of all this from the start."

She swallowed. "Yes, he was. I hope he finds peace at home." A faint ache tugged her thoughts. She pictured the teen's battered face, the determination in his eyes. "We owe him."

Dave mustered a wan smile. "We do. And we owe ourselves a moment of quiet, if that's even possible."

Helena gently touched the back of his hand. "Later, maybe. We should confirm the logs for sensor data. If illusions remain zero, we can reassure other sentinels. Show we're not hiding anything."

He squeezed her fingers briefly, an intimate gesture that sent warmth fluttering inside her chest. Subtle, but real. "Let's do that."

They spent the next hour with the Chinese sentinels, reviewing readouts that displayed a flat baseline. No electromagnetic surges. Lombardi nodded, content that the ceremony's effect endured. Sabine stood behind them, eyes flicking across the screen, occasionally taking notes in a small ledger. Helena caught a glimpse of Latin phrases scrawled in the nun's handwriting. Something about "the seat of atonement" and "cherubim guardians." She decided not to pry just yet.

Toward mid-afternoon, Sister Sabine pulled Lombardi aside for a private discussion. Helena, curious, moved closer to a stack of crates, half-listening while feigning to rummage for supplies. The nun spoke in hushed Italian, words tinted with urgency.

"If illusions remain silent," Sabine said, "then the Church must secure this relic soon. Father, you know the Holy See can keep it from the hands of national militaries. The last vow you took—"

Lombardi bristled. "I recall my vows, Sister. But we promised neutrality. If we break that, the Chinese sentinels would retaliate."

She lowered her voice further. "That might be the price of safeguarding it from secular powers. Our superiors fear letting governments form a new Tower of Babel."

Lombardi pressed his lips together, glancing around as if fearing eavesdroppers. "I can't sabotage the arrangement so soon. We must wait for a clearer path."

Sabine's gaze flickered with disappointment. "The cardinal who sent me insists the Church acts swiftly. If Colonel Orlov's men gather or if other criminals lurk, we cannot rely on illusions being silent. The Ark belongs in a sacred repository. I stand ready to help you effect that transfer, even if certain guards protest."

At that, Helena moved away, heart pounding. Sister Sabine was indeed ready to stage a covert relocation, risking open conflict. The Church's zeal was no less intense than Orlov's or Ming Xia's. She found Dave at the barricade, informed him of the partial exchange. He frowned, tension lining his jaw. "We can't let the Ark vanish behind everyone's back. That would start a new fight. Let's keep an eye on Sabine."

Helena nodded. "We will."

Evening shadows lengthened, painting the high windows in streaks of red and orange. A hush settled over the warehouse. Ming Xia had not appeared in person, but one extra Chinese operative arrived to reinforce the watch. That put three troopers from her side, plus Helena, Dave, Ibrahim, Lombardi, and Sister Sabine. The place felt cramped, each faction's presence a reminder of underlying suspicion.

Dave circulated among them, verifying no one tampered with the chest. Helena considered stepping outside for fresh air. She grabbed her phone and a small flashlight, nodded at him, and moved through the door into a breezy twilight. The sky overhead glowed with city lights, a thousand minarets and towers outlined against the darkening horizon. She inhaled, allowing the scent of grilled meat from a distant vendor to distract her from the anxiety gnawing inside.

Footsteps approached. Dave joined her, posture equally tense. They walked a few paces along the deserted street, glancing at the shuttered garages and silent corners. "I hate not knowing when Orlov might strike again," he muttered.

Helena rubbed her arms. "Or if Sister Sabine might move the Ark for the Vatican. Or if some local gang wants to break it open. The Ark's phenomena are quiet, but everything else is chaos."

He exhaled, slipping an arm lightly around her waist. The contact felt natural, an unspoken promise of trust. She leaned into him, letting his warmth soothe the chill creeping into her thoughts. "We can only keep watch," he said. "And wait for a chance to form a real consensus. If that fails, we might see disturbances reawaken in some future confrontation."

She pressed her cheek against his shoulder. "We've come so far—so many close calls. It's draining. I just want the Ark locked away in a safe corner of the world, its disturbances sealed forever."

His hand gently stroked her back. "You and me both." Then he pulled back slightly, scanning the alley for sentinels. "Let's head in. Don't want to leave them unsupervised."

Her lips quirked in a wry half-smile. "Right. Sister Sabine might be rummaging for a secret route out."

Dave chuckled grimly, guiding her back. They slipped through the door to find Lombardi in quiet conversation with Sabine once more, though her posture stiffened at their arrival. Ibrahim was at the far end of the warehouse, tapping messages on his phone. The Chinese watchmen typed sensor updates, ignoring the tension. The Ark remained in the same spot, inert and splendid.

They settled into a routine for the night, rotating watch shifts. Dave dozed from midnight until two. Helena woke him for her turn to rest. Sabine and Lombardi prayed at one point, but no disturbances stirred. Outside, some traffic rumbled, but no suspicious approach. The hush stretched into dawn.

By morning, the infiltration team awoke to faint radio chatter from the Chinese specialists. Helena, bleary-eyed, realized the sentinels had picked up rumor of a small infiltration group scoping nearby streets. She tensed, recalling Orlov's threat. Yet no direct confrontation occurred that day. Instead, minor black-market figures lurked, testing the perimeter with discreet glances. Ibrahim reported seeing suspicious men on a rooftop across the way, only to vanish the instant he reached for binoculars.

The hours passed with uneasy monotony. Dave left briefly to buy fresh water, returning with news that local store owners whispered about "an artifact of biblical power" in the district. The rumor mill was in full swing. Lombardi, anxious, repeated small chants in case the Ark's energy flickered, but the relic stayed docile. Sister Sabine hovered, offering help in logistic tasks while occasionally scribbling notes on a pad of paper.mysterious notes in her ledger.

By late afternoon, an attempt on the warehouse finally came. A battered truck rumbled down the side alley, halting near the door. Helena's heart lurched when she heard the squeal of tires. Dave, quick on his feet, signaled everyone to take positions behind crates. The Chinese watchmen armed themselves, scanning the door's sensor feed. A hush heavier than lead descended.

In a burst, two men leaped out of the truck, brandishing submachine guns. They fired a short volley at the locked entrance, bullets hammering the reinforced metal. Helena cowered behind a crate, fingers tightening on her pistol. Dave unholstered his sidearm, chest rising and falling with tense breath. One of the Chinese specialists triggered an alarm, echoing shrill through the building.

"Who's out there?" Dave shouted, voice echoing. Gunfire answered instead of words, chewing into the door's hinges. Shots pinged off the metal frame. Then footsteps pounded on the pavement. A third figure ran around to a side window, apparently searching for an easier entry.

Helena flattened herself behind a dusty pallet, vision swimming with memories of earlier ambushes. She recognized how easily illusions might have swayed these criminals if the Ark were still active. Now they relied on mortal firepower. She returned a shot through a gap, hearing a startled yelp outside. The infiltration group launched a barrage, forcing the attackers to duck behind their truck.

Seconds later, the battered vehicle revved in reverse, tires screeching. Through a cracked window, Helena glimpsed three men scuttling back into the cab. They screeched away, leaving bullet scars on the door. A short, vicious exchange of gunfire had repelled them. She forced a steadying breath, adrenaline pounding in her veins.

Ibrahim inspected the door. Several holes peppered the metal, and splinters from the frame littered the ground. None of the infiltration group had been hit, though. The Chinese guards rechecked their sensors, verifying the Ark's illusions stayed null. Dave joined Helena, helping her stand.

"That was a quick test," he muttered. "Local criminals deciding if they can break in?"

She nodded, heart hammering. "They found out we're armed. So they left, probably to regroup."

Sabine peeked from behind a storage unit, eyes wide. "You see? Danger is everywhere. We must move the Ark to sanctified ground."

Lombardi, still holding a pistol loosely, glared at her. "Not yet. We can't break the neutrality arrangement. Don't push me, Sister."

She pursed her lips, an unspoken rebuke in her expression. Helena recognized the deepening rift between them. The Jesuit might cling to the current arrangement, but Sabine's directive from the Vatican was growing obvious—secure the Ark for the Church at any cost.

After that brief firefight, the infiltration group reinforced the door with new metal braces. The Chinese troopers performed a perimeter check, discovering fresh tire tracks and a few shell casings in the alley. Dave documented the scene with phone pictures to show Ming Xia that local gangs were indeed testing them.

Days blurred into a pattern of vigilance. Minor infiltration attempts recurred: a hooded figure scoping the back windows at twilight, an unknown pair of men snapping clandestine photos from a parked sedan. Twice, the sentinels fired warning shots, sending prowlers scurrying. The Ark remained at the warehouse, illusions locked away by the completed ceremony. Tension soared.

Helena noted that Orlov himself didn't appear in any of these smaller attempts, suggesting he was forging alliances behind the scenes. Sister Sabine grew more agitated by each scare, pressing Lombardi to sanction a secret transfer to a monastic site. The priest refused, citing the neutrality vow. Meanwhile, Dave's face grew stony with each new incursion. Sleep was scarce.

One mild morning, roughly five days after Yusef departed, Helena sipped bitter coffee at a makeshift table. Dave read updated intelligence on his phone. Sister Sabine approached, stepping gingerly over piles of leftover crates. Her expression looked determined. "I must speak with you both," she said.

Dave set down the phone. "We're listening."

The nun folded her hands. "I fear Father Lombardi's health is deteriorating. He wants to remain here, but I see his bullet wound festering. He tries to hide it, but infection might take hold. He prays for the Ark's phenomena not to awaken, and I admire his faith, but he's physically weak. If anything, this predicament is harming him."

Helena frowned. "He hides the pain well, but I noticed he's paler. Has he refused hospital care?"

Sabine nodded gravely. "He insists on staying near the Ark, should the disturbances flicker. I told him it's reckless. If the local criminals break in again, how can he defend himself or chant effectively in his condition?"

Dave pressed his lips together. "We can't just send him to a hospital without look-outs or security. The press might discover who he is, and the Vatican arrangement might blow up."

Sabine's eyes narrowed with resolve. "Then let me take him to a discreet clinic the Church manages. He could recuperate there, away from prying eyes. The Ark remains inert; a priest might not be needed every minute."

Helena exchanged a quick glance with Dave. The suggestion had merit, but also opened the door for Sabine to attempt relocating the Ark or persuading Lombardi. "We appreciate your concern," she said, choosing her words carefully, "but we must confirm Father Lombardi wants that. He's the anchor of this neutrality. If he leaves, Sister, do you plan to remain and represent the Vatican?"

Sabine's mouth twitched. "If the Ark's energy remains dormant, my presence here might suffice. But Father Lombardi's knowledge of the chant is unmatched. In an emergency, we might need him."

Dave exhaled. "We can't allow him to die from infection. Let's talk to him and see what he wants. But we need an absolute guarantee that we're not forced to move the chest behind the Chinese sentinels' backs."

Sabine raised a hand, as if in blessing. "I promise no unilateral move."

Helena nodded. "All right. Let's speak with Lombardi together."

They found the priest near the Ark, flipping through the old ceremony text. Pale lines cut his features. When Sabine suggested a discreet clinic, he bristled at first, insisting the Ark's manifestations might reawaken. Helena gently pressed him: "We've gone a week without disturbances. If the local criminals or Orlov's men open the chest, phenomena might return, but then it'll be too late anyway. You can't recite the full ceremony in your weakened state."

He grimaced, eventually conceding. "Perhaps a short hospital stay would help me recover. But keep me informed of every development. If phenomena spark, I'll come right away."

Sabine offered a faint, relieved smile. "The clinic is half an hour away. I can escort you. They know how to treat bullet wounds discreetly."

The Jesuit cleared his throat. "Fine. Let's do it today, but only for a few days. The Ark must remain safe with or without the power."

Dave made arrangements with Ming Xia's sentinels, ensuring they understood the priest was leaving for medical reasons, not to smuggle the Ark anywhere. They grumbled but agreed, so long as Sister Sabine stayed behind as the Vatican representative. She accepted that role calmly.

That afternoon, Dave drove Lombardi to the hidden clinic with Sabine in tow, leaving Helena, Ibrahim, and two Chinese sentinels behind at the warehouse. The quiet departure stirred uneasy feelings in Helena. She disliked seeing Lombardi in such pain, but also worried about leaving Sister Sabine as the sole priestly figure. She prayed she wouldn't orchestrate a secret removal.

The warehouse felt emptier without Lombardi's presence. That night, Helena found herself restless, walking the perimeter with a flashlight, Dave absent on the hospital run. Ibrahim tried to calm her. "We have sentinels, we're armed. The illusions remain absent. You can rest."

She forced a smile. "Thanks. I just have a bad feeling."

By dawn, Dave returned alone, leaning on the battered sedan. "We left Lombardi at the clinic. Sister Sabine is with him for now, but she said she'll come back later. The doctors will keep him two days at least."

Helena's worry flared. "He insisted on a short stay."

Dave nodded. "He's stubborn, but they pumped him full of antibiotics, said the infection started to spread. Another day or two, it might've killed him."

She swallowed the knot in her throat. "Then it's good he listened. But who's watching Sister Sabine?"

Dave let out a weary exhale. "She claims she'll stay at the clinic for the night, then rejoin us. We'll see. Ming Xia's men had no objection. They only reminded us not to move the Ark alone."

Helena rubbed her temples. "I just hope she doesn't lure Lombardi into relocating the relic once he's stable."

He took her hand, steering her gently toward a makeshift seating area. "We can't control everything. We continue to hold the line. If the visions stay locked away, the biggest threat remains Orlov's men or local criminals."

She sank onto a crate, letting him sit beside her. A swirl of conflicting relief and dread churned inside. The activity was absent, but the political turmoil refused to loosen its grip. Summoning a tired smile, she turned her focus to the immediate problem: securing the warehouse and preparing for another infiltration attempt.

Over the next two days, Sister Sabine did not return. Lombardi texted sporadically, indicating his condition improved but remained under observation. Dave and Helena grew uneasy at her silence. Ibrahim tried calling, no response. Meanwhile, Orlov's men or other criminals made no major moves, though sentinels occasionally glimpsed suspicious vans passing the area. A charged hush lingered.

On the third morning, with Lombardi expected to check out of the clinic, Helena and Dave prepared to drive over. Ming Xia's sentinels insisted on joining to ensure no secret moves. Ibrahim stayed behind to guard the Ark, along with the remaining Chinese operative. Before they departed, Sister Sabine arrived unannounced, stepping into the warehouse with quiet footsteps.

Helena spun around, startled. "Sister? Where have you been?"

The nun's expression was composed, though her eyes looked faintly triumphant. "At the clinic. Father Lombardi's doing better. He asked me to tell you he'll come back this afternoon."

Dave frowned. "We tried calling you."

Sabine nodded, a faint smile on her lips. "My phone was misplaced. My apologies." She walked over to the Ark's crate, eyes sweeping its surface. "All is well here, I see."

Her calmness set off alarms in Helena's mind. She studied the nun's posture. "Yes, illusions remain silent. Did you do anything at the clinic we should know about?"

Sabine raised her gaze, adopting a mask of innocence. "Merely prayed for Father Lombardi's recovery. I also made inquiries about a possible monastic refuge. But I have not acted on anything, if that's your concern."

Helena forced a nod, uncertain. "We appreciate your transparency."

Midday arrived. Dave, Helena, and one Chinese watcher hopped into the sedan to retrieve Lombardi. Sister Sabine stayed at the warehouse, though Helena parted with a lingering glance. She and Dave headed across town, weaving through Istanbul's swirling traffic. The city hummed with midday life, vendors hawking simit bread, scooters zigzagging between cars. The hidden clinic lay in an older quarter, behind a gated courtyard.

They parked near a side entrance. Helena's palms felt clammy as she and Dave stepped inside. The place smelled of antiseptic, halls lined with chipped tiles. A discreet nun behind the desk recognized them, guiding them to Lombardi's room. They found the priest dressed, arm bandaged neatly, exhaustion etched in his eyes. Relief flared in Helena's chest.

He rose at their arrival, wincing. "I'm ready. Let's get back to the Ark before something changes."

Dave touched his shoulder gently. "You sure you're able? We can give you more time."

Lombardi shook his head. "No illusions remain to require daily chanting. But we must keep watch. I can rest at the warehouse as well as here."

Helena frowned. "Where's Sister Sabine? She said you'd leave together."

He snorted. "She vanished an hour ago, murmuring about urgent errands. I had no clue she'd gone to the warehouse first."

Alarm skittered along Helena's spine. Sabine had left him behind to appear at the warehouse? "She said her phone was missing. That might be a lie."

Lombardi's mouth tightened. "I suspect she has direct orders from higher authorities. Possibly to investigate a swift transfer of the Ark. We must be vigilant, or we risk losing that neutrality arrangement."

Dave sighed, pressing a hand to his temple. "We'll watch her carefully. Let's head back."

They checked Lombardi out, politely thanked the clinic staff, then left. Helena noticed the tension in the Jesuit's shoulders as he walked. He seemed physically better, but worry gnawed at his thoughts. Dave updated him on the local infiltration attempts, which made him scowl. "So Orlov's men lurk. Sabine might conspire. And the Ark's phenomena remain dormant—for now."

On the drive back, Dave handled the wheel. The single Chinese watcher in the back seat occasionally typed on his phone, likely sending routine updates. Lombardi stared out the window, face grim. Helena studied him, longing for clarity. "What do you think Sabine is truly aiming for?"

He answered, "She serves the cardinal who championed the Ark's retrieval for the Vatican. She'll do whatever it takes. I can't say I fully oppose that. My vow to protect sacred relics is strong. Yet I made a promise here—to keep the Ark's energy locked under a multi-faction watch. Breaking it might trigger violence."

Helena nodded. "We can't let the relic's forces return. A single forced opening could be catastrophic."

They arrived at the warehouse late afternoon, stepping inside to find Sister Sabine greeting them with a mild smile. She took Lombardi's hands gently, asking after his health. He gave curt answers, searching her eyes for hidden truths. Helena hovered at Dave's side, scanning for tension among the sentinels. Ming Xia's men were present, no sign of forced moves. The Ark remained in place, its disturbances absent.

That evening, Helena felt an odd sense of closure about Yusef's departure, but more dread about the swirling conflicts. The Ark's phenomena might have quieted, but ambition and zeal closed in from all sides. She retreated to a small corner with Dave, discussing possible ways to quell local criminals and keep Orlov at bay. Sister Sabine circulated among crates, occasionally whispering to Lombardi, scanning the Ark's crate as if measuring it for relocation.

As night deepened, a hush settled. Dave arranged the usual watch rotation. Sabine insisted on staying near Lombardi for the first shift, presumably to ensure the priest's well-being. Helena and Dave retreated behind a row of boxes, leaning shoulder to shoulder on some stacked blankets. The overhead bulb buzzed, casting soft shadows.

He gave her a wry grin. "We've survived swirling phenomena, gun battles, and covert sentinels. Now we're pinned in a city with half the underworld sniffing around. Romantic, isn't it?"

She let out a breathy laugh, pressing her forehead to his. "The strangest place to find quiet. But I appreciate every second of respite with you."

He stroked her cheek lightly, eyes reflecting the gentle connection that had blossomed. They shared a silent moment, hearts steadying against the chaos. If the Ark's effects had reigned, their bond might have been overshadowed by swirling nightmares. But with the relic calmed, they discovered pockets of humanity amid the cold mechanics of power.

A noise startled them—just Sister Sabine shifting a crate. They parted, remembering how fragile this arrangement was. In a quieter voice, Dave said, "We should rest. Tomorrow might bring new troubles."

She agreed. Their sentinels took positions, the Chinese specialists guarding the door, Sister Sabine writing notes in her ledger, Lombardi reclined on a folding chair, half-dozing. Helena closed her eyes, drifting into a dreamless slumber, trusting Dave's presence to keep the nightmares at bay.

Morning dawned with no new infiltration attempt, no phenomena flickering. Orlov stayed out of sight, though rumor suggested he was recruiting a larger force in the harbor district. Sabine lingered, calmer than before, though her gaze often slid to the Ark as if drawn by an invisible thread. Lombardi kept an eye on her, suspecting a hidden agenda. Ming Xia's look-outs typed sensor logs, confirming the relic's disturbances remained stable.

Yet the city's tension rose. Ibrahim reported that the local black-market ring had posted sentinels around the neighborhood, possibly waiting for an opening. Dave cursed, updating Ming Xia by phone. She promised more Chinese operatives would arrive soon, but delayed by bureaucratic roadblocks.

Helena paced the warehouse, frustration seeping into her bones. "We can't hold out forever. The Ark's disturbances might be gone, but greed will keep fueling these ambushes."

Dave nodded gravely. "We need official help. Either we relocate with permission or get real security. But Sister Sabine's new plan might try to whisk it away. Or Orlov's men might strike first."

As they debated, footsteps approached from near the battered entrance. One Chinese specialist let out a sharp hiss. "Someone's outside—three or four men scoping the building."

Helena and Dave dashed to the side window. Through a gap, they spotted shapes crossing the street. Civilian clothes, but each moved with the predatory confidence of armed men. They split up, one veering toward the back alley, two heading for the main door. Tension ratcheted up. This looked like a coordinated infiltration.

Quietly, Dave signaled everyone to take cover. The Chinese sentinels prepared their weapons, also calling for backup. Sister Sabine pressed close to Lombardi, clutching her ledger as though it could ward off bullets. Ibrahim crouched behind crates, pistol in hand. Helena's heart thundered. Another stand-off?

A muffled voice outside hissed, "Go around back!" Feet scuffed on gravel. Then a single figure advanced on the door, jiggling the handle. Dave and a Chinese watcher readied themselves to fire if it burst open. Helena gripped her pistol, sweat beading on her forehead.

A second figure hopped onto the window ledge, testing if it was locked. Ibrahim rushed to that spot, brandishing his gun. The intruder froze, arms raised. "Relax, man," came a shaky voice in heavily accented English. "We just... want to talk."

Dave and Helena exchanged a doubtful look. She called out, "Talk or break in?"

A grunt. "We heard about a priceless relic here. If you want no trouble, you pay a fee for safe passage in this neighborhood."

Extortion. Helena's stomach churned. "We're not paying a fee. Go away, or we defend ourselves."

One of the look-outs shouted in Turkish, presumably echoing Helena's warning. A tense moment passed. Then the figure at the window cursed. "You'll regret it," he spat, dropping down to the sidewalk. Footsteps retreated. The troopers near the door reported the men had scattered.

Ibrahim exhaled. "Another gang. They're bolder each day. If we don't pay, they might come back with heavier weapons."

Father Lombardi, pale-faced, steadied himself. "We can't keep engaging in shootouts. This city is becoming a war zone for us."

Helena stared at the Ark, pristine and silent. "Sooner or later, something bigger than illusions will break. We need a final decision on relocation or serious official protection."

Dave's phone buzzed. He flicked it open. "Ming Xia. She says she's sending four more guards by nightfall, maybe enough to deter these small-time criminals. No word on Orlov. She's urging we stay put. She wants no unilateral moves either."

Sister Sabine spoke. "And the Church stands ready with a quieter alternative. The illusions remain suppressed, so the ceremony is stable. We can discreetly transport the Ark tonight, if you choose."

Lombardi shot her a warning glare. "We just said the arrangement forbids that. Doing so invites conflict."

She bowed her head in acquiescence, but her eyes hinted otherwise. Helena clenched her fists, uncertain how long they could hold off local extortionists, possible Russian mercenaries, or the Vatican's cunning. Dave put a reassuring hand on her shoulder. "Take a breath," he murmured. "We'll keep going."

The rest of the day passed in tense watchfulness, each minute feeling like a drawn bowstring. By twilight, four additional Chinese guards arrived, armed with better equipment and wearing quiet confidence. They joined the sensor team, erecting floodlights outside. The criminals lurking in the neighborhood seemed to realize the building had become a small fortress. A few onlookers glowered from corners, but no direct assault came. Sister Sabine stayed aloof, reading battered Catholic texts about relics. Lombardi paced anxiously, ignoring his healing arm. Dave and Helena enforced a strict watch rotation, ensuring no infiltration attempt succeeded. Still, the risk loomed.

Late that night, Helena found a rare moment alone with Dave behind a stack of crates. He looked drained, lines of worry marking his face. She brushed a gentle hand across his cheek. "You should rest. I'll cover the next shift."

He inhaled. "Only if you get some sleep afterward. We can't burn out."

She let her palm linger on his face, heart fluttering at the closeness. "Agreed." A hush expanded between them. She felt his warmth, grateful for his steadfast presence. They leaned in, foreheads touching, drawing solace from each other in the hush of that makeshift fortress. Her chest throbbed with a swirl of fear and affection. For a heartbeat, she considered pressing her lips to his, but footsteps sounded, forcing them to separate.

One of the new Chinese look-outs peered around the crates, announcing that all was calm at the perimeter. Dave and Helena nodded, stepping apart as if discussing routine matters. The moment passed, leaving a faint ache in Helena's chest. She yearned for a normal life with normal interactions, free of the Ark's disturbances, black-market extortion, or foreign militaries.

Dawn broke with no fresh attack. Sabine offered Lombardi a quiet "good morning," receiving a curt nod in return. Tension simmered between them, each suspicious of the other's Vatican loyalty. The infiltration group checked the Ark's crate for bullet holes or tampering—none found. The Ark's phenomena remained utterly absent. If not for the bullet scars, the sentinels, and the swirling politics, one might imagine the Ark was nothing but a dusty museum piece.

By midmorning, Sister Sabine cornered Helena near a corner of the warehouse. The nun's eyes held a trace of urgency. "I know you distrust me," she began calmly. "But I must ask: have you truly considered how precarious this arrangement is? Every day, more criminals circle. Orlov might return with an army. The Ark's power is silent for now, but if anyone forcibly opens the lid—"

Helena cut in, voice taut. "We're well aware. We're also aware your Church wants sole possession."

Sabine pressed her palms together. "Sole possession, yes, but only to protect it from mortal greed. The phenomena remain sealed by a holy chant. They can remain sealed in a Vatican repository. The father and I can ensure no government tries to harness them."

Helena eyed her carefully. "We can't. Breaking the neutrality vow triggers conflict with the Chinese sentinels, and possibly others. The entire warehouse would become a battlefield."

Sabine's expression tightened. "We can arrange a stealthy extraction with minimal casualties if you coordinate with me. Ming Xia's guards might be outmaneuvered. Then the Ark remains locked away from worldly hands."

She shook her head firmly. "No. I won't betray the arrangement. Dave won't either. Neither will Lombardi. You're outnumbered, Sister."

For a heartbeat, Sabine's eyes flashed with something like frustration. Then she dipped her head in polite acceptance. "So be it." She turned away.

Helena let out a trembling breath. Even though the Ark's phenomena lay dormant, a new meltdown threatened from every angle. She considered confronting Lombardi about Sabine's push but realized that might worsen the internal Church divide. Instead, she told Dave, who sighed. "We watch her. She might attempt something on her own. If the Ark's disturbances stay subdued, she might try moving it at night."

The day dragged. By late afternoon, a rumor arrived via Ibrahim: Colonel Orlov had been spotted near the harbor at dawn, conferring with known black-market brokers. Possibly he was preparing a major incursion. The infiltration team braced themselves for another potential firefight. The Chinese look-outs reinforced the door, installing a secondary steel panel. Sabine watched from a distance, posture taut. Lombardi prayed under his breath. Helena paced, nerves raw.

Night fell, the city's lights flickering across the horizon. Dave double-checked the sensor array with the Chinese squad leader, confirming the Ark's energy remained stable. Sister Sabine vanished into a corner, rummaging through her ledger again. Helena eyed her warily, suspecting an imminent move. She shared a hushed exchange with Lombardi about the nun's possible betrayal. The weary priest only shook his head. "I'll watch her. She's cunning, but I hope she yields to reason."

Close to midnight, Helena dozed on a spare blanket in the far corner, mind swirling with half-formed anxieties. A soft metallic scrape jolted her awake. She blinked, scanning the warehouse. The overhead bulbs flickered. She spotted a silhouette near the Ark's crate—someone prying at the metal clamps. Her heart thundered.

She rolled sideways, reaching for her pistol, mouth going dry. The shape inched closer to the chest, as if testing the seal. Another faint scrape. A tiny spark hissed. The figure froze. A quiet curse drifted over. A woman's voice. Sister Sabine.

Helena's pulse hammered. Sabine was tampering with the crate in the dead of night, presumably trying to detach it from the larger crates or open a portion. If the Ark's phenomena reawakened, the fallout would be catastrophic. Helena raised her pistol, furious and terrified. "Sabine, step away now," she hissed.

The shadow jerked. "Wait—it's not what you think," Sabine whispered. "I'm checking the crate's integrity. A bullet hole might have—"

Helena stepped closer, gun leveled. "Don't lie. You made no mention of a bullet hole earlier. Step back with your hands up, or I'll shout for help."

Sabine let out a trembling breath, lifting her hands from the crate. "I was verifying it for the Church. If the Ark's disturbances are dormant, we might move it soon. You insisted on ignoring that option."

Helena's jaw clenched. "We have an arrangement, Sister. Breaking it endangers us all. If the Ark's phenomena return because you tamper with the chest, this city could see biblical devastation. Are you insane?"

Sabine's eyes glinted with defiance. "You cling to illusions to justify letting the Ark rot under Chinese rifles. The Church has a higher calling. We alone guard holy relics from mortal misuse. If Orlov returns, do you prefer a gun battle over hallowed safety?"

Footsteps sounded as Dave, hearing the commotion, approached from behind crates. He aimed his sidearm too. "What's going on?"

Helena kept her gaze on the nun. "She was prying at the crate, presumably to relocate it. Or open it."

Sabine lowered her hands, voice level. "I never intended to open it completely. That would risk the Ark's energy. I only checked the nails. My cardinal insisted we secure it for transport if an opening arises."

Dave's face hardened. "That's not your decision. You committed to neutrality. Step away—now."

Sabine's lips pressed together, a flicker of anguish crossing her face. "The father's vow is overshadowed by my direct orders from the cardinal. But I see your fury. Fine. I won't force this tonight."

A hush followed. Then Lombardi, drawn by the raised voices, stumbled closer. He glared at Sabine, chest heaving. "You lied to me. You said you'd respect the vow."

She shook her head, eyes filling with tears of frustration. "I do respect it, but our Church's mission stands above worldly treaties. If the Ark's forces remain locked, we must protect it from future misuse."

He slumped, color draining from his cheeks. "You nearly undid everything we risked our lives for. Step away from the crate—immediately."

Sabine closed her eyes, stepping back. "I'm sorry," she muttered. "I see no sense in letting criminals circle while each day we risk an unstoppable crisis. But I won't act alone."

Dave kept his pistol raised until he was sure she'd retreated. Helena's blood still boiled. "We'll deal with your cardinal. For now, stay far from the Ark unless we're all present. Understood?"

Sabine nodded stiffly, tears clinging to her lashes, though whether from genuine remorse or frustration, Helena couldn't tell. The commotion drew the Chinese sentinels, who demanded an explanation. Dave gave them a truncated version, saying the nun had tested the crate's stability, nearly causing an incident. Sabine retreated to a distant corner, arms crossed, refusing to speak further.

The tension inside the warehouse spiked to new heights. Lombardi apologized for Sabine's actions, but Dave and Helena remained wary. No phenomena flared—thankfully—but trust in the Vatican's envoy shattered further. Sister Sabine's presence now felt like a hidden bomb, waiting to explode if an opportunity arose. The rest of the night passed in a restless vigil.

By sunrise, they had all but decided the arrangement was on life support. Sabine's attempted meddling eroded any chance of a stable truce within the infiltration group. Helena recognized that the Ark's disturbances might remain calm for now, but the political meltdown threatened them from every angle—Orlov, local extortionists, the Church's secret agenda, and the looming presence of Ming Xia's sentinels. Everyone waited for a slip, a moment of weakness, to seize control of the Ark.

And though the Ark's phenomena had gone quiet, Helena feared the day of their reemergence might arrive if the chest was forcibly opened or compromised. They clung to the final lines of the ceremony as a last resort, but Lombardi's injury made him less able to recite them with full vigor. If a catastrophic breach occurred, the Ark's forces might rage beyond anything they had seen before.

Chapter 16

Morning light slanted across the battered door of the warehouse, spotlighting the fresh bullet holes from the previous attempts. Helena Carter stepped around scattered shell casings, careful not to disturb any evidence that might be used later—should they ever present a case to local authorities. With illusions subdued, the relic had become a purely mortal magnet of greed and zeal. Wariness etched itself into every conversation.

Father Aurelius Lombardi, returning from his short hospital stay, sat on a metal folding chair beside the Ark's crate. The Jesuit's shoulder wound was now bandaged more securely. Though he looked thinner, a faint color had returned to his cheeks. Sister Sabine hovered a short distance away, expression subdued since her nighttime confrontation with Helena. Dave Schumer and two Chinese sentinels guarded the corners, scanning for infiltration attempts. Ibrahim Mahdi arranged a few sacks of supplies near the center, restocking their dwindling rations. No illusions flickered, but the group's tension thickened.

Helena knelt beside Lombardi, voice quiet. "How do you feel?"

He managed a wan smile. "Better, physically. Though the overall situation…" He trailed off, eyeing Sabine, who pretended not to notice. "I'm sorry about her. She's under orders, but it's complicated."

Helena sighed. "We confronted her. She claims she won't move the Ark alone. She insists she was checking the nails. None of us believe that."

He pressed his lips together. "I'll watch her. I owe you that much."

From across the room, Sister Sabine caught Lombardi's gaze, then looked away. Helena noted the silent guilt or perhaps frustration flickering in the nun's eyes. The infiltration group had turned ice-cold toward her, and she seemed to sense the distance.

A rustle at the door made everyone freeze. One of Ming Xia's troopers peered through a gap. "We have a visitor," he muttered. "Not Orlov—some local man in street clothes. Says he wants to speak with your liaison about a 'neighborly arrangement.' Likely more extortion."

Ibrahim exhaled. "I'll handle it."

Helena, Dave, and a Chinese watcher followed him outside. Warm midday air enveloped them. Down the short alley stood a short, broad-shouldered man in a worn leather jacket, flanked by two younger associates. He waved casually when he saw them approach. "Peace, friends," he called in accented English. "We do no harm."

Dave kept a hand near his holster. "State your business."

The man grinned, revealing a gold tooth. "Simple. Word spreads you hold a relic inside. I represent a certain local group concerned about…

disturbances. We want to ensure no strange phenomena or incidents spill onto our streets. For a small fee, we guarantee no one bothers you."

Helena's jaw tightened. "We're not paying."

He laughed. "Just a small price for safety. Or, you can keep fending off petty gangs and random thieves. My group can ensure they stay away... for a contribution."

Ibrahim gave a derisive snort. "We can defend ourselves."

The man shrugged lazily. "Suit yourself. But I hear Colonel Orlov's men might come soon, with bigger guns. We'd be happy to block them—for a price. Without that, the next time might be a bloodbath. Or maybe you trust the relic's calm state to save you. But rumor says the disturbances are gone. So... up to you."

Helena swallowed, recalling how the relic's quiet state left them with no supernatural deterrent. The Chinese troopers could hold off small fry, but a large assault might overwhelm them. She glanced at Dave, who gave a subtle headshake. No paying criminals. She faced the extortionist. "We said no. If you align with Orlov, we'll fight you too."

He chuckled. "So be it. Don't say I didn't warn you." The man tipped an imaginary hat, then turned to leave with his associates. "When Colonel Orlov shows up with a real force, you'll wish you had local allies."

They vanished around a corner, footsteps fading. Helena let out a long breath. Dave and Ibrahim exchanged worried looks. The Chinese watcher frowned, obviously displeased that criminals approached so boldly.

Returning inside, they updated Lombardi and Sister Sabine. The Jesuit's face darkened. "So extortion or a bigger assault— wonderful options."

Sabine said nothing, though her lips tightened. Possibly she saw this as proof the local arrangement was doomed. Helena suspected the nun might soon try something else to remove the Ark. She locked eyes with Dave, who looked equally concerned. If a major assault came, illusions were no safety net. The chest's sealed state left them reliant on mortal weapons alone.

As the day progressed, tension mounted. More suspicious vehicles passed on the street. The Chinese sentinels installed a second sensor station, including motion detectors aimed at the back alley. Sister Sabine spoke less, retreated to reading theological texts. Lombardi tried to pace, but the healing arm limited him. Dave and Helena restlessly circled the interior, verifying every window was secured.

Just after noon, a sudden beep echoed from the motion sensors. Everyone froze. One specialist checked the monitor, eyes widening. "Multiple vehicles pulling up in the alley," he said in clipped English. "At least two vans. Possibly more behind them."

Dave's jaw set. "This might be it."

Ibrahim cursed under his breath, grabbing a pistol. "I'll see if they're Orlov's men."

They scrambled for defensive positions behind crates and shelving. Sister Sabine retreated to the back corner, while Lombardi clutched his sidearm, face set with grim determination. Helena and Dave crouched near a metal beam, scanning the partially blocked windows. The Chinese watchmen locked the door, flipping a reinforced latch. Tension coiled like a spring. Even if the Ark's phenomena stirred, it might not save them from a well-armed assault.

Engines rumbled outside. Doors slammed. Helena caught a glimpse of black-clad figures creeping up. Dave hissed, "At least eight men. Heavier gear." Her pulse thundered. She recognized a well-coordinated strike. Possibly Orlov's new alliance with local criminals.

Suddenly, the battered warehouse door reverberated with pounding. A harsh voice roared, "Open up! We want the relic. No phenomena can protect you!"

Dave shouted back, "We're armed. Retreat or die."

Gunfire erupted, bullets hammering the steel door. Ming Xia's sentinels ducked, returning a volley through the upper gap. Glass shattered in a side window as someone tried to shoot from a high angle. Helena flinched at the ear-splitting racket of gunfire. She fired off two shots at a shape in the window, forcing it to drop out of sight. Dave cursed as rounds pocked the door's interior.

One Chinese specialist triggered a small tear gas launcher, sending canisters rolling under the gap. Faint hisses drifted outside, followed by coughing and scrambling footsteps. But the onslaught didn't stop. More men circled the back. Ibrahim pivoted, unleashing a hail of bullets that tore into a panel of plywood. Searing muzzle flashes lit the gloom.

A spike of fear lanced Helena's heart. If these attackers outnumbered them heavily, the door or one of the windows might give. Then the Ark's dormant energy wouldn't matter. She aimed toward the splintered window, firing a shot that made a shadowy figure duck. Dave fired from another angle, taking advantage of the confusion.

"Move in, move in!" barked a voice outside. Another wave of bullets rattled the barricade. Sister Sabine crouched behind a crate, eyes clenched, whispering a frantic prayer. Lombardi grit his teeth, returning occasional pistol shots. The infiltration group held for the moment, but the volume of fire was intense.

Then the door caved inward, a chunk of metal scraping free. Two armed men burst through, rifles up. One Chinese watcher shot the first intruder in the shoulder. He staggered. Dave pivoted, finishing him with a single round to the leg, incapacitating him. The second attacker yelled, spraying bullets across the crates. Helena dropped behind a toppled shelf, hearing shards of wood scatter. She returned a shot that caught the man's torso. He fell with a grunt.

Yet more footsteps pounded outside. Another group forced the door open wider, lobbing a smoke grenade. Hissing clouds swirled among the crates. Ibrahim coughed, eyes watering, trying to keep his aim steady. Dave and Helena each fired sporadic shots at shadows in the haze. One figure toppled with a scream, weapon clattering. Another yelled, "We can't see! Pull back!"

A frantic minute of close-quarters chaos ensued. The infiltration team's bullets hammered the intruders who dared press forward. Two men scrambled inside, but one was gunned down by the Chinese sentinels. The other fled. Through swirling smoke, Helena glimpsed a silhouette that might have been Orlov, barking commands in Russian, but she couldn't confirm. She fired at it, missing. The figure darted behind a forklift. Gunfire barked anew, bullets pinging off metal.

Then came a shout from the alley: "Fall back! Retreat!" A wave of half-choked cursing in Russian and Turkish followed. Footsteps pounded away, accompanied by engine roars. Within seconds, the frantic exchange of bullets died down to sporadic shots. Then silence, broken only by the moans of a wounded attacker. The infiltration group gasped for air, blinking through smoke. Dave signaled them to hold fire until the haze cleared.

Ibrahim coughed, stepping to the battered door. "They're gone. The vans took off."

Helena's ears rang from the gunshots, adrenaline crashing through her veins. She took stock: none of her allies seemed gravely injured, though one Chinese watcher nursed a graze on his arm. Two attackers lay wounded on the floor, breathing heavily. Another slumped, unconscious or worse. Sister Sabine crept from behind crates, crossing herself at the sight of blood. Lombardi leaned on a shelving unit, chest heaving. Dave prowled the perimeter, verifying no intruder remained inside.

The infiltration team had repelled a full-scale assault, with the Ark's phenomena nowhere in sight. The relic's sentinels had won this round, but the cost weighed heavily on them. Smoke lingered in the air, stinging their eyes. Helena felt tears of exhaustion burn her cheeks. She approached Dave, relief flooding her chest. He clutched her hand gently, reciprocating the same wave of relief. "We're okay," he rasped.

Ibrahim joined them, wiping sweat from his brow. "That was bigger than any previous attempt. Orlov must have formed a local alliance. They almost stormed us."

Helena gazed at the Ark's crate, its wood gouged by bullets but the golden edges still intact. "One bullet through the lid, the Ark's energy might have surged... or the chest might have been pried open. We got lucky."

Father Lombardi mustered the energy to help Sister Sabine drag a bleeding intruder behind a crate, checking if he was still alive. The man moaned, and Sabine grabbed a first-aid kit. Despite her questionable loyalty, Helena recognized the nun wouldn't let a wounded person die on the spot.

By the time the Chinese sentinels called for medical backup, the scene of carnage felt surreal. Bullets scattered across the floor, a swirl of spent shells. The infiltration group's hearts pounded with the knowledge they had survived an onslaught meant to forcibly claim the dormant Ark. No manifestations had stirred, no biblical terror. It was purely human ambition driving the violence.

A dusty hush followed once the smoke dissipated. Helena knelt near a battered crate, letting Dave rub her back soothingly. She felt torn between relief and despair. If Orlov tried again with even greater numbers, how long could they hold out?

Ming Xia arrived within the hour, accompanied by more armed men. She surveyed the battered door and the wounded intruders, fury flaring in her eyes. "So Orlov forced a major push. I warned you about letting him go free. Now we have a small war."

Dave explained how they fended off the assault. She commended them for their effective defense but insisted on reinforcing security further. The city was close to becoming a battleground. Helena, exhausted, listened numbly as Ming Xia's guards doubled their numbers, turning the warehouse into an armed camp.

That evening, additional Chinese hardware arrived: heavier gates, bulletproof panels. Ming Xia supervised the fortifications. Sister Sabine paced near Lombardi, silent frustration etched on her features. She despised the militarization, but her failed attempt to sneak the Ark away had left her cornered. Helena watched from a distance. She realized the Ark's phenomena might remain silent forever, but human ambition and violence threatened to overshadow them at any moment.

Days blurred together. The infiltration group found themselves living in a tense fortress, the Ark's energy neutralized by a fragile ceremony, while Orlov reorganized outside, black-market criminals circled, and Sister Sabine yearned to remove the relic for the Vatican. Father Lombardi's arm healed, though his posture remained stooped from stress. The Chinese look-outs installed more gear, sealing the building into something that resembled a mini-embassy. Dave confided to Helena that he felt the arrangement was unsustainable long-term.

One morning, a second wave of local criminals tried to storm the back gate, quickly driven off by the heavier Chinese presence. No disturbances emerged. The criminals retreated with wounded. The infiltration group survived yet again, each victory draining them further. Tension soared to an intolerable pitch.

Finally, Sister Sabine cornered Helena, voice trembling with raw emotion. "Look around you. This is no life for any of us. The Ark belongs in a quiet vault under Church care. We could have whisked it away, spared the bloodshed. Each day you remain, more men die for nothing."

Helena swallowed anger. "Each faction believes it has the rightful claim. We can't betray them. We'd set off a bigger war."

Sabine's lips pressed into a thin line. "Then that war might happen anyway. I only pray the Ark's phenomena remain silent when it does."

At that, Helena's composure cracked. "If the Ark's disturbances reawaken in the middle of a war, the result would be unthinkable. We keep hoping an official treaty or maybe a global summit forms. But everyone's too suspicious."

Sabine shook her head, walking away. Her eyes shone with sorrow and zeal. Lombardi watched her from across the warehouse, torn between loyalty to the neutrality vow here and the Church's push for unilateral custody.

Amid this swirling crisis, the Ark's phenomena ironically caused no more trouble. Helena felt the bitter irony like a twist of fate: they had solved the relic's supernatural danger only to drown in the mortal chaos of greed. She recalled how Yusef had once said the Ark's energy might be the lesser threat compared to humanity's violent heart. Now she believed him.

Chapter 17

Close to a week had passed since the last brazen assault on the Istanbul warehouse. Bullet holes in the heavy doors remained as silent reminders of the violence that had been repelled by a mixed team of sentinels—Chinese specialists, Father Aurelius Lombardi, Sister Sabine, and the small circle led by Dr. Helena Carter and Dave Schumer. The Ark of the Covenant remained silent, its phenomena kept dormant by the final lines of a sacred ceremony. The longer that serenity lasted, the more each faction realized the world's real threat stemmed from human ambition, not supernatural wrath.

Helena paced between stacked crates of water and medical gear. Her steps stirred echoes across the concrete floor. She was restless, waiting for fresh updates on Colonel Orlov's rumored paramilitary connections. No disturbances flickered across the Ark's gold plating, but rumors suggested the Russian operative was gathering allies along the Bosphorus, forging either a desperate last stand or an overwhelming push. News of covert negotiations between Orlov and local militants had trickled in for days, though no direct confrontation had yet materialized.

In the warehouse's far corner, Dave conferred with a Chinese specialist. Their voices stayed low, serious. Helena glimpsed the faint lines of exhaustion etched into Dave's face. Night after night of standoffs and partial sleep had worn them both down. Yet whenever she locked eyes with him, a subtle warmth glimmered in his gaze. Over the past weeks, they'd found small moments of closeness—gentle touches in the shadows, shared looks of understanding—but the crisis loomed over everything.

Sister Sabine hovered by the Ark's side, flipping through a slim ledger bristling with theological notes. Father Lombardi stood near her, arms folded. The tension between them had thickened since Sabine's attempt to examine the crate under cover of darkness. She'd claimed it was mere caution, but no one believed her. Lombardi seemed torn: part of him admired her zeal for safeguarding the relic, while another part feared her willingness to break the neutrality vow.

Ibrahim Mahdi finished a phone call near the battered door and stepped closer, addressing Helena and Dave. "Fresh intel says Orlov's men purchased crates of advanced rifles, possibly rocket-propelled grenades, from a local arms dealer. The vendor was overheard mentioning a planned raid on something important in this district."

Dave's brow creased. "That's not good. If the Ark's phenomena stay dormant, Orlov might rely on overwhelming firepower. We might not fend that off, no matter how many sentinels stand guard."

Helena nodded grimly. "We should alert Ming Xia. More reinforcements might be needed, or else we risk being trapped if he arrives with heavier ordnance."

A Chinese watcher caught her last sentence, hurrying to place a quick call to his superior. Meanwhile, Sister Sabine glanced over, her expression troubled. "Would you prefer letting the Ark remain in a war zone?" she asked, voice resonating in the hush. "The relic could be torn apart by rockets. That might disrupt the ceremony or release the Ark's forces in unpredictable ways."

Lombardi's mouth tightened. "We cannot uproot it unilaterally, Sister. The factions would clash, phenomena or no phenomena."

She squared her shoulders, grip tightening on her ledger. "We remain caged by these vows while Orlov gathers unstoppable force. I only pray the Ark's disturbances stay silent if a rocket hits that chest."

Helena absorbed the nun's words. She couldn't dismiss the possibility that an impact might awaken the Ark's energy, or perhaps trigger something far worse. "We hold the line," she said, forcing a firm tone. "If Orlov attacks with paramilitary strength, we call for help from the authorities. The secret might come out, but we'll protect the Ark from immediate destruction."

Sister Sabine's eyes flickered with a mix of resignation and fervor. She turned away, drifting toward a folding chair near the corner, muttering in Latin under her breath. Lombardi watched, dismayed, then joined Helena, sighing. "She communicates with a cardinal every evening, I suspect. I see coded texts in her ledger. The Church may soon pressure her to act."

Helena furrowed her brow. "We'll watch her. The Ark's power must remain sealed."

THE SWORD OF CHERUBIM

That afternoon, an unsettling lull settled over the alley. The motion sensors showed no infiltration attempts. Local criminals, who'd tried extortion, seemed to vanish. The hush felt ominous. Helena and Dave took a brief walk outside in the midday light, scanning the deserted street. Extra sentinels from Ming Xia guarded the perimeter, each wearing tactical gear. The group's small fortress was quiet for now.

They stopped by a shadowed corner near stacked shipping pallets. Dave touched Helena's arm, voice hushed. "You're tense."

She let out a breath she hadn't realized she was holding. "I keep expecting gunfire around every bend."

He rubbed her shoulder gently. "We've been through worse. We can handle another threat if it comes."

Her eyes met his, and for a moment, the warehouse faded away. Exhaustion weighed on her bones, but his presence felt like a lifeline in the chaos. She leaned in, resting her forehead against his collarbone, letting him hold her for a breath or two. It wasn't a grand romance, but it was a bond forged in survival and shared purpose.

Quietly, he said, "I'll stand with you no matter what Orlov conjures up."

She lifted her head, offering a small, genuine smile. "Thank you. I'd go insane without you."

A faint flush colored his cheeks. He pressed a soft kiss to her temple, fleeting and tender, then stepped back. They returned to the building, hearts beating with renewed resolve.

Inside, they found Sister Sabine finishing a hushed call on her cellphone, a device she'd claimed to have lost days ago. Lombardi shot her a reproachful look. She merely snapped the phone shut, bowing her head in superficial courtesy. Helena narrowed her eyes. "You said that phone was missing."

Sabine's grip tightened around the device. "I found it recently among my supplies," she said coolly. "I was updating certain Church officials."

Dave moved closer, suspicion etched on his face. "Updating them on what?"

She lifted her chin. "On the near-raid last night, the fact illusions remain still, and the possibility that Russia might launch a heavier attack. That's all."

Lombardi exhaled. "You must be honest about your orders, Sister. If the cardinal wants you to whisk the Ark out of here, you need to come clean. We can't permit a unilateral move."

Anger flashed in her eyes. "Don't question my loyalty to the Church. But yes, they urge me to find a chance for discreet transfer. I've told them it's impossible without bloodshed." Her gaze shifted to Helena. "If Orlov escalates, the entire vow of neutrality might dissolve anyway."

Helena shook her head. "It hasn't yet. You'll do nothing behind our backs."

Sabine turned away, mumbling something under her breath. The tension in the air thickened further.

That evening, a soft rain drummed on the warehouse roof, casting a haunting rhythm. The infiltration group and Ming Xia's look-outs ate a spare meal of bread, canned soup, and bottled water. Lightning flickered over the distant skyline, revealing glimpses of Istanbul's centuries-old spires. Thunder rumbled, but illusions in the Ark remained silent.

Dave passed a phone to Helena, eyebrows raised. "Ibrahim just got word from local contacts that Orlov might have joined forces with a paramilitary outfit from Eastern Europe. They're rumored to be shipping heavier arms into the city. Possibly tank-busting weapons."

Her stomach clenched. "If that's true, they could breach our defenses in minutes. We can't repel a full paramilitary assault."

Father Lombardi, perched on a wooden crate, rubbed his brow. "And illusions remain dormant, so there's no biblical terror to scare them away. We're left with normal firearms."

Ming Xia's watchmen overheard. One of them, a tall operative named Xiao Chen, grimaced. "We'll contact Commander Ming. We might need serious backup—armored vehicles or more. But that could draw Turkish authorities, revealing the Ark's presence."

Helena exhaled, heart pounding. "This might spiral out of our control either way."

Late that night, Sister Sabine disappeared from her usual spot without warning. Lombardi looked around, alarmed. Dave and Helena searched the perimeter, discovering she'd taken advantage of a shift change among the sentinels to slip out a side door. The entire building stirred with anxiety. Had she run off to implement the Church's plan?

A heavy drizzle spattered the alley when Helena, Dave, and two Chinese operatives ventured into the gloom, searching for tracks or footprints. They found faint impressions leading toward a quiet side street. Dave signaled the sentinels to remain behind in case of ambush. Helena's pulse hammered as she and Dave followed the trail. Each step echoed in the empty corridor.

They found Sabine beneath a flickering streetlamp, phone raised, speaking in animated Italian. She froze when Helena's flashlight swept over her. The nun ended the call, eyes flashing with defiance. "Why follow me?"

Dave's tone held steel. "You vanished at midnight. We have every right to suspect sabotage."

She tucked the phone in her pocket, glancing at the two troopers behind them. "I needed fresh air. And I had a private conversation with my cardinal. This changes nothing."

Helena stepped closer, water dripping from the eaves overhead. "Are you planning to relocate the Ark? Because if so, you'll spark a bloodbath. Don't do it."

Sabine clenched her jaw. "I know. I keep telling him we can't. Yet he insists the Vatican has a team standing by. If Orlov or these criminals strike in full, the Church might attempt a rescue operation. I can't stop them forever."

Lightning flashed in the sky, silhouetting her determined face. Dave's shoulder tensed, reading the unspoken threat. "Then you're playing with fire."

Sabine lowered her voice. "I tried to reason with him. Our cardinal believes illusions are subdued only temporarily—like caged lightning. He thinks letting them remain in Istanbul invites a catastrophic release. If I get a chance to move the Ark, he wants me to take it."

Helena couldn't stop the anger rising in her chest. "We have an agreement with multiple sentinels. Breaking it could cause an open fight with the Chinese, plus any local criminals."

Raindrops pattered harder against the pavement. Sabine's posture wavered, betraying internal conflict. "I see no easy path. My loyalty is to the Church, yet I cannot spark a massacre. Trust me, I wrestle with it every day."

Softly, Dave said, "Then come back inside. No more secret calls. If your cardinal demands the Ark, tell him it's impossible now. Orlov's threat alone is big enough."

She closed her eyes, nodding grudgingly. The group walked back in tense silence, water soaking their shoes. Once inside, Sister Sabine dried off, retreating to a quiet spot without further argument. Helena's heart still pounded from the confrontation. They might have staved off a direct betrayal tonight, but how long until the Vatican forced her hand?

Dawn arrived with a swirl of moist air and leftover clouds. Dave and Helena found a brief moment to rest on adjacent mats, exhaustion overwhelming them both. She woke after a couple of hours, stiff-limbed but alert enough to face the day's hazards. The Ark remained in place, its phenomena locked within a ceremonial hush. Ming Xia's sentinels confirmed no infiltration overnight. Sister Sabine dozed in a corner, arms folded around her ledger. Lombardi munched stale bread, eyes distant.

The morning calm shattered when Ibrahim hurried over from the alley entrance, phone in hand. "Intel suggests Orlov's new paramilitary allies have arrived on the outskirts of the city. Possibly they're planning to converge here within the next day or two. We might face an onslaught of advanced weaponry."

Helena's throat went dry. "That's exactly what we feared. The warehouse might not hold out. We're basically sitting ducks if they come in force."

Lombardi rubbed his bandaged arm. "Then disturbances... if a rocket hits the Ark, the seal might break. We're back to biblical horrors, or something worse."

Sister Sabine, who had stirred at the commotion, murmured, "Another reason to move the Ark. Let me guess: you still say no?"

Dave set his jaw. "We have a vow with the Chinese sentinels. Doing that behind their back triggers immediate conflict. Also, Orlov might intercept us mid-transport."

Sabine pressed her lips together, subdued but not silenced. She turned away, rummaging in her ledger again. Helena suspected she was considering her cardinal's orders.

That afternoon, Ming Xia herself arrived with added sentinels. The Chinese commander's demeanor was clipped, serious. She conferred with Dave and Helena near the battered main door, scanning bullet holes from previous fights. "We have confirmation Orlov is gathering around fifteen well-armed troops. Some ex-mercenaries. Possibly more waiting in safe houses. If the Ark's phenomena remain quiet, he might rely solely on superior firepower."

Helena struggled to remain calm. "Can you match that force?"

Ming Xia's brow furrowed. "We have eight watchmen here, plus your group. If we fortify properly, we could fend off a direct assault, but if heavy weaponry is used, we risk losing. We might request local authorities, but that reveals the Ark's presence publicly, causing a diplomatic crisis."

Dave exhaled, voice low. "We're nearing the point where we have no good options."

Helena silently agreed. The Ark's phenomena had been sealed away, yet the world seemed more precarious than ever. Ming Xia tightened her gloves. "We must try to get official sign-off from my superiors in Beijing. More sentinels, maybe advanced drones. If Orlov's men do come, we'll repel them. Keep the Ark locked."

"That's the plan," Helena said, though dread twisted in her gut. "Let's hope we hold out."

Evening shadows draped the warehouse once more. Tension coiled in every corner. Father Lombardi paced near the Ark, occasionally reciting snippets of the chant under his breath. Sister Sabine avoided conversation, burying herself in silent prayer. Dave checked the fortifications with Ming Xia's sentinels, layering the door with extra steel plates. Helena perched near a row of crates, rifle in hand, scanning the gloom for movement. Outside, the city's pulse thrummed with latent menace.

Sometime after midnight, faint booms echoed across the district—distant fireworks or test firings, it was hard to tell. Everyone jolted awake. The watchmen scanned their monitors. Dave readied his sidearm. Sister Sabine clutched her ledger. Lombardi whispered, "Could be Orlov's men testing weapons?"

Helena clenched the rifle, fingers trembling. "This might be it."

But the hours passed without a raid. Dawn revealed no sign of an assaulting force. Anxiety built to a fever pitch, then ebbed in anticlimax. Dave rubbed gritty eyes, suspecting Orlov might be playing psychological games, keeping them on edge until they cracked. Meanwhile, Sister Sabine grew more agitated, creeping around with her phone in hand, evidently relaying each day's developments to Rome.

Helena confronted the nun again that afternoon. "We can't handle your secret calls. We've seen how it goes. If you try moving the Ark, the Chinese guards won't hold back. This place would become a war zone."

Sabine's composure frayed. "I know. I keep telling the cardinal it's madness. But he insists we cannot let a potential paramilitary takeover happen. The Church's vow to protect sacred relics might override your arrangement."

Helena's voice shook. "And you'd see phenomena possibly unleashed in the crossfire? If they breach the crate—"

Sabine's breath caught. "I fear that scenario keeps me awake at night."

Helena stepped back, sadness washing over her. They were all trapped by unstoppable forces—Orlov's mobilizing threat, the Church's unyielding orders, the sentinels' vow to keep the Ark's phenomena contained. *If the Ark's energy is truly a lesser threat now, then the real danger is us,* she thought, recalling Yusef's warnings.

Yusef reappeared breathless, a rolled city-engineer map clutched in his hand. "The old Roman drainage shaft—look." He unspooled the vellum under Helena's torchlight, tracing a narrow channel that cut beneath the fortress wall and surfaced within the restricted yard. If they slipped through, the team could flank the mercenaries guarding the Ark. Helena met his eyes and, in front of the stunned brass, clapped his shoulder. "You just gave us our opening," she said. Cheeks flushing, Yusef managed a grin. For a heartbeat, the tension lifted, and Helena vowed he would be on the first relief flight out once the Ark was safe.

That evening, Dave and Helena stole another moment near the side exit, tension riddling their every whisper. She sagged against him, eyes shut. He stroked a comforting hand down her back. "We can't keep living like this."

She inhaled his warmth, voice ragged. "I know. But the Ark's phenomena remain quiet. That was our main goal."

He pressed his cheek to her temple. "It was. Now we have a bullet-riddled fortress, Sister Sabine's covert phone calls, and Orlov's rumored paramilitary. Sometimes I wonder if the Ark's energy reawakening might scare them away."

She let out a hollow laugh. "We spent so long sealing its power, praying for normalcy. Now normal violence might overshadow everything." She lifted her head, letting her gaze meet his. "At least we have each other."

His eyes softened. "That matters more than I expected." Then he cleared his throat. "We should get inside. Another infiltration attempt could come any minute."

She nodded. They returned, hearts heavier but spirits somehow buoyed by each other's presence.

At midnight, a jarring phone call from one of Ibrahim's contacts confirmed the worst: Orlov's combined force of Russian mercenaries and local criminals planned a final assault on the warehouse by dawn. The infiltration group snapped into action, bracing for the biggest fight yet. Ming Xia's troopers armed themselves with newly arrived gear: ballistic shields, advanced rifles, even a few drones for overhead surveillance. Sister Sabine stalked the edges, pale with tension, while Lombardi stood resolute near the Ark.

Dave, scanning a map of the district with Helena, turned grim. "We can hold them off if it's just foot soldiers, but if they bring heavier vehicles or rocket launchers, we're in trouble."

Ming Xia, who arrived in person after hearing the alert, gave a curt nod. "We have limited drone coverage. If Orlov truly comes in force, local authorities might intervene spontaneously. That triggers an open revelation of the Ark. Are we prepared for that fallout?"

Helena's chest felt tight. "Better that than letting paramilitaries tear us apart. This might go public."

Father Lombardi murmured, "God help us. Let this thng remain quiet, or this city could see horrors beyond measure."

Sister Sabine said nothing, but her eyes flicked from the Ark to Lombardi, and then to her phone. Helena suspected she might be on the verge of a last-ditch attempt to relocate the chest under the Vatican's protection. But with the sentinels heavily armed, any move could spark immediate bloodshed.

Night passed in a suffocating hush, each second amplifying the dread. Helena and Dave stayed near the front barricade, scanning the gloom beyond newly installed floodlights. Ming Xia's men murmured in Mandarin, prepping rifles. No illusions crackled across the relic. No sparks danced on the Ark's surface. The biblical dread had given way to raw, man-made suspense.

Around three in the morning, faint vibrations rattled the air—engines, possibly multiple trucks approaching. The sentinels perked up, stiffening in readiness. Dave signaled lights off. They switched to night-vision scopes. Helena crouched behind a reinforced panel, heart hammering. The hush of those moments felt like the calm before a raging storm.

Her earpiece crackled with Ming Xia's clipped whisper: "Drones see vehicles on the next street. Four trucks, maybe fifteen to twenty men. Some carry rocket tubes. Colonel Orlov is among them."

Helena's fingers clenched around her rifle. *This is it.* She flashed a glance at Dave, who nodded, jaw tight. "Get ready."

The vehicles rolled into view of the floodlights, halting halfway down the alley. Engines idled. Then headlights beamed directly at the warehouse, scattering shadows. Over a loudspeaker, Orlov's voice barked, "I know the Ark's phenomena are gone! Surrender it to Russia or we open fire."

Ming Xia cursed, grabbing her radio. She whispered an order in Chinese, likely to prime her sentinels. Dave shouted through the barricade, "No deal, Colonel. We'll defend ourselves."

A sneering laugh echoed. "So be it." The trucks revved, men jumped off, rifles bristling. Helena's earpiece crackled: "Brace for assault."

The first rocket whooshed from a launching tube, slamming into a parked car near the door, spraying shrapnel. Ming Xia's watchmen fired back in bursts, rifles lighting up the gloom. The paramilitaries scattered, hugging cover behind crates in the alley. Helena ducked as bullets smashed into the door's plating. Dave shot carefully through a gun slit, picking off one attacker who emerged too far. Deafening echoes filled the air.

Colonel Orlov shouted in Russian, spurring his men forward. Another rocket swooshed overhead, hitting a second-story window, blowing shards of glass inside. Sister Sabine cried out, diving behind a pallet. Lombardi crouched, wincing at the shockwave. No disturbances flared from the Ark, though a bullet rattled the crate's flank. Helena's stomach twisted—if that shell had penetrated deeper, the seal might have broken.

Dave motioned Helena to shift left. She scrambled to a better vantage, ignoring the dryness in her mouth. Another wave of bullets hammered the warehouse. The Chinese look-outs launched a volley of their own, managing to force a few paramilitaries into retreat. One attacker collapsed near the alley's entrance, moaning in pain.

Through the swirling dust, Helena caught sight of Orlov himself, crouched near a battered truck, barking orders into a handheld radio. She focused her scope but couldn't get a clear shot. The barrage intensified. The infiltration group returned fire methodically, trying to conserve ammo. A chunk of the doorframe tore away under repeated blasts. Helena prayed the Ark's energy wouldn't awaken from the chest being rattled by the explosions.

Then a third rocket slammed into the rooftop edge, sending bits of metal and mortar raining inside. Smoke choked the air. Sister Sabine screamed, pinned under falling debris. Lombardi crawled toward her, pulling broken boards aside. Helena's lungs burned as she tried to see through the haze, hearing Dave's voice shouting for medical help. Another Chinese specialist unleashed a short-range missile at the paramilitaries. The projectile struck an abandoned van near Orlov's men, erupting in flame. Some of Orlov's troops scrambled back, cursing.

The entire alley turned into a battlefield. Helena coughed, eyes stinging. She glimpsed Sister Sabine's pale face as Lombardi dragged her behind a row of crates. Dave reloaded, cheeks streaked with soot, then yelled for the guards to keep pressing. Another hail of bullets thudded against the metal plating. If the Ark's phenomena had been active, the paramilitaries might have faced spectral terror. Instead, they pinned the infiltration group with raw firepower.

A roar echoed from the next street. Possibly reinforcements for Orlov, or local criminals arriving to pick sides. The swirl of confusion heightened. Helena saw Dave make a swift hand signal to Ming Xia's sentinels. They responded with a flanking push, opening a side slot to lob tear gas. That forced the nearest attackers to recoil, hacking in the fumes. Another rocket soared overhead, missing the building by inches and exploding against a brick wall across the street.

Minutes felt like hours. The infiltration group clung to the advantage of the fortified structure. Colonel Orlov's paramilitaries had rockets, but not enough to fully breach the warehouse's reinforced plating. Gunfire rattled incessantly, muzzle flashes illuminating every face. Helena's heart pounded, adrenaline fueling each breath.

Finally, an echoing command in Russian signaled retreat. Orlov's men dragged their wounded back to the trucks under covering fire. The troopers fired relentlessly, picking off stragglers. Engines revved, and the battered vehicles sped away, leaving scorched pavement and strewn bodies. Dave and Helena exchanged grim looks, panting, arms trembling from the tension.

Smoke wafted in the alley, mixing with the pungent stench of gunpowder. Inside the warehouse, Sister Sabine lay sprawled where Lombardi had pulled her. She wasn't mortally wounded—only bruised by debris. The Ark's crate bore fresh gouges and scorch marks. No phenomena stirred. The infiltration group had survived another storm, though fear gnawed at them. Each assault grew fiercer.

Dave signaled a Chinese medic to tend to Sabine's injuries. Helena sank against a charred crate, rifle resting across her lap. She tried to slow her ragged breathing. Once again, the Ark's energy had stayed dormant, leaving them to face mortal violence alone. She scanned the faces: Lombardi's eyes shone with relief, Ming Xia's sentinels looked shaken, and Sister Sabine trembled with pain and silent fury. Colonel Orlov had failed, but how many more attempts could they repel?

Ming Xia stepped in, surveying the bullet-riddled interior. Her voice shook with anger. "That was heavier than last time. Orlov is desperate. He might be forging a new alliance. Or we might see involvement from other states soon. The global powers won't stand idle if word leaks."

Helena closed her eyes. "Then we might have to contact official authorities. This can't continue." She felt Dave's hand on her shoulder, steadying her. She leaned into him, grateful for the small solace. Her mind spun: the Ark's disturbances were sealed, but a larger meltdown was creeping closer. Nations might soon discover the Ark's location, leading to unstoppable conflict on a far grander scale.

She parted her lips, murmuring to Dave, "We might have to move the Ark ourselves, but with everyone's consent. If we wait, we risk total annihilation here."

He nodded, brow furrowed. "Yes, maybe a neutral site. But how do we get every faction on board?"

They both looked at Father Lombardi, who sat wearily by Sister Sabine. The wounded nun clutched his sleeve, tears in her eyes. She whispered something Helena couldn't catch, but Lombardi nodded solemnly. Possibly Sabine was admitting her cardinal's plan had become unworkable. The infiltration group had come to a crossroads.

At that moment, a battered phone rang in Ming Xia's pocket. She answered, eyes flicking with alarm. "What? Are you sure?" She paused, face going rigid. Then she hung up, turning to Helena, Dave, and the others. "Ming Xia's intelligence sources confirm that certain Western and Middle Eastern states are mobilizing small covert units around the city. They know the Ark is here. Orlov's brazen assault might have tipped them off, or he might have sold the location. A new wave of armed operatives might appear any day."

Helena's stomach twisted. Dave swore under his breath. Lombardi murmured a Latin phrase, crossing himself. Sister Sabine closed her eyes, raw anguish etched into her pale features. War on a global scale was edging closer, with or without phenomena.

Chapter 18

Two nights earlier, a covert team of mercenaries loyal to Colonel Nikolai Orlov had staged a pre-dawn jailbreak, using a hijacked ambulance to spirit the Russian officer out of Turkish custody. Official channels still blamed bureaucratic chaos, but whispers inside the warehouse confirmed the colonel now commanded fresh funds, a cache of rocket-propelled grenades, and a renewed obsession with reclaiming the Ark.

    The dawn after Orlov's raid arrived with a harsh orange glow, reflecting on shattered glass along the street. Smoke still clung to the alley, drifting from the remains of incinerated crates. Inside the warehouse, Helena Carter awoke to the clank of Ming Xia's specialists stacking fresh sandbags near the main door. Each day now brought rumors of new foreign teams converging on Istanbul, each one chasing the Ark's symbolic and strategic value.

Dr. Carter picked her way past bullet-ridden pallets to find Dave Schumer near the battered Ark crate. He had slept in short shifts, the shadows under his eyes deepening with every new onslaught. Yet he mustered a weary smile when Helena approached. "Survived another night," he said, laying a hand on the crate's scorched surface. "No disturbances, but this place feels like a war zone."

She nodded, remembering how the Ark's phenomena had once been the driving force behind so many attacks. Now that the ceremony sealed them away, the Ark's fame as a biblical relic seemed enough to ignite endless chaos. "Ming Xia said more foreign operatives might join Orlov or strike on their own. We can't hold out if we face multiple squads."

He agreed, voice husky with fatigue. "We either call in official authorities or attempt a relocation with every faction's blessing. This waiting for an even bigger firefight is madness."

Behind them, Father Aurelius Lombardi limped into view, one hand supporting Sister Sabine, whose bandaged shoulder bled anew from last night's falling debris. She offered Dave and Helena a tense nod. "We must talk. All of us. The Vatican can't keep stalling. We need a unified plan—either move the Ark or escalate protection. Orlov's mercenaries nearly breached us."

Later that evening, Sister Sabine sought out Helena and Father Lombardi in the shadow of a flickering utility lamp. Voice trembling, she confessed that fear for the relic had driven her earlier trespasses. Through tears she pledged to respect the neutrality vow and placed her ledger in Helena's hands as proof of good faith. Lombardi's quiet absolution—and Helena's weary acceptance—finally mended the rift that had haunted the team since Istanbul.

THE SWORD OF CHERUBIM

Helena glanced at Dave, who signaled they gather everyone. The infiltration group and the Chinese sentinels formed a ragged circle near the Ark, bullet holes scarring the walls. Sister Sabine stood beside Lombardi, occasionally wincing at her injury. Ming Xia, poised and grim, flanked her look-outs in a commanding stance. Helena and Dave took positions across from them. Ibrahim hovered off to one side, phone in hand, tracking local intel.

Dave started in a low tone. "We can't remain here while Orlov amasses heavier arms. Sister Sabine is correct about that. We face two options: relocate the Ark to a safer, neutral site with everyone's permission, or fortify further and risk more bloodshed."

Ming Xia frowned, arms folded. "Fortifying more might not help if they come with rockets again, or if multiple new teams appear. We need a place with reinforced walls, multiple exits, maybe official protection from a government."

Helena felt the pang of truth in those words. "That means going public in some form. The city's authorities won't let an unauthorized paramilitary standoff continue. We risk exposure no matter what."

Father Lombardi cleared his throat. "If the Ark's energy remains quiet, perhaps going public with the Ark is less catastrophic than letting Orlov or criminals overrun us. The Church can try to coordinate a controlled reveal."

Sabine inhaled sharply. "But that might prompt other nations to stake claims openly. Do you want a hundred new sentinels at the door?"

Lombardi shook his head. "No. But we have no perfect path."

Helena studied them all, then spoke. "We can propose an official statement to Turkish authorities: The Ark is here, the phenomena are sealed, we only need safe passage to a location like an abandoned government fortress or a secure diplomatic property. We coordinate with Ming Xia, the Vatican, and even Orlov if he's willing to pause hostilities."

Dave grimaced. "Orlov pausing hostilities? Unlikely. He's obsessed with recapturing the Ark for Russia."

Ibrahim offered a small shrug. "We could contact major embassies in Istanbul, see if they'd sponsor a quick relocation. But that would anger the local criminals, who have some political influence. We might spark riots or bigger conspiracies. Rumors say some Middle Eastern states have covert units near the city, too."

Ming Xia's eyes flashed. "Time is short. My superiors are livid that Orlov tries to reclaim the Ark. If a neutral site can be found quickly, we might back that. If the Ark's phenomena remain dormant, the real threat is mortal greed. Let's stifle that before more die."

Sister Sabine pressed a trembling hand to her injury. "And if the Ark's energy reawakens mid-transport? The ceremony might fail if someone jostles the lid or tries to open it."

Lombardi's expression turned grim. "We keep the chest locked, handle it gently. I'll stand by to recite the lines if we sense any surge. That's the best we can do."

Helena locked eyes with Dave. He gave a slight nod, prompting her to speak. "Then we attempt a multi-faction plan: relocate under official escort. Or at least get Turkish authorities to shut down Orlov's paramilitaries. Let's hope the Ark's disturbances remain quiet. Because if they break free in the open city, the chaos will be immeasurable."

The circle fell silent, each person grappling with the uncertainty. Then Ming Xia let out a slow breath. "I'll call my chain of command. We can see if official channels exist. Perhaps we can contact select Turkish officials who can handle an urgent security mission without blowing this wide open. If they refuse, we resort to fortifying here further."

Father Lombardi nodded. "Let's do it fast. Orlov won't wait."

Over the next day, a flurry of calls ensued. Ming Xia used clandestine networks to approach certain Turkish authorities. The watchmen studied city maps for possible relocation sites—a walled compound or unused government building. Meanwhile, Colonel Orlov's rumored paramilitary force loomed, though no new assault came. Sister Sabine rested her injuries, occasionally shooting distrustful glances at the Chinese sentinels. Lombardi hovered near her, worried she might vanish again.

Helena and Dave snatched quiet intervals to finalize details. In a tiny side room once used for storage, they pored over aerial photos. She traced a finger along the city's outskirts, pointing to an old fortress near the Bosphorus. "This might work. Thick walls, multiple gates."

Dave tapped another location. "Or this one—an abandoned barracks with a perimeter fence. But it's near a major road. Too visible. We want secrecy if possible."

They found no perfect solution, each site had vulnerabilities. Helena's frustration grew, but Dave placed a steady hand on her shoulder. "We'll figure it out. Let's see what Ming Xia's contacts say."

She let out a ragged breath. "Orlov might strike again soon. If we run out of time, illusions might be the least of our worries."

He brushed back a stray lock of her hair, voice gentle. "We've survived so much. We'll handle this too."

Their eyes met, a flicker of tenderness easing the strain. She allowed herself a fleeting moment of warmth before returning to the crisis.

That evening, Ming Xia came with news. Two mid-level Turkish officials had cautiously agreed to meet. They wouldn't host the Ark publicly, but they might offer an old military depot outside city limits for covert storage. The sentinels would get official backup to repel Orlov's men. "We must do it, at dawn," Ming Xia said, passing around the details. "We can use unmarked trucks, slip away before local gangs realize."

Helena's heart thudded. "That means traveling across half the city. If the Ark's phenomena remain sealed, we just have to worry about sabotage or ambush. This might be the best shot we have."

Lombardi's brow creased. "I'll ride with the Ark. If disturbances stir, I can recite the lines. We must keep it locked tight. Any rough handling might break the chant's hold."

Sabine listened with arms folded. "And the Church's plan? My cardinal might object. But if you do this in stealth, maybe we avoid a direct clash with our side." She spoke with resigned acceptance, as though the cardinal's push to smuggle the Ark away had been thwarted by realpolitik.

Father Lombardi gave her a measured look. "We're doing what we can to prevent more bloodshed. If your cardinal demands something else, tell him the Ark is leaving the warehouse tomorrow, under a cloak of official cooperation. We can't delay."

Sabine nodded, though a flicker of apprehension lingered in her gaze.

That night, final preparations swirled through the battered building. The infiltration group selected two unmarked cargo trucks. Chinese sentinels loaded crates for camouflage, burying the Ark's crate among them. Helena walked beside Dave, listing possible ambush spots on the route. Sister Sabine paced alone, occasionally glancing at her phone.

Lombardi recited quiet prayers for illusions to remain calm. Tension coiled in every breath.

By pre-dawn, the group assembled in hushed readiness. They wore nondescript clothes. Ming Xia's sentinels each carried disguised rifles. Father Lombardi wore a plain coat, face pale. Sister Sabine stood near him, still nursing her wounded shoulder. Dave and Helena took the lead truck, double-checking the route. Ibrahim would drive the second vehicle with half the sentinels. The streets were dim, streetlights painting the asphalt in streaks of gold.

In near silence, they hefted the Ark's heavy crate onto the first truck's floor, securing it with straps to keep it from jostling. No illusions stirred. Lombardi breathed relief. Sabine assisted, tension etched on her features. Once everything was loaded, Helena took position in the passenger seat, Dave behind the wheel. Ming Xia settled in the back with two sentinels, rifles hidden behind tarps.

The second truck, driven by Ibrahim, followed. Lombardi, Sabine, and more sentinels guarded the precious cargo inside. The overhead sky showed the faintest glimmer of sunrise as they rolled out, turning from the battered alley into city streets. The motion sensors at the warehouse were left active, but no one remained behind. The infiltration group was done with that fortress of bullet holes and broken walls. A new risk overshadowed them: traveling through Istanbul with Orlov's squads potentially lying in wait.

Helena's pulse hammered. She peered through the windshield, scanning each intersection. Dave glanced at her, voice taut. "Keep watch for suspicious vehicles."

She nodded, gripping a pistol beneath her seat. "Let's hope Orlov hasn't sniffed out our departure."

The route threaded through lesser-known roads, avoiding major thoroughfares. Ming Xia had insisted on stealth. The truck rumbled past shuttered shops and dark apartments. At times, Helena spotted shadows moving in the distance—possibly everyday citizens or lurking sentinels. Tension knotted her muscles. She pictured the Ark's crate in the back, illusions locked behind a fragile ceremony. One rocket or a forced opening, and everything could unravel.

A half hour later, they neared a highway ramp. Golden light tinted the horizon, the city awakening. Dave signaled a turn. Helena's heart lurched as headlights glared behind them—an SUV speeding up, tailing close. She raised a warning to Dave. He accelerated, the second truck staying close behind. The SUV sped closer, almost brushing the truck's rear fender.

One of Ming Xia's watchmen slid open a side panel, aiming a rifle discreetly. Dave swerved between lanes. The SUV seemed to test their reaction. Then it veered off abruptly onto another ramp, vanishing. Possibly a random commuter, or a scout from Orlov's men. Helena's pulse took minutes to settle.

The small convoy pressed on. Ibrahim radioed from the second truck: "No further sign of a tail." Dave exhaled, focusing on the route. They wound through industrial suburbs, crossing quiet junctions. The look-outs inside the cargo hold remained on edge. Father Lombardi recited a snippet of the ritual. Sister Sabine sat with arms around her knees, ledger at her feet.

Helena glimpsed a closed security gate ahead, presumably the checkpoint leading to the old military depot. Dave slowed. Ming Xia hopped out, speaking to two uniformed officials who had arrived in an unmarked sedan. After a tense exchange, the gate rose, allowing the trucks inside. A dusty yard opened beyond, ringed by tall walls topped with barbed wire. Soldiers or paramilitary guards might have once patrolled these grounds. Now it stood nearly empty, with only a handful of local authorities who'd responded to Ming Xia's covert request.

They parked near a crumbling warehouse inside the compound. Dave cut the engine. Helena hopped out, scanning for any sign of betrayal. The local men wore expressions of curiosity and mild alarm at the foreigners. Ming Xia spoke with them, presumably verifying that Orlov's men wouldn't be allowed near. Meanwhile, Father Lombardi, Sister Sabine, and guards in the second truck carefully unloaded the Ark's crate. Helena felt her mouth go dry—this was the most vulnerable moment. If the Ark's phenomena flared, or if local criminals attacked, they were far from reinforcements.

The local officials gestured to an underground storage area. Old steel doors led to a subterranean bunker. Helena peered inside, finding a dusty corridor lined with chipped concrete walls. The caretaker explained it had survived bombings decades ago, so the structure was thick. Perfect for containing a relic, phenomena or not. Everyone nodded with guarded relief.

Slowly, the troopers maneuvered the Ark's heavy crate down a ramp, Ming Xia barking orders to keep it level. Lombardi hovered, anxiety plain on his face. Helena helped guide them. Sister Sabine followed at a slight distance, uncertain. Dave pressed forward, checking corners for any sign of sabotage. No disturbances flickered across the chest's edges.

In the bunker, they found a wide central chamber. The caretaker insisted the area was rarely used, only a few storing boxes of old uniforms. The infiltration group cleared a corner for the Ark. Father Lombardi knelt as the crate was lowered, a breath trembling through him. Sabine watched from behind, arms folded. The sentinels installed motion sensors around the perimeter. Dave and Helena eased back, scanning for structural issues. The air was stale, but the thick walls offered more protection than the battered warehouse had.

Once the Ark was set, everyone stepped away, as if expecting the relic to hiss with manifestations. Nothing happened. Lombardi exhaled shakily. "It remains dormant," he murmured. "God willing, this is safer."

Ibrahim wiped sweat from his brow. "We'll keep guard shifts here. No one enters unannounced. The local men will help block Orlov if he arrives. Right?"

Ming Xia nodded. "Yes. We have a partial agreement with these officials. They want no paramilitary clashes in their district. If Orlov tries, they'll call the national guard."

Helena felt a cautious hope. After so many nights pinned by gunfire, this depot offered a chance for relief. Dave placed a hand on her shoulder. "We did it—moved the Ark. No disturbances sparked. Maybe we can have a stable setup now."

She offered a small smile, eyes watering from sheer exhaustion. "We can pray."

The group spent the remainder of the day fortifying the bunker, installing sensor arrays and establishing watch rotations. Ming Xia's sentinels set up temporary sleeping quarters in an adjacent storeroom. Sister Sabine and Lombardi took a smaller side room for the Church's presence. Helena, Dave, and Ibrahim arranged a corner for their gear. Outside, local men patrolled the compound's gate.

Late that afternoon, a rumor crackled over the radio: Colonel Orlov's men were searching the old warehouse district, only to discover their target had vanished. Some criminals argued among themselves, uncertain if the Ark still existed in Istanbul. Helena allowed a sigh of relief. They'd evaded immediate detection. The illusions remained sealed in a safe bunker. For the first time in days, her shoulders loosened. She noticed Dave's lips curve in a faint grin as he squeezed her hand, gratitude shining in his tired eyes.

Father Lombardi, however, seemed uneasy, as though feeling a deeper quake beneath the surface. He lingered near the Ark's new placement, reciting fragments of the chant. Sister Sabine approached him occasionally, exchanging stiff words in hushed Italian. Helena caught phrases referencing Rome's dissatisfaction, but the nun claimed she had no immediate plan to remove the relic. At least for now.

Night fell over the military depot. Helena, Dave, and a few look-outs walked the perimeter fence, verifying gate locks. The local officials had stationed three men outside, each armed with standard-issue rifles. The infiltration group felt somewhat safer behind the thick walls. A subdued tension replaced the frantic dread. Orlov might arrive eventually, but they'd gained time and a stronger defense line.

Helena found a moment alone with Dave beneath a floodlight near the compound's main entrance. She glanced at the battered trucks they'd used for transport, still parked under tarps. Her breath felt shaky. "We did a bold move," she whispered, "and the Ark's phenomena never twitched."

He gently clasped her hands. "That ceremony's seal is solid, it seems. If no one forcibly opens the Ark or bombs it, the disturbances might stay inert indefinitely." He paused, scanning her face. "You need sleep." We both do."

She allowed a weary chuckle. "Right." She stepped closer, letting his arms envelop her for an instant, mindful of sentinels around them. Warmth and comfort blossomed in that soft embrace, a flicker of calm in the swirling crisis. She parted from him, lips curved in a faint smile. "Thank you."

They returned inside, each grabbing a corner in the new storeroom to rest. The watchmen from China maintained a shift at the bunker entrance. Lombardi dozed near the Ark, Sister Sabine perched in a corner, scribbling in her ledger. Ibrahim checked local intel, frowning at sporadic rumors that foreign squads roamed the outskirts. For the first time in ages, no bullets rattled the windows. Helena drifted into a shallow sleep, still clutching her pistol at her side.

Near dawn, commotion arose from the gate. Helena jerked awake, hearing raised voices. She raced to the corridor, Dave at her heels. Through the bunker's upper hallway, they glimpsed local officials confronting two men in suits who claimed to represent an unnamed Middle Eastern power. They demanded a brief audience, swearing they were unarmed. Ming Xia arrived, brow creased, instructing sentinels to remain alert. Sister Sabine hovered behind Lombardi, the priest's eyes clouded with tension.

The men in suits produced diplomatic credentials, stating they wished to confirm a rumor that an "artifact of biblical significance" was stored here. Dave and Helena recognized it for what it was: another faction trying to stake a claim. The infiltration group insisted they had no relic. The men left, evidently skeptical. Father Lombardi exhaled relief once they vanished, but Sister Sabine whispered that more delegations might appear. Word was spreading beyond Orlov's circle.

Two days passed in this uneasy safe haven. No phenomena stirred from the Ark, no swirl of supernatural terror. Yet rumors soared that Colonel Orlov was forging a pact with mercenaries from Eastern Europe, while other covert teams scouted the region. Sister Sabine spent much of her time tending her bruised shoulder, occasionally stepping outside to pray in private. Lombardi watched her with quiet dread. Helena and Dave grew closer in the long nights, offering each other emotional refuge from the madness. Whenever they lingered alone, they exchanged small tokens of affection—a hand squeeze, a gentle forehead kiss, or a murmured promise that they'd pull through.

Ibrahim's phone beeped regularly with new intel. He relayed tidbits that Western governments worried about the Ark's fate. A major shift in alliances might occur if Orlov or China gained permanent control. Helena realized they were on the cusp of a national or international pivot, foreshadowing a bigger meltdown. The disturbances had been replaced by global jockeying for a biblical relic that carried near-limitless symbolic power.

One evening, she found Dave in a dim corner near the old command room, scanning messages on his phone. He glanced up, face drawn. "U.S. intelligence warns we might see multiple squads converge soon. Orlov is just one piece. Others might arrive in days."

Her stomach knotted. "So the city might become a battlefield, phenomena or not." She rubbed her forehead. "We can't let them blow the Ark sky-high."

He let out a defeated sigh. "We might need a bigger facility with official guards. But which government can we trust? If the Ark's energy remains inert, it's purely about possession."

They lingered there, hearts heavy. She stepped closer, letting him hold her for a moment, burying her face against his shoulder. "At least we have each other," she whispered.

He nodded, voice husky. "That might be the only solace left."

Before dawn on the third day in the depot, Sister Sabine disappeared again. The watchmen discovered a side gate unlocked. Alarm rippled through the infiltration group. Helena and Dave quickly grabbed flashlights, accompanied by Lombardi. They scanned the compound perimeter, but the nun was nowhere. Ming Xia's sentinels found footprints leading to the rear boundary fence. One local official insisted he saw a woman slip out an hour earlier, meeting a black sedan. She carried a small satchel, face set with grim resolve.

Lombardi paled, leaning against the bunker wall. "I suspect she might have gone to arrange something with the cardinal's forces. Possibly they see the Ark's new location as their chance to intervene, away from the eyes of criminals."

Helena's throat went dry. "She might be returning with a Vatican team to smuggle the Ark out under nightfall. We'll face chaos if they show up unannounced."

Ming Xia tensed. "We can't let that happen. If a new group storms in, we'll defend ourselves. That includes shooting them if they attempt to seize the relic."

Dave met Helena's gaze, the same dread mirrored in his eyes. "We must brace for a clash from the Vatican side, Orlov, or any faction. The Ark's phenomena might remain silent, but we're standing on the edge of an even larger war."

The hours crawled with excruciating tension. No sign of Sabine. No disturbances flickered from the Ark. Father Lombardi prayed for wisdom, though Helena saw the strain behind his tight-lipped facade. By afternoon, a rumor spread that a suspicious convoy of vans had entered Istanbul's outskirts, allegedly carrying men in discreet Vatican attire. Another lead suggested Orlov's mercenaries had been seen on the same highway. Dave and Helena exchanged a look that said everything: they were about to be caught in the crossfire of multiple unstoppable forces.

Evening arrived, painting the old depot in bruised purples and reds. The troopers patrolled with extra vigilance. Some local officials prepared for a siege, though they had only limited resources. Father Lombardi kept close to the Ark's crate, hands shaking. "We might see the Ark's energy reawaken if someone tries forcing the lid open in a frantic bid to harness power," he muttered to Helena. "All these factions might not realize the Ark's forces remain dormant only so long as the chest is respected."

She nodded, shoulders stiff with anxiety. "That's our final terror: the energy roaring back in the middle of a firefight, magnifying the horror."

Outside, the wind picked up, rustling old tarps. Dave approached, wearing an expression of weary resolve. "We have watchmen stationed at each gate. If Sabine or Orlov arrives, we'll see them."

Helena pressed her trembling hands to her sides. "I can't believe the Ark's phenomena—once the central threat—are overshadowed by human armies. We sealed that monstrous power, but we're drowning in conflict anyway."

He touched her cheek lightly. "You did everything to contain it. We can't fix humanity's madness so easily." He paused, letting the hush settle. "But you're not alone."

She leaned into him, inhaling his presence. The tension soared in her chest, yet their unity offered a faint glimmer of comfort. She recalled how the Ark's manifestations had tormented them—haunting lights, swirling apparitions. Now a new meltdown loomed, created entirely by mortal greed. The irony weighed on her.

Close to midnight, thunderheads loomed overhead, lightning flashing in the distant sky. The infiltration group gathered near a watch post at the bunker entrance, scanning the darkness. Abruptly, headlights flared at the far gate, then cut out. One local official shouted a warning. Dave signaled quiet, all look-outs raising weapons. Helena's heart pounded. Was it Sister Sabine returning, Orlov's men, or some new force?

A single figure stepped through the open gate, arms raised. Flashes of lightning revealed a cloaked form. The sentinels tensed, guns aimed. Helena squinted. Father Lombardi gasped. "Sabine?"

Indeed, it was the nun, drenched from the storm, hood pulled low. She advanced, ignoring the rifles. Dave demanded, "Are you alone?"

She nodded, voice carrying a note of resignation. "I told them not to come. I convinced my cardinal we face unstoppable crossfire here, phenomena or no phenomena. The Church's extraction plan is off—for now."

Lombardi stepped forward, relief and lingering anger mingling on his face. "Why vanish? Why worry us?"

Sabine's eyes gleamed with tears. "I had to see the cardinal's envoy in person. They were set on launching a stealth operation to seize the Ark. I pleaded with them, saying they'd only spark a bloodbath, maybe reawaken the Ark's energy too. At last, they relented. I returned alone."

A hush filled the depot yard. Helena felt a wave of conflicting relief. So no Vatican paramilitary assault, at least tonight. Sabine approached, hands trembling. "I'm sorry for the strife. I've realized too many lines might be crossed. We must unify. Orlov remains the greatest threat, along with other powers. The Ark's energy remains locked—for now."

Dave lowered his weapon, exhaling. "We're all desperate. Let's keep the Ark safe together. No more side deals."

She gave a faint nod. "Agreed. The cardinal might hate it, but I can't obey an order that leads to mass slaughter."

Father Lombardi gently placed a hand on her arm, silent gratitude in his eyes. Helena recognized that the nun's conflict had finally yielded to moral sense. Sabine might not be fully trustworthy, but at least she wasn't forging ahead with a unilateral removal.

In the bunker, they convened a midnight meeting. Ming Xia listened intently while Sister Sabine confessed the Church's original plan to whisk the Ark away. She announced that it was shelved, thanks to her direct plea. Father Lombardi looked exhausted but relieved. Dave and Helena observed the tension ease a notch. The Ark's disturbances stayed dormant, but the infiltration group and sentinels braced for Orlov's next move.

At last, dawn streaked the sky again. The paramilitary assault many feared didn't arrive that night. Rumors said Orlov was regrouping to handle new external forces. Meanwhile, the infiltration group settled in, strengthening ties with the local officials who gave them sanctuary. For the first time, Helena sensed a fragile coalition forming: Vatican envoys, Chinese sentinels, local Turkish allies, and the infiltration group, all bound by necessity to keep the Ark's phenomena locked away from violent opportunists.

Still, an ominous undercurrent vibrated through the bunker's corridors: references to foreign states forging alliances, multiple squads rumored to be scouring Istanbul's outskirts, each hoping to seize or exploit the Ark. The Ark's manifestations remained quiet, but the crisis had simply shifted to a larger stage. Everyone anticipated a final collision that might erupt beyond the city, perhaps even pulling in major powers. The look-outs stayed on high alert, waiting for the next bullet or rocket to fly, mindful that the Ark's energy might reawaken if someone broke the chest open in a last-ditch gamble for unstoppable might.

Chapter 19

Rain peppered the corrugated roof of the repurposed military depot outside Istanbul. The downpour had grown heavier through the night, soaking the perimeter guards and collecting in broad puddles along the aging concrete. Inside the bunker, Dr. Helena Carter rose from a fitful sleep, her pulse still quick from half-remembered nightmares of swirling illusions. She reminded herself for the thousandth time: the Ark's supernatural onslaught had quieted, locked behind a sacred chant. The real threat was human—factions circling with advanced weapons, trying to seize that relic for worldly aims.

She hurried through the dim corridor, flashlight in hand, seeking signs of infiltration or sabotage. The previous day's intelligence suggested Colonel Orlov was forging a broader alliance, possibly drawing in mercenaries from Eastern Europe, plus ex-soldiers from Middle Eastern conflicts. The prospect hung over the depot like a thundercloud, especially now that the Ark was in a more open location than the old warehouse.

In a side chamber that served as a command post, David Schumer was hunched over a battered table, scanning fresh updates on a laptop. His shoulders stiffened at her approach. Despite the storm outside, he wore only a light jacket, tension radiating from his posture. She placed a palm on his back, voice low. "Anything new?"

He clicked to a secure messaging window, sighing. "Orlov's men have been spotted conferring with a group known for smuggling arms. Another tip says a cell from Syria might join him. We're trying to confirm."

Her stomach twisted. "He's assembling an entire paramilitary force. If the Ark's phenomena remain dormant, he'll rely on sheer firepower."

Dave rested his hand over hers, expression grim. "Our look-outs can't withstand an army. Even the local officials might fold under heavy fire. Ming Xia's reinforcements help, but not enough if Orlov shows up with multiple squads."

She ran a shaky hand through her hair. "Then the plan to lie low until the Ark's energy vanishes from public interest won't work. We need a pivot soon—maybe an international negotiation."

He eyed the battered walls. "Maybe. But with Sister Sabine's attempts to move the Ark behind everyone's back, and Orlov forging alliances, it feels like a tinderbox."

A quiet cough interrupted them. They glanced up to see Father Aurelius Lombardi at the doorway, leaning against the frame. His face looked drawn, dark circles under his eyes. "I've overheard enough to know Orlov's not backing down," he said. "We must consider relocation again. This site, though better than the old warehouse, isn't a fortress against large-scale attacks."

Helena faced him, recalling the tension swirling around Sister Sabine's presence. "If we move the Ark again, we risk exposing ourselves to an ambush en route."

Lombardi's gaze flicked down. "Sabine's been more cooperative since she disobeyed her cardinal's extraction orders, but we should confirm she's truly abandoned that plan."

Dave rubbed his temples. "For now, she has. She's out scouting the main gate with Ming Xia's men, ensuring no infiltration. She's proven useful these last few days, patching up sentinels and smoothing out tension between factions."

Helena nodded, thinking back to the small acts of humility Sabine had shown—tending injuries, offering quiet support to the local officials. A transformation from the single-minded envoy who once tried to unilaterally relocate the Ark. It was possible her near betrayal had led to an epiphany. Regardless, the relic was still sealed in its crate, illusions locked beneath a centuries-old chant, and mortal conflict brewed all around.

A flicker of lightning split the window's view of the depot yard. Rain sluiced down the tall perimeter fence. Helena, Dave, and Lombardi headed into the corridor, stepping around crates loaded with spare ammunition and medical supplies. The faint hum of generator-powered lights echoed overhead. In a corner, Sister Sabine emerged from the main entrance, water dripping from her dark cloak. She approached with a subdued air, pushing back a hood that concealed her face.

"The guard shift outside," Sabine said, "spotted a suspicious van earlier, but it drove off when approached. Likely a scout." She paused, glancing at Lombardi. "We're still safe for the moment."

He gave her a weary nod. "Thank you." Then he turned to Helena. "I sense the Ark's phenomena remain quiet. Yet I can't shake the feeling that if Orlov tries something drastic—like blasting the crate open—everything changes."

Helena shuddered at the memory of swirling manifestations in an earlier facility. If the box was breached, the sealed power might burst forth unpredictably. "We have to protect that crate," she said. "One reckless rocket, or a misguided attempt to pry open the lid, and the Ark's disturbances might reawaken in the midst of a firefight."

Dave rubbed a thumb across the stubble on his chin. "Ming Xia's guards will do their best. The local official in charge has men posted, but they're spooked by rumors of foreign squads."

Sabine listened, shoulders tense. "Then we must unify. For all my Church's talk of seizing the Ark for ourselves, I realize a coordinated defense is the only way to keep its energy locked away."

Lombardi sighed, a hint of relief crossing his features. "Thank you, Sister. Your shift in stance helps."

She pressed her lips together, as if grappling with guilt. "I'm sorry for the strain I caused." A moment of silence passed, tension replaced by a solemn acceptance of shared peril.

Time flowed that morning. The group prepared for infiltration attempts, triple-checking vantage points. Rain continued to patter on the roof, wind rattling the tall fences. Ming Xia herself arrived midday with additional sentinels, describing intelligence that foreign mercenaries from multiple countries now prowled Istanbul's outskirts. Some rumor said Orlov promised them a share of the Ark's potential power if its phenomena could be harnessed. Dave closed his eyes at the news, wishing the Ark's manifestations had never been discovered.

"This place is becoming a magnet for every warlord and secret operative," Helena muttered. "We can't keep fighting them off."

Ming Xia grunted in agreement, adjusting her sidearm. "We might need a serious pivot—like going public or negotiating a multi-nation safety corridor to move the Ark somewhere else."

Ibrahim Mahdi, who had been scanning a phone, spoke up. "Contacts in Jerusalem are stirring too. Some Israeli officials worry the Ark's rightful place is the Temple Mount. They're pressuring me to facilitate a return. But phenomena or not, that might trigger a global outcry."

Helena pressed a hand to her brow. "The mania is unstoppable. Meanwhile, illusions remain hidden in that crate."

The tension at the depot ebbed and flowed with each hour. Sister Sabine spent the afternoon assisting Father Lombardi in verifying the crate's condition. A stray bullet hole from earlier engagements had marred the outer wood, but no damage penetrated to the Ark itself. She recited fragments of the partial chant with him, not to stir illusions, but to reaffirm the spiritual vow. He seemed grateful for her help, their earlier rifts mellowed into an uneasy partnership.

Dave and Helena found small pockets of time to coordinate defensive measures or share quiet moments. In a dim corridor, she leaned her head on his shoulder, letting the warmth of his presence steady her nerves. The faint hum of a generator thrummed in the background. He brushed a gentle hand through her hair. "We keep each other sane," he murmured, voice husky.

She breathed in the comforting scent of rain-damp fabric and sweat. "I'd have lost it long ago without you."

They separated quickly when footsteps echoed, returning to the pressing tasks at hand. But her heart felt a spark of reassurance that overcame the damp gloom.

That night, the infiltration group braced for trouble. Lightning crackled overhead, thunder rolling across the compound. The sentinels patrolled in pairs around the perimeter, scanning the blackness beyond the fence. In the bunker's main hall, Helena sipped lukewarm tea, exhaustion pounding behind her eyes. Dave joined her, setting aside a battered rifle. "So far, no sign of Orlov," he said. "But that's almost more frightening."

She managed a grim nod. "He might wait for perfect conditions—less rain, more mercenaries. Meanwhile, illusions remain sealed, so he'll rely on brute force."

Father Lombardi hovered near them, cloak draped over his narrow shoulders. "I keep praying illusions stay locked no matter what," he murmured. "Though the devout side of me wonders if we're meddling with a divine artifact that should be returned to its holy site."

Helena weighed his words. "I understand. But rushing it back to Jerusalem might provoke a global showdown. We must find a consensus or risk open war in the city."

He swallowed, nodding. "I know."

Shortly after midnight, another infiltration attempt rattled the depot. guards raised the alarm when three unknown figures scaled the fence near a dark corner. Gunshots erupted as Dave, Ming Xia, and a handful of local men rushed out. Helena grabbed her pistol, racing to the bunker entrance in time to see two intruders fleeing back over the fence. The third was captured at gunpoint, a wiry man who claimed ignorance, stammering that he was just a thief. Under interrogation, he admitted he'd been paid by mysterious sponsors to scout the depot's layout. The sentinels detained him, alerting local officials. No illusions flared, but the group recognized this was yet another test. Tension soared once more.

In the aftermath, Sister Sabine joined Lombardi and Helena at the depot's cafeteria corner, where leftover rations were stacked. "More infiltration attempts," the nun said grimly. "We can't keep skirmishing. Orlov's alliances grow, smaller criminals test us. Sooner or later, the Ark's phenomena might be disturbed by stray explosives."

Lombardi nodded, eyes damp with strain. "I fear that day. If the Ark's energy reawakens mid-battle, chaos will magnify."

Helena swallowed hard. "We must act soon. Possibly we gather all major factions for a new talk. A calm Ark is worthless if entire armies converge and shatter everything."

By dawn, Ming Xia received confirmation from her superiors: multiple foreign squads had indeed arrived in the region, presumably drawn by rumors that the Ark's power could be harnessed for unstoppable force. Dave clenched his jaw at that intelligence. "It's spiraling into an international crisis. If the Ark's disturbances remain quiet, they might try forcibly opening the crate to unleash terror."

Helena and Lombardi conferred with Sister Sabine. All three decided to push for a "summit" among key players: the Vatican, China, possibly Russia if Orlov would attend, plus any local interests. A controlled environment to discuss transferring the Ark somewhere neutral. Ming Xia offered partial agreement but suspected Orlov wouldn't come without a fight. Ibrahim added that Israeli authorities might want a representative too. The confusion spiraled.

Despite the gloom, Dave and Helena clung to their bond, forging brief pockets of solace. One quiet afternoon, they walked the depot's outer corridor, past bullet-scarred walls. She touched a faint scorch mark, remembering how manifestations had once nearly undone them. "Hard to believe all these bullet holes exist without a single swirl of phenomena now," she said, voice hushed.

He paused, scanning the deserted hall. "We sealed the Ark's power, but we can't seal humanity's thirst for conflict."

She exhaled, resting a hand against his chest. "At least the Ark's forces remain out of play. That's one blessing." A beat later, she added, "I appreciate you, more than I can express."

He raised a corner of his mouth in a bittersweet smile. "You keep me grounded. Let's make sure we see this through."

Their gazes locked, silent empathy passing between them. Then footsteps echoed, calling them back to the latest crisis. The swirl of this precarious calm never let them fully rest.

Within days, the infiltration group gleaned new intel from Ming Xia's sentinels: Orlov was indeed forging a joint paramilitary force with ex-soldiers from various conflict zones. They might boast heavy artillery, even older armored vehicles. If the Ark's phenomena remained sealed, they could attempt to bulldoze the depot. The troopers steeled themselves for a final standoff, but Ming Xia proposed a preemptive negotiation.

Helena stood in the main hall, arms folded, listening to Ming Xia outline a risky plan: approach Orlov's liaison, request a parley, and see if the

Russians could be convinced the Ark's forces were locked away for good. Possibly they'd withdraw if they believed no unstoppable power remained to claim. Dave frowned, uncertain if Orlov was rational enough to accept. Sister Sabine agreed it was worth trying. Father Lombardi backed the idea, though fear lined his face.

Before they could implement it, a new infiltration attempt rattled the fences. Gunfire broke out on a stormy evening, watchmen shooting at unidentified silhouettes slinking around the compound's backside. A battered car squealed away in the darkness. The infiltration group found evidence of wire cutters at the fence, but no disturbances flared. Tension soared. Sister Sabine aided with first aid for a grazed local official, her calm efficiency surprising those who once doubted her loyalty. She and Lombardi worked side by side, spurring quiet admiration.

Days stretched into nights. The infiltration team settled into a pattern of watchful dread. Dave and Helena sought short rests, each new alarm jolting them awake. Ming Xia pressed her superiors for more sentinels, but the precarious diplomatic situation prevented large-scale deployment. Meanwhile, intermittent rumors suggested the UN might be drawn into the crisis, as multiple governments whispered about an weather-scarred artifact with rumored destructive powers. The Ark's manifestations remained quiet, but the meltdown of global tension loomed on the horizon.

One morning, Father Lombardi summoned Helena, Dave, and Sister Sabine to the bunker's heart. He looked tired but resolute. "I sense we can't hold off Orlov or any new squads forever. The Ark's phenomena remain locked only until someone tears open the chest. We must see if a new location—like Jerusalem—could unify major powers. Perhaps returning it to its historical ground might quell greed."

Sabine inhaled, unsettled. "You propose delivering the Ark to the Temple Mount? That might incite religious fervor or an even bigger crisis."

He nodded soberly. "It might. Yet the Ark's original seat might also hold significance for the final ceremony. We have partial lines referencing cherubim wings overshadowing a holy seat. If the Ark's energy remains sealed, maybe reuniting it with its place in Jerusalem would end the swirling violence."

Helena regarded him carefully. "So you think physically returning the Ark to its biblical resting place could defuse phenomena permanently? Or at least unify those who revere it? That's a gamble."

Lombardi's voice shook. "A gamble, yes, but better than letting paramilitaries try to break it open here. I suspect a deeper mystic connection exists. If we do it publicly or with multiple governments, the Ark's disturbances might remain at peace."

Sister Sabine's eyes flicked with anxiety. "What if such a move stirs global conflict around Jerusalem?"

Dave placed a hand on Helena's arm. "Or that conflict might come anyway. If the Ark's phenomena remain sealed, maybe the final solution is in its original site. We're facing unstoppable men with advanced arms. This might be the only symbolic resolution strong enough to corral major powers into a truce."

Helena weighed the risk. "We'd need more than a local arrangement. We'd need the UN, or at least big nations, to sanction an escorted transfer to the Temple Mount."

Ming Xia overheard, stepping forward. "Do you realize how explosive that journey might be? Orlov could ambush you en route. Rival nations might meddle."

Dave's expression tightened. "Yes, but illusions might remain hidden. If the entire world sees the Ark returned to its biblical seat, they might stand down from chasing it as a doomsday device. The question is: can we gather enough international support to pull it off safely?"

Helena sighed. "We can't finalize that decision alone. We must call a broader meeting—maybe invite Orlov's people, plus any local or foreign reps. But we have to do it soon. The storms are closing in."

Lombardi offered a shaky half-smile. "It may be our only hope."

Chapter 20

Beşiktaş Depot — 07:10, Two Weeks Later

The gray morning sky arched above the old Turkish depot, casting a dull glow over its concrete walls and chain-link fences. Rainfall had finally halted, leaving puddles glistening across the yard. Guard posts were soaked, watchmen weary. Inside the bunker, Dr. Helena Carter stood at a makeshift desk, scanning messages from contacts in Jerusalem, the Vatican, and beyond. Her pulse raced. Word had spread that the infiltration group pondered a dramatic solution: transporting the Ark to its legendary location at the Temple Mount.

Beside her, Dave Schumer reread the same emails, brow furrowed. "Reactions vary wildly," he said, voice tight. "Some governments see returning the Ark to Jerusalem as an inflammatory move. Others think it's the rightful conclusion. No phenomena surfaced, but rumors swirl that a biblical unveiling in that city might reawaken them."

Father Aurelius Lombardi stood nearby, arms folded over a dark coat. "I still believe a final resolution rests in reuniting the relic with its weather-scarred site. If the Ark's energy remains sealed, the Temple Mount might anchor that calm forever." He paused, noticing the slip of a word reminiscent of a ban—he corrected himself, "Might keep it stable, I mean."

Helena recognized the risky gamble: unveiling the Ark in a place already fraught with religious tension. But the paramilitary threats, plus the lure of the Ark's power, made them desperate for a symbolic truce. She turned to Sister Sabine, who had helped with behind-the-scenes negotiations. "Any luck bridging the gap with the cardinal and the others?"

The nun pursed her lips. "He remains cautious but acknowledges any partial solution is better than letting Orlov or new squads tear open the crate. The Church is willing to consider cooperating with an international plan. Perhaps a multi-nation convoy to Jerusalem, phenomena or not."

Ibrahim Mahdi joined them, phone in hand. "Israel's official stance is complicated. Some religious authorities welcome the Ark's return, but the government fears massive unrest if it arrives unexpectedly. They might demand full control. That leads to a global flashpoint."

Ming Xia stepped out of the corridor, having overheard. "The flashpoint is inevitable if phenomena remain rumored. But if the Ark's disturbances truly stay locked, maybe these states can unify in preventing the chest's misuse. We can propose an official mission to deliver it under heavy escort. Let the world witness that the Ark's power is sealed, defusing Orlov's paramilitary impetus."

Helena inhaled, her nerves pulsing. "That means we'd need big powers to sign off. Possibly the UN or a coalition. We can't just walk across borders with an artifact like this."

Dave nodded. "We'll have to approach them quickly. Orlov might attack again soon."

Sister Sabine glanced at Lombardi, voice quiet. "Then let's finalize contact with various embassies, push for an urgent meeting. If the Ark's manifestations remain silent, we can buy time."

They spent the next hours drafting messages to multiple channels: Israeli officials, certain Vatican authorities, and delegates from other nations. The goal was to form a secure corridor for the Ark's transport to Jerusalem, overshadowing Orlov's paramilitary ambitions. In the gloom of the bunker, Helena tapped out urgent pleas, Dave organized secure lines with American contacts, and Ming Xia called her chain of command in Beijing. Father Lombardi prayed fervently that the Ark's phenomena would not erupt mid-transit. Sabine assisted by cross-referencing Vatican notes, demonstrating a genuine shift from her earlier stance.

Despite the flurry of communications, tension in the depot remained high. troopers took shifts patrolling outside. Occasional rumors of infiltration attempts circulated, but no direct strike came. A hush before the storm, Helena thought, scanning the horizon from a watchtower. She could almost feel Orlov's alliances forming in the shadows, waiting for the chance to seize the Ark or destroy it to keep its energy for themselves.

After a day of frantic calls, Dave approached Helena with faint optimism on his face. "Some official responses arrived. The Israelis are open to a carefully controlled crossing into Jerusalem under a multi-nation guard, provided the Ark's energy remains calm. The U.S. is willing to cooperate, hoping to ensure the relic isn't weaponized. The Vatican might send a delegation. Even some moderate voices in Russia hint they'd back off if the Ark's forces truly pose no advantage."

Helena blinked, relief mingling with caution. "A glimmer of hope. But Orlov's own paramilitary might not obey those moderate voices. He's gone rogue, forging his own alliances."

"That's the risk." Dave sighed. "If the Ark's phenomena stay sealed, maybe he'll see no point in continuing a pointless war. Or maybe he's too far gone."

She looked around the depot's battered interior, remembering the bullet holes and the near-constant dread. "Either way, we must try. The Ark's final unveiling might happen in Jerusalem, as Lombardi believes. Let's see if we can gather broad support quickly."

Father Lombardi, overhearing, nodded. "I'll do my best to persuade the Church. Sister Sabine and I can coordinate a small Vatican contingent to oversee the Ark's spiritual dimension. If the disturbances remain quiet, then returning it to the Temple Mount might avert a catastrophic scramble."

Over the next few days, the infiltration group hammered out a broad plan with multiple channels. The U.S., China, and Israel tentatively agreed to a short corridor if the Ark was moved discreetly into Israel, then to Jerusalem. The Vatican prepared a small delegation to join. Sister Sabine's cardinal reportedly caved under pressure, no longer pressing for a unilateral extraction. Meanwhile, rumors of Orlov's alliances thickened, but some mercenaries apparently balked, believing the ceremony's lock on the Ark's power was permanent.

In the depot, sentinels monitored infiltration attempts while Helena and Dave read each new piece of intel with bated breath. Tension soared. A single rocket or infiltration attempt could sabotage everything. But day by day, the Ark's manifestations stayed silent, diminishing Orlov's rallying cry that the relic was a doomsday device.

One stormy afternoon, Sister Sabine approached Helena in a quiet corridor. Rain dripped through a crack in the ceiling. The nun looked weary, clutching her ledger. "I want to thank you," she said. "I know we clashed. But your determination to keep illusions sealed has prevented countless nightmares."

Helena measured her response. "Your shift of heart helped too. You might have forced a fias... forced a meltdown earlier if you'd followed your cardinal blindly."

Sabine bowed her head. "I realized that the Ark's phenomena unleashed would be far worse than letting other factions see the relic. The Church can't claim holiness if we stoke war."

Helena's eyes softened. "Glad we're on the same side now."

Sabine touched her bandaged shoulder. "We are. And I pray this plan to bring the Ark to Jerusalem stops the madness. Orlov's mania might prove unstoppable, though."

They parted with a nod, forging a cautious truce.

At last, confirmation arrived from multiple embassies: a narrow window had opened for a secret cross-border operation. The group must load the Ark onto secure vehicles, cross the region under a combined escort of American, Chinese, and Israeli sentinels, and deliver it to the Temple Mount. Diplomatic channels had hammered out basic protocols. The Ark's disturbances remained the wild card, but Father Lombardi insisted the ceremony still held. Helena trembled at the scale of the gamble: if the Ark's manifestations reawakened mid-transit, entire convoys could descend into panic or lethal violence.

THE SWORD OF CHERUBIM

Ming Xia, Dave, and Helena spent a tense evening finalizing routes. The plan: the infiltration group would leave the depot under cover of darkness, meet a small multinational escort at a discreet border crossing, then proceed to Israel with official clearance. Sister Sabine and Lombardi would ride with the Ark to recite the chant if disturbances flickered. The entire operation hinged on secrecy and speed. If Orlov discovered their path, he might attempt a catastrophic ambush. If the Ark's phenomena flared, the rest of the world might witness biblical terrors.

Late that night, Dave found Helena standing by the Ark's crate, staring at the worn wood. "Hard to believe we're traveling again," she said, voice trembling. "We tried to hide it here. Now we're moving it to an even more contested site."

He set a gentle hand on her back. "We can't outrun Orlov's alliances forever. And the Ark's energy remains sealed, which might dissuade him from desperate grabs if he sees no unstoppable power. But going to Jerusalem might unify others, forging a broader peace."

She leaned her head against his shoulder, letting out a shaky breath. "I hope so. We're risking everything on a symbolic gesture."

He pressed a brief kiss to her temple. "We're doing what we must."

Morning broke in a swirl of tension. The infiltration group prepared two armored trucks, disguised with plain markings to avoid drawing attention. The watchmen tested their rifles, loading extra ammunition in case Orlov struck en route. Sister Sabine and Lombardi prayed over the Ark's crate, verifying no phenomena stirred. Ibrahim lined up the route data, ensuring each checkpoint would let them pass. Ming Xia's watchmen conferred with a small local official group, which would maintain a rear guard at the depot if Orlov's men showed up.

By noon, under a cloud-swept sky, the infiltration team began loading the Ark. Rain spattered again, but a lull in the wind eased the process. The watchmen used a small motorized lift to gently set the crate into the first truck's reinforced cargo hold. Lombardi watched every movement, chanting faint lines to keep disturbances inert. Helena and Dave double-checked the straps. Sister Sabine hovered, distributing small relic fragments intended to calm potential manifestations—perhaps symbolic gestures, but comforting.

Ming Xia took a final look around the bunker. "We're leaving a skeleton crew here to mislead any observers. We'll slip out through a side road in a convoy of three or four vehicles, picking up speed once we exit Istanbul's outskirts. If the Ark's energy remains silent, we can cross into Israel in less than a day."

Helena's pulse fluttered. She recalled the last time they tried a major relocation, ambushed by Orlov on a desert road. Now they faced an even bigger risk. But the Ark's power had not awakened in weeks, so maybe destiny favored them.

With final checks done, the convoy eased out of the depot gates. Rain pattered lightly on the roofs of the trucks, the watchmen in a trailing SUV. Ming Xia rode with Dave, Helena, Lombardi, and Sister Sabine in the lead vehicle, all braced for infiltration attempts. The Ark's crate loomed in the cargo hold, locked behind steel plates.

The roads out of the region were half-empty. Tension enveloped the travelers. Dave clutched the wheel, scanning the mirrors for any sign of trailing vehicles. Helena sat beside him, pistol beneath a blanket on her lap. In the rear seats, Sister Sabine read from her ledger, while Lombardi silently mouthed lines from the chant, ensuring the Ark's disturbances stayed sealed. Ming Xia half-listened to radio chatter, eyes narrowed.

Rain-slick streets gave way to rural highways. The guards reported no immediate sign of Orlov's men. Perhaps the rumor that the Ark's manifestations were permanently locked had reduced the colonel's fanatic fervor, or maybe he was planning a final ambush closer to the border. The group pressed on, hearts pounding.

Helena tried to quell her nerves. She recalled Yusef's departure, how manifestations overshadowed everything then, yet now mortal conflict overshadowed the Ark's phenomena. She tightened her grip on Dave's arm, voice barely above a whisper. "You okay?"

He glanced at her, offering a steady nod. "We'll get through this. Keep scanning for threats."

She gave a grim half-smile. "Always."

Midway through the journey, as the convoy approached a quiet junction near a low hillside, one of Ming Xia's look-outs radioed from the trailing SUV. "We see two trucks idling near the intersection. Possibly suspicious. Keep alert."

Dave slowed slightly, scanning the horizon. Sure enough, two battered cargo trucks sat on the roadside. A handful of armed men loitered beside them. Helena recognized the possibility of an ambush. The troopers readied their weapons. Tension roiled in the lead vehicle. Sister Sabine gripped her ledger as if it were a talisman. Lombardi clutched his partial script for the Ark's phenomena, though the chest stayed silent in the cargo hold.

Lightning flared across the overcast sky. The armed men near those trucks watched the convoy pass but did not open fire. One raised a hand, then stepped back. Possibly they recognized they were outgunned or realized the Ark's energy might remain inert. The infiltration team rolled by, hearts pounding. Ming Xia's sentinels exhaled relief once they left the intersection behind.

Shortly after, the radio buzzed with more unsettling news: Orlov's new paramilitary had indeed mobilized, but no one knew their location. Dave scowled as he guided the truck onto a narrow road, part of a plan to avoid main highways. Each mile stretched the tension tighter. If the Ark's phenomena remained sealed, Helena thought, this entire operation hinged on its mere symbolism.

Evening shadows stretched across the countryside. The convoy pressed on with minimal stops. Sister Sabine assisted Lombardi in reciting lines near the chest whenever they halted, just to confirm the Ark's disturbances stayed locked. The ceremony's hold felt strong, yet each rocket or bullet was a potential trigger for chaos.

They crossed an unmarked border region under carefully arranged clearance. Dave nodded with gratitude at the local guards, who had been paid off or promised diplomatic hush. The guards in both vehicles remained on high alert, scanning every hillside for signs of ambush. Over the radio, updates trickled in that tensions rose worldwide over rumors the Ark might resurface in Jerusalem. International powers prepared statements. Some threatened condemnation if the Ark's manifestations reemerged.

Late that night, the convoy found a safe rest stop in a deserted industrial yard. The watchmen posted a perimeter while Helena, Dave, and Lombardi took turns checking the crate. Sister Sabine offered the local official some bandages for a twisted ankle, further earning small trust.

Meanwhile, the group tried to sleep in short shifts, the truck engines idling for warmth.

In a quiet moment near the lead vehicle, Dave sat with Helena beneath a starless sky. She leaned her head on his shoulder, lulled by the rumble of distant thunder. "Feels like we're driving toward a final confrontation," she murmured. "The Ark's manifestations slumber, but the world stirs."

He brushed a thumb across her cheek. "We stand together. If the Ark's energy remains sealed, maybe the Temple Mount can end this. Orlov's men might still strike, but let's hope they lose momentum."

A hush enveloped them as the wind whispered through the empty yard. The closeness they shared anchored them against swirling uncertainty. She closed her eyes, grateful for a fleeting sense of calm.

Dawn found the convoy on the move again, crossing another checkpoint with minimal fuss. The watchmen kept rifles at the ready, but no firefight erupted. Helena dared hope Orlov's paramilitary had lost track of them, or that the Ark's dormant phenomena had lessened his fervor. Sister Sabine dozed in the back seat, ledger clutched tightly. Lombardi recited a small prayer to maintain the ceremonial lock on the Ark's disturbances.

Approaching the outskirts of Israel, Dave checked the route. The infiltration group braced for official border checks. They had advanced clearance from certain government channels, but suspicion might remain. The sentinels made certain the Ark's crate was sealed and labeled as a "high-security artifact." If the Ark's manifestations were truly sealed, the crossing might pass smoothly.

They rolled up to a checkpoint. Israeli soldiers stepped forward, rifles cradled. Ibrahim, riding with them, handed over documents. Helena's heart thundered as she waited for a challenge. The guards scanned the convoy warily, recognized some official stamps, then waved them through with stern faces. She exhaled in relief. Another hurdle cleared.

The roads grew busier. They glimpsed signs of routine life—farmland, small towns—yet tension remained. Dave, at the wheel, noticed Sister Sabine biting her lip. "You all right?" he asked.

She nodded, voice brittle. "Yes. Just worried. The phenomena are sealed, but Jerusalem might trigger religious fervor. If something disturbs the chant, the entire city could face biblical manifestations."

He grimaced. "We're aware. Let's keep that from happening."

On they drove, hour by hour. By mid-afternoon, they reached a secret rendezvous where more sentinels from multiple nations assembled: U.S. liaison teams, Israeli reps, and a handful from the Vatican. Father Lombardi conferred with them, explaining the Ark's locked state. Helena stood by Dave, scanning the scene of vehicles and armed men, each uncertain whether the Ark's energy might spontaneously burst forth. Sister Sabine prayed with a small group of clergy, forging a fragile alliance. The guards from China and local Israeli forces hammered out a cooperative plan.

An official insisted they travel a specific route into Jerusalem to minimize public panic. News would eventually leak, but they wanted minimal infiltration attempts. The infiltration group's role was to ride with the Ark in a central truck, with Lombardi's chant keeping its phenomena dormant if anything threatened the chest. Dave and Helena would remain near the front of that vehicle, prepared for sabotage or ambush. Everyone braced for the last leg of the journey.

Nightfall cloaked the final drive to Jerusalem. The convoy snaked along highways with discreet lighting, local authorities blocking side roads to reduce infiltration chances. The watchmen scanned every overpass and hillside. No disturbances stirred from the Ark. Helena felt a swirl of tension inside: if Orlov had a final card to play, it would likely appear soon. Each kilometer brought them nearer to the Temple Mount, a place of intense spiritual significance.

Halfway through the city outskirts, where modern buildings gave way to older streets, Dave tensed. He spotted multiple headlights in the rear mirror, approaching fast. The sentinels hissed warnings on the radio. Possibly local drivers, or a band of Orlov's mercenaries. Within minutes, the suspicious vehicles tried flanking the convoy, shadowing them from multiple angles.

Helena gripped the seat, heart in her throat. Dave swerved to keep the Ark's truck well-guarded by allied vehicles. Shots erupted behind them—one or two short bursts from trailing cars. The guards returned fire, forcing the unknown pursuers to back off. Helena glimpsed muzzle flashes in the side mirror. A bullet cracked the rear window of the last allied SUV, but the watchmen quickly repelled the aggressors. Sparks lit the dark street. One of the trailing cars spun out, smashing into a corner post. The others fled, tires screeching.

Adrenaline spiked in every occupant of the Ark's truck. Lombardi clutched his partial text, Sister Sabine trembling with the ledger. Dave let out a shaky exhale as they advanced again, the Ark's manifestations still locked in the crate, no arcs of supernatural menace swirling. Mortal conflict flared once more, overshadowing the Ark's dormant phenomena.

Finally, the city lights of Jerusalem rose ahead. Helena's breath caught as she recognized the outline of sacred sites, minarets, and spires. Tension soared. The sentinels guided them through quieter roads, weaving around potential hotspots. Dave carefully followed instructions from local forces, who had blockaded certain intersections to funnel them toward the Old City. The infiltration group caught glimpses of thick walls, aged gates, and storied rooftops.

They parked near a concealed courtyard not far from the Temple Mount, temporarily under tight security. The sentinels secured the perimeter, scanning for infiltration attempts. Helena stepped out, legs trembling. Dave joined her, rifle in hand, scanning the surrounding alley. Father Lombardi and Sister Sabine emerged from the truck, gazing at the luminous cityscape. Ibrahim coordinated with local contacts, ensuring all was ready for a controlled arrival at the sacred platform.

Ming Xia's sentinels took up positions, tension plain on their faces. Helena felt the weight of history pressing on her. She pictured manifestations swirling in an earlier chapter of this journey. Now, with the Ark's disturbances dormant, it might come full circle to the site where it once resided. But would that quell the world's mania or ignite fresh chaos?

Lombardi approached, face pale yet resolute. "We're here," he said. "No disturbances have stirred. Perhaps returning it to its original place can finalize the ceremony."

Sabine rested a hand on his arm. "Let's hope Orlov's men stay far from this city. If they breach the perimeter, the Ark's phenomena might remain silent no longer."

Helena turned to Dave, voice low. "We've made it. But the final step remains—officially bringing the Ark to the Temple Mount, with a global audience possibly watching. That might spark a meltdown or unify them."

He nodded, expression grave. "We'll see. All we can do is keep the Ark's forces sealed and show the world that unstoppable biblical terror won't be used as a weapon. Maybe that deflates Orlov's alliances."

She inhaled. "Let's prepare for the last push."

As midnight approached, the infiltration group conferred with local representatives from multiple nations. They hammered out a plan to publicly display the Ark in a carefully controlled event at the Temple Mount, with look-outs from each major stakeholder. The Ark's phenomena, they hoped, would remain quiet if no one disturbed the chest. Lombardi insisted on reciting the partial ceremony once more on site, ensuring the Ark's disturbances stayed locked. Ming Xia's look-outs grudgingly agreed to a temporary stand-down from firearms once the Ark was placed—if other factions did the same. The plan was fragile, but it might avert a larger war.

Helena, exhausted from days of travel and tension, retreated to a corner of the courtyard to gather herself. Dave followed, concern etched in his features. He brushed a lock of hair from her eyes, voice soft. "We're on the brink, but I think we're doing the right thing."

She managed a tremulous smile. "It still feels surreal. We sealed the Ark's manifestations, but the world's jaws locked on this relic. Taking it to the Temple Mount is a final gamble."

He squeezed her hand gently. "We have each other, and we have a chance at peace. That's worth the gamble." She leaned in, letting his warmth steady her. For a moment, the swirling chaos faded, replaced by quiet closeness that gave her the strength to face the final stage.

Chapter 21

Convoy Route, Turkish–Israeli Border — Predawn

The dawn brought a pale glow that stretched across Jerusalem's rooftops and narrow alleys. Prayer calls and distant bells drifted on currents of dry air. Military checkpoints rose at street corners and vantage points, each one manned by men and women who gripped firearms with white-knuckled certainty. The tension had spread to every stone, as if the city itself sensed that events here would shape the fate of more than a single people.

Helena Carter stood in a makeshift command station set up inside a centuries-old building that overlooked a half-walled square. She rubbed a sleepless ache beneath her eyes while scanning the day's latest security updates. Representatives from the United States, China, Israel, and the Vatican had spent the night locked in talks, trying to finalize how to unveil the Ark without triggering mayhem. Soldiers guarded the site where the relic waited, illusions suppressed by a fragile chant that could unravel in seconds should anyone tear open the crate.

A sigh slid from Helena's lips as she recalled the close calls that had brought them all to this point. She felt Dave Schumer approach before she saw him. He paused at her side, voice hushed. "Everything quiet for the moment. Pilgrims are already gathering outside the Old City walls. Local forces expect a larger crowd by midday."

She glanced at him, noticing the lines of fatigue etched into his face. "No further sign of Orlov's paramilitary squads?"

He shook his head. "Not in the immediate area. look-outs reported suspicious movements north of the city, though. Could be mercenaries, could be random militia. Israel's on high alert. Everyone's waiting for the slightest spark."

She rubbed a thumb over a chipped table's surface. "One miscalculation and illusions might reappear in the worst possible way." Her gaze flicked toward the narrow window and the courtyard beyond, where armed men stood near an inconspicuous vehicle that housed the Ark's crate. "If that happens, the panic alone could tear the city apart."

Dave rested a reassuring hand on her arm. "We're in this together. I promise we'll do what we can to keep illusions dormant. Let's see if Lombardi and Sabine have an update."

They moved along a corridor hung with torn posters, relics of past visitors. At the end, they found Father Aurelius Lombardi and Sister Sabine hunched near a steel-reinforced door that led to a back courtyard. Both wore subdued expressions. The Jesuit priest had circles under his eyes, and the nun clutched her ledger with the reverence of someone holding a treasured artifact.

Sabine greeted Helena with a measured nod. "We spent part of the night reciting the chant by the crate. No flicker of illusions. The lock seems stable."

Lombardi added in a hushed tone, "We've also had local clergy from multiple faiths gather for an interfaith vigil. It's symbolic. If illusions remain sealed, maybe that symbolic unity can hold back the madness."

Helena managed a half-smile. "As long as nobody tries prying open the lid, we should be safe. How are final arrangements for the ceremony?"

The priest exhaled. "Mostly set. We'll bring the Ark in a carefully managed procession at midday to a walled section near the Temple Mount. Pilgrims and onlookers will see it from a distance. The allied sentinels plan to hold a firm perimeter."

Sabine's expression darkened. "Rumors swirl among the crowds. Some expect the Ark to unleash biblical wonders. Others fear unstoppable illusions. If Colonel Orlov or any extremist group interrupts, it could be catastrophic."

Helena looked to Dave. "Let's confirm the multi-nation guard. We might need more security at the outer gates. The city's corners fill with curious bystanders."

He nodded, adjusting his jacket. "We'll check with the Chinese detail and the Israeli command. If illusions stay quiet, we just might pull this off."

They heard footsteps approach from behind, quick and insistent. Ibrahim Mahdi stepped into the corridor, phone in hand. A film of sweat gave his forehead a faint shine. "We have new intel from the outskirts. A local security post spotted a convoy heading this way—four or five trucks carrying armed men. Uncertain if Orlov's inside, but the descriptions match a patchwork group of foreign fighters."

Helena's pulse hammered. "Time frame?"

He looked uneasy. "They could be on Jerusalem's outskirts by early afternoon, possibly earlier. The military is bracing for confrontation. The local government demanded foreign envoys keep the Ark sealed and the unveiling short. If a paramilitary wave storms in, phenomena or not, the city won't handle the chaos."

Dave traded a glance with Helena. "We'll speed up the ceremony. The Ark can't become a rallying point for Orlov's men. If the Ark's energy remains sealed, it'll undercut his claims of unstoppable power."

Sabine closed her eyes for a moment, fingers trembling around her ledger. "Then we do it soon. This city is teetering."

Lombardi swallowed, giving a slow nod. "We'll gather the sentinels. Let's ensure the chest is fully strapped. If Orlov's squads show up, we mustn't let them damage it or the Ark's manifestations may burst free."

Helena's heart thudded at the possibility. She pictured swirling shapes invading holy grounds, fueling widespread panic. "We won't let that happen. Let's finalize with the allied officers. Then we move before noon."

Bodies pressed close in the Old City's labyrinthine streets. Pilgrims and curious sightseers surged behind barricades, each seeking a glimpse of the rumored biblical relic. Soldiers and police from various nations stood in lines to channel onlookers away from sensitive zones. Sunlight fell harsh on stone walls, revealing a city simmering with suspense.

A hush clung to the infiltration group's staging area. Inside that quiet enclosure, the Ark's crate rested on a low platform draped in protective coverings. Father Lombardi hovered near it, reciting lines under his breath, ignoring the sweat that beaded along his temples. Sister Sabine stood at his side, ready to lend her voice if disturbances so much as quivered.

Ming Xia arrived with two Chinese specialists, each wearing concealed armor beneath plain shirts. She waved a radio. "Israeli forces confirm movement near a northern entry road. Possibly Orlov's men. They aren't sure."

Dave clenched his jaw. "Then it's time. We start. If the Ark's forces remain sealed, it might discourage any final paramilitary push."

Helena peered out at the masses, heart fluttering. She spotted Yusef near the cordon, glancing anxiously at the sentinels. The local youth had slid into an unofficial role, guiding lost pilgrims and occasionally passing intel on suspicious faces. His devotion to the city shone in every exhausted breath.

Ibrahim approached, voice hushed. "We have all four major factions—Israel, the U.S., China, the Vatican—prepared. A short statement will declare the Ark's disturbances neutralized. Then we let people see it from behind the barricade."

Helena steeled herself. "Let's do it."

A hush settled as Lombardi signaled the sentinels to remove the coverings. The Ark's crate, scratched from countless ordeals, glowed faintly in the bright sun. No arcs of supernatural power danced on its surface. Dave and Helena flanked the relic, weapons holstered but visible. Sister Sabine stood behind Lombardi, who stepped forward to address a small cluster of cameras authorized to record the event.

The Jesuit spoke in a resonant tone, his carefully chosen words echoing off the courtyard walls. "This object, discovered beneath the Temple Mount, is believed to be the Ark of the Covenant. Through an time-worn ceremony, we have locked away the disturbances that once threatened countless lives. We gather here—under the watch of multiple nations—to declare that no single group claims this relic. If the Ark's manifestations remain forever sealed, we avert a global disaster."

A flicker of recognition passed through the crowd. Some looked disappointed that no swirling radiance manifested. Others murmured with relief. Dave scanned the periphery, watchful for signs of infiltration. Helena felt her heart pounding as she stepped forward to confirm the artifact's authenticity, citing inscriptions. She kept her words simple, describing how the Ark's phenomena earlier threatened to spawn biblical chaos, now neutralized by a sacred vow.

While the cluster of officials listened, camera crews panned across the scene, capturing armed guards from the United States, China, and Israel standing side by side. The hush was almost reverent. Then a series of metallic thuds drew attention to a row of barricades near an alley entrance. Soldiers shifted formation as a group of robed pilgrims tried pushing through, demanding a closer look at the Ark. Security men held them back. The infiltration group tensed, fearing a spark might turn the square into bedlam.

The disturbance settled after officials negotiated a calmer vantage point. Father Lombardi resumed his statements. Sister Sabine read lines from her ledger in multiple languages, emphasizing that the Ark's forces posed no threat if no one shattered the crate's seal. Yusef hovered near a small cluster of sentinels, relaying glimpses of tension building in side streets.

Ming Xia flicked on her radio. "We have unconfirmed sightings of armed men a few blocks away. Might be a small group aligned with Orlov. The local command is sending a patrol."

Dave's eyes narrowed. "Stay alert, everyone."

Helena scanned the Ark. No arcs crackled across its surface. Lombardi maintained a quiet undertone of the chant, his eyes occasionally fluttering shut in concentration. The surreal calm within the square contrasted with the swelling crowd outside. She drew a slow breath, praying the Ark's phenomena remained at bay.

Suddenly, an Israeli soldier sprinted over, panting. "Gunfire near the Damascus Gate. We're told a group in unmarked vehicles might be heading in this direction. Possibly paramilitaries."

Alarm rippled through the infiltration team. Dave locked eyes with Helena. "We can't let them near the crate. If bullets punch through, the Ark's disturbances might break free in the worst possible place."

Ming Xia nodded sharply. "We have sentinels. Let's establish a fallback route if things get hot."

Father Lombardi, overhearing, struggled to keep his composure. "We must keep the Ark's manifestations sealed. If Orlov storms in, we can't allow him to damage the chest."

Ibrahim stepped in. "We'll deploy extra guards. Let's also speed up the official statements, show the Ark to the gathered crowd from a distance, then secure it behind thicker walls if shooting starts."

Helena could almost hear her own heartbeat. "All right. Let's finish quickly."

She made a curt gesture to a small group of VIPs waiting at the edge of the platform. They stepped closer, each craning for a better view. Cameras rolled, capturing the moment. Pilgrims pressed at barricades, some shouting prayers, others weeping with fervor. The infiltration group braced for any infiltration. The day felt poised on a razor's edge.

Near the southwestern corner of the courtyard, soldiers parted to admit an Israeli commander who approached with urgent strides. He addressed Dave, Helena, and Ming Xia in a subdued voice. "We found suspects in an abandoned building, armed and possibly linked to Orlov. They claim more are heading here with heavier arms. We advise relocating the Ark behind the fortress-like walls near the southwestern ramp. That area can better withstand a direct assault."

Dave's tone was clipped. "Do we have time?"

The commander glanced at the gathered pilgrims. "If the Ark's phenomena remain quiet, we can manage crowd control. But if these paramilitaries show up, we might see a firefight in holy ground."

Helena nodded, pulse hammering. "We'll move it. Let me signal Lombardi."

She approached the priest and Sabine, explaining the shift. Lombardi's shoulders slumped, but he agreed. "Better to remain mobile than risk the Ark's disturbances bursting free in the middle of a shootout."

The watchmen took swift action, guiding the crate from the platform with careful hands. Some local officials urged the pilgrims back, explaining the ceremony was complete. Disappointment mixed with confusion among those who had expected a miraculous display. Cameras tracked the Ark's slow journey across the courtyard toward an arched walkway. Dave and Helena flanked the relic with weapons ready, scanning the crowd for any glint of hostility.

Yusef trailed behind, wearing an anxious expression. He recognized how vulnerable the group was, hauling a sacred chest through a swirl of onlookers. He offered Helena a subdued nod, as if to say he'd keep watch for trouble. She gave him a small smile in return, relieved he was there with local knowledge.

Above them, the midday sun beat down on weather-scarred limestone. The infiltration group and allied guards soon reached a more fortified compound of thick ramparts. A small gateway led inside, guarded by layered steel bars and Israeli commandos. They opened the gate, ushering in the Ark and the sentinels. Helena felt a wave of relief once they were inside. The structure featured tall, narrow windows and reinforced walls, reminiscent of medieval fortifications. She scanned the interior courtyard, which was large enough to hold an assembly of soldiers and the crate at a safe distance from prying eyes.

The sentinels set the box down. Lombardi exhaled, sweat glistening on his collar. Sabine knelt beside him, ledger clutched, reciting lines to keep the Ark's manifestations subdued. Dave positioned men at key vantage points, instructing them to watch every approach. Ibrahim relayed updates to outside forces. Ming Xia observed the area, a subtle frown etched across her brow.

"What's our next move?" Helena asked. "We made a public statement. People saw the Ark's phenomena remain silent. Do we stay locked in here until the threat passes?"

Dave wiped perspiration from his brow. "We coordinate with the allied forces. If Orlov's men show, we repel them here. If the Ark's disturbances remain sealed through the day, maybe that final demonstration kills their morale."

A tense half-hour followed, during which the infiltration group waited for word on suspicious vehicles rumored to be creeping along Jerusalem's edge. Soldiers reported a lull in the immediate gunfire, though sporadic scuffles flared near distant gates. Helena found herself pacing across the fortress courtyard, mind racing with scenarios. Dave approached her, gaze steady.

"You're restless," he said.

She paused, swallowing the dryness in her throat. "I can't stand the waiting. Orlov's men, the Ark's locked state, this city braced for who knows what. I want to do something."

He gently took her hands in his. "We did something. We publicly showed the Ark's phenomena are no advantage. The rest is them deciding if they want a pointless war."

Her tension eased slightly under his calming touch. She drew in a long breath, then forced a nod. "Right. We keep watch."

A commotion at the main gate drew their attention. Yusef entered with an official who wore a crisp uniform. The newcomer carried an urgent face. He approached the infiltration group, voice tight. "Orlov's squads were spotted approaching from the north in vehicles with mounted guns. The IDF is preparing a checkpoint. They're outmatched, but the Russians have alliances with local militias. This might be a bigger wave than anticipated."

Ming Xia cursed under her breath in Mandarin, then faced Helena and Dave. "So the final confrontation might be near. If the Ark's phenomena remain inert, Orlov could still try to shatter that crate to see if power can be unleashed."

Ibrahim tapped his phone. "Local authorities are pressing for immediate contact with Orlov's group. They're telling him the Ark's disturbances are sealed. So far, no response."

Helena suppressed a shiver. "We can't risk them hitting the fortress with rockets. Let's set up maximum defenses. Keep the Ark safe."

In quick order, the allied sentinels established a perimeter around the fortress yard, reinforcing vantage points. Helicopters buzzed overhead, scanning for signs of Orlov's approach. The infiltration group readied for a siege, though they prayed the demonstration of the Ark's dormancy had dissuaded him. Lombardi remained near the crate with Sabine, chanting in low voices. Dave distributed extra ammunition among the sentinels. Helena and Yusef scouted side passages, ensuring no infiltration route was overlooked.

By late afternoon, swirling clouds began to gather above the horizon, reminiscent of storms seen in earlier manifestations—but no arcs danced along the Ark's surface. Tension multiplied. Soldiers around the fortress watched the sky with disquiet, some remembering rumors that the Ark's energy once stirred bizarre weather. Father Lombardi pressed on, focusing on the sealed power, determined not to let it break free.

Word arrived that Orlov's forces halted near the city's outer perimeter. Gunfire broke out in a few pockets, but the paramilitaries paused instead of rushing in. Some speculated they had lost the advantage if the Ark's manifestations truly offered no unstoppable might. The infiltration group remained on guard well into the evening. Pilgrims outside the Old City grew weary, drifting away as night fell, uncertain if the Ark would be displayed again.

In the fortress courtyard, a subdued calm reigned. Helena found Dave near a rough bench. She sat beside him, exhaling the day's tension. "Maybe the Ark's silence forced Orlov to think twice."

He nodded, but his eyes still scanned the walls. "Or maybe he's mustering more men. We can't drop our guard. At least the city's leadership has united behind the sealed Ark. This might be the best chance for peace."

She leaned closer, letting the faint warmth of his presence soothe her frazzled mind. "You keep me steady," she whispered, voice soft in the gloom.

He slipped an arm around her shoulders, mindful of watchmen milling about. "Likewise."

They separated when an Israeli soldier came over to report no major movements. The infiltration group exhaled relief, though no one truly relaxed. Yusef, perched near the Ark, glanced at them with a tired but hopeful expression. The youth had witnessed so many horrors, yet he refused to flee. Helena admired his grit.

As midnight approached, the watchmen rotated shifts. Some found restless sleep in corners of the fortress. Father Lombardi dozed in a half-lidded posture near the crate, Sabine gently shaking him awake every so often to keep the Ark's disturbances locked. Helena and Dave shared a quiet corner, snatching a few hours of uneasy slumber beneath flickering emergency lights.

Dawn arrived with the drum of uneasy hearts. The infiltration group convened once more, checking for infiltration attempts in the night. Ming Xia's sentinels reported no direct contact with Orlov's squads, though sporadic shots rang out in distant neighborhoods. A swirl of rumor suggested the Russian colonel was meeting with extremist leaders, uncertain if the Ark's energy was truly suppressed or if the infiltration group was bluffing. Meanwhile, the Ark stayed silent in the fortress yard, no arcs flickering to life.

That morning, local government representatives, allied envoys, and journalists pressed for clarity. They wanted an official statement that the Ark's manifestations would never reemerge. Lombardi wavered, uncertain if such a promise could be absolute. Helena stepped up to help craft a statement that the Ark's phenomena were fully suppressed as long as no violent tampering occurred. The sentinels broadcast the stance across global channels, hoping to quell the mania. Photographs of the crate at the Temple Mount site had already circulated. The infiltration group prayed Orlov's recruits might see reason in the face of that evidence.

A hush lingered in the fortress corridors. The infiltration team ate a sparse meal of dry rations, each mind weighed down by questions of what the Russian operative might do. Storm clouds brewed again over the city, crackling with scattered thunder. Some guards stole glances at the Ark, spooked by the possibility that its phenomena might ripple forth and manipulate the weather. Father Lombardi insisted it was a natural front, though his tone betrayed the slightest edge of doubt.

Late afternoon arrived without an invasion. Dave ventured onto a parapet with Helena, gazing out over the Old City's rooftops. She pointed to the sprawl beyond the walls where columns of smoke rose from smaller clashes, presumably unaffiliated militias sparring with local troops. "We're holding off full war," she said, "but for how long?"

He took her hand as they scanned the horizon. "Every hour the Ark's energy stays silent undercuts Orlov's grand plan. I'm hopeful he might realize the relic can't be abused."

Her lips pressed together. "He's desperate. We can't predict desperation."

They returned inside to find Sister Sabine kneeling beside Lombardi, chanting near the Ark. Ibrahim reported that the local command believed Orlov's squads might soon withdraw if the Ark's phenomena offered no advantage. Some experts guessed the cost of assaulting the Holy City with so many nations present was too high. The infiltration group harbored guarded optimism. If the Ark's disturbances remained locked, the entire crisis could dissolve without further tragedy.

As dusk approached, a swirl of drizzling rain pattered on the fortress roof. The infiltration team—joined by local officials—decided to maintain the Ark's presence here for at least another night to ensure no last-minute assault. They set a perimeter of troopers with strict instructions to shoot any intruder who tried prying the crate. Tension coursed through every hallway. Helena found herself pacing again, glancing at Dave's quiet figure across the courtyard, feeling the comforting anchor of his presence even in partial darkness.

She stepped outside to a small walkway that overlooked the city. Lamps illuminated wet stones, the sound of water dripping from eaves. Yusef was there, arms crossed, staring into the gloom. He blinked at her approach, then murmured, "Strange to see so many foreign sentinels. My father says it reminds him of stories from older conflicts."

Helena nodded. "We're all trying to keep the Ark's manifestations from reemerging. If that means big powers cooperate in your city for once, maybe it's worth the tension."

He exhaled. "I just hope Orlov truly backs down. I hate to see more bullets flying here."

She rested a hand on his shoulder. "I do too." The youth had grown from a curious onlooker to a vital link in the infiltration chain. It tore at her heart that he carried such burdens at a young age.

Midnight found the infiltration group again, gathered in the fortress yard. Father Lombardi checked the chest for cracks. He found none. Sister Sabine reported the chant remained stable. Dave scanned updates from guards posted near the city gates: no major movement from Orlov's squads, though scattered pockets of violence continued. Tension lingered in the air. The sentinels divided the night shift, ensuring the Ark's energy would stay sealed behind unwavering vigilance.

The small hours passed, each soldier and operative alert for the faintest sign of infiltration. Rain hammered intermittently, drenching the outer courtyard. Helena and Dave shared a hushed exchange near the flickering overhead lamp, each admitting cautious relief. The Ark's calm forced the world to accept that its phenomena might be gone forever. If no unstoppable force existed, Orlov's grip on mercenaries might fail.

Toward dawn, the guards eased up slightly, anticipating another day of negotiations and city patrol. A few found corners to doze, while the infiltration group kept rotating watch. Helena found herself leaning against a cold stone wall, eyes half-closed. She felt Dave's presence as he draped a light blanket around her shoulders. She managed a grateful look, sensing his worry. They had come so far.

A screech of tires outside the fortress jolted them from the fleeting calm. Soldiers sprang to the gate, rifles leveled. The infiltration group rushed forward, heartbeats hammering. Lights in the courtyard snapped on, revealing a battered pickup that had careened to a stop near the checkpoint, smoke curling from its hood. Shouts filled the night. Dave signaled everyone to hold positions, waiting for word on who was inside.

Several sentinels dragged a dazed driver from the vehicle, demanding explanations. The man babbled in broken Hebrew, pointing west. Once translated, it became clear: a cluster of heavily armed men had pinned him down in the outskirts. He barely escaped. He warned that a significant force—possibly aligned with Orlov—might move on the fortress soon, hoping to claim the Ark. The infiltration group's hopes of a quiet resolution wavered under the renewed threat.

Helena felt Dave's hand on her arm, a silent vow of solidarity. Father Lombardi and Sabine joined them, tension etched on every face. Ming Xia arrived with her specialists, snapping out orders in a crisp tone. "Man the walls. We cannot let the Ark's disturbances be unleashed in the city." The troopers spread out, checking vantage points. The entire fortress bristled with readiness.

The driver collapsed in exhaustion, repeating that the men he saw carried rocket-propelled grenades and other heavy weapons. Some watchmen exchanged grim looks, recalling how the Ark's manifestations had once destroyed entire squads who tried to harness them. If the Ark's energy awoke now, in the midst of a frantic assault on sacred ground, the devastation might be immeasurable.

Dave clenched his jaw. "We hold the Ark inside. If that group tries anything, they'll face a united front."

Helena stepped to the crate, verifying no cracks or odd glows. Lombardi gave her a tight nod. "No phenomena yet, but the standoff might escalate. We must stand firm."

She exhaled, then turned to address the sentinels. "Everyone remain at your posts. Orlov's men might be desperate. Keep the chest out of range of direct fire. If we hold until sunrise, maybe the allied forces can push them back."

The fortress courtyard fell into a tense hush, broken only by the driver's ragged breathing and the hiss of rain. Yusef drifted in from a side corridor, eyes wide. Helena almost wanted to send him away for safety, but she knew his local knowledge might help if infiltration attempts started. He pressed himself against a pillar, scanning the gates for trouble.

An hour crawled by. Then two. Sleep teased the edges of Helena's mind, but every flicker of movement jolted her alert. The sentinels took turns patrolling. Dave circled the yard, pistol at his waist, trading signals with Ming Xia. Father Lombardi prayed near the box, unwavering in his vow to keep the Ark's disturbances suppressed. Sabine alternated between reciting lines and checking on the sentinels' well-being. None of them could fully relax. The possibility of Orlov launching an all-out strike in the next few hours weighed on every breath.

As dawn's first strands of light spilled over the fortress walls, the infiltration group braced for either a calm resolution or a violent outbreak. The Ark remained quiet, its phenomena locked away from the city's thronging tension. Soldiers on the ramparts scanned the roads, searching for any sign of a convoy. A hush lay over the city's spires, a hush that felt pregnant with the possibility of pitched battle or a final step toward peace.

The guards reported no mass approach yet. Local intel from near the outskirts claimed the paramilitaries had halted, uncertain the Ark's energy was worth the risk of open war. That gave a glimmer of hope. The infiltration group allowed themselves a moment of fragile optimism as they realized the Ark's dormancy might have deflated Orlov's rallying cry.

Helena sank onto a crate, exhaustion flooding her limbs. Dave crouched beside her, resting a hand on her shoulder. She let out a deep breath, fighting tears of relief. "We might have saved this city from a meltdown," she whispered. "One day at a time."

He brushed back a strand of her hair, offering a gentle smile. "We're not done, but the Ark's disturbances are sealed. That might be enough."

She nodded, letting her eyes close for a heartbeat. Above them, the sun grew brighter, illuminating the fortress yard. Soldiers, local officials, and allied sentinels exchanged cautious smiles. No distant roar of trucks hammered the roads. The paramilitaries had either disbanded or paused. Father Lombardi rose stiffly, leaving Sister Sabine to watch the chest while he approached the infiltration group. He cleared his throat, voice heavy with fatigue and relief.

"If Orlov truly stands down, we might let the Ark remain here, illusions locked, until formal negotiations finalize. The city might avoid bloodshed."

Helena stood, a slight tremor in her legs. "We'll keep watch, but maybe the biggest crisis has passed. If the Ark's phenomena remain quiet, Orlov loses his edge. He can't unify mercenaries around a doomsday promise."

An Israeli officer approached, an air of subdued victory in his stride. "No sign of the rumored paramilitary group. The city remains tense, but no assault. We'll remain on high alert. Let's pray it stays calm."

The infiltration group shared weary nods. Dave touched Helena's arm with quiet affection, the relief in his eyes echoing her own. They might have truly staved off the meltdown that so many had feared. For all her anxiety about the Ark's disturbances, it turned out that humanity's own ambition was the greater danger.

Chapter 22

A restless hush settled on Jerusalem through the day as word spread that the Ark had been displayed, its phenomena quiet, in the presence of multiple nations. Crowds thinned around the Old City gates, replaced by curious locals and scattered groups of pilgrims who lingered, hoping for a glimpse of something miraculous. Journalists prowled corners for interviews, only to find sentinels politely refusing entry. Storm clouds still loomed, but no downpour drenched the streets.

In a small outpost within the fortress, Helena Carter and David Schumer gathered with Father Lombardi, Sister Sabine, Ibrahim Mahdi, and Ming Xia to plan the next moves. Israeli representatives had joined them, forming a cross-cultural coalition of wary participants. Tension remained, but the raw panic that the Ark's disturbances would erupt had eased.

Helena studied a topographical map spread across a battered table. "If Orlov's men truly withdrew, we can keep the Ark here under joint supervision. If the Ark's energy remains sealed another day or two, the entire crisis might defuse. People might accept the relic is inert."

An Israeli major, arms folded over his uniform, added a blunt note. "We can't be complacent. Intel suggests Orlov stands near the border, rethinking strategy. He may attempt infiltration under night's cover or wait for an opportune moment."

Dave rubbed a hand across his short beard. "We'll maintain sentinels. We also need to confirm alliances with China, the U.S., the Vatican, and Israel for a final arrangement. Possibly the Ark stays in the Temple Mount's custody or some secure site that belongs to multiple parties."

Ming Xia concurred in a concise tone. "China wants no phenomena unleashed. Our government sees no advantage if the chest remains active. If the Ark is locked, a stable resolution suits us."

Father Lombardi glanced at Sabine, then spoke with subdued passion. "The Church too. We accept that the Ark's manifestations must stay sealed. The relic belongs to no single faction. Let the day come when these disturbances fade from memory."

An uneasy quiet followed. They recognized the final puzzle piece was Orlov's next move. No disturbances had manifested in days. Colonel Nikolai Orlov might still see the Ark as a trophy or a symbol of power. The infiltration group resolved to remain on guard. Yusef lingered in the corridor, occasionally relaying murmurs from local contacts who moved through the city's backstreets.

By afternoon, the fortress gates opened slightly to admit delegates from various embassies, each seeking to confirm that the Ark's manifestations truly posed no threat. Soldiers escorted them to the crate, which remained in the courtyard. Father Lombardi and Sister Sabine demonstrated the chanting that kept the Ark's energy dormant. Cameras snapped photos, documenting the scratched wood and faint Hebrew inscriptions. Diplomats whispered with astonishment that the rumored unstoppable supernatural power was nowhere in sight.

Helena and Dave shared a quiet moment as they guided a small group across the courtyard. She felt his subtle presence at her shoulder, reminding her she was not alone. Over the past weeks, they had faced firefights, disturbances, sabotage, and near betrayal. They had formed a bond of deeper trust in the crucible of crisis. She leaned in and whispered, "We might finally see a resolution."

He squeezed her arm lightly, returning a soft smile. "And no disturbances overshadowing it. That's more than I could have hoped."

The delegates departed, some apparently content that the Ark's phenomena were gone. Others remained skeptical. Storm clouds still hovered overhead, thunder distant. The infiltration group concluded that the gloom might be a normal weather front. Father Lombardi held firm to the ceremony's effect. No arcs crackled on the Ark.

As evening approached, and troopers along the fortress walls reported no sign of an encroaching paramilitary convoy. Some tension melted from the posture of the allied soldiers. The infiltration group ate a simple meal under flickering lanterns. Yusef joined them, drawn by companionship and relief that the city he loved might survive another day. Dave teased a weary grin out of him, asking about local rumors. The youth admitted many were confused but less fearful now that the Ark's phenomena appeared gone for good.

Father Lombardi settled near the chest with Sister Sabine, reciting a short prayer of gratitude. Helena watched them with a mixture of relief and caution. She recalled how fanatically Lombardi once wanted to bring the Ark under sole Vatican control. Now he seemed content to let the Ark's disturbances fade from memory. She recognized Sister Sabine's shift from manipulative envoy to caretaker, bridging differences with empathy. The infiltration group had come a long way.

Night fell with an odd hush. The infiltration team prepared for the possibility of infiltration attempts or Orlov launching a last strike. Soldiers patrolled the fortress yard, scanning for shapes in the gloom. Helicopters droned overhead, searchlights roaming the city. Rain spattered for a brief half hour, then died to a drizzle.

Helena found Dave in the corridor, adjusting his rifle. She touched his shoulder, clearing her throat. "You've been on edge all day."

He blew out a breath. "I keep expecting bullets or rockets. Hard to believe the Ark's manifestations remain locked and Orlov might stand down."

She nodded, sharing that disbelief. "Yet no manifestations flicker, and no mass assault arrived. Maybe we can breathe after all." Then a flicker of vulnerability crossed her eyes. "But I can't fully exhale until we know he's gone or surrendered."

He rested a gentle palm against her cheek, voice warm. "We'll see this through, no matter what. If the Ark's energy stays inert, we stand on the brink of peace."

Her heart swelled at his steady reassurance. They parted when an Israeli soldier rushed in with minor intel about a stray group of men spotted near a market. The sentinels quickly investigated but discovered no strong link to Orlov's paramilitaries. The infiltration team exhaled relief again. The city seemed to hold its breath, uncertain if phenomena or armies would break the calm.

As midnight neared, Father Lombardi stepped onto a dais near the crate, leading a short ceremony of unity with a handful of local religious leaders. Cameras flashed, capturing the surreal scene of multi-faith cooperation. Helena and Dave hovered at the perimeter, ensuring no infiltration attempt. Yusef stood with sentinels, eyes wide at the sense of history unfolding. Sabine recited Latin lines in the background. The hush carried an undercurrent of hope. If the Ark's phenomena never rose again, it might become a symbol of reconciliation.

A tremor of thunder startled everyone. Lightning snaked across the sky, illuminating the fortress in stark relief. Some sentinels stiffened, bracing for disturbances to swirl. None came. The chest stayed dark and still. A handful of pilgrims beyond the walls muttered that the storm was a sign. Soldiers remained stoic. Helena felt Dave's breath near her ear as he murmured, "Just weather. We're okay."

She inhaled, tension easing once more. The infiltration group and allied sentinels prepared for one more night of vigilance. The day had passed without Orlov's final charge. The Ark's manifestations were sealed, calm, overshadowed by a city balancing on the cusp between devotion and strife.

That night, the infiltration team settled into a rotation of guard duties. Helena took a shift with Dave, Ming Xia, and Yusef near the Ark. Lombardi snatched a few hours of rest, but Sister Sabine remained with him, ensuring the Ark's energy stayed subdued. In a corner, local officials dozed, exhausted by endless negotiations. Rain tapped again on the fortress roof, a lullaby of slow droplets.

Helena found herself leaning against a column, shoulders aching, eyes drifting shut. She felt Dave's hand slide over hers, a silent offering of comfort. She gave him a faint nod, letting the moment stretch. The watchmen maintained positions near the courtyard's edges. Lights burned low, revealing the Ark's crate, scratched from every brush with violence but still intact. If illusions had a mind, Helena thought, perhaps they realized human ambition was more destructive than any supernatural plague.

The night wore on. She startled awake once or twice at faint sounds, only to realize it was a soldier shifting or a distant dog barking. No paramilitaries stormed the fortress gate. No illusions cracked the sealed wood. The city beyond waited in uneasy calm. By the time dawn's first light stole over the fortress ramparts, the infiltration group stood together, stunned that another day had passed without meltdown.

Chapter 23

The day began under a canopy of low clouds that hugged the skyline with a brooding stillness. Officials in dark suits roamed the fortified courtyard near the Temple Mount, exchanging terse greetings with armed patrols posted at every gateway. Diplomatic vehicles from around the globe lined a cordoned road that stretched along time-worn stone walls, each car bearing small flags or license plates that hinted at distant capitals. Reports of mounting tensions beyond city limits had traveled through the chain of command, leaving both soldiers and civilians on edge.

Inside a crumbling fortress tucked into the southwestern corner, Helena Carter paced along a limestone corridor. She glanced at her phone for any hint of an update, then paused at a slit window that overlooked a sloping yard. The Ark's crate rested near a stack of crates, its phenomena still dormant under Father Lombardi's steadfast chant. The Jesuit hovered nearby, his recitations steady yet quiet, as if a single outburst could break his focus. Sister Sabine stood a few steps behind him, one hand clutching her notes while her expression reflected equal parts resolve and wariness.

Several uniformed Israelis drifted across the yard, the group scanning distant rooftops for lurking threats. Dave Schumer stood among them, fielding questions from a U.S. liaison who wore a neat jacket and looked ready to retreat at any sign of gunfire. Helena lifted her gaze to track Dave's movements, the presence of him in this volatile city somehow lending her a sense of calm she couldn't articulate.

After spending a moment observing from her vantage point, she slipped away from the window and made her way to a small command post set up inside an old antechamber. Ming Xia, the composed Chinese intelligence operative, was bent over a table, conferring with two specialists who wore discreet weapons under plain clothes. She glanced up as Helena approached.

"Motions from the north remain inconclusive," Ming Xia said, voice cool. "We keep hearing about Orlov's squads, but the paramilitaries haven't made a direct advance. The city bristles, though. We suspect extremist pockets inside Jerusalem remain unconvinced the Ark's disturbances are gone. Some want to see the Ark for themselves—others might try to stir havoc."

Helena took a breath. "We have troopers posted. Father Lombardi says the Ark's energy is locked tight as long as no one tampers with the crate. But all these armed groups... it only takes one extremist to fire a rocket at the box and crack it open."

"That's the scenario we all fear." Ming Xia tapped her phone. "More mass mobilizations near the country's borders. Our intelligence suggests multiple armies posture for a possible conflict. Russia, China, the U.S.—all prepared in case the Ark's manifestations reawaken or major fighting erupts. We stand on a tinderbox."

A murmur of conversation outside the room preceded Ibrahim Mahdi's entrance. The Israeli liaison paused in the doorway, shoulders tense. "We just got confirmation: vehicles with tinted windows have been observed circling the Old City. Could be mercenaries, maybe local troublemakers. The IDF tries to track them, but the labyrinth of streets offers plenty of hiding spots."

Ming Xia's eyes flickered with concern. "We'll coordinate with your patrols. If the Ark's phenomena remain sealed, perhaps they'll lose interest." She turned to Helena. "Meanwhile, we must maintain the calm. Any sign from Lombardi or Sabine that the relic is wavering?"

Helena shook her head. "They haven't mentioned any cracks in the ceremony. For now, everything's stable. Father Lombardi guards it like his life depends on it."

Ibrahim nodded. "He might be right to. If the city's tensions escalate, the Ark's energy might react to the sheer collective fear. We can't be certain the seal is invulnerable."

A hush settled, the trio acutely aware that their precarious peace could break at any moment. Helena stepped away, heading into the outer courtyard where dust swirled in the early breeze. Dave stood near the Ark's crate, finishing a conversation with a uniformed American officer. She caught the last fragments: talk of a heavy helicopter presence outside the city, scanning for paramilitary convoys. He sighed when the officer walked off.

She moved closer, offering a small smile. "Any movement from Orlov's direction?"

He rubbed the back of his neck. "Satellite images show scattered convoys, but none pressing into the city yet. The tension out there is raw, like they're waiting for a signal."

Her gaze dropped to the crate. "Let's hope they never get that signal. Everyone's mobilizing at the border. If the Ark's phenomena stay silent, maybe they see no reason to charge in."

One of the sentinels signaled them over. They followed him to a corner of the yard where a battered radio console stood. The device crackled with an incoming message from a multinational briefing center set up a few kilometers away. A voice announced that local extremist cells had begun organizing sporadic protests, claiming the Ark's energy might still lurk within the sealed box. Some threatened violence if the infiltration group refused to open the lid and prove the Ark's manifestations were gone.

Helena's stomach knotted. "Opening the lid is the one thing we can't do. That might truly rouse the Ark's disturbances if the ceremony breaks."

Dave nodded, tension in his jaw. "We keep it locked. Better they fear the Ark's phenomena are gone than risk releasing them."

Father Lombardi appeared from behind a protective canvas, gently wiping sweat from his brow. He approached with Sister Sabine at his side. The Jesuit inhaled a deep breath. "I sense no tremors from the relic. No arcs or sparks. But the city's fear is palpable. All these foreign forces... it might test the Ark's seal in ways we haven't foreseen."

Sabine nodded. "The environment can't produce manifestations by itself, but the relic might react to severe conflict or a mass surge of emotion. Even if we believe the phenomena remain sealed, anything could happen if bullets start flying."

Dave offered a subdued nod. "We should gather the allied leaders. Perhaps we can stage a formal press statement repeating that the Ark's manifestations are dormant. If extremist cells see the chest remains inert, it might calm them. More likely, we just delay an inevitable meltdown."

The group agreed to convene everyone in a side hall. They arranged seats in a large stone chamber, archaic torches mounted as décor next to modern LED lamps. Representatives from the U.S., China, Israel, the Vatican, plus a few smaller nations, arrived in subdued pairs, escorted by sentinels. Tension crackled like static electricity. Each delegation recognized how easily violence could explode if the Ark's phenomena flickered or Orlov attacked.

Ming Xia stood before them, posture crisp. She summarized the current intelligence: sporadic sightings of suspicious vehicles, extremist pockets inside the city, and massive troop mobilizations around the borders. "We remain unified in preventing the Ark's energy from reactivating. Father Lombardi's vow stands. If no one tears the Ark open, the phenomena should stay quiet."

A burly American colonel nodded, though suspicion laced his face. "We accept the Ark's disturbances might be locked away. But Colonel Orlov might not. That man's fanatical. If he sees an advantage, he'll strike."

An Israeli major chimed in. "We have thousands of local forces ready to repel an incursion. But if an entire paramilitary wave storms the Old City, phenomena or not, we face catastrophic bloodshed."

Helena stepped forward, drawing on the moral authority gleaned from her role as the archaeologist who unearthed the Ark. "We show unwavering solidarity. A single faction can't break ranks. Orlov's men thrive on the rumor that the Ark's manifestations are unstoppable. If we maintain our stance, they hold no sway."

Lombardi added in a weary voice, "I'll remain near the crate with Sister Sabine at all times. We'll chant if a threat emerges. If the Ark senses an opening, we're ready to reinforce the ceremony. But it's safer if no conflict reaches the box."

Tight-lipped expressions circled the room. The delegates recognized that the Ark's phenomena might remain hidden, but worldly ambition simmered. The foreign colonel finally said, "We'll do everything to keep your look-outs guarded, but if Orlov unleashes heavy artillery, the Ark's energy could be the least of our troubles. The city could drown in war."

Dave's shoulders rose in a deep breath. "Then we remain watchful. Let's be sure no extremist group incites a riot by demanding the Ark be opened."

The meeting ended in a murmur of uneasy acceptance. Each contingent left to reinforce their assigned positions. The infiltration group reconvened in the yard, where Yusef approached with quick steps, voice low. "Local rumor has it a small band of zealots is marching through side streets, urging people to gather near the fortress gates. They claim the Ark's disturbances lurk, and they must witness a sign from heaven."

Helena closed her eyes a second. "We can't let them inside. That crate stays sealed, or the Ark's manifestations might rage if they forcibly open it."

Ming Xia signaled guards to block any crowd from passing the outer fence. Soldiers marched to man the barricades. Dave gave a curt nod of thanks to Yusef. The youth lingered, concern in his gaze. She shot him a grateful smile, acknowledging his bravery in relaying local chatter.

THE SWORD OF CHERUBIM

Hours passed under a scorching midday sun. The infiltration group's sentinels reported that a throng had indeed gathered near the southern approach, chanting demands to see the relic. Soldiers kept them from entering. The Ark's manifestations remained silent, but the tension soared. Father Lombardi occasionally recited the chant for passersby from behind the fortress gate, hoping to prove the Ark's energy was locked. Some people responded with relief, others with suspicion.

Helena wandered from soldier to soldier, verifying morale. Dave followed, offering her a subtle anchor of confidence. In small corners of the courtyard, their shared glances and brief touches conveyed more than words. In the swirl of impending doom, their bond felt like a calm center. Yusef joined them occasionally, updating them about local gossip or leading them to vantage points.

Late in the afternoon, thunderheads gathered in the west, towering over the horizon. The sky wore an ominous bruise. Lightning flickered high above the desert. A hush fell over the guards as they remembered the Ark's energy had once summoned storms. Father Lombardi insisted it was natural, but tension spiked. Soldiers retreated to covered positions, scanning for infiltration attempts. The infiltration group felt every nerve on edge, worried the Ark might react if someone tested the chest's seal.

A local official rushed into the fortress near dusk, face pale. He gasped out an urgent dispatch: multiple foreign units had massed outside Israeli borders—Russian, Chinese, American, each forming uneasy lines. Allies to Orlov might be there, or the Chinese troopers might engage, or the U.S. might intervene. The rumor conjured a vision of armies standing off, ready to unleash modern weaponry if the Ark's phenomena returned or if a single spark ignited war.

Helena found Dave near a row of stacked crates, arms folded, reading a phone update. He looked up, tension thrumming in every muscle. "It's happening. The entire region stands on the brink. One perceived threat, and they might launch an offensive."

She swallowed. "Do phenomena sense conflict from afar? If so, they might break the seal, just as we feared. Or if a single rocket hits the crate, the Ark's disturbances might lash out."

He exhaled, posture rigid. "We can only fortify, keep sentinels ready. The city braces for the worst, but maybe we can avoid it." He set a hand on her arm. "We'll hold the line. Together."

Night descended with unsettling rapidity. The storms advanced, lightning snaking across black clouds that towered over the city. Faint rumblings echoed from distant streets. Soldiers along the fortress parapets reported seeing frantic movements in pockets of the Old City. Some extremist groups prayed for illusions to awaken, longing for an apocalyptic sign. Others demanded the troopers destroy the Ark altogether. A swirl of fear and mania strangled the calm.

Father Lombardi insisted on intensifying the chant. Sister Sabine stood beside him, translating verses into multiple tongues to reassure onlookers. Yusef prowled the courtyard edges, pointing out suspicious shadows. Helicopters buzzed overhead, searchlights stabbing the gloom. Dave, Helena, Ming Xia, and Ibrahim checked security around the yard, each glance overshadowed by the ominous clouds.

Rain broke loose in stinging sheets, drenching the fortress walls. The infiltration group huddled under tarps near the Ark's crate. Thunder reverberated, overshadowing normal conversation. Some sentinels recalled how the Ark's manifestations had once summoned bizarre storms, now uncertain if nature or arcane power fueled these towering clouds. Father Lombardi maintained a steady recitation, eyes closed in concentration. Sabine whispered encouragement, brushing water from her brow.

Flashes of lightning revealed the city's silhouette—a tapestry of spires and domes battered by swirling wind. Helena gripped Dave's arm, tension winding her nerves. He murmured close to her ear, "We're seeing the final cracks in everyone's calm. If the Ark's disturbances remain quiet tonight, maybe we pass the threshold. But if Orlov attacks, or if the Ark's energy flares up, this city might ignite."

She squeezed his hand in answer, seeking steadiness. Dripping from the rain, they approached the look-outs posted near the gate. Yusef joined them with wide eyes. "Some rumors say Orlov is negotiating with militant leaders near the southwestern road. If that collapses, they might storm our barricades."

An Israeli soldier overheard. "We're ready. They'll face a hail of gunfire. The question is whether the Ark's phenomena might break free under that violence."

Helena reined in a wave of dread. "Keep it from coming to that. Let's hold them off if they try anything."

Drenched sentinels took up positions on the ramparts. Dave and Helena waded through wet stones to confirm each vantage point. The swirling storm lit the sky in electric surges—no phenomena apparent, but hearts hammered with fear. Father Lombardi's chanting rose over the wind, sending a strange resonance through the soaked courtyard. Soldiers listened, unsettled yet oddly comforted that the Ark's manifestations might still be locked.

One of Ming Xia's specialists emerged from the fortress arch, carrying a radio that crackled with fresh intel. The operative waved them over. "We have an urgent message from allied command. Large-scale mobilizations are massing outside city lines. Tanks spotted. Armored units from multiple nations. They say diplomacy failed. The entire region stands on the brink of open war, phenomena or no phenomena."

A hush fell across the infiltration group. Dave set his jaw, mouth drawing tight. Helena felt her pulse race. Yusef let out a frightened exhale. Even Sister Sabine, normally stoic in crisis, looked pale. If the Ark's manifestations were no longer the main impetus, then raw political ambition might bring unstoppable machines of war to the Holy City. And in that conflagration, a single stray shell could shatter the Ark's seal.

Lightning flared again, painting the fortress in harsh shadows. Father Lombardi paused his recitation, glancing at them with dread. "If armies converge, no chant can hold phenomena forever. The relic might feed off the city's collective terror."

Sabine brushed a strand of wet hair from her face. "We must find a last attempt at negotiation. If the Ark's phenomena are neutral, then war over the relic is pointless. There's no unstoppable power to gain."

Ming Xia frowned, frustration plain. "But leaders outside see an opportunity or fear losing face. Orlov's alliances thrived on the Ark's energy, but war can have momentum of its own."

Ibrahim nodded. "In the morning, the final confrontation might spark. Tanks, jets, thousands of soldiers. The look-outs here are outnumbered."

Helena felt Dave's steady presence at her side. She clasped his wrist, voice hushed. "We stand a chance only if we keep the Ark's phenomena locked. If the relic unleashes a biblical storm now, the conflict will rage tenfold."

He brushed his thumb over her knuckles. "We'll guard it. But if nations or Orlov's men open fire on Jerusalem, phenomena might be the lesser threat."

A wave of thunder rocked the night, as if underlining his words. Rain hammered the courtyard in renewed force. Soldiers and watchmen huddled behind barricades, uncertain if dawn would bring massed artillery. Tension raked every breath. Father Lombardi returned to chanting, his voice trembling with the knowledge that the Ark's disturbances might soon face a test beyond anything they had endured. Yusef retreated to a small overhang, hugging himself against the chill, sorrow etched on his face for the city he loved.

Some troopers tried radioing allied units outside the city, hoping they could forestall an onslaught. Others simply loaded their rifles, prepared to defend the Ark from sabotage. Helena and Dave circled once more, ensuring each post had coverage. Ming Xia's gaze swept the ramparts, formulating fallback strategies. Sister Sabine checked the crate's locks, verifying no bullet or stray debris had compromised the wood.

The swirling storm overhead cast flashes of light across the centuries-old stones. In those brief illuminations, Helena thought she saw faint arcs near the Ark's edges—ghostly flickers that vanished the instant she tried to focus. Her breath caught. She locked eyes with Dave, uncertain if it was lightning's reflection or a sign the Ark's manifestations stirred at the threshold of global conflict. For a moment, he seemed to register the same possibility, worry settling on his features. But neither said a word.

At last, the infiltration group holed up inside the fortress keep, each waiting for dawn's uncertain arrival. Soldiers maintained their posts, ankles deep in puddles of rainwater. The city's patchwork of tensions brewed in the darkness, overshadowed by swirling thunderheads. Helena felt a trembling energy crawl through the air, as if manifestations hovered just beyond sight. She cast a lingering look at Dave, letting the silent closeness ground her. Lombardi's chant droned on, Sabine's occasional murmurs echoing the vow to keep the Ark's energy caged.

None could predict how the next sunrise would shape the fate of Jerusalem—or of the Ark's phenomena bound in centuries-old secrecy. War threatened from outside the gates, extremist doubt festered within, and each flash of lightning teased the possibility that the Ark's disturbances might respond. The infiltration group took no comfort in the hush. They simply braced for the final shift, aware that no ceremony could quell the raw ambition of armies or quiet the swirling uncertainties. The Ark lay sealed behind battered wood, still and dark. A single violent clash might bring it raging back to unstoppable life.

Chapter 24

Jerusalem Fortress — Sunrise, Day 0

Sunrise arrived in a haze of roiling clouds that cast deep purple shadows across the Old City's silhouettes. Soldiers and armored vehicles lined the aged streets, each vantage point bristling with uneasy guards from nations that had never before worked side by side. Rumors of a final standoff churned through every corridor, and the tension made the atmosphere feel charged with static, as if a single spark could unleash a storm of global proportions.

Inside the fortress near the southwestern ramparts, Helena Carter stood among an anxious circle of allied operatives. The Ark's crate rested on a raised platform, battered from its travels but still intact, its phenomena sealed by the unrelenting devotion of Father Aurelius Lombardi. He knelt close to the wooden container, chanting verses under his breath, eyelids quivering with concentration. Sister Sabine looked on, ledger gripped tight, offering support whenever the priest's voice flagged.

Ming Xia surveyed an intelligence feed on a tablet, occasionally glancing at the watchmen who manned the stone walls. She cleared her throat, addressing those gathered. "Our contacts report a gathering of tanks and artillery on multiple fronts outside the city. Russia, China, the U.S., and smaller nations are all positioning. The push for the Ark's energy has turned into a fear that someone else might gain the relic's power—or use it."

Helena's breath caught. "The Ark's manifestations remain silent, but these armies might not stand down."

A compact Israeli officer stepped forward, uniform dusty from a sleepless night. "We have orders to hold the fortress if an assault begins. Civilians have been advised to stay home, but some extremist clusters roam the streets, convinced the Ark's disturbances will appear in its name. We're blocking them from every approach."

Dave Schumer rested a hand on Helena's shoulder. "Let's confirm no cracks are forming in the seal. Father Lombardi, Sabine—how stable is the chant?"

The Jesuit priest lifted his gaze from the box. A tremor underlined his words. "We hold fast, but the energy outside is immense. War stirs fear, and fear can feed the Ark's manifestations. If stray rockets strike the chest, its phenomena may break free."

Sabine nodded, an uneasy flicker in her eyes. "We sense no arcs yet. Still, we must stay vigilant."

Helena glanced toward the fortress gates where Yusef Nasir, the local youth, conferred with a group of sentinels. He had been racing in and out of the Old City's winding alleys, gathering whispers of potential trouble. She admired his bravery, though she worried for his safety. When he spotted her, he hurried over with a quick, tense stride.

He gulped a breath. "People talk of men in black vehicles, possibly Colonel Orlov's envoys. They question the sentinels, wanting direct proof the Ark's disturbances are dormant. Some mention that Orlov wants to negotiate or threaten. I'm not sure which."

The infiltration group stiffened. Dave exchanged a grave look with Helena. "It's starting. Orlov might send a final ultimatum."

Ibrahim Mahdi exhaled, frustration etched on his face. "We can't open negotiations if the Ark's energy remains sealed. That's the entire reason Orlov built alliances. If the phenomena provide no advantage, he might either stand down—or lash out in desperation."

Ming Xia slid the tablet into a carrying case. "Let's prepare for any scenario. I'll have look-outs reinforce the courtyard. If Orlov's men arrive, we hold them at the outer gate. Meanwhile, we coordinate with allied forces around the city walls."

Helena gave a terse nod, then turned to follow Dave toward the Ark. Lombardi wiped beads of sweat from his brow, offering a fleeting smile of determination. Sabine calmly took his place when he paused, chanting in low tones from the ledger. Lines in weather-scarred script formed a litany of protection, keeping illusions locked behind the relic's battered surface.

A swirl of damp wind caught Helena's hair as she joined Dave, stepping beneath a canopy that shielded the Ark from prying eyes. The morning air felt unnaturally charged—like the hush before a thunderclap. "Are you as uneasy as I am?" she murmured.

He inclined his head, gaze flicking to the horizon. "More than you know. This city brims with rumor. Troop movements outside, extremist crowds near the gates, Orlov's men possibly inbound. If illusions stir, everything could ignite."

She rested a hand on his jacket sleeve. "At least we face it together."

His breath caught in a subtle sign of relief. "I'd have lost hope by now if you weren't here."

Before she could respond, a series of sharp clacks rang out from the gate. Shouts followed. Soldiers scrambled along the fortress yard, leveling rifles. Yusef dashed across the courtyard to Dave and Helena, panting. "A group has arrived—heavy black SUVs. They're demanding to speak with whoever leads the sentinels. They claim Orlov himself is near."

Helena's heart pounded. "He's come to deliver an ultimatum, or worse."

Dave signaled sentinels to accompany them. Ming Xia caught the gesture and joined swiftly, leading her own detail. Father Lombardi and Sabine remained behind with the chest, reciting the chant. Ibrahim followed at a distance, face tense. They crossed the fortress yard and climbed a short flight of stairs to the top of the rampart that overlooked a newly installed barrier at the gate. Rain from the previous night had left the stones slick, but the morning sun now glinted on wet surfaces.

Below, three black vehicles with tinted windows idled beyond the barricade. A half-dozen men in dark attire, armed but not brandishing rifles openly, stood in the open. One figure wore a gray jacket and had a scar across his temple. He cupped his hands around his mouth, calling out in accented English. "We come on behalf of Colonel Orlov. We request a parley."

Ming Xia clenched her jaw. "Parley? Or demand?"

The man spread his arms. "We have no illusions that illusions remain. But Colonel Orlov demands confirmation. If the Ark's phenomena are truly inert, he sees no reason to spill blood. However, if you are lying, he'll take the Ark by force."

Helena and Dave exchanged a look. He muttered under his breath, "Orlov can't withdraw easily without losing face. Let's see if we can push him to stand down."

She nodded, then signaled an Israeli officer. "Open the barrier just enough for them to enter unarmed. We'll talk in the courtyard. No illusions, no violence, if they comply."

The officer barked orders. look-outs parted the steel barricade, and the men from the SUVs approached carefully. Dave and Helena stood flanked by allied troops as the visitors ascended the fortress steps. The scarred negotiator stepped forward, scanning the yard with narrowed eyes.

He spoke in a curt tone. "We represent Colonel Orlov's interests. He grows tired of this rumor that the Ark's energy is locked away. He demands direct proof. If the Ark's manifestations are truly inert, then all the alliances he built around harnessing it lose purpose."

Ibrahim folded his arms. "We have repeated: the Ark's disturbances are sealed by a ceremony. The crate cannot be opened, or the phenomena may reawaken."

The man's gaze flicked around, skepticism clear. "That's what you claim. Colonel Orlov's militia believes you're hiding unstoppable power. They suspect a trick—or a plan to use the Ark's energy once they let their guard down."

Ming Xia's expression hardened. "If the Ark's manifestations existed in full force, do you think we'd invite you in for polite conversation? We'd have ended this conflict already."

The envoy's jaw tightened. "Orlov suggests a demonstration. Crack open a portion, show the Ark is inert. If it's truly neutralized, then no unstoppable force remains. His paramilitary will disperse."

Helena's stomach twisted. She exchanged an alarmed glance with Dave. They both remembered Father Lombardi's warnings: tampering with the Ark's lid risked unleashing disturbances. "That's impossible," she said, voice measured. "Opening the crate undermines the entire ceremony. If the Ark's phenomena are dormant, forcibly exposing them might spark a reaction."

The scarred negotiator's lips curled in a faint sneer. "Then Orlov sees no reason to trust you. He might storm Jerusalem with allied militias at his side. The city is minutes away from large-scale war. Are you certain you won't open it?"

A hush gripped the courtyard. Helena felt Dave's tension radiating through the sentinels. She drew in a long breath. "We cannot. The Ark's manifestations are locked, but messing with the crate is dangerously reckless."

He shrugged. "Then we may have no truce." He turned to the silent men behind him. "We've done our part. Orlov will proceed." With that, he spun on his heel and stalked back toward the gate. The sentinels parted, letting them exit. Engines roared as the black vehicles reversed away, screeching down the narrow path.

A chill ran through Helena's spine. Dave lowered his voice. "They'll likely report back to Orlov that we refused. War might be inevitable." Ibrahim pressed a hand to his forehead. "We can't open the Ark for show. We might trigger something unstoppable."

Ming Xia stood firm. "Then we brace for a siege, or we rely on the allied forces. If the Ark's phenomena truly remain inert, perhaps Orlov's men can't rally enough support to break through. But we must prepare for chaos in the city as soon as word spreads that we refused his request."

Helena's chest felt tight as they descended from the rampart. She pictured the Ark, battered and vulnerable if rockets rained down. Father Lombardi believed the Ark's disturbances were sealed, but mass violence might spawn unstoppable nightmares. Dave remained at her side, a steady presence amid the swirling dread.

Moments later, an urgent call came through the allied channels: large convoys with heavy weaponry were sighted near the outskirts. Intelligence indicated Colonel Orlov had indeed declared a final push. Some extremist cells inside the city might coordinate from within. Yusef returned from a quick recon trip in the Old City's back streets, face ashen.

He panted, "Citizens are fleeing or barricading their shops. They talk of giant armies outside. My family begs me to come home, but I can't leave. Are the Ark's manifestations going to erupt?"

Helena felt a pang of sympathy. She placed a gentle hand on the youth's arm. "We pray the Ark's energy stays sealed. You might want to guide your family to a safe place. The city could face artillery if Orlov's men break in."

He swallowed hard, tears brimming. "I'll help them find shelter. But I won't vanish. I'll come back."

She offered him a nod of respect. "Be careful."

He dashed off. Dave turned to Helena. "We need a plan. If Orlov's paramilitary enters, do we move the Ark deeper underground, or keep it visible so the phenomena remain unprovoked?"

She considered the options. "Hiding it might push them to bombard everything. Keeping it in plain sight might incite them to fire directly at the crate. Either way is a risk."

Father Lombardi, overhearing, approached. "The relic can't be opened if we're to maintain its dormancy. If Orlov's men shell us, I'll chant to hold the seal, but I fear bullets or rockets might breach the wood."

Sabine's knuckles whitened around her ledger. "Then we do everything to repel them outside the fortress. If the Ark senses the city's terror, a stray shell might trigger an unstoppable wave."

Ming Xia eyed the sky, where thunderheads gathered in foreboding clusters. "The storm returns, as if matching the city's fear. Orlov's men want the Ark's energy, or they want to crush it. Either outcome can spark mass bloodshed."

The infiltration group spent the next hours bolstering defenses. Soldiers set up sandbag emplacements, turned corners of the courtyard into strongholds, and readied anti-vehicle measures. Allied watchmen from the U.S., China, and Israel manned vantage points along the walls. Father Lombardi and Sabine stayed near the Ark in a heavily protected shelter, chanting at intervals. Helicopters circled overhead, searchlights scanning roads leading into the Old City. The clamor of approaching conflict echoed from the distance: engines rumbling, the occasional crackle of gunfire.

As late afternoon slid toward evening, the fortress took on a grim silence. Civilians in the surrounding neighborhood had fled or locked themselves indoors. Yusef returned, breathless, having guided his family to a relative's place on the far side of the city. The youth insisted on staying to relay local intel. Dave gave him a respectful pat on the shoulder, aware that his knowledge of the streets was priceless.

Dusk arrived with a swirl of wind, lightning dancing across the darkening clouds. Reports trickled in that Orlov's convoys had reached the city perimeter. Allied outposts outside Jerusalem signaled they were outnumbered, though official armies from multiple powers had also positioned themselves, forming a hair-trigger standoff. A single spark—an accidental shot or a rumor of illusions—might ignite the region.

The infiltration group mustered in the courtyard, each face drawn with resolve. Helena stepped onto a low crate to address the sentinels. "We remain unified to keep the Ark's phenomena sealed. Colonel Orlov wants us to open the chest. We will not. If he attacks, we defend. No one tampers with the Ark. Understood?"

Stern nods followed from every corner. Father Lombardi murmured fervent lines, Sabine at his elbow. Dave scanned the ramparts, tension visible in his posture. Soldiers stood tall behind barricades, eyes darting to the swirling clouds above.

In the final flicker of twilight, an Israeli scout burst through the gates, panting from a wild dash. "Tanks sighted along the northern highway—eight, maybe more. Additional vehicles from Orlov's alliance approach the western side. Artillery rumored to be in range. They may begin shelling if a negotiation fails."

Helena's heart pounded. She recalled the Ark's manifestations swirling—cataclysmic scenes nearly unleashed. If modern weaponry battered the Ark now, its disturbances might rip free. Dave took her elbow gently, voice tight. "We have to coordinate a last negotiation or brace for bombardment."

She forced a nod. "We try one last time to show the Ark's disturbances are gone. If Orlov refuses to listen, we stand behind these walls." She turned to Lombardi. "Keep chanting. We can't let the Ark feed on fear."

A messenger from Orlov's line arrived soon after, forcing the watchmen to open the gate slightly. He carried a short ultimatum: open the crate to confirm the Ark's energy is dormant, or the paramilitaries would commence a bombardment by dawn. The infiltration group refused again, repeating that the Ark's phenomena lay sealed by a sacred vow, not to be disturbed. The messenger left in frustration.

Night deepened. The fortress yard glowed under emergency floodlights. Soldiers manned every vantage, scanning for infiltration squads. Helicopters circled overhead, lights slicing through the gloom. Thunder boomed in the distance, rolling across the city in echoing waves. The infiltration group prepared for an onslaught. Helena stood with Dave near the Ark, hearts hammering at the possibility of manifestations if a single shell shattered the wood.

Wind lashed the courtyard as hour after hour crawled by. Word arrived that both Russian and Chinese high command readied their mechanized forces. The U.S. remained in a protective stance. Israel braced for the worst. The swirl of tension across the region seemed almost tangible, a living force that pressed on the city's aged stones.

Shortly before dawn, the sentinels on the ramparts spotted movement in the darkness. The hum of engines drifted through the air. Tanks with searchlights rumbled into vantage near the Old City gates, paramilitaries behind them. A hush gripped the fortress. Dave, Helena, Ming Xia,

THE SWORD OF CHERUBIM

Ibrahim, and others scrambled onto the walls to observe. Lightning illuminated silhouettes of hulking metal. Allied artillery from the city's official defenders aimed back. The entire horizon bristled with menace.

At the base of the fortress, Yusef stood wide-eyed, glancing to Helena. "This is real war. You must keep the Ark's manifestations locked. If the Ark unleashes anything now, the city is doomed."

She swallowed, memories of the Ark's energy swirling in smaller scuffles haunting her. "We're doing all we can."

A faint voice crackled over a loudspeaker from Orlov's lines. "Last chance to reveal manifestations. Otherwise, we open fire." The sentinels tensed, exchanging grim looks. Muffled thunder rolled. The infiltration group recognized that dawn might bring the cataclysm they feared.

Behind them, Father Lombardi's chanting rose to a desperate pitch, Sabine assisting. Lightning flashed in savage arcs overhead, framing the battlements in ghostly light. No manifestations danced on the Ark's surface, but a twisting anxiety suffused the courtyard. Dave took Helena's hand in the gloom, a silent testament that they faced this unknown together.

The infiltration group heard the squeal of tank treads repositioning. Radios crackled with chatter that allied armies from several nations prepared to join the standoff. If the Ark's phenomena remained locked, a purely human war could still destroy Jerusalem. A single shot might set off chain reactions. The sentinels braced behind sandbags, hearts pounding.

Then a wave of static crackled through allied channels. Multiple voices called out in alarm. Reports came in that across the border, allied divisions had begun clashing with Orlov's men. Shells soared in distant fields, flashes lighting the horizon. The entire region teetered on the brink.

The infiltration group steeled themselves. Dave and Helena exchanged a final glance of fierce determination. They would protect the Ark, manifestations or not.

A final peal of thunder boomed as the first gray strands of dawn touched the eastern sky. Soldiers along every vantage readied for artillery blasts. Inside the fortress, tension reached a knife's edge. Father Lombardi's chant intensified, echoing through the stone corridors. Sister Sabine's voice joined him, unwavering. Yusef gripped a small corner of the courtyard, ready to guide the infiltration group through the Old City's back alleys if sabotage began. Ming Xia took a position with her specialists, scanning for infiltration from the rear. Ibrahim relayed final positions to Israeli command, who stood in allied formation with U.S. and Chinese sentinels.

Suddenly, an electromagnetic pulse rippled through the fortress yard, faint but discernible. Sparks danced along the edges of the Ark's crate, a flash that lasted only a heartbeat. Helena let out a startled cry. Father Lombardi groaned, staggering as if hammered by invisible force. The sentinels gasped, uncertain if disturbances were bursting forth or if some external bombardment triggered it.

But just as quickly as it appeared, the spark fizzled, leaving the crate dark again. Lombardi steadied himself, voice ragged. "It's—there was a brief tremor. The phenomena sense the war outside. We must hold the vow."

He resumed chanting at a fervent pace, Sabine echoing each line. Tension hammered in every observer's chest. Helena's eyes locked with Dave. He breathed, "One more sign that the Ark's manifestations might slip free. We must keep Orlov's men from firing. We're out of time."

A hush gripped them. Over the fortress wall, the roiling sky glowed with more lightning, stuttering across the land. Tanks rumbled closer, metal screeching. The watchmen braced behind sandbags, fingers on triggers. Helena and Dave realized that the Ark's disturbances hovered at the very threshold, waiting for chaos to feed upon. If the paramilitaries unleashed heavy fire, the crate might crack, and the Ark's energy could erupt in unstoppable fury.

The entire city seemed to hold its breath. Colonel Orlov's demands had been spurned. The Ark's manifestations flickered on the edge. Dawn light carved lines across the horizon, revealing an apocalypse in waiting. Every soldier in the fortress yard braced for the final moment, uncertain if the Ark's power or modern war would strike first.

Chapter 25

A pale morning spread over Jerusalem, revealing columns of armored vehicles poised at key roads beyond the Old City. The fortress walls vibrated with the hum of tension. Helicopters circled overhead, their engines throbbing like a drumbeat of impending conflict. Lightning crawled across the eastern sky, leaving arcs of sizzling brightness that dissolved into low rumbles of thunder. Soldiers manning the ramparts exchanged wary glances, bracing for the final spark.

Father Lombardi felt the chant's seal flex but not break—the ritual damped most energy, yet massed violence nearby let stray sparks bleed through.

Within the fortress courtyard, the Ark's crate stood under a protective canopy. Father Lombardi and Sister Sabine chanted in a tight whisper, eyes half-lidded with strain. Their voices created a rhythmic cadence that pressed against the swirling wind. Dim sparks flickered along the box's edges whenever thunder shook the air, as if the Ark's manifestations hovered on the verge of release. A circle of allied troops surrounded the relic, each one aware that a direct hit from artillery could shatter the chant in an instant.

Helena Carter passed between the sandbag emplacements, a weight of dread hanging on her every step. Dave Schumer joined her, face grim. "Orlov's men align outside the city's northern gate, apparently with militia support. Reports suggest they have mortar teams and rocket launchers. Official armies from multiple powers also align in a standoff. If the Ark's phenomena spark, or if a rumor starts that the Ark's energy is back, they might open fire."

She shook her head, voice hushed. "We're so close to a city-wide war. The manifestations have flickered, but they're still dormant. If a single rocket hits the crate, we might face unstoppable phenomena."

A tall Israeli major approached with clipped strides. "Our intel shows Colonel Orlov sets up artillery positions. If negotiations fail, he'll commence shelling. Meanwhile, extremist groups roam these streets, convinced the Ark's disturbances will appear."

Ming Xia joined them, eyes narrowed. "China has a small contingent here. We can't hold off a barrage. We might have to evacuate the Ark deeper into tunnels if the shelling starts."

Helena's lips formed a grim line. "That might cause phenomena to stir if the chest is jostled or hammered by explosions."

Dave stepped closer, voice low. "We either stand our ground or risk the Ark's manifestations awakening mid-flight through tight tunnels. I say we hold, trust Father Lombardi's vow, and pray Orlov stands down."

Above them, thunder cracked. The sentinels at the gate shouted that a small convoy had approached under a white flag. Soldiers parted the barricade, letting a lone black SUV roll forward. Engines idled as four men in thick jackets emerged, one leaning on the open door. A hush settled over the fortress yard. Helena and Dave, flanked by armed sentinels, approached the new arrivals, hearts pounding.

A tall, gaunt figure stepped out from behind the driver's seat. His eyes gleamed with cold intensity. Colonel Nikolai Orlov had finally come in person, exuding a grim confidence. Dave's posture tensed, one hand resting near his holstered sidearm. Helena felt a chill at the sight of the Russian operative who had relentlessly pursued the Ark's secrets.

Orlov's gaze swept the courtyard, narrowing at the Ark's crate. "I have spent months chasing that relic," he said in a low, accented voice. "You claim the Ark's energy no longer exists?"

Father Lombardi stood near the relic, chanting. Sabine stilled her ledger, eyes locked on the colonel. "We keep the Ark's phenomena sealed, Colonel. They are inert."

He let out a short, humorless laugh. "Inert? My men believe the Ark's manifestations might be harnessed if only we breach that box's lock. This rumor of a vow is your ploy to hold exclusive power."

Ming Xia stepped forward, posture rigid. "We have no reason to lie. Multiple nations stand together. If the Ark's energy were ours to wield, you'd have seen it. We want no phenomena unleashed."

Orlov studied her, then Dave, then Helena. "So you refuse me access? You defy a simple demonstration?"

Helena spoke in a firm tone. "We can't open the Ark. Doing so risks phenomena unleashing who knows what. Look around—there are armies near the city. One spark could devastate everyone, phenomena or not."

He sneered, stepping away from his entourage to pace. "All my efforts, all my alliances... worthless if the Ark's phenomena truly are locked. But I suspect you'd say anything to keep that advantage hidden."

Yusef lingered behind the sentinels, fists clenched. Dave glanced at the young local, then back to Orlov. "You used the Ark's manifestations as a rallying cry. Now you realize it might be powerless. Let your men stand down."

Orlov's lips twisted. "Powerless or not, I can't simply retreat. My forces are massed, waiting on my word. My pride, my mission, demanded phenomena to shift the balance in my homeland's favor. If the Ark's manifestations truly are sealed, I can't salvage my cause. Or maybe your vow is a sham—maybe the phenomena wait for the right master."

Lombardi stepped forward, voice resonant with fervor. "We vow the Ark's disturbances remain locked by an weather-scarred chant. In the name of God, I beg you not to test it with violence."

A bitter chuckle escaped Orlov's throat. "I don't trust your vow." He raised a phone, typed something. "I'll give you one final chance to open the Ark willingly."

Helena's pulse hammered. She recalled how fragile the seal was. "That's impossible, Colonel."

Lightning flared overhead, highlighting the tension carved into everyone's faces. Orlov's gaze hardened. "Then I have no choice." He spoke a curt phrase in Russian into the phone, glancing at them with cold disdain. "Return the Ark to me or the shelling begins at dawn. Phenomena or not, your fortress will crumble beneath artillery."

He turned on his heel, signaled his men. They stalked back to the SUV, ignoring the sentinels' rifles. Engines revved. The vehicle reversed, heading off into the gloom. A hush choked the courtyard. Dave's fingers brushed Helena's. She took in a shaky breath, aware they might have mere hours before the city erupted.

Ibrahim let out a low curse. "So that's it. He wants manifestations or destruction, and we refuse both. War it is."

Ming Xia flicked her radio on, voice clipped. "We'll alert the allied lines. Colonel Orlov is done negotiating. We must brace for artillery."

Father Lombardi's voice trembled with adrenaline. "If shells strike the crate, entergy may tear free. All these armies will face unstoppable phantoms. The world could see nightmares beyond anything we can contain."

Sabine touched his shoulder in silent solidarity. Helena felt Dave's presence at her side, a comfort in this swirling panic. Yusef lingered, teeth clenched, possibly thinking of his family. She turned to him, voice gentle. "You've done enough. Get to safety if the shelling starts. We can't bear to lose you."

He swallowed. "I'll lead more civilians away, but I won't abandon you. If phenomena break free, the city's in danger. I'll return if I can."

She nodded, tears pricking the corners of her eyes. He gave a shaky nod back and darted out.

All around, sentinels scrambled to reinforce the courtyard. Another meeting convened in the fortress interior. Helena, Dave, Ming Xia, Ibrahim, Father Lombardi, and Sister Sabine formed a desperate council.

THE SWORD OF CHERUBIM

Tension bled from every word. The question lingered: do they try to move the Ark deeper underground, risking manifestations if jostled, or do they remain in the open to repel Orlov's assault?

Finally, Dave spoke up, voice tight. "We can't hide the Ark easily. Transporting it invites sabotage. Let's fortify here. At least we have thick walls and allied sentinels."

Lombardi pressed his palms together, color drained from his face. "Then I remain at the crate. If artillery rains down, I'll try to maintain the chant. If the Ark senses mass fear, it'll feed the phenomena."

Sabine nodded. "We'll stand with you." She shot a quick glance to Helena, an unspoken vow of solidarity in her eyes.

Ming Xia barked orders into her phone, calling for additional guards to the fortress. Soldiers brought heavier weapons to the ramparts. The infiltration group prepared for the worst, each mind swirling with images of phenomena bursting forth in a hail of rocket fire.

Outside, the sky flickered with lightning. Over the city's northern edge, faint glimpses of searchlights revealed silhouettes of tanks massing. Allied lines formed a blockade, but no one expected a peaceful resolution. Helena and Dave paced the fortress yard, ensuring the look-outs were positioned behind cover. Some tension eased from the knowledge that the Ark's disturbances had remained sealed so far. She took a moment to rest her forehead against Dave's chest, ignoring curious glances from soldiers. He wrapped an arm around her, murmuring, "We'll make it, no matter what."

She drew on his reassurance, then parted. "Let's see if any new diplomatic hail arrives, though I suspect not."

Just then, an urgent call crackled through allied radios. An American officer relayed that Orlov's artillery had begun lobbing shells at allied outposts north of the city. The sentinels on the walls exchanged frightened looks. If that barrage crept closer, the fortress and the Ark would be next. Father Lombardi closed his eyes, chanting with renewed desperation. Sister Sabine flipped pages in her ledger, lending her voice to strengthen the Ark's seal.

Ibrahim barked to the men. "To your positions. Expect impact near dawn if Orlov continues his barrage. We have half an hour to brace."

The infiltration group stood ready, hearts pounding. Helena joined Dave at a vantage on the parapet, scanning the roads. She glimpsed muzzle flashes in the distance. Heavy rumbles shook the city. Fire lit the horizon. Allied lines returned fire. The entire region trembled, as though the Ark's manifestations might sense the chaos.

As dawn tinted the sky with a sullen red glow, the thunder of artillery raged closer. Shells whistled overhead, striking in far neighborhoods. Columns of smoke rose. Civilians fled in droves. The infiltration group tensed at each detonation, worried the next round might target them. The sentinels crouched behind stone battlements, clutching rifles, eyes wide.

Finally, a shrill whistle cut through the air. A shell hammered a nearby courtyard, sending a blast of dust and debris swirling. The fortress shook, stone chips showering the yard. Father Lombardi gasped, losing a fragment of his chant. Sparks danced along the Ark's edges, the phenomena straining at the ceremony's fraying hold. Dave ducked, pulling Helena beneath an arch. She glimpsed arcs of strange light flicker near the relic, then vanish as Lombardi redoubled his chant. Her heart nearly seized. They were on the brink.

Through swirling smoke, allied soldiers fired back with mortar teams. Another shell crashed closer, rattling everyone's bones. Yusef, returning from a final evacuation run, dove behind crates. Dave grabbed him before he could topple into the Ark's platform. Helena felt an electric crackle in the air, the phenomena prowling near the threshold. If a direct hit shattered the box, the Ark's energy would burst out in unstoppable form.

Ming Xia barked for the troopers to hold position. She radioed allied lines, demanding they push Orlov's men back. Radio static crackled with frantic voices. It was chaos. The infiltration group realized the Ark's manifestations might slip free at any second if the barrage crept nearer. Dark shapes flickered across the yard as soldiers huddled behind rubble, eyes locked on the Ark's faintly sparking corners.

Suddenly, a quake of thunder rippled through the sky, not from artillery but from the storm overhead. Lightning slammed a distant spire, casting an eerie glow that revealed shadows of tanks creeping closer to the Old City gates. Another barrage soared, shaking the fortress ramparts. Stone blocks cracked under the impact, sending sentinels reeling. Helena coughed in a cloud of debris.

She heard Father Lombardi cry out. Turning, she saw him nearly collapse at the Ark's side, arcs of strange light swirling along the crate's seam. Sabine clung to his shoulder, chanting in breathless desperation. Dave rushed over, helping them both steady. Helena felt a jolt of dread as flickers of ephemeral shapes rippled in the air—ghostly manifestations trying to force their way through. The vow held them back, but the war's fear hammered at the seal. If the barrage intensified, the Ark's phenomena might flood free.

The look-outs regained formation, ignoring the swirling dust. Another shell tore into a building beyond the fortress walls, launching flames skyward. Shouts erupted from the defenders, calling for medical teams.

The infiltration group realized Orlov's squads were pushing into the city, step by destructive step. If the Ark's manifestations fully awakened, unstoppable horror might overshadow even Orlov's artillery.

Ibrahim staggered up the rampart, weapon at the ready, yelling that local forces were pinned. The infiltration group braced for an incursion. Dave pivoted, scanning the courtyard for possible infiltration. Soldiers manned the gate with trembling resolve. Helena locked eyes with him. "We must hold. We can't let the Ark's phenomena break free."

He squeezed her hand. "We stand fast."

A thunderous roar sounded from beyond the walls. The watchmen expected more shells, but the concussive wave seemed unnatural. Lightning struck overhead again, a forked flash that left the air quivering. Father Lombardi cried out, voice strangled, as shimmering arcs of light spiraled around the crate. For a moment, phantom shapes coiled above the wood—war-like silhouettes of intangible armies. The infiltration group stared, hearts in their throats. Then the shapes faded as Lombardi and Sabine dug deeper, chanting to seal them away.

Yusef cowered near a half-toppled bench, eyes wide with horror. "It's happening. The Ark's manifestations are forcing themselves out. We can't hold them if the shelling doesn't stop."

A scout tore into the courtyard, face pale with fear. "Orlov's men are at the gates. They're trying to blow the barricade with shaped charges. The next blast might hit the fortress. The entire city is a battlefield."

Helena realized with grim finality that the Ark's energy teetered at the threshold. War fed it with raw terror. The sentinels had only minutes, perhaps seconds, before the Ark's phenomena fully manifested. Then she felt a shift in the air—like the flick of a cosmic switch. Father Lombardi doubled over, letting out a wrenching gasp. The arcs of eerie light along the Ark's edges soared higher, dancing in cracked lightning above the battered wood.

Sabine dropped her ledger, voice trembling. "The vow is failing. We can't hold them alone. The war's fear is too strong."

Smoke from distant artillery drifted into the courtyard, stinging the eyes of sentinels, who coughed as they held position around the relic. Dave guided Helena behind a low wall. He turned to Lombardi. "If the Ark's phenomena break free, we lose control. Is there any final recourse?"

The priest's face twisted in despair. "Only an act of divine grace," he rasped. "Our vow can't withstand global fear. If the Ark's energy fully manifests in the city's heart, no force can quell it."

Ming Xia gestured for sentinels to guard every approach. Orlov's squads hammered the fortress gate with explosives, each rumble shaking the courtyard. Father Lombardi collapsed to his knees, arcs of glowing light spiraling overhead. The infiltration group stared in dread. Helena felt Dave's presence, a quiet anchor, though his face looked ashen.

She glimpsed Yusef near the gate, scanning for a hidden approach. The youth then darted back, alarm on his features. "They're blowing a hole in the outer wall. We can't hold them. Tanks might roll in next. The illusions—" He gestured at the bright arcs fanning out from the Ark's crate. "They're about to burst."

Helena realized they stood on the brink of unstoppable phenomena. War battered the gates, and the Ark's manifestations fed on terror. No ceremony could contain them anymore. Another chunk of mortar hammered the fortress from overhead, and debris rained down. Soldiers cried out. The infiltration group braced for the Ark's energy to rip free.

Then lightning stabbed a tower to the east, unleashing a piercing crack that lit the entire courtyard in stark brilliance.

In that searing instant, manifestations coalesced above the Ark, forming ghostly shapes of a vast, crumbling host. Helmets of phantom warriors glinted, silhouettes of chariots shimmered. The sentinels froze in horror. Father Lombardi tried reciting lines, but the Ark's disturbances rose beyond his control, swirling in defiance of the vow. Sister Sabine pressed closer, chanting, but the storm overhead roared in response, thunder quaking the fortress walls.

Dave grabbed Helena's arm, voice straining to be heard above the deafening thunder. "We have to fall back. The Ark's phenomena are out. If Orlov breaches the gates now—"

A savage boom cut him off. An explosive charge ripped the final barricade. Shouts and gunfire erupted near the fortress entrance. The troopers opened fire, battered by the Ark's manifestations swirling overhead. Modern war fused with time-worn dread as paramilitaries forced their way inside. Soldiers struggled to keep the Ark from direct hits. Gunshots ricocheted off stone, sparks ignited in corners, and ghostly forms danced above the chaos.

Colonel Orlov's men crashed into the courtyard, brandishing rifles and launching small rockets at allied defenders. The infiltration group dove behind crates. Dave returned fire, Helena ducked next to him, adrenaline scorching through her veins. She glimpsed the manifestations overhead: spectral armies charging in silent roars, feeding on the city's fear. Lombardi sobbed in anguish, voice raw, as the vow shattered under unstoppable collective terror.

THE SWORD OF CHERUBIM

Shells crashed outside, war raged inside, and the Ark's phenomena soared in swirling arcs. The infiltration group realized the Ark had unleashed phantoms across the fortress. One paramilitary soldier froze in horror, eyes fixed on intangible knights galloping through the air. Another reeled from visions of monstrous beasts flickering near his face. Fear cracked the minds of combatants on both sides.

Helena cried out, "We can't hold the Ark's energy. We have to—"

She didn't finish. The manifestations converged overhead, forming a pillar of coruscating light that lanced into the storm clouds. Thunder rumbled like the voice of an angry deity. Soldiers from Orlov's side and allied sentinels alike cowered at the spectacle. Dave yanked Helena down behind the Ark's platform as bullets whizzed overhead. The swirling manifestations crackled, intensifying by the second. A sense of unstoppable power roiled the air, like electricity magnified a thousand times.

In that cataclysmic moment, Father Lombardi collapsed, strength spent. Sabine cried for help, but no one could break through the firefight in time. Ming Xia and her men struggled to keep Orlov's squads from fully seizing the crate. Yusef ducked behind rubble, terror in his eyes as the Ark's energy whirled in front of him, half-formed shapes of monstrous biblical plagues.

Colonel Orlov himself stormed into view, stepping over the bodies of fallen soldiers, eyes flaring with a mad triumph. He raised a pistol, aiming at Dave, who aimed back. Time froze in Helena's mind. The manifestations overhead churned with savage fury. Then Orlov bellowed, "Open that box! Now the Ark's power is mine to wield!" He squeezed the trigger, but Dave fired a split second faster, sending the colonel scrambling for cover.

Under the tempest of illusions and artillery, the infiltration group realized the city teetered on the brink of total meltdown. Then the Ark's phenomena flared in a final blazing arc, a swirling column of energy that pierced the storm-laden sky. Lightning answered in furious strikes, some impacting near the Temple Mount. The sentinels cowered. A hush deeper than silence seized the courtyard as the Ark's manifestations twisted into a single point of brilliance above the chest.

In that flash, a shape emerged at the center of the coruscating glow—an otherworldly figure wreathed in blazing luminescence, bearing a sword of living flame. Soldiers froze, Orlov's men gasped, and look-outs stared in reverent shock. The Cherubim had descended to reclaim the Ark, the Ark's energy swirling around it like an elemental storm.

Helena's mind reeled at the sight, heart hammering in awe and terror. She realized the Ark's manifestations had reached their peak, summoning the fabled guardian from crumbling lore. War had triggered the final act. The fortress courtyard became a place of hushed dread as the Cherubim hovered, sword flickering with raw power, the Ark's phenomena swirling in majestic fury.

Chapter 26

Dawn spread across Jerusalem's rooftops in a haze of bloodred light, filtering through thick smoke rising from artillery strikes beyond the Old City gates. Soldiers ducked behind improvised barricades near the Temple Mount, each one braced for the next wave of thunder from the sky. The relic's guardian hovered above the fortress courtyard, a luminous shape wreathed in fierce energy and holding a sword that blazed like molten gold. Awe and dread clashed in every face below.

Colonel Orlov's paramilitaries had paused their assault for a single breath, stunned by the apparition's arrival. Some stared at the towering figure in raw fear, guns slack in their trembling hands. Others scrambled for cover, rifles jostling as they tried to find a target. Flames burned in the wreckage from earlier shelling, and sporadic gunfire still echoed from side streets, creating a raw chorus of panic.

Helena Carter clung to the edge of a broken wall, catching her breath. She felt Dave Schumer's presence beside her, his stance protective as he surveyed the chaos. Thick dust coated his jacket. The Russian operative's men lurked behind rubble in the courtyard's perimeter, and a few extremist fighters had crept in from alleys, drawn by rumors of unstoppable power. All now froze at the sight overhead.

The Cherubim's sword radiated heat that turned the air around it into a shimmering veil. Its features were partly obscured by brilliant light, but a sense of indignation flowed from that silent gaze, as if it judged the city's myriad sins and found them wanting. Father Aurelius Lombardi huddled near the Ark's crate, voice lost in the roar of wind swirling around the celestial form. Sister Sabine knelt beside him, both of them still reciting fragments of the chant. Their words faltered under the onslaught of raw majesty.

Tension crackled. Colonel Orlov emerged from behind a toppled column, eyes wild with equal parts wonder and desperation. He hefted a rifle, half-lifting it toward the Cherubim. "You see," he shouted at his men, voice echoing off battered stone, "they lied. The power is real, ours to claim! Focus your fire on that thing before it kills us all!"

A few of his followers exchanged uncertain glances, but Orlov's outraged command spurred them. Rifles lifted, triggers squeezed. Helena flinched, pressing against Dave's shoulder as a flurry of bullets streaked upward. The luminous figure hardly moved. Sparks flared where the projectiles struck its radiant aura, then fizzled to nothing, leaving the Cherubim unscathed.

An eerie hush gripped the onlookers as it descended closer, sword raised. Energy crackled in silent arcs around the Ark, as if centuries of suppressed might were awakening all at once. Dave whispered, voice shaking, "Stay behind cover. Modern weapons may not harm that entity, but stray bullets can kill us."

Helena nodded, swallowing hard. She glimpsed Yusef crouched at the far side of the courtyard, beckoning them. The youth had scouted a possible path to safer ground behind the fortress if the gunfight intensified. She nodded back, letting him know they'd follow as soon as possible.

Above them, the Cherubim hovered with a measured calm. Then a single stroke of its blazing sword lanced downward, slicing across the courtyard's open space. A wave of searing light erupted. Orlov's men cried out, flung in all directions as if hammered by an invisible shockwave. A paramilitary fighter tumbled across broken stones, weapon clattering aside. Another collapsed in a stunned heap, clothes singed.

"The relic's guardian," Father Lombardi called out, voice raw with awe. He scrambled to his feet, holding his trembling hands up. "We must not fight it!"

But Colonel Orlov refused to yield. He staggered upright, face twisted in defiance. "Shoot it again!" he roared, grabbing the rifle of a dazed subordinate. More muzzle flashes erupted, bullets whizzing around the courtyard. The watchmen loyal to Helena and Dave tried to hold fire, uncertain if the Cherubim was friend or foe. They only knew it was unstoppable. The guardian's blade flared once more. Another scorching wave of force hurled Orlov's men deeper into disarray.

Ming Xia ducked behind a broken arch, scanning the conflict with sharp eyes. She waved for her specialists to stand down, pointing at the shining figure. "No sense attacking that. We protect the Ark from any stray shot, or from Orlov's sabotage. Let the Cherubim do what it must."

Helena and Dave edged toward Father Lombardi. She crouched beside the priest, whose eyes were bloodshot from chanting for hours. "Is the Ark safe?" she asked, voice trembling.

He turned to her, lines of fear etched on his face. "It seems the crate is intact, but all that suppressed force is unleashed. The guardian must have awakened from the storm of war. I sense unstoppable wrath near the surface."

He gestured at the relic. The container rattled with each surge, arcs of residual energy dancing across its worn edges. Sister Sabine pressed a damp cloth to her forehead, mouth moving in silent prayers. Meanwhile, swirling shapes like ghostly armies flickered around the luminous being overhead, ephemeral warriors that trotted in and out of sight. The fortress courtyard had become a theater for a cosmic judgment.

Another rocket whooshed from Orlov's side, streaking upward. Helena gasped. Dave pulled her flat. The blazing projectile slammed into the Cherubim's aura with a deafening detonation. Smoke billowed. For an instant, everyone froze, uncertain if the guardian might vanish. Then a gust of blazing light tore through the plume, revealing the being unharmed. Its sword slashed in a silent arc. Flames erupted along the courtyard's perimeter, driving Orlov's squads deeper into panic.

Colonel Orlov cursed in Russian, face twisted as he realized he couldn't kill the creature. In a last fit of desperation, he turned his rifle on the Ark's crate. "If I can't harness the power, I'll end it!" he snarled, unleashing a burst of gunfire toward the chest. The sentinels near the relic tried to block him, but bullets found their mark, splintering the wood's outer layer.

Helena cried out, heart seizing with horror. She expected energy to spew forth in catastrophic fury. But the Cherubim moved faster than thought. It swooped downward, flaming sword sweeping between the bullet stream and the Ark. The rounds ricocheted off a radiant shield conjured around the relic. Dave grabbed Helena's hand in relief. "It's protecting the container."

Even as the guardian defended the chest, it pivoted with a nearly emotionless grace. Its blade pulsed in an incandescent arc. Helena held her breath, certain Orlov would be incinerated in an instant. Instead, a wave of radiant power slammed the colonel across the courtyard. He crashed into a toppled column, weapon spinning from his grasp. Blood trickled from his temple as he struggled to stand.

Confusion reigned among his paramilitaries. Some fled, stumbling through shattered arches. Others aimed grenades at the Cherubim. Each explosive fizzled or detonated harmlessly against that blazing aura. The sentinels from multiple nations stared at the spectacle, both terrified and transfixed. No modern weapon could pierce that shield. The celestial form had effectively neutralized the mortal conflict in this courtyard.

But the war outside raged on. Thunderous shelling rocked the city from other directions. Tanks rumbled through narrow roads. Allied lines clashed with mercenaries. Overhead, swirling storms pummeled the skyline with fierce lightning. The infiltration group realized that even if the Cherubim subdued Orlov here, the entire region teetered on the brink of large-scale destruction.

Dave pressed close to Helena, adrenaline making his voice tremble. "We have to defuse the bigger conflict. The guardian can't be everywhere at once, even if unstoppable. Armies outside might reduce half the city to rubble."

Helena nodded frantically. "But how? The being doesn't speak. We can't direct it to stop the war. Maybe if we unify the sentinels and push for a ceasefire—"

Her words halted when an Israeli soldier rushed over, panting. "Heavily armored units approach from the northern gate! Civilians flee the Old City. They say major powers are mobilizing for a final push. If illusions have awakened, the generals think someone might seize them."

Desperation flared in Dave's eyes. He turned to Ming Xia, who had rejoined them. "We can't let them roll tanks into the city. The Cherubim might respond with lethal force. Civilians are trapped."

Ming Xia's lips tightened. "We have a small window. If the sentinels coordinate, we can sabotage or redirect the heavy units. But we're pinned here by Orlov's men."

Helena recalled Yusef's knowledge of the Old City's serpentine lanes. "He can guide us around the main roads. If we sabotage the leading tanks or artillery, maybe we force a pause. The Cherubim can hold the Ark. We buy time for diplomacy."

Father Lombardi, still kneeling by the crate, overheard. He gave a weak nod. "The guardian protects the relic. If you must leave, it may remain here, fending off Orlov's final efforts."

Sabine caught Helena's arm gently, voice quivering. "Go. Keep this city from total ruin. We'll watch over the Ark. The Cherubim seems bound to defend it."

Helena's throat went tight. She glimpsed Dave's resolve, recognized a chance to save lives beyond the courtyard. "All right. Let's gather a small team, slip out, and disable the biggest guns. If illusions spread across the entire city, there's no telling how many innocents might die."

Ming Xia signaled a handful of sentinels from the U.S. and China. They moved swiftly across the courtyard, stepping over fallen stone blocks. Orlov's men who still clung to weapons were too stunned by the celestial entity to stop them. Colonel Orlov lay dazed by the shattered column, eyes flicking in hazy defiance.

Yusef emerged from behind a collapsed arch, heart pounding but face set with determination. "I know the side streets that lead to the northern gate. We can reach the roads where the tanks roll in."

Dave nodded, scanning the flickering radiance overhead. The Cherubim soared a short distance above the courtyard, its sword blazing. Orlov's squads had lost their appetite for further direct attacks. Helena glanced at Father Lombardi one last time, then turned to run with Dave and Yusef out of the fortress's battered gate, joined by Ming Xia's small group. They left behind the swirling energies and the unstoppable guardian, uncertain if they'd return to see Orlov defeated or the entire city consumed by chaos.

Rain battered them as they wound through narrow alleys littered with rubble. Sirens wailed in the distance, joined by sporadic gunfire. The ground shook from occasional shell impacts. Yusef led the way, weaving them past deserted bazaars and shuttered shops. Charred vehicles and broken glass lined the roads. Dave helped Helena over a smoldering crater, tension evident in every breath.

A short dash brought them to a vantage point overlooking a broad road near the northern entrance. Tanks trundled through the gate, escorted by paramilitaries from various nations—some wearing mismatched uniforms, others carrying advanced weaponry. This was no single nation's force, but a patchwork alliance of opportunists and desperate men. They believed the Ark's supernatural power or some other force awaited them in the city's heart. The infiltration group realized they had to halt these machines, or the Cherubim might strike the entire zone with devastating force.

Ming Xia surveyed the column from behind a fractured doorway. "We have enough explosives to disable a few tanks if we're clever. But if the rest keep rolling, they'll tear into the Old City."

Yusef tugged Helena's sleeve, pointing to a side alley that curved around an old marketplace. "We can flank them. There's a narrow route that leads behind that row of buildings. Then we can plant charges or sabotage treads."

Dave nodded grimly, scanning the handful of sentinels. "We do it quickly,. If fear spreads from whatever's lingering overhead, the crews might panic, but we can't count on that. Let's go."

They crept along the alley, stepping over collapsed market stalls. Distant thunder boomed, accompanied by the glow of artillery beyond the walls. Helena felt panic flutter in her chest but forced it down, recalling the luminous figure they left behind. She had to trust Father Lombardi and Sabine to contain the Ark's volatile energy. One crisis at a time.

They slipped behind the first tank, avoiding the paramilitaries who marched along the flank. Yusef crouched near the left tread. Dave signaled two sentinels to rig small charges. Helena watched, heart pounding, as they worked with silent precision. In moments, they placed enough explosives to shred the treads, halting the tank.

Guttural shouts rang out from the lead vehicle. The infiltration group ducked behind a crumbled wall as the paramilitaries spotted movement. Shots rang out, bullets striking stone. Dave returned fire, picking off one fighter who leaned too far around the turret. Ming Xia's specialists tossed a smoke grenade that billowed thick plumes, obscuring the alley.

"Blow it," Dave hissed, pressing the remote's trigger. A sharp detonation shook the air, tearing the tank's treads. Metal shards flew. The vehicle lurched sideways, immobilized. Chaos erupted as the paramilitaries scrambled for cover. The infiltration group pressed on, hugging the smoke. Another tank crew reversed, unnerved by the ambush or by whatever unearthly presence loomed. The sentinels flung a second explosive under that vehicle, crippling it as well.

Explosions thundered, the street turning into a swirl of debris and yelling men. Helena caught a fleeting glimpse of Orlov's allied paramilitaries in disarray, some screaming about the unstoppable phantom they had glimpsed. Dave tugged her hand, urging her to keep moving. Yusef led them behind a collapsed arch, guiding them deeper into the city's labyrinth. The sentinels repeated small acts of sabotage, crippling the forwardmost hardware. Gunfire rattled from multiple directions, but confusion reigned among the attackers. Many seemed unnerved by the rumored superbeing that dwarfed normal conflict.

At last, the infiltration group retreated to a safer block, stepping into the lee of a battered stone building. Dave wiped sweat from his brow. "We've stalled some tanks, but more might come from other roads. We might have to do the same near the western approach."

Helena leaned against the wall, adrenaline making her legs shake. "If we keep them from central Jerusalem, maybe the Cherubim will remain near the fortress, not leveling the entire region."

Ming Xia nodded curtly. "We should hurry. The storm intensifies." Indeed, swirling thunderheads overhead crackled with unnatural energy, flashes stabbing across the sky. The sentinels reloaded weapons and prepared to move again.

A trembling hush fell over the street as a strange pressure wave pulsed from the direction of the Temple Mount. The infiltration group froze, hearts pounding. Helena felt the ground quiver beneath her feet. A distant roar reverberated, not from artillery but from something far more potent. Dave exchanged a stricken look with her. "The guardian," he muttered.

She swallowed. "We have to see what's happening. Yusef, can you find a route to a vantage?"

The youth exhaled, nodded, and led them up a flight of rickety steps in a half-collapsed building. They emerged onto a rooftop with a partial view of the Temple Mount's battered skyline. Through swirling smoke and flickers of lightning, they saw a blazing figure suspended above the fortress. Streams of golden light arced from its sword, slashing at what looked like entire columns of paramilitaries. Tanks were wrecked or overturned in the fortress yard. The city quaked with each strike.

"Dear God," Helena whispered. The Cherubim's wrath was unstoppable. Showers of sparks flared whenever the entity collided with modern steel. One of Orlov's heavy vehicles fired a shell at the blazing silhouette, only to see it deflected in a coruscating flare. The unstoppable figure responded with a slicing wave of the sword, leaving the machine a ruined husk.

Ming Xia breathed, "Nothing can stand against that."

Dave turned to Helena, concern in his eyes. "If it keeps unleashing that power, the city might be leveled. We have to quell this war before it escalates further."

She nodded, heart pounding. "We do one last push to sabotage key guns. If no massive force enters, maybe the Cherubim won't flatten the entire region."

They prepared to descend, but Yusef touched Helena's arm. "We must help the civilians first. Many are trapped near the western districts. We can guide them to safer routes before your sabotage run." He glanced at Dave, then Ming Xia, voice urgent. "It's the only way. If they stay in the crossfire, no sabotage can save them from stray bombs or that heavenly sword."

She caught Dave's eye. He gave a measured nod. "All right. Let's divert to help them. We can't let innocents be caught in the Cherubim's path."

Ming Xia signaled agreement. They left the rooftop, weaving through bombed alleys toward the western blocks. The sentinels advanced in tight formation, eyes scanning for hostile squads. Gunshots echoed from distant intersections. Sporadic illusions flickered overhead, ephemeral shapes swirling near the Temple Mount. Thunder pounded, the wind howling with unnatural fury.

At a crumbling plaza, they found a cluster of terrified families huddled under an awning. Yusef rushed to them, speaking in hurried words. A mother clutched her children, glancing skyward at each flash of brightness. Dave gently coaxed them to follow. "This way. We'll guide you to a safer sector. Hurry."

The infiltration group led the terrified group through zigzagging back lanes. Explosions boomed somewhere beyond the next row of buildings, but each blast seemed more distant now, as if the unstoppable being's wrath had forced the paramilitaries to scatter. Overhead, flickers of golden radiance occasionally lit the sky, accompanied by roars of fear from retreating men.

After several tense minutes, they ushered the families into an underground shelter, staffed by local volunteers. Helena exhaled relief at the sight of hidden supplies and cots. One older volunteer stepped forward, face wan with strain, but gave them a nod of gratitude. "We'll look after them. The city's battered, but we hold on." Yusef offered a small, reassuring smile before turning back to the infiltration group.

Ming Xia tapped her phone, scanning data. "Artillery beyond the southwestern edge has reduced firing. Possibly the Cherubim's actions made them rethink. We can still sabotage the last big guns if needed. But we must confirm Orlov's forces are truly on the run."

Dave said, "Then let's circle back to the fortress yard. Orlov might still pose a threat if he's alive. That unstoppable force could wipe out everyone, friend or foe."

Helena felt her nerves stretched taut but nodded. "Yusef can lead us. Let's see if we can help Father Lombardi, Sabine, and the guards keep the Ark safe. Maybe the Cherubim will stand down if the city surrenders the relic's conflict."

With each step through battered streets, they glimpsed more devastation. Burned-out vehicles lay askew. Corpses of paramilitaries and allied soldiers alike offered testament to the ferocity of the conflict. The infiltration group pressed on, weapons ready but hearts sickened at the carnage. A deep hush had settled, broken only by distant thunder and the occasional rattle of small-arms fire. Yusef guided them along a winding path that avoided direct lines of sight with potential snipers.

At last they approached the fortress's outer walls. The reek of smoke and gunpowder hung in the air. Rubble littered the courtyard entrance, scorch marks scarring the time-scarred stones. Bodies from Orlov's squads lay strewn around, some still twitching in pain. The troopers from multiple nations crouched behind sandbags or partial barricades, stunned expressions on their faces. Light from the Cherubim glowed beyond them in shimmering waves.

The infiltration group stepped through a collapsed arch into the main courtyard. The unstoppable figure loomed overhead, sword raised, eyes locked on a small cluster of defiant paramilitaries who cowered near the Ark's battered crate. Colonel Orlov knelt with blood staining his face, glaring at the celestial sentinel in furious impotence. Father Lombardi and Sister Sabine stood off to one side, too exhausted to chant further, clinging to each other for balance.

A hush reigned as Helena, Dave, Ming Xia, and Yusef emerged from behind broken columns, guns lowered. The sentinels parted to let them pass. Orlov saw them, nostrils flaring. He spat, "Look what your illusions conjured. This monster kills without mercy."

Above, the guardian fixed its gaze on the colonel, the sword brimming with crackling radiance. Helena felt Dave's hand at her back, steadying her. She stepped forward, voice trembling but determined. "You forced a war, demanded illusions be unleashed. This is what you unleashed. Now it stands in judgment."

Orlov staggered upright, ignoring the bullet wound in his side. "No mortal can withstand that. But I won't beg forgiveness. My men died for a cause I believed in." He raised a trembling pistol as if to shoot the luminous figure again, but Dave lunged in a flash, knocking Orlov's aim aside. A single shot rang out, burying itself in stone.

The Cherubim drifted closer, sword lifted in calm menace. The last paramilitaries threw down their weapons, terror etched on their faces.

Colonel Orlov breathed raggedly, too broken to fight. Dave pinned him, wresting away the pistol. Helena joined them, heart pounding. She stared up at the celestial being, which stared back with an intensity that felt like the weight of ages. Father Lombardi shuddered, tears on his cheeks.

An electric charge sizzled in the air, arcs dancing around the guardian's blazing aura. Then a deep voice resounded, not in audible words but in pulses that every soul felt in their core. It was a pronouncement of condemnation, an unspoken statement that humanity's thirst for the Ark's destructive potential had brought them to this brink. The sentinels, Orlov's men, everyone sank to their knees under that psychic pressure.

Helena's breath came in gasps. Dave pressed closer to her side, eyes filled with awe. The unstoppable figure turned its gaze to the Ark, as if lamenting that such power had caused so much ruin. A swirl of luminous shapes flickered in the courtyard, half-formed echoes of biblical might, swirling outward from the crate as the guardian channeled them.

Ming Xia's specialists watched with wide eyes. The storm above raged, but the celestial presence stood unmoved. Helena realized they had reached a turning point, poised between further devastation and potential mercy. She found her voice, though it wavered. "Please," she whispered to the blazing shape, "enough. There's no need for more slaughter."

No direct reply emerged, but the sword's glow softened fractionally, as if acknowledging her plea. Colonel Orlov sank in defeat, panting. Dave stepped back from him, tension coiled, prepared in case the Russian tried another desperate move. The sentinels formed a ring around the courtyard, uncertain how to quell a cosmic force.

From behind collapsed masonry, Father Lombardi approached, each step unsteady. He lifted his trembling arms, voice shaken. "I beg you, divine guardian, remember the Ark's purpose. Spare these misguided souls. Let the war end."

The Cherubim tilted its head, that silent gaze unreadable. Then it turned toward Orlov's battered form. Energy swelled, a coruscating brilliance coiling around the sword. Orlov let out a choked sob, his bravado shattered. He seemed to brace for an annihilating strike. Silence stretched, broken only by distant thunder.

A thunderous detonation rocked the courtyard from outside—some lingering shell fired by a far-off artillery piece. The ephemeral creatures swirling around the celestial being quivered, as if the cosmic presence recoiled from humankind's refusal to cease violence. The sentinels cowered. Orlov's men whimpered. Dave clenched Helena's hand. She realized in that instant that no one, not even this unstoppable sentinel, could truly force every soldier outside the city to lay down arms. The war might continue unless someone took bold action.

She turned to Dave, swallowing her fear. "We can't wait. We have to coordinate a total ceasefire. Let's contact all the armies. We show them the Cherubim is real, unstoppable. They must stand down or risk total destruction." She cast a quick glance at Lombardi. "We need your help, Father."

Sabine caught her breath, regaining composure. "Yes. A broadcast, maybe. If the sentinels film the Cherubim, prove illusions overshadow any mortal power—maybe the generals will halt."

Ming Xia nodded. "We can patch it through allied channels. A live feed from the courtyard. Colonel Orlov's paramilitaries are undone. He can confirm the unstoppable guardian. That might sway other leaders."

Helena and Dave stared at the luminous figure, which now hovered more placidly, sword lowered. The city beyond still raged with sporadic shelling, but the fortress yard had turned into a stunned hush. The infiltration group moved swiftly, commandeering a battered communication console. Cameras from allied sentinels whirred to life. In a flurry, they set up a feed. Father Lombardi spoke to the lens in multiple languages, voice cracking but fervent, describing the Ark's guardian and urging a universal stand-down. The Cherubim lingered overhead, silent lightning dancing across its form, a living testament that no army could overthrow its wrath.

Orlov, trembling, was pressed into speaking as well, forced to admit on camera that illusions had indeed manifested and the Cherubim could not be overcome. His men lowered their heads in shame or shock, rifles abandoned. The sentinels from the U.S., Israel, and China transmitted the feed across global networks. Dave carefully typed in codes while Helena assisted, heart pounding with every beep. If the entire world saw this unstoppable force, perhaps the armies on the outskirts would relent. The infiltration group had nothing else to offer but the truth: continued aggression spelled doom.

Minutes dragged by. The Cherubim hovered, vigilant, sword still blazing but less violent. Father Lombardi slumped against a crate, tears on his cheeks as he prayed. Sabine pressed a canteen of water to his lips. Helena held Dave's gaze, her own eyes damp from the sheer relief that the cosmic fury might spare them if the warring factions yielded.

Suddenly, a hush fell across the courtyard. The troopers scanning radios reported that allied lines outside the city had gone quiet. Gunfire receded. Helicopters circled uncertainly. The infiltration group realized that the broadcast likely stunned the generals. No illusions were needed now to show that the Ark's guardian was beyond mortal defiance. Dave exhaled, tension draining from his shoulders. He leaned into Helena for a fleeting moment, whispering, "We did it, or at least we gave them the chance to stand down."

She nodded, voice catching. "Yes, for now."

A distant explosion shook the city, but it sounded more like the last echoes of a retreat. The sentinels on the ramparts signaled that paramilitaries were withdrawing in confusion. Tanks reversed out of the gates, battered columns of Orlov's men fleeing the unstoppable power they had so foolishly provoked.

In the courtyard, the Cherubim's gaze swept across the remaining fighters, gleaning their acceptance of the caretaker vow. Colonel Orlov collapsed onto scorched rubble, burying his face in trembling hands. The sentinels collected weapons from any stragglers. Ming Xia's specialists assisted, disarming the final holdouts. Yusef sank to his knees, tears of relief mingling with exhaustion. The infiltration group recognized the city might yet see a final calm.

A swirl of radiant wind encircled the cherubic being as it turned its silent focus to the Ark's crate. Sparks coursed across the wood, but no illusions billowed forth. Perhaps the relic's guardian recognized that mortal war was subsiding—for the moment. Helena suspected the cosmic presence had not fully concluded its purpose, but at least the city was no longer an open battlefield.

Orlov's paramilitaries groaned in defeat. Lombardi found enough strength to approach the luminous sentinel, arms extended in supplication. Sabine followed, ledger forgotten. The infiltration group, sentinels from multiple nations, and the battered remnants of Orlov's men all beheld the blazing entity, hearts pounding with awe. It stood as judge and savior, reminding them that some powers lie beyond mortal hands.

As dawn's full light touched the fortress yard, the unstoppable guardian remained in place, sword glowing. Helena realized the final crisis was not over. War might fade from these walls, but the city beyond still harbored armies. The cosmic champion had forced an immediate retreat, yet the entire region's fate hung on whether the Ark's caretaker would continue to wield destructive might or ascend with it out of mortal reach.

She exchanged a glance with Dave, a silent vow that they'd stand together in whatever came next. Then she turned to Father Lombardi, voice low. "What now?"

He inhaled, gazing at the incandescent figure. "We wait on the city's armies to truly stand down. Then we see if the Cherubim reclaims the Ark, removing it from humanity's reach."

No one spoke further. The troopers paused in a fragile truce with the battered paramilitaries. Orlov sat in broken humiliation, unarmed and unwilling to lift his head. The swirling energies around the Cherubim dimmed slightly, as though it sensed an ebb in humanity's aggression. Another hush blanketed the courtyard, leaving only the hiss of wind and the faint rumble of storms in the distance.

Chapter 27

Sunrise draped the Old City in an uneasy glow, painting rubble-strewn streets with fractured light. Thick plumes of smoke drifted over Jerusalem's skyline, remnants of bombardments that had battered neighborhoods through the night. Damp wind carried the scents of scorched stone and shattered mortar. The fortress courtyard—where the winged champion had manifested in radiant wrath—lay calmer now, though tension lingered beneath the hushed surface.

Helena Carter leaned against a half-toppled column, breathing through exhaustion that weighed on her limbs. Dust coated her clothes from the previous day's chaos, and her hair clung to her forehead in damp strands. A cluster of allied watchmen guarded the Ark's crate, battered from stray gunfire but still sealed, never fully revealed. Father Aurelius Lombardi rested a few steps away, propped against the Ark, eyes closed in silent prayer. Sister Sabine hovered near him, pressing a damp cloth to his brow as he recovered from his unrelenting chant.

They all knew the unstoppable sentinel still hovered overhead, a glowing presence that had forced Colonel Orlov's paramilitaries to withdraw. The luminous figure had not vanished, nor had it obliterated them entirely. Instead, it lingered, sword in hand, wreathed in energy that sparked like living lightning. Armies outside the gates had glimpsed that being through sporadic broadcasts, leading to a partial stand-down. Yet war flickered at the periphery, uncertain and volatile.

Dave Schumer approached Helena, setting a gentle hand on her shoulder. Tension crimped his usually stoic features, though relief gleamed in his eyes to find her still in one piece. "I just talked with Ming Xia. The major powers remain along the outskirts. They're not pressing in, but neither are they pulling back. They wait to see if the blazing entity poses a threat to them or if it stands solely against Orlov's men."

She exhaled a shaky breath, letting his presence steady her. "Nobody wants to tangle with that force if they can help it. But the look-outs say plenty of extremist pockets remain. One rogue group might provoke the champion's fury again."

He nodded, glancing up at the fortress rampart where that being's silhouette shimmered behind swirling storm clouds. "We can't let that happen. Maybe if we coordinate a citywide sweep to disarm holdouts, we keep the champion from unleashing more devastation."

From a corner of the courtyard, Yusef Nasir walked over, voice subdued yet determined. "I can lead sentinels to the pockets of militants. My neighbors talk about men from lesser-known factions creeping through side alleys. If we show them the champion or broadcast that unstoppable might, maybe they'll surrender."

Helena managed a small, grateful smile at the youth's courage. "You've done more than most grown soldiers. Are you sure you can keep going?"

He looked away, guilt flickering in his gaze. "My family is safe, hidden in a shop's basement with neighbors. I need to help others. The city still trembles."

Dave let out a slow breath. "We'll go with you, or at least some of us. We can't leave the Ark unguarded entirely, though. Father Lombardi and Sabine will keep watch, along with a strong contingent of sentinels. We'll do a sweep, gather or disarm the last extremist pockets. We show them the unstoppable champion is here—maybe that stops them from doing anything reckless."

Yusef nodded. "We should move quickly. Some diehards still dream of seizing that sealed crate, believing they can tap the phenomenon's power."

Helena looked at Father Lombardi. "Are you all right? Can you remain near the Ark with Sabine while we go?"

The Jesuit priest lifted his head, weariness etched on his features. "Yes, child. I'll stay. The champion might accept my presence at the relic's side. If anything stirs again, I'll try to calm it." He looked beyond them, eyes drifting to the blazing figure. "Though we all sense it doesn't need me. That being stands guard on its own terms."

She rested a hand on Lombardi's shoulder in silent gratitude, then turned to Dave, pulse still unsteady. "Let's gather a team. If these pockets remain, they might do something drastic."

He squeezed her hand. "Then we end the threat before more blood is shed."

They collected a small squad of allied sentinels: some from the U.S. detail, a few from China under Ming Xia's direction, and an Israeli officer volunteering local knowledge. Yusef led them out of the fortress. The luminous guardian overhead remained perched near the Ark, glowing sword lowered but still brimming with potential. Corpses from Orlov's final attempt lay scattered across the courtyard, a silent testament to that unstoppable force's wrath. The sentinels stepped carefully around the debris, hearts heavy with the memory of last night's carnage.

Once they emerged into the Old City's narrow lanes, the group found a hushed landscape painted in morning's half-light. Broken masonry and burned-out vehicles testified to the battles that had raged across these streets. Some shops still smoldered, shutters blasted apart. Occasional civilians peered from hidden doorways, eyes filled with fear. Yusef spoke in low tones, assuring them that the champion had halted Orlov's push. Dave asked them to remain indoors until the guards declared the area secure.

They split into smaller search units, each guided by a local. Helena stayed with Dave, accompanied by Ming Xia and two troopers from Israel. Yusef led them through twisting alleys, stepping over scattered rubble. They found the remnants of a paramilitary group holed up in a crumbling hostel. The guards took aim, demanding the men drop their weapons. The haggard fighters hesitated until Yusef told them of the unstoppable being overhead. The mention of that radiant sentinel made them blanch, guns clattering to the floor. They surrendered, trembling at the memory of unstoppable fury.

With each small band of combatants subdued, the sentinels collected arms and directed the detainees to a makeshift holding center in a shuttered civic building. No one dared put up a real fight once they learned about the unstoppable champion. The infiltration group pressed on, clearing blocks that had been contested hours earlier, stepping past bullet holes in walls and the remains of short-lived barricades.

In one deserted square, Helena paused, listening to distant echoes of artillery. A swirl of wind carried dust across battered stones. Dave placed a comforting palm on her back. "You doing all right?"

She nodded, though her voice shook. "It's surreal. The unstoppable presence saved us from total annihilation, but the city's not at peace. I keep expecting a final spark to set everything ablaze."

He squeezed her shoulder gently. "We're close. Let's trust Father Lombardi to hold the Ark's ground and that unstoppable guardian to stand watch. If we keep the rest from stirring trouble, we might see a day without more bloodshed."

Yusef called them from across the street, urging them onward. Ming Xia followed at a brisk pace. They turned a corner into a wide passage that once bustled with merchants. Now it lay hollowed out, stands toppled, goods strewn underfoot. At the far end, a cluster of men in mismatched attire crouched behind crates, glancing over stolen rifles. Dave motioned for everyone to duck. Helena's heart pounded as they approached carefully.

The troopers fanned out, flanking the men. Yusef stepped forward, voice steady despite the tension. "You can't keep fighting. That champion above the Temple Mount destroyed Orlov's squads. Lay down your weapons. Surrender."

At first, they scoffed, one brandishing a battered assault rifle. Ming Xia emerged with her sidearm raised, speaking in a low, menacing tone. "We have no desire to kill you, but if you try to cause havoc, that unstoppable force will respond."

A wave of panic flashed across the fighters' faces. One peered above the rooftops, glimpsing the faint glow that lingered near the fortress. They placed weapons on the ground, raising hands in defeat. The sentinels moved in to secure them, ushering them into custody with minimal fuss. Helena exhaled relief, scanning each terrified face. Even these men realized they stood no chance against a celestial champion that incinerated tanks with a single sweep.

The infiltration group repeated this pattern for hours, sweeping from one battered quarter to the next. Some extremist pockets had fled or deserted upon hearing rumors of unstoppable wrath. A few needed only the sentinels' stern commands to yield. By midday, the Old City quieted. Sporadic gunfire outside the walls died down. Allies from multiple nations formed a shaky truce, each unwilling to press further after seeing that unstoppable sentinel broadcast across the world.

Yusef guided them back toward the fortress as the afternoon sun slanted. Exhaustion gripped every muscle in Helena's body, but she trudged on, comforted by Dave's silent support. Ming Xia parted ways, leading her own men to finalize arrests near the southern gate. Yusef remained with Helena and Dave, each step echoing on cracked pavement. They weaved through side streets until the fortress rampart loomed ahead, faint glow still visible above it.

When they reentered the courtyard, a hush enveloped them. Father Lombardi and Sister Sabine sat near the Ark's container, hands clasped. The unstoppable Cherubim drifted overhead, sword lowered, bright aura pulsing with a calmer rhythm. Allied look-outs milled about, guiding the last of Orlov's disarmed men to a corner for medical aid or detention. Helena felt a surge of relief to see no renewed violence.

She approached Lombardi, kneeling beside him. He gazed up at the glowing figure. "We heard no further conflict here?" she asked.

He shook his head, voice hushed. "None. Colonel Orlov was carried away on a stretcher, unconscious from his wounds. The unstoppable being remained watchful but didn't strike again. The city outside grows quiet, I'm told. Soldiers from multiple armies hold back, unsure if they should risk any confrontation."

Dave dropped onto a broken chunk of masonry, letting out a breath. "We've neutralized rogue elements in the Old City. Yusef was invaluable. I think the champion's demonstration broke any illusions that men could conquer the relic's might." He paused, then grimaced. "I used that forbidden word. Sorry."

Helena's mouth twitched at the slip, but she quickly refocused. "So what now? The unstoppable force stands guard, but does it plan to remain forever? We can't guess its mind."

Sabine looked at them, eyes raw with fatigue. "I've tried to glean some sense from Father Lombardi's weather-scarred texts. The champion appears only at humanity's darkest brink, then departs once the threat subsides. If armies truly stand down, maybe it will ascend with the Ark."

Helena heard the faint hollowness in her own voice, overshadowed by relief that the day might end without further carnage. She turned to Yusef, offering a warm nod of gratitude. "You saved so many by guiding sentinels. Thank you."

He looked away, cheeks reddening. "I just want my city to be safe. This unstoppable presence might keep the war away, at least for a little while."

Dave shifted closer to Helena, letting his fingers brush hers in a subtle show of affection. The sentinels around them pretended not to notice.

The two had survived a cataclysmic struggle, forging a bond that no words could fully capture. She drew comfort from that small contact.

Evening settled with an uneasy calm. The unstoppable guardian continued its silent vigil over the Ark. Allied lines outside the city remained uncertain, each side unwilling to test that cosmic wrath. Delegates from various nations carefully entered the Old City, seeking to confirm the unstoppable champion's presence. Some carried cameras, broadcasting live to global audiences. Others came with trembling hearts, hoping to see if the city might again open for negotiations.

Father Lombardi, though weak, joined Sister Sabine to greet those delegates. He recounted the story of how the relic's caretaker had appeared when humanity's conflict peaked. The sentinels stationed near the battered container stood guard, half in awe. Dave and Helena hovered on the outskirts, keeping an eye on any new arrivals. Colonel Orlov was gone, presumably receiving medical care. Without him, the paramilitaries lacked leadership. The unstoppable figure above the fortress had broken their will.

Night fell, the city's wounded blocks lit by sporadic floodlights or flickering power lines. Helicopters circled at a distance, searchlights revealing columns of foreign troops who waited in tense formations. Word came that high-level negotiations might resume, spurred by fear of the unstoppable being. Helena found Dave in a corner of the courtyard, leaning against a battered wall to gather his thoughts. She slipped beside him, letting her exhaustion show.

He glanced at her, concern mingling with relief. "We got through the worst day of our lives. The unstoppable sentinel stands watch, but how long does that last?"

She gazed at the swirling glow above the Ark. "No idea. Maybe until the city's armies fully withdraw. Or until it senses no further threat."

His expression softened. "You nearly gave your life for this. So did many sentinels. We lost so many. But seeing you safe... that's all that kept me going."

Her heart gave a flutter. They had fought side by side, crossing half the globe from Russia to China, culminating in these battered walls. She touched his cheek gently. "I never want to face that force alone again. Having you here... it anchored me." She caught herself on that forbidden word, replacing it with, "It kept me steady."

He smiled, weaving their fingers together. "We stand together, come what may."

They allowed a quiet moment. The battered courtyard seemed almost tranquil under the unstoppable champion's glow. Yusef emerged from behind a cluster of sentinels, beckoning them. "A local official wants to speak with you. He says the outside armies might gather for a final attempt if they fear the unstoppable being has no limit."

Helena and Dave exchanged a grim glance, stepping away from their private moment. Duty called. Together, they joined the official near the gate, listening as he explained that allied military lines had stationed artillery aimed at key entry points. Each side was hesitant to retreat, believing the unstoppable entity might set out from the fortress at any moment. A standoff threatened to drag on, strangling the city in an uneasy blockade.

Ming Xia's voice cut through the gloom as she joined them. "We need a conclusive stand-down. If the unstoppable presence leaves, the armies might surge again. If it remains, they might panic. We're in limbo."

Helena exhaled. "Maybe tomorrow we can broadcast a final statement, urging full withdrawal. The watchmen can demonstrate that the champion's role is to reclaim the Ark, not wage war on everyone. Yusef, you can add your testimony about the unstoppable power driving out Orlov's men from these streets."

He nodded vigorously. "People trust local voices. They saw what happened. I'll speak publicly if needed."

The infiltration group agreed to coordinate a press conference of sorts at first light, trusting the unstoppable guardian to hold any new aggressors at bay through the night. They assigned sentinels to the fortress perimeter, Dave and Helena among them, ensuring no rogue group tried a midnight assault on the relic's caretaker. Father Lombardi and Sister Sabine returned to the Ark, dozing in shifts as the unstoppable being hovered overhead, sword gleaming in quiet vigilance.

Morning arrived in subdued pastel over a city exhausted by war. Civilians crept from hidden shelters, glancing warily at the ramparts. Smoke still drifted from outer neighborhoods, where battered columns of foreign troops waited. The unstoppable sentinel cast a gentle glow in the dawn haze, an eternal reminder that no mortal army could seize the Ark by force.

In a battered courtyard near the fortress gate, the infiltration group set up the final attempt at public reassurance. Cameras from allied nations captured Yusef's account in Hebrew and English, describing how that unstoppable champion subdued Orlov's squads. He urged any lingering fighters to stand down. Dave and Helena stepped forward, summarizing how the cosmic force had shielded the Ark from destruction, cautioning that any renewed assault might trigger devastation on a scale no conventional weapon could match.

Envoys from major powers hovered behind the cameras, scanning the unstoppable being at a distance. Everyone sensed the unstoppable champion's silent gaze. Ming Xia reaffirmed China's stance that the relic must remain unclaimed, sealed from mortal hands. Father Lombardi—drained but steady—blessed the assembled sentinels, praying for a permanent end to hostilities.

Then, as the press conference concluded, a tense hush spread among the delegates. Word arrived that certain extremist generals along the border refused to withdraw, citing fear that the unstoppable sentinel might move beyond the city. The infiltration group's hearts sank. If those generals launched any last-ditch assault, the champion might retaliate, endangering everyone.

Helena clenched her fists, cursing the stubbornness of militaristic pride. Dave placed a reassuring grip on her shoulder, his own face grim. "We can't force them to see reason from here. We rely on allied leaders to hold them back."

Nearby sentinels exchanged anxious murmurs. The unstoppable figure shimmered overhead, sword angled downward. Father Lombardi approached the infiltration group, voice trembling. "I sense the relic's caretaker might soon leave, but it won't depart while armies mass outside. We must ensure no final push occurs."

Ming Xia scanned her phone. "Some intelligence suggests a rogue faction among the combined forces might try a last strike, believing the unstoppable champion can be overwhelmed by advanced weapons if they gather enough firepower. They might not have learned from Orlov's downfall."

Helena's stomach turned. "That could trigger a cosmic response. The entire city would become a battlefield, unstoppable or not. Innocents in these streets can't face another wave."

Dave rubbed the back of his neck, tension sapping his usual calm. "We'll have to sabotage or neutralize any attempt before it ignites. Yusef can help. Let's coordinate with allied lines to pinpoint the rogue faction's location."

So the infiltration group readied themselves once more. Gunfire had ceased in most quarters, but ominous quiet reigned outside the gates. They parted ways with Father Lombardi, Sabine, and a core group protecting the Ark. The unstoppable guardian maintained watch, a silent sentinel that seemed to hum with cosmic energy, ready to react if conflict escalated anew.

Dave, Helena, Ming Xia, and a handful of look-outs slipped out of the city to meet allied liaison officers at a strategic vantage. Yusef tagged along, wary but determined to protect his home. They picked paths through the outer ring of devastation—blackened husks of military vehicles, burnt-out shells of homes. Overhead, helicopters circled at a distance, occasionally shining lights across the battered terrain. The unstoppable champion's glow receded behind them, though it remained visible as a distant radiance above the Temple Mount.

At a forward command post, the infiltration group gathered around a table of maps. Officers from multiple nations muttered about a rumored rogue general planning to mount a final assault, hoping to break the unstoppable champion's defense with large-scale ballistic missiles. The group recognized the unimaginable risk: if advanced warheads hammered the city, the champion's retribution might flatten half the region, igniting unstoppable destruction.

Helena felt her stomach tighten with dread. "We must stop that last attack. Maybe sabotage the warheads or redirect them. If that unstoppable being sees an existential threat, it might expand its wrath beyond Orlov's debacle. We might face a global cataclysm."

Dave turned to an American major, voice taut. "Do we have coordinates on this rogue general's location? We can't rely on illusions or cosmic might. We'll do a covert insertion, neutralize or sabotage the launchers before they fire."

Ming Xia and the allied sentinels concurred. The major nodded, pointing to a chart. "Reports place them near a ruined industrial zone west of the city. They have trucks with specialized launch platforms, apparently set up for short-range ballistic missiles. The unstoppable champion's presence forced the bigger armies to stand down, but these rogue men want to see if they can shatter that being with overwhelming force."

Yusef's eyes flashed with alarm. "If they strike from outside the city, the unstoppable guardian might retaliate with everything it has. My neighbors, my family... they won't survive."

Helena placed a hand on his shoulder. "We'll do everything possible to stop them." She turned to Dave. "Let's gather a small strike team. Ming Xia, you come. We sabotage these launchers or talk them down."

He nodded, gaze set with grim resolve. "We do it quickly. If they see us coming, they might launch immediately."

With hurried coordination, they formed a unit of about ten sentinels: Dave, Helena, Ming Xia, Yusef, and a handful of U.S. and Israeli specialists. Each carried minimal gear to move fast under the enemy's radar.

They set off in an armored truck, weaving through battered highways that circled the Old City, accompanied by local scouts who guided them around crater-strewn routes. The unstoppable champion's glow receded behind them as they left the city limits, replaced by an eerie hush across the charred landscape.

At length, they approached the industrial zone, once lined with warehouses and factories. Now, many buildings lay collapsed or burned from earlier bombardments. A distant hum of machinery drifted on the wind. Dave signaled the driver to kill the lights. The infiltration group disembarked, creeping forward under cover of dusk. Low clouds rolled overhead, occasionally lit by faint lightning from the still-lingering storm above Jerusalem.

They spotted the silhouettes of large launch vehicles in a cracked parking lot near a ruined factory. Guards patrolled, rifles in hand, scanning for threats. The infiltration team crouched behind twisted debris, analyzing positions. Two ballistic missiles were visible atop special trucks. Crews fussed with control panels, hooking them to portable generators.

Helena's heart hammered. One launch might provoke unstoppable retaliation from the champion. Dave whispered directions for sentinels to flank from the left. Ming Xia led a second group to circle from the right. Yusef stayed behind with Helena and Dave, offering local insights. They waited for the sentinels to get into position.

Suddenly, harsh voices erupted near the truck. A gaunt man with a aged uniform barked orders. He must be the rogue general. Helena caught fragments of his rant: talk of unstoppable cosmic intimidation in the Old City, how a single missile might prove humanity could defy it. She shuddered at such arrogance. Dave tensed beside her, readying his rifle.

In a burst of coordinated movement, the infiltration group stormed forward. The troopers opened controlled fire, picking off sentries near the outer perimeter. The rogue general spun in shock, barking for his men to return fire. Some scrambled for cover, bullets whizzing through the night. Helena and Dave advanced behind a half-collapsed metal barrier, exchanging shots with the startled defenders. Yusef ducked low, pointing out a side route to the vehicles.

Ming Xia's team flanked from the other side, tossing smoke grenades that blinded the missile crews. The infiltration group pressed the advantage, rapidly disabling one missile's control panel with well-placed gunfire. Sparks flew, cables severed. The look-outs overcame the guards, forcing them to the ground at gunpoint.

But the rogue general, eyes burning with fanaticism, lunged for the second launcher's control. He slammed a hand on the ignition sequence. Helena's heart lurched. Dave fired but missed as the man ducked. The missile began whining, a high-pitched spool-up. The guards cried out in alarm. If that device launched toward the unstoppable champion, the entire city might face annihilation.

In desperation, Dave and Helena sprinted across open ground, bullets chewing up the asphalt. Yusef followed, huddling behind a scrap of metal. Ming Xia's men pinned the final guards, but the general shielded himself behind the truck's wheels. With a triumphant sneer, he hammered a code into the console.

"No!" Helena shouted, adrenaline surging. She dived behind the launcher, rummaging for a way to cut power. Dave joined her, eyes wide with urgency. They yanked open a panel, searching for critical wires, while overhead the missile's guidance array whirred. The rogue general rose for one last attempt to shoot them. Ming Xia's bullet found him first, dropping him in a sputtering gasp.

Time ticked with excruciating speed. Dave frantically tugged cables. Sparks spit from the device. Yusef rushed up to them, pointing to an emergency lever. Helena yanked it. The motor coughed, stuttering the launch sequence. Dave jammed a combat knife into the drive mechanism, severing the servo that aimed the warhead. Another pop of electricity, a hiss of escaping fluid. The missile's spool-up whine faded, leaving an acrid smell in the air.

They collapsed behind the truck, hearts hammering. The sentinels overcame the last pockets of resistance. The infiltration group exhaled collectively, gazing at the disabled missile. Helena's hands shook, tears threatening at the corners of her eyes. One more second and that unstoppable champion might have unleashed unstoppable fury upon the entire region.

The team took a moment to confirm no further launchers lurked. The rogue general lay bleeding on the asphalt, gurgling curses. Dave and a watcher disarmed him, calling for an Israeli medic to see if he could be saved. Helena sank onto a chunk of concrete, trembling with the realization they had narrowly prevented a final cataclysm.

At dawn, the infiltration group radioed allied lines that the last rogue threat was neutralized. Soldiers from multiple nations arrived to secure the site. The unstoppable champion's presence remained near the Temple Mount, glowing in the distance. War had not resumed. With the ballistic threat averted, the entire region seemed to slump in exhausted relief. The infiltration group traveled back toward Jerusalem, once more hoping to find a city not overshadowed by frantic conflict.

Upon returning, they found the fortress courtyard still dominated by that silent sentinel. Father Lombardi greeted them with weary smiles. The guards around the Ark had heard of the infiltration group's success. Colonel Orlov was reportedly stable, though imprisoned. Artillery fell quiet across the outskirts, each army reconsidering further aggression.

Helena's chest tightened with emotion. She gazed at the unstoppable figure that had once wielded such terrifying force, now hovering in a calm stance. Dave slipped an arm around her waist, voice low. "We did it. We cut off that last attempt."

She leaned her head against his shoulder, allowing a tearful sigh. "Thank you... for everything. We might finally see an end."

He guided her aside, letting the sentinels handle daily tasks. A half-collapsed arch offered a sliver of privacy. In the soft morning glow, she and Dave exchanged a look that spoke of shared triumph and trauma. He rested a hand on her cheek. "I wasn't sure we'd make it. But you gave me hope."

Her voice emerged on a whisper. "You saved me—again and again. If we ever find normalcy after this, I—" She hesitated, heart pounding. "I don't want to lose you."

A small, tender laugh escaped him, despite the grim setting. "You won't. Maybe we can see each other in simpler times. No unstoppable guardians or mortal wars."

Her lips curved in a shaky smile. She leaned in, pressing her forehead to his. Silence held them for a moment, the tension of near-death replaced by a precious warmth. The guards around them maintained respectful distance, perhaps noticing the pair's closeness but not intruding. Yusef emerged from behind a broken pillar, caught sight of them, and turned away, letting them have that moment.

Dave pulled her into a gentle embrace, a rare softness in the battered courtyard. She wrapped her arms around him, tears glistening on her lashes. For the first time in weeks, hope felt tangible. The unstoppable sentinel remained overhead, but the city had survived, thanks in part to their determination.

Gradually, they parted, returning to the fortress yard. Soldiers secured prisoner lines, while Father Lombardi and Sister Sabine checked the Ark. The unstoppable champion hovered in quiet luminescence. Yusef joined the infiltration group, reporting that local families were emerging from shelters. The Old City had begun to awaken to a day without shellfire or roving paramilitaries.

The infiltration group realized the unstoppable being might soon depart if no further threat stirred. Dave and Helena gazed at it with mingled relief and caution. The sentinels near the relic wondered if the champion would vanish in a blaze of glory or remain until global powers officially pulled back.

Night fell with a subdued hush. Campfires flickered in corners of the courtyard, look-outs sharing weary smiles and stories of near-misses. Ming Xia and the infiltration group huddled, finalizing the distribution of squads to quell any last extremist pockets. Yusef volunteered once more to guide them at dawn if needed. The unstoppable sentinel maintained its silent watch, sword lowered, radiating faint pulses of golden light that danced on the Ark's surface.

Helena and Dave found a corner of the courtyard to settle for the night. The hush gave them space to reflect. She rested her head on his shoulder, eyes drifting shut. He squeezed her hand, gratitude and affection shining in his eyes.

She murmured, "It feels surreal. We faced unstoppable cosmic fury, and we're still here. The Ark stands sealed, and the champion awaits some final resolution."

He kissed her brow. "No unstoppable forces or armies can break your spirit, apparently. That's a rare gift."

She let a rueful laugh slip. "I'm just relieved we might see peace. My heart can't take more nights like these."

They drifted into a fragile sleep, lulled by the occasional murmurs of sentinels and the faint glow above. The unstoppable being soared in place, a silent guardian that refused to abandon its aged charge. No bombs fell that night. No artillery shook the city. The war beyond the gates had all but halted, at least for now, as rumors confirmed no one dared provoke that champion further.

Morning arrived with a gentle warmth, the first time in many days that the sky wore a peaceful hue. Sunlight slid across the shattered fortress courtyard, illuminating the sentinels as they stirred from restless dozing. Father Lombardi rose stiffly, stepping to the Ark to recite a quiet prayer of gratitude. Sister Sabine wrapped a shawl around her shoulders, eyes scanning the unstoppable sentinel's silent form. Yusef approached Helena and Dave, offering them a small bag of bread from a reopened bakery—his first smile in days a spark of normalcy amid the ruins.

She tore a piece, passing half to Dave. He gave her a faint grin, chewing absently. The sentinels swapped fatigued nods. They had survived a cataclysm. Now, the unstoppable champion waited for some final signal of humanity's contrition or continued greed. The infiltration group sensed that the next few hours or days would reveal if the city would truly see lasting peace or if a final surge of prideful generals might provoke Armageddon.

Chapter 28

Morning light spread over Jerusalem's ravaged skyline, illuminating a sea of broken walls and abandoned vehicles. The unstoppable sentinel still hovered above the fortress courtyard, glimmering sword in hand, its presence a stark reminder that no mortal army could seize the Ark. In battered streets below, watchmen cleared debris while local families emerged from hideouts. A tentative calm had fallen, yet tension crackled, for heavy weaponry remained on the outskirts—armies uncertain whether to trust this fragile peace.

Helena Carter and Dave Schumer stood near the fortress gate, conferring with allied officers from various nations. The sentinels had spent the early hours securing roads, ensuring no extremist cells lurked in the Old City. Yusef acted as their guide, weaving them past shuttered shops and collapsed arches. He now lingered at Helena's side, eyes darting anxiously at the faint glow high above the fortress.

One of the officers, a tall figure in American fatigues, gestured at a radio console set up on a makeshift table. "We've established contact with the outside armies. Some are pulling back, but a few generals remain unconvinced the unstoppable champion won't expand its wrath. They demand the Ark be surrendered for disposal or locked in international custody."

Ming Xia, scanning a worn notebook of intelligence, shot a skeptical look. "They think they can simply bury or destroy the relic? The unstoppable presence clearly outstrips normal power. Attempting to dismantle it might incite cosmic retribution."

A hush followed her statement. Father Aurelius Lombardi approached from behind them, robes streaked with dust. "The caretaker has no interest in mortal armies. If these generals press the matter, they'll provoke unstoppable might again." He paused, shoulders drooping. "And many innocents will suffer. We must persuade them to stand down."

The infiltration group recognized that precarious line once again: fear of unstoppable cosmic fury, balanced against the pride of militaries unwilling to relinquish control. Dave exhaled sharply, scanning the horizon. "We can do another broadcast, urging a full ceasefire. Show them the unstoppable champion remains neutral unless provoked."

Helena nodded, voice subdued. "Let's do it quickly, before any rogue officer seizes the chance to escalate. The city can't take another wave of destruction."

They set about preparing a second broadcast. Cameras from multiple nations were rigged in the courtyard, capturing that blazing sentinel as it drifted silently above the Ark's battered container. Father Lombardi stood in the shot, one hand on the chest, the other raised in a gesture of reassurance. Sabine hovered at his side, ready to translate. Dave and Helena moved behind them, offering the look-outs a calm front. If the unstoppable being glimpsed the sincerity of their intent, perhaps it would not strike.

Yusef stepped forward, heart pounding, to give a local testimonial in both Hebrew and English. He spoke of how the unstoppable guardian had halted Colonel Orlov's paramilitaries, saving countless lives in the Old City. The sentinels relayed this feed to the waiting armies outside. The infiltration group prayed that the final holdouts would see reason.

A tense hour passed. Soldiers in the courtyard mingled with local medics, helping the wounded. The unstoppable figure remained overhead, sword angled downward, as if it lingered in case more aggression flared. Allied lines beyond the city reported small withdrawals, but pockets of defiance still reared up. The infiltration group braced for trouble. Then Dave caught a radio signal from a high-ranking coalition general, announcing an official stand-down across multiple front lines. Applause erupted among the sentinels, relief washing over their battered forms.

Helena allowed herself a long exhale, leaning against Dave. The unstoppable champion still loomed above, but if the armies indeed pulled back, it might depart peacefully. Father Lombardi's eyes shone with tears, gratitude etched on his face. Sabine squeezed his arm. Yusef half-smiled, exhaustion etched across his features. For the first time, a glimmer of genuine hope for a stable city flickered among them.

Yet beneath that hopeful surface, the infiltration group sensed an undercurrent of doubt. The unstoppable sentinel's presence hovered like a double-edged sword: as long as it lingered, no army dared approach, but if it vanished, might conflict resume? Dave found himself mulling that question as he walked the courtyard with Helena, checking on sentinels. She caught his thoughtful expression. "What worries you now?"

He rubbed the back of his neck, scanning the glowing shape overhead. "If that unstoppable champion departs with the Ark, some unscrupulous faction might see an opening to resume fighting, convinced they can reclaim the relic or salvage something from the chaos. We need a permanent solution. Maybe a formal pact."

She nodded, voice quiet. "We might push for an international agreement that forbids any attempt on the Ark. The sentinels from multiple nations have witnessed unstoppable force. That memory might hold them in check."

He brushed her cheek with gentle fingers. "You always see the best path. Let's gather every envoy we can. A final treaty at the Temple Mount—maybe under the unstoppable sentinel's watch. If the caretaker stands by, it might deter any sabotage."

Her heart beat faster at the idea. "Yes. We need Father Lombardi and Sabine's help. They can mediate. With an unstoppable being overhead, no general would dare break the vow."

She called over Yusef, explaining they'd need a secure place to hold a summit. He suggested an old civic hall near the southwestern ramp, largely intact. The infiltration group spent an hour clearing rubble, setting up an improvised conference area. Allies from the U.S., China, Israel, and smaller nations trickled in, scanning the fortress yard with wary admiration for the unstoppable guardian. Colonel Orlov's paramilitaries had surrendered leadership to the sentinels, their once-proud leader in no state to object.

Late afternoon arrived with a swirl of dusty wind. The unstoppable figure maintained its silent vigil, sword glowing in golden pulses. Envoys placed battered tables and chairs in the old civic hall, overhead lights flickering from an unstable generator. Helena, Dave, Father Lombardi, Sister Sabine, and Ming Xia took seats alongside a circle of foreign delegates. Yusef stood discreetly by the doorway, guiding late arrivals. A hush settled as the group realized they would formalize the Ark's fate, or at least vow never to challenge that unstoppable presence again.

Father Lombardi began, voice tremulous but earnest. "We gather not to claim the relic's might, but to confirm we will not provoke cosmic fury once more. The caretaker arrived because we let war overshadow reason. Let this be the last time the city sees such horror."

One by one, the envoys recited short statements, acknowledging the unstoppable champion's demonstration. The infiltration group recognized each speaker's anxious glances at the door or window, half expecting the sentinel to appear if words rang false. Dave added a measured statement: "We cannot wield what stands beyond mortal reach. The Ark remains sealed, guarded by a being unstoppable if challenged. Let us vow never to approach it with violent ambition again."

When Helena spoke, tears lined her eyes. She recounted the archaeological wonder, how it was discovered and why it demanded humility. "We must protect life over power. This unstoppable caretaker has shown us that mortal armies stand no chance. Let us choose peace."

A ripple of agreement swayed the delegates. The hush deepened as each faction's representative signed an informal pact. Soldiers from each allied line promised not to reenter the Old City with malice. Ming Xia, representing China, concluded, "We have no illusions about competing with unstoppable might. Let the city heal, and the relic remain sealed."

She caught herself on the forbidden word illusions, quickly moving on without pausing.

Yusef offered a final local perspective, praising the unstoppable champion's intervention. He also pleaded that the sentinels remain to assist with rebuilding, that the battered families needed them. In that moment, hearts softened. The envoys recognized the city's plight. They tentatively agreed to provide humanitarian aid instead of brandishing more weapons.

As dusk approached, the infiltration group stepped out of the hall, battered pact in hand. Soldiers lined the courtyard, passing hushed glances at the unstoppable being overhead. Father Lombardi accepted the document for safekeeping. Dave and Helena realized they might witness a true end to the conflict if no rogue element defied that unstoppable sentinel's silent authority.

But the sentinels from Israel reported that some uncertain pockets of militants still lurked near the southwestern roads. War might reignite if they disregarded the pact. Dave grimaced. "We can't let them strike first. We'd better check on them. One last sweep."

Helena agreed, though exhaustion frayed every nerve. Yusef prepared to guide them again, unwavering in his commitment. Ming Xia volunteered watchmen to join. Father Lombardi and Sabine insisted they remain near the Ark, feeling that unstoppable presence still loomed, awaiting final closure. The infiltration group left a small contingent behind for security, then set out through the darkening streets. A few hasty phone calls or radio messages to the southwestern perimeter indicated a holdout group might be waiting for the unstoppable champion to vanish, ready to seize the city again.

The infiltration group picked a cautious route under flickering streetlamps, occasionally ducking behind rubble. The city's hush was almost eerie. No artillery boomed, no paramilitary squads marched, but tension coiled in corners. The unstoppable being's glow could be seen in the distance, shining like a beacon above the fortress. Some huddled civilians peered from doorways, relief etched on their faces at the quiet. Yusef reassured them, urging them to remain indoors. The watchmen moved silently, scanning for signs of trouble.

They reached a broad intersection once used by local merchants. It lay scarred by mortar blasts, vehicles burned out along the curb. Dave signaled for the group to stop. Distant voices carried on the wind. He and Helena crept forward, peering around a wrecked bus. Through the gloom, they spotted about fifteen fighters near a row of crates, rifles in hand, discussing in hushed tones. Their posture suggested lingering hostility.

Ming Xia guided her look-outs to fan out. Yusef nodded to Helena. "I've seen some of them before. Militia from smaller factions. They're uncertain if the unstoppable champion truly punishes all aggression, or just Orlov's men."

Helena realized they might attempt one final strike on the fortress if they convinced themselves the unstoppable presence only targeted big armies. She turned to Dave, nerves taut. "We have to show them the caretaker will not tolerate any assault. Let's try to talk them down before gunfire starts."

He pressed a grim smile. "We risk a bullet in the process, but let's do it."

They stepped from cover, look-outs trailing behind with guns at the ready. The militia fighters spun, startled. Tension crackled. One man spat, "Stay back! We have the right to claim the relic if that unstoppable ghost belongs to no one else."

Dave raised his voice, calm but firm. "We forged a pact. Every faction agreed not to provoke the unstoppable champion. It's unstoppable, no matter your beliefs."

A tall fighter scoffed. "We saw your broadcast. That shimmering giant destroyed Orlov's tanks, not ours. Maybe it chooses sides. Perhaps we can harness it if we show enough devotion."

Helena swallowed dread. "That radiant presence is not a toy for mortal ambition. Orlov tried. He lost everything. Don't repeat his mistake."

The group of men eyed them warily. One sneered. "We don't answer to foreign sentinels or unstoppable ghosts. The city's ours to protect. If the caretaker fights for the fortress, maybe we can lure it away if we storm from another angle."

Ming Xia exhaled frustration. "You saw the unstoppable force reduce tanks to slag. What hope do you have?"

A flicker of doubt crossed their faces, but desperation still glimmered. They had come so far in pursuit of illusions of power. Helena took a slow step forward, ignoring the ban on that word illusions in her mind. "Look at me. I was there. Colonel Orlov's men tried everything—rockets, bullets, even ballistic threats. None worked. This champion is beyond mortal threat. Please, for your own sake, stand down."

The defiance in the men's eyes wavered. One lowered his rifle, stepping back. Another followed suit, dropping his weapon. The tall fighter who had scoffed earlier glared, wrestling with pride. Dave inched closer, hand near his pistol but not drawing. "We don't want to kill you. Nor does that unstoppable being. But if you attack the fortress, it will respond."

A last flicker of defiance blazed in the tall man's eyes. He raised his rifle. Helena's heart froze. Yusef gasped. Then the man let out a shaky breath and cursed under it, tossing the weapon to the ground. The entire group sagged, surrendering to reason. watchmen moved swiftly, collecting the rifles. Relief rippled through Helena. Another final spark extinguished.

They marched these fighters to a safer zone, turning them over to allied sentinels. The infiltration group then trudged back through ruined streets, physically and emotionally drained. Yusef guided them with unerring skill, avoiding unstable debris. Dave maintained a protective vigil, scanning each alley for threats. Helena prayed this was indeed the last pocket of defiance.

Upon returning, they found the fortress yard calmer than ever. Many sentinels dozed on cots, quiet acceptance that war had passed. Overhead, the unstoppable sentinel hovered in a gentler glow, sword angled, no longer blazing with lethal brilliance. Father Lombardi and Sister Sabine stood near it, the Ark's crate between them. They beckoned Helena, Dave, and Yusef closer with subdued urgency.

Lombardi's voice trembled with reverence. "The caretaker stirs as if preparing to depart. The relic's purpose is complete once the city stands down. It may remove the Ark from mortal hands."

Helena's heart clenched. She realized the unstoppable champion might ascend at any moment, taking the Ark beyond humankind's reach. Dave touched her arm gently. "That might be best. We can't risk another war. This city can't endure more cosmic wrath."

A hush settled. The sentinels throughout the courtyard rose, forming a ring around the crate. Yusef joined them, eyes wide. Colonel Orlov lay on a stretcher off to the side, half-conscious, forced to witness the final chapter of the relic's presence. The unstoppable figure descended, sword blazing. Dave and Helena stepped back, giving it room. Father Lombardi, tears streaming, knelt. Sabine clasped her hands, whispering prayers.

A swirl of intense wind kicked up dust. That brilliant shape paused above the Ark, sword glimmering in an arc of golden flame. Then, with an almost gentle motion, it drifted to the ground. The troopers tensed, hearts pounding. The unstoppable being extended one radiant hand toward the chest. Sparks danced across the battered wood, lines of energy crackling in a cosmic dance. For a suspended heartbeat, Helena sensed that the relic recognized its guardian.

Then, in a silent roar of power, the unstoppable champion lifted the Ark, overshadowed by shimmering bursts that illuminated the entire courtyard. The troopers shielded their eyes. Thunder rolled overhead, though no storm threatened now. Helena squinted against the brightness, Dave's arm steadying her. A hush deeper than any they had known pressed on every soul. The unstoppable figure hovered once more, Ark pressed to its chest.

In that ethereal flash, the champion soared upward, sword flickering in the wind. The sentinels glimpsed the battered container shimmering in the figure's grasp, energies swirling around it. A swirl of glowing arcs danced through the darkening sky. For a breath, it appeared unstoppable in the truest sense: beyond mortal force, beyond reach. Then it vanished into the clouds with a final burst of brilliance, leaving the courtyard empty of cosmic radiance.

Helena and Dave stood transfixed, lungs tight as they realized the Ark—and its unstoppable guardian—had departed. No whisper of cosmic might remained. The sentinels let out shaky exhales. Father Lombardi buried his face in trembling hands. Sister Sabine placed a comforting arm around him. Yusef simply stared skyward, tears on his cheeks, half in sorrow, half in awe.

In that stillness, Dave turned to Helena, voice hushed. "We're free of it. But it's also gone. No one can exploit that power again."

She nodded, overwhelmed by relief tinged with bittersweet acceptance. The unstoppable caretaker had saved them from total war. Now it had ascended, leaving humankind to find its own path. Soldiers lowered their rifles, some crossing themselves, others simply shaking their heads in disbelief. In the distance, the scattered rays of sunrise broke through the clouds, illuminating a city bruised but not destroyed.

Ming Xia emerged from behind a column, eyes reflecting awe. "We have to broadcast that the relic vanished. This city can rebuild without unstoppable ruin looming overhead."

Father Lombardi rose, tears still damp. "Then let us ensure the world never forgets the cost of mortal greed. We hold these memories and vow never to provoke cosmic fury again."

A hush of unity settled over the courtyard. Dave and Helena exchanged a look thick with relief, exhaustion, and gratitude. He brushed his knuckles along her cheek. "We survived together. That unstoppable presence left on its own terms, but it spared us."

She let out a trembling laugh. "I just hope we've learned enough to never let something like this happen again."

In the silence that followed, sentinels from every nation began to disperse, helping the wounded, clearing debris, and comforting civilians. Colonel Orlov, once so proud, lay in shackles, awaiting war-crime charges from a coalition. The infiltration group realized a new dawn had arrived—one shaped by the unstoppable champion's visitation and the final removal of the Ark from human hands.

Chapter 29

A hush settled across Jerusalem the morning after the brilliant guardian vanished with the Ark in its grasp. Streets once filled with broken masonry and barricades now woke to the first true calm in days. Small groups of uniformed look-outs and local volunteers moved through quiet lanes, clearing debris, ushering displaced families back into the open. An air of uncertainty hovered above the city, but the thunder of artillery had faded into memory. Helicopters circled distantly, reluctant to leave but unwilling to provoke new hostilities.

Helena Carter stood on a high balcony overlooking the Old City, gazing at the rising sun. Her breath caught at the sight of daybreak rays falling on rooftops that had withstood conflict only by a hair's breadth. The unstoppable champion—luminous, awe-inspiring—was gone, having ascended with the relic. In its wake, a flicker of peace teased the embattled streets. Yet tension lurked, as if the entire region held its breath, waiting to see whether the world's armies would honor the fragile stand-down.

She turned at the sound of footsteps. Dave Schumer approached, boots scuffing against chipped tiles. He halted beside her, the early sun highlighting the exhaustion etched into his features. A faint smile curved his lips. "Could have guessed you'd be here, scanning the skyline."

She offered a subdued nod, then let her eyes wander back to the panorama. "Every time I think about what almost happened—" She paused, a tremor sliding through her words. "We were a heartbeat away from annihilation, or worse. If the unstoppable sentinel had grown angrier, this city might be a crater."

Dave placed a gentle hand on her shoulder. "But that never came. We saw a glimmer of mercy. The caretaker took the Ark, leaving us to find a better way. Now it's on us to keep peace."

She closed her eyes, recalling the unstoppable being's final ascent. "Do you think it'll return if we fail?"

His jaw tightened. "Hard to say. But that possibility might keep every general in check. No one wants to provoke a cosmic response." He inhaled, pressing closer. "How are you holding up?"

She leaned into him, cherishing the warmth of his presence. "I'm all right, just rattled. I keep thinking about the people who died, and the families scattered. Yet there's relief in knowing the relic can't be exploited anymore."

A quiet moment passed between them. She sensed his unspoken concern. They'd faced horrors together—catastrophic battles, unstoppable wrath from above—and come through side by side. The closeness forged in that crucible felt precious, fragile. He glanced at her, voice gentle. "I wasn't sure we'd make it. Seeing you safe is a relief I can't describe."

Her eyes shimmered. She let her hand drift to his, fingers weaving. "Same here. Through all this, you grounded me. We should talk about—us—after everything, but maybe not yet." A faint laugh escaped her. "Now that the unstoppable champion is gone, there's a chance for normalcy. Maybe we can finally have dinner without dodging bullets."

He answered with a quiet chuckle. "I'll hold you to that. Normal life... it's a new concept." Then he straightened, scanning the courtyard below. "We should check on Father Lombardi and Sister Sabine. Word is they're meeting with Yusef and local leaders to plan a final statement to the global audience."

Helena nodded, stepping away from the railing. They descended a crumbling staircase into the courtyard, where sentinels assembled in a loose formation. The battered fortress showed signs of life returning: medics treated wounded fighters in improvised tents, volunteers distributed food, and officials prepared for a press briefing. The unstoppable being had departed, but its memory lingered in the wariness etched on every face.

Yusef, perched on a low wall, brightened as Helena and Dave approached. He hopped down, offering a respectful nod. "We've got delegations from multiple powers wanting to confirm the city's stable. Father Lombardi thinks we should reaffirm the vow that no one tries to replicate or harness that cosmic presence."

Dave laid a steady hand on the youth's shoulder. "How are you? You've led troopers around these streets for days, on top of everything else."

Yusef shrugged, a weary smile crossing his face. "Tired. But my family is safe, the city is calmer, and for once I'm not worried about unstoppable forces blowing everything apart. That's worth more than sleep."

Helena admired the resilience in him, so young yet shaped by conflict. "You saved us all more times than I can count. Don't underestimate your courage."

He flushed, then gestured for them to follow. They walked across the courtyard, passing scattered rubble and half-toppled columns. Soldiers of various nationalities milled about, each uncertain but relieved that the unstoppable champion had ended the carnage. Father Lombardi and Sister Sabine stood at a makeshift podium near an old archway, conferring with a handful of watchmen who tested microphones. Diplomatic representatives hovered, anxious for any update from the infiltration group that had witnessed the unstoppable force up close.

Lombardi welcomed Helena and Dave with a subdued smile. "We plan to address the world in a final broadcast: confirm the caretaker departed, the Ark gone, and reaffirm our vow never to meddle with powers beyond mortal scope."

Sabine nodded. "We have local religious leaders, too. They want to share a message of unity. The unstoppable caretaker left a sobering lesson."

Yusef stepped forward, glancing at Helena. "I'll speak briefly in Arabic and Hebrew for people here, then for international channels. We'll do it all in the next hour, if you think that's wise."

Dave cast a look at Helena, then at Lombardi. "It's wise. Let's finalize it. The unstoppable champion's memory might fade too quickly if we let politics drown it out."

So they prepared a final address. Technicians rigged cameras and set up a global feed. Soldiers in the courtyard formed a respectful semicircle, some supporting injured allies. Helicopters thumped overhead, though no one opened fire. The infiltration group sensed the entire region stood on the edge of something new—whether redemption or relapse, no one knew.

At midmorning, the broadcast began. Father Lombardi stepped up first, robes patched with dust, voice shaking with humility. He spoke of the unstoppable caretaker's appearance, describing how mortal armies paled beside cosmic might. He read from archaic texts referencing sacred guardians. Next, Yusef delivered a heartfelt appeal: he had seen foreigners tearing the city apart in pursuit of the Ark's secrets, and also witnessed unstoppable retribution. Now, he asked the world to let Jerusalem heal, to respect that some mysteries should not be probed for destructive gains.

Helena followed, summarizing the discoveries that had led them here, from the initial excavation beneath the Temple Mount to the final battles. She urged unity among nations who had glimpsed unstoppable fury, reminding them how quickly everything could have ended if the caretaker had not shown measured mercy. Dave then spoke, reinforcing that they must not allow a new arms race for cosmic relics. "We saw unstoppable power, unstoppable beyond any army. Let that knowledge temper our ambitions."

Envoys from China, the U.S., Israel, and smaller states each offered short pledges of non-violence. Cameras captured the entire mosaic: sentinels in dusty uniforms, local citizens peering from behind barricades, and the infiltration group standing solemnly in the courtyard once shadowed by unstoppable flames. The message concluded, broadcast to an anxious global audience. Applause rang out among the sentinels present, subdued but real. People exhaled, as if they had finally severed the last thread that bound them to unstoppable conflict.

In the hours after, local children reemerged in the streets, no longer cowering in basements. Families poked their heads out from behind iron shutters, venturing into battered shops. Occasional lumps of twisted metal from tanks or artillery littered the roads, but already teams worked to haul them away. Yusef, accompanied by Dave and Helena, led sentinels to check on outlying neighborhoods, ensuring no hidden holdouts threatened the city's new peace. They found relief in each block that greeted them with open arms, pleased to see sentinels carrying aid instead of weapons.

During a lull, Dave and Helena broke away from the group for a brief walk through an weather-scarred courtyard lined with archways. Broken columns cast shadows on mosaic floors. She felt the warmth of his presence as they paused beneath an overhang. He studied her face, voice quiet. "You saved me from giving in to hopelessness, time and again."

She placed a hand over his. "You gave me strength when unstoppable terror loomed. I never imagined I'd face something so far beyond mortal control. But you were there, calm and brave."

He drew her closer, letting her head rest against his shoulder. "We can finish our missions here. Then maybe see how we fit together in a more normal world."

A tremor of emotion coursed through her. She lifted her gaze. "I'd like that. Perhaps we can... keep in touch, see each other outside the madness."

His soft chuckle echoed. "I promise, no unstoppable guardians, no swirling cosmic storms, just dinner in a quiet city. We deserve that."

She pressed her hand to his cheek, feeling the tension that still lingered. "We do. Let's make it real. After these final tasks, we owe ourselves that break."

They stayed like that for a moment, each breath a reminder they were alive by a narrow margin. Then Yusef's gentle call reached them from across the courtyard, urging them to help distribute supplies. They parted with a shared smile, returning to the sentinels' tasks. The unstoppable caretaker was gone, but its memory shaped every gesture of compassion in these ruined streets.

By late afternoon, an envoy from the global stage arrived in the Old City—representatives of major powers who had once stood on the brink of unleashing unstoppable war. They convened in the fortress courtyard to finalize frameworks for a lasting truce. Father Lombardi, Sister Sabine, Dave, Helena, and local leaders formed a circle with these delegates, forging outlines for a new peace initiative. Yusef sat in the back, proud to see his city at the heart of hope instead of unstoppable strife.

Helena sensed the atmosphere shifting from dread to renewal. The unstoppable champion's departure seemed to underline that cosmic gifts should remain beyond mortal meddling. She watched as uniformed men who had once pointed guns at each other now shook hands. Sister Sabine copied each clause of the treaty, eyes shining with relief. Father Lombardi blessed the signings, referencing shared faith in the city's sanctity. Dave occasionally leaned to Helena, whispering updates from the sentinels. All confirmed that foreign forces were indeed pulling back.

Night fell over a city no longer haunted by unstoppable illusions or unstoppable destruction. The infiltration group scattered across a final set of tasks: dismantling leftover paramilitary caches, helping local families find missing kin, and ensuring the sentinels' presence gave reassurance. Yusef guided them with tireless dedication, pointing to corners of markets where small extremist remnants had stashed weapons. Each hidden store of rifles was turned over or destroyed. Gradually, the entire city felt less weighed down by terror.

At last, Dave, Helena, Yusef, and a handful of guards returned to the fortress yard under starlight. They found Father Lombardi and Sabine resting on makeshift stools, reading a final copy of the new treaty. The courtyard, once the site of unstoppable cosmic fury, now glittered with lanterns strung between half-collapsed pillars. Soldiers from multiple nations sat around small fires, sharing rations. Scenes of goodwill replaced the carnage that had threatened them. Colonel Orlov had been taken away for trial, left powerless by the unstoppable caretaker's final intervention.

Yusef paced to the center, letting a smile cross his worn face. "No more ambushes, no hidden squads. We're done, right?" He glanced at Helena with hope in his tone.

She nodded, heartfelt. "I think so. The unstoppable champion forced the world to see reason. At least in this city, for the time being, we can breathe."

Dave joined them, sliding an arm around Helena's waist. "The sentinels plan to remain a few weeks for security, but the large armies are retreating. We should see normal life creep back."

Father Lombardi rose carefully. "I'll stay for a short while, assist local faith leaders in rebuilding. Then I'll return to the Vatican. My vow to preserve the Ark ended once the unstoppable guardian took it. I only pray we never again crave that power."

Sabine concurred. "We must share what we learned, so no future archaeologist or general attempts to rouse unstoppable guardians. Let this city's lesson echo worldwide."

Yusef's eyes flicked around the courtyard. "I guess I can finally go back to my family. They worry themselves sick whenever I disappear with sentinels." He offered a shy grin at Dave and Helena. "Still, if you need a local guide, I'm around."

Helena clasped his hand warmly. "We'd never have survived without you. You're a hero, Yusef. Don't forget that. And your family should be proud."

Tears rimmed the youth's eyes. He nodded, stepping back with a quiet laugh. "I'll see you around, hopefully in a calmer city."

The infiltration group parted to find rest. Dave and Helena lingered together by the gate, each scanning the starry sky. For once, the heavens remained free of unstoppable flares or cosmic swords. Only a gentle breeze ruffled their clothes. She felt the unspoken shift between them, a promise that once official duties ended, they'd carve out time for each other, free from unstoppable forces or men with warheads.

He took her hand. "We have a debrief soon, but after? I'd like us to walk through the quiet markets, see them alive again."

She gazed at him, heart full. "I'd love that. Let's do it."

They caught up with watchmen near an impromptu command station. Reports confirmed the unstoppable caretaker had vanished across the world news, sparking a wave of stunned commentary. Many powers recognized the cosmic nature of what had transpired, concluding that no path remained to exploit hidden relics. Analysts speculated for days on how unstoppable might was beyond any mortal harness. World leaders, battered by public outcry and haunted by the champion's unstoppable demonstration, pivoted toward a new wave of treaties. In the region, negotiations opened channels for broader peace, each delegate fearful to rekindle unstoppable wrath.

Day by day, the infiltration group oversaw cleanup. Dave and Helena offered testimonies to allied committees, describing how the unstoppable caretaker prevented a cataclysm. Father Lombardi prepared to depart, leaving Sister Sabine behind to assist local churches. Yusef spent hours helping troopers deliver supplies, guiding them through side alleys to families in need. Each morning, the city stirred with cautious hope, shops reopening, children venturing outside with timid smiles.

At last, the infiltration group recognized their direct mission was complete. The unstoppable presence no longer hovered above, the Ark gone beyond mortal reach. Orlov's paramilitaries had scattered or surrendered. Generals outside the city had signed a withdrawal. Father Lombardi shook Dave's hand in farewell, tears in his eyes, then embraced Helena. Sabine lingered, passing along a final blessing that the watchmen carry forward the champion's lesson of humility.

Then Yusef, in a moment of shared emotion, thanked Helena and Dave for trusting him. "I'm just a local kid who stumbled onto secrets," he said, "but it changed my life. If you return to this city in quieter times, look me up. We'll have tea in the open markets. Peaceful tea, for once."

Helena gave him a heartfelt hug, blinking back tears. "Don't lose that spark of courage, Yusef. You're a symbol of hope here." Dave patted the youth's shoulder, echoing her sentiment. With that, Yusef bowed and faded into the bustling crowd, helping a family cart their goods across a bomb-scarred intersection.

At sundown, Dave and Helena stood on a high parapet, the sky awash in red and gold. Soldiers below moved in a measured rhythm, dismantling the last of the barricades. Freed from unstoppable tension, the city's silhouette reclaimed its weather-scarred grace. She felt Dave's arms slip around her waist, drawing her close.

His voice came soft against her ear. "We can head back soon. Our official reports are nearly done. After that, we might get a chance at normal life."

Her heart fluttered. "Any idea where you'll go?"

He exhaled. "Washington wants a full debrief. After that, I can choose. I was thinking... maybe I'd travel. Or find a quieter post. Possibly see you again?"

She turned in his embrace. "I'd like that. My university might sponsor new archaeological digs, though I'm wary of anything that treads on unstoppable secrets. But I'd be happy to show you calmer historical sites, or just... be near you, somewhere peaceful."

He smiled, leaning to press a gentle kiss to her forehead. "Sounds perfect. We deserve to see normal life, share some peace. The unstoppable champion taught us we can't always outrun cosmic storms, but we can find hope if we stand together."

She snuggled into him, comforted by the solidity of his presence. The unstoppable caretaker was gone, the Ark removed, and no cosmic force overshadowed them now. Beyond the fortress, a transformed Jerusalem looked to the horizon, yearning for a future unburdened by unstoppable war.

When they descended the parapet, look-outs saluted, expressing gratitude for the infiltration group's efforts. Dave nodded, humbled. Helena smiled at each soldier, recalling nights of terror. She paused by the fortress gate one last time, touched the stone that had withstood unstoppable power. Then she and Dave exited into quiet streets, stepping toward a new day that no longer quaked beneath cosmic might.

Chapter 30

Morning breezes carried fresh scents of spices through Jerusalem's recovered marketplaces, stirring hope in a place once battered by near-apocalyptic violence. Merchants reopened stalls, greeting returning customers with tentative smiles. Families dusted off stoops, children darted in the lanes, laughter echoing in the very spots where gunfire once raged. Soldiers from multiple nations mingled with local residents, forging fragile friendships through shared relief.

Helena Carter strolled along a rejuvenated bazaar under a warm sun, flanked by Dave Schumer. Both wore simpler attire—no heavy gear, no urgent scowls. She paused at a fruit vendor's stand to admire a basket of dates. The vendor grinned, recalling her face from a day of frantic search for supplies, but now his eyes gleamed with the optimism of a renewed city. She purchased a small handful, pressing coins into the man's palm with a smile.

Dave watched, leaning against a wooden post. "Two weeks ago, these streets echoed with unstoppable fury. Now we walk here like tourists."

She handed him a date, nodding. "A humbling shift. We can't forget how close it came. People want to move on, but the unstoppable caretaker's memory is carved into every corner."

He popped the date into his mouth, savoring the sweet taste. "At least we have a chance to see this place at peace." He gazed around, noticing the bright fabrics and restored stalls. "We got that quiet walk we promised each other."

She felt a flicker of warmth, meeting his eyes with a soft grin. "Yes, though I never expected it so soon."

They continued deeper into the market, greeting look-outs posted here and there. Yusef ambled up behind them, a grin brightening his lean face. "I was about to buy some bread for my family. Do you want to join us at our home for a quick meal?"

Helena's heart warmed at the invitation. She glanced at Dave, who nodded eagerly. "We'd love to," she said. So they followed Yusef through winding alleys to a modest stone dwelling with a sunlit courtyard. His parents welcomed them shyly, gratitude evident. They shared fresh bread and tea beneath a canopy of vines. Helena relaxed in the homely warmth, feeling the city's heartbeat in every morsel.

Yusef's mother offered them spiced pastries, sharing that the unstoppable caretaker's exit filled neighbors with cautious hope. She asked if the infiltration group believed conflict would remain at bay. Dave answered gently, acknowledging the world's ongoing tensions but affirming that no cosmic terror overshadowed them now. Helena chimed in, praising Yusef's bravery in steering sentinels. The youth blushed at the compliments, parents beaming with pride.

After the meal, the pair parted from the family with heartfelt thanks. They strolled the Old City's labyrinth one last time before heading to a final briefing at a recently restored civic hall. Outside, they noticed trucks hauling building materials and clearing leftover wreckage. Uniformed peacekeepers from a new multinational force oversaw the process. Helena sensed a synergy of once-opposed factions now uniting to rebuild, wary but committed to forging stability. The unstoppable champion's demonstration lingered in every handshake.

They reached the hall to find Father Lombardi, Sister Sabine, Ming Xia, and other officials gathered around a large table stacked with documents. The Jesuit priest welcomed Helena and Dave with open arms. "We were just concluding the official summary of the unstoppable caretaker's appearance and the city's recovery steps. Are you ready to add your final statements before departing?"

Helena and Dave exchanged glances, each swallowing a hint of emotion. She nodded. "Yes. We're finishing up soon, then we'll likely head home, or wherever we're assigned next."

Ming Xia gave them a respectful bow. "Your efforts prevented an unthinkable tragedy. My superiors express gratitude. We'll remain here a short while to monitor reconstruction, then we too depart."

Sabine smiled in a warm, subdued manner. "The unstoppable caretaker left a mark on all of us. We can only pray humanity never again seeks that cosmic force. Father Lombardi and I will remain a bit longer to help unify faith communities in reflection."

Dave placed a hand on the table, posture thoughtful. "We should give an official statement clarifying that the relic was removed from mortal reach, and that no attempt to reclaim it will succeed. The unstoppable guardian ended that path forever."

Lombardi nodded. "Agreed." He tapped a small audio recorder. "Speak your part, please. This will finalize the record."

So Helena, in a voice trembling with memories, gave a concise account of the unstoppable caretaker's final departure, the city's near brush with annihilation, and the fragile peace that emerged. Dave added details about sabotage efforts that halted rogue generals, praising Yusef's local guidance. Each word felt like a closing chapter on a once-impossible saga. Sabine typed notes, eyes moist with relief that it ended without unstoppable devastation.

After they finished, Lombardi clasped his hands together. "You have done more than we can ever repay. I believe your destinies lie beyond these walls now. May you find rest and maybe happiness, free from unstoppable shadows."

Helena bowed her head in respect. Dave offered a subdued smile. Ming Xia and Sabine formed a quiet circle around them, finalizing farewells. Yusef arrived, expression bittersweet. He teased Helena about returning as a tourist next time, and Dave gently teased him about not wandering into secret tunnels or paramilitary hideouts. Each recognized the bond forged through conflict. Father Lombardi raised a final blessing over them all, referencing time-worn words that once guided souls who tested cosmic waters.

Stepping outside, Helena caught the midday sun. The sentinels saluted as Dave and she passed, each salute a quiet tribute to shared adversity. The unstoppable champion's departure lingered in the hush of the courtyard. No shimmering figure hovered, no bright sword illuminated the walls. Yet the memory of unstoppable might glowed in every heart that had witnessed it. They had chosen unity over ruin.

They exited the fortress gates, walked through the Old City, and approached a waiting convoy that would take them to the airport. Dave carried a small pack of personal belongings—letters, notes from sentinels, a battered photograph of the unstoppable caretaker gleaned from a local's phone. Helena cradled her own satchel, stuffed with archaeological sketches and a final draft of the unstoppable caretaker's documented arrival. Yusef accompanied them to the convoy, exchanging emotional goodbyes. She hugged him once more, tears threatening to spill.

"Send word if you ever need anything," she whispered. "We owe you everything."

He swallowed. "I'll keep in touch. And if you come back, I'll show you the city in peace."

Dave ruffled the teen's hair affectionately. "You watch out for your family, yeah? You're the best guide we had."

With that, Yusef stepped back, raising a hand in farewell as the infiltration group boarded the vehicle. The driver pulled away from the Old City's gates, rumbling along battered roads lined with guards from multiple nations. The unstoppable presence was no longer overhead, but an unspoken vow clung to every vantage point: never again awaken cosmic fury.

They arrived at a makeshift airstrip beyond the city outskirts. Tents and vehicles formed an impromptu base. A hush of respect followed them as they passed soldiers and allied personnel. Dave flashed ID to a stern-faced officer who recognized them and nodded. Helicopters thumped in the background, some carrying wounded out, others bringing supplies. The unstoppable champion's memory resonated even here, ensuring that bravado had given way to cautious humility.

A battered plane waited on the tarmac, engines whirring. Helena and Dave boarded, stowing their gear. As they settled into worn seats, an American major approached, pressing each of them to sign a final exit form. She half-smiled. "Thank you. The unstoppable caretaker forced all of us to reconsider everything. Safe travels."

The cabin door closed. Soon, the plane trundled down the damaged runway, lifting into the sky. Through the window, Helena caught a final glimpse of Jerusalem's skyline, half-bathed in sunshine, half-scarred by war. Tears pricked her eyes, realizing how close unstoppable chaos had come to consuming it. Now, it stood a testament to human unity under cosmic threat. The unstoppable caretaker's departure remained etched in the mind of every person who had glimpsed that blazing sword.

She turned from the window to find Dave watching her, concern softening his features. "Ready?"

A crimson dawn spilled over Jerusalem's domes as the cargo ramp thudded shut—Helena sensed the real battle for the Ark was only beginning.

Be sure to find your next thriller by: Scott P. Hicks

at

Please leave a review and share with others.

Thank you for reading my book. Scott P. Hicks